REBEL SISTERS

Also by
TOCHI ONYEBUCHI

War Girls

Beasts Made of Night

Crown of Thunder

REBEL SISTERS

WITHDRAWN

TOCHI ONYEBUCHI

RAZORBILL

RAZORBILL

An imprint of Penguin Random House LLC, New York

First published in the United States of America by Razorbill,
an imprint of Penguin Random House LLC, 2020

Copyright © 2020 by Tochi Onyebuchi

LIBRARY OF CONGRESS CATALOGING-IN-PUBLICATION DATA
Names: Onyebuchi, Tochi, author.
Title: Rebel sisters / Tochi Onyebuchi.
Description: New York : Razorbill, 2020. | Sequel to: War girls. |
Audience: Ages 12+ | Summary: Living a comfortable life in the Space
Colonies, Ify, now nineteen and a medical administrator, must return to
wartorn Nigeria, where she last saw her sister, to investigate why
young refugees from that nation are carrying a deadly virus.
Identifiers: LCCN 2020023214 | ISBN 9781984835062 (hardcover) |
ISBN 9781984835086 (ebook)
Subjects: CYAC: Science fiction. | War—Fiction. | Refugees—Fiction. |
Sisters—Fiction. | Cyborgs—Fiction. | Blacks—Fiction. | Nigeria—Fiction.
Classification: LCC PZ7.1.O66 Re 2020 | DDC [Fic]—dc23
LC record available at https://lccn.loc.gov/2020023214

Printed in the United States of America

1 3 5 7 9 10 8 6 4 2

Design by Tony Sahara

Text set in Fairfield LT Std

To Chinoye and Uchechi

REBEL SISTERS

PART

I

CHAPTER

1

Centrafrique, Outer Alabast Colony: 2181

Wesh? Je suis enjaillé de toi. Ça avance ndank-ndank. Je wanda . . . deuxieme bureau . . . Il est sorti nayo nayo. Je vais te see tomorrow. The words mingle and the voices echo inside the receiving station, shuttles docking with a whoosh and clank, passengers alighting with their checkered nylon-canvas bags. Ify squints and touches her temple, activating the Whistle, the communication device linked to the Augment embedded into the base of her neck, and flips through the languages in her translation software—Arabic, Wolof, Finnish, French. Yet it all comes to her as gibberish. A riot of words to mirror the mess of colors before her in Porte Nouveau, the capital city at the center of Centrafrique and, according to Céline, the brightest jewel in the crown of Outer Africa's future. Ify looks to her friend, who grins at the bustle of the city on the other side of the receiving station's entrance, at the Adjogan drums and singsong blaring from street speakers, the teenage boys—all arms and legs— lounging on hoverboards with dishes of chicken yassa balanced on their chests, chuckling and speaking around mouthfuls. The scotch bonnet peppers are so hot Ify's eyes start to sting from several hundred paces away. Someone shouts a string of words, and Ify hears "shoga," and two older men—cyberized—walk over to an old woman crouched over a misfiring broadcast transmitter. The men walk with the ease of people in love. The taller one gazes admiringly at his partner, who stoops to help the woman fix her BoTa and hear the rest of the football match. Farther down the broad thoroughfare, Ify sees the spires of chapels and the domes of mosques and, past that, the tops of what look like broad-based swirling cones with antlers sticking from their tops to absorb solar energy. Centrafrique Polytechnic Institute.

"What are they speaking?" The whole time, Ify has been scrolling through languages. Xhosa, Mande, Sandawe, Vandalic. "Is it French?"

Céline turns her smirk on Ify and slaps her shoulder with the back of her hand. "Ah-ah! You think these people would sully their tongues with such a bankrupt language?" Then she laughs and loosens up, her eyes softening into an apology. "It is everything. You know how we Africans are. We don't choose, we collect." She mimes opening a cupboard and picking out ingredients. "Some onions, some olives, okra, sofrito, and whatever else is in the cupboard." Then she mimes pounding on a surface. "Grind up some maggi cubes." She spreads her arms. "Then throw it all in the pot." A glint of seriousness flashes like a comet in her green eyes. She lowers her voice to a kind murmur. "When was the last time you saw this many Africans in one place, eh?"

Shame warms Ify's cheeks.

Céline puts a gentle hand to the back of Ify's neck. "Come. Let me show you the rest of my kingdom." After a beat, she starts giggling.

And Ify does too.

"Spend too much time around those whites in Alabast and you'll forget who you are." Céline says it with a smile to soften the rebuke.

Together, they leave the shuttle-receiving station behind. The deeper they walk into Porte Nouveau, past the communities that have sprouted up around the massive, shimmering, raised pentagram-shaped prism that somehow manages to accommodate traffic from railway trains, maglev matatus, and space shuttles, the less the city seems like chaos and the more it feels like something familiar. Something ordered. A feeling of recognition hums in Ify's bones, and a single word whispers in her head.

Home.

■ ■ ■ ■ ■

The lights are off in the room that is to be Céline's new office. For now, the room is barren, a white box cast in shadows so deep that her skin and Ify's both glow blue. Behind Ify, Céline paces its length, fingers tapping her chin. With a thought, Ify adjusts the temperature of her bodysuit a few degrees warmer than the room's temperature. Ease floods into her and loosens muscles tensed against the soft chill of the central air conditioning.

"I think my desk will go here." Céline stands in the room's center. "With two chairs here in front of it. And a chaise longue by the wall there. And plants! Plenty of plants." She turns to see Ify staring out the floor-to-ceiling windows at the stars outside. "Ah, Ify. Never one for interior decoration, eh?"

Ify's mind jolts back to the room with a start. She throws a smirk over her shoulder, then returns her gaze to the inky jewel-studded black outside. "There's no Refuse Ring."

Céline joins her. "We're not like Alabast," she says with pride. "Outer space, *ce n'est pas une poubelle*." Pride fills her face. "It's insulting to treat space like our waste basket. Our compost is harvested into energy that powers the Colony. In case the sun were ever to die, we'd be safe. And, well, you know how I feel about plastics."

Ify remembers the horror that had stricken Céline upon watching their classmates at the Institute in Alabast drink from one-use plastic bottles, toss away their plastic iFlexs as soon as an upgrade was available, even seal their dead in metal coffins lined with a special plastic supposedly meant for preservation before being shot out into space to join the rest of the Refuse Ring that circled the Colony. *They never finish what's on their plates*, Céline had said to Ify, over and over with a mournful shake of her head as they walked from class to class. Even the campus transports were riddled with plastics.

"And the Gokada hoverbikes I saw on the way here?" Ify asks, remembering the motorbikes laden with two, sometimes three passengers, weaving their way around bigger matatus and sometimes even city trains, all noise and rude shouts and giggling responses, cutting through the otherwise well-ordered traffic. Powered by some bootleg energy source she couldn't detect. "More jujutech?" she jokes, invoking those items, objects, and wonders that seemed to make science and magic indistinguishable.

"Eh, sometimes a city grows faster than you can regulate it."

Ify keeps her gaze on space. "You sound more than ready to become a Colonial administrator."

"Four years I've trained and studied. But I will not do like they do in Alabast. For once, Centrafrique will have an administrator who looks like them, who understands them. Not one who constantly tries to fit them in an Alabast-sized cercueil. Their coffins are too small for us anyway. And you? You'll continue in medicine?"

"Doctor, lawyer, or engineer," Ify says, laughing. "Those are the only career options for us. Anything else is a failure to the tribe." She resists the temptation to adjust her Whistle and have the mix of languages around her translated into something she can understand. "But I've grown to like it." She smiles. "I think it suits me. The refugee population in Alabast is only growing. And someone needs to care for them. Like you, I think it is important that they are cared for by someone who understands their struggle." She squints. "Someone who understands where they are coming from."

"And in four years, they will graduate at the top of their class, just like you."

"I hear the playing in your voice, Céline. Four years is a long time. Plenty of time to work, to grow, to become myself. Though the Biafran War is over, other wars continue. All over Earth, it is the same. Pain and death and destruction. Here in space, you can find peace. Your struggles will not chase you here. And if there's anything I can do to help these people move on, I will do it." She realizes she's grown serious, so she forces a smile. Any mention of the war she had fled prompts memories of her arrival in Alabast all those years ago, alone, wrapped in a rug in the cargo hold of a space shuttle, shivering, with dried tears streaking her face, constantly asking for her sister, Onyii. She scoops up the memory and tosses it into a mental lockbox out of habit. She turns to Céline. "I must get back. Medical directors get even less leave time than their subordinates."

Céline smiles, and in it, Ify sees all the camaraderie that has built up between them over their four years studying and living together. Céline had come from Francophone West Africa only a year before Ify's arrival and had lived with an Alabast family but was the only Earthland African in their neighborhood unit. She'd only spoken in occasional snatches of story about what she'd had to endure from her white classmates, from her white neighbors, from the authorities—always white—who would hound her family and check her immigration status. It had not been easy. But it had made Céline the perfect companion for Ify. Four years had made them family, so close that they shared every defeat and, together, basked in every victory.

"*J'suis fier de toi,*" Ify says, without the aid of her translator. *I'm proud of you.*

"Ah, look at you, meeting me where I live." Céline shows her teeth, then pulls Ify into a soft but strong embrace. When she breaks away, she says, "Promise me you will visit. You will not find better fried plantains in all of outer space."

Without warning, tears brim in Ify's eyes. "I promise."

CHAPTER
2

I am telling this story to you, but I am telling it to myself too. I am telling it to myself because it is important to be remembering. That is what the robot say who pull me from underneath the mountain of bodies where it is so hard to breathe that my chest is paining me fierce. It is like knife in my chest over and over and over, and I am not knowing for how long I am lying like this. But I am remembering that the first thing I am seeing is tiny hole of light coming from sky. Everything is shadow, and this is how I know I am being covered. And I am first thinking that this is what night is. That it is just blackness with tiny hole of light. But it is bodies. Many bodies piled on top of me. And then I am remembering the bodies are falling away. It is sounding like someone is dragging their foots on the dirt road, then it is sounding like a shirt rustling in wind, like someone is wearing a shirt too big for them and running down dirt road, and when I think of this thing, I am thinking that the person wearing this shirt should be giggling. I am liking the sound in my brain.

As more and more body is coming away, I am seeing that light is bigger. Big big. So big it is paining my eyes to look at. I am wanting to raise my arms to block out the light, but I cannot move them because there are more bodies on top of them.

I am not hearing any words anywhere, not even wind, just crunching of stones and rustling like clothes and shuffling like feet wearing slippers on road until many bodies tumble away at once and I am seeing blue and white and gold and red, and I must close my eyes because it is too much. And air is feeling cold on my skin because there is no more pile of smelling bodies crushing me. But air is also paining me like many many knife on my skin. It is burning, and I am hearing sizzle like meat is cooking.

Then, hand is pulling me out of where I am lying and I see robot for the first time. It has arms and legs and a big round chest like an upside-down belly. It has no lips, just two lines on the sides of its face for where the plates are coming together. They are like grooves, and I am wanting to reach and touch them, because some memory in my bones is wanting me to do this, but I cannot raise my arm, because I am too weak.

Robot is raising me up and down so that my feet just touch the ground, but when it is letting me go to stand on my own, I am falling like sack of yams. Small small stones on ground are digging into my cheek, and I am trying to push myself up. But I must try many many times before I am able to sit on my knees. And that is when I am seeing them.

Many many robots. Not like army of robots. But family of robots. They are all looking the same, and they are the only thing I am seeing in this place that is moving. Not even beetle or blade of grass is moving here. Only the light in the eyes of the robots. That light is like single bar of white moving back and forth. I am thinking that this is how they are speaking to each other. With light.

My teeth are chat-chatting but I am sweating like it is second skin, and, even though there is quiet everywhere, there is noise like jagga-jagga inside my head. Like train is running back and forth between my ears.

One robot is walking to me with crunch-crunch footstep and is lowering themself to me. And long wire is coming out of its back and I am seeing that it is hose, because it is opening at its end and sliding past my teeth and into my mouth. And water is swimming down my throat.

I am coughing so hard my chest is paining me again, but I am wanting water, so my body is scrambling like mouse to take hose, and I put it to my mouth and it is feeling like entire world—like sun and earth and sky—is smiling on my body, because pain is leaving me.

Another robot is close to me and it has a different hose. I am thinking I will be drinking more water, but this one sprays me in shower so hard it is knocking me back on ground. It is like raining all over my body, but pain is leaving me, and I am smiling, and suddenly, I am seeing vision of child in too-big shirt running down dirt road. The shirt is flapping like flag is wrapping around them, and there is water everywhere in this vision, and the child is shining with the rain. Suddenly, I am back in the desert and all around me is dead bodies, but I am feeling like it is raining on my body, and I am hearing sound, and it is me giggling and giggling and giggling.

CHAPTER
3

Without Céline in one of the window seats or in a desk chair, Ify's private first-class cabin in the shuttle heading back to Alabast seems cavernous. Ify has shut the windows and adjusted the interior lighting for the perfect amount of brightness to keep her awake and focused on her work.

She sits cross-legged on her king-size bed (again, too big) with a series of tablets arrayed in a semicircle around her, holographic images and charts springing up from them in glimmering blue. In one display, a three-dimensional diagram of a human brain rotates with annotations spitting out from it, noting which part of the brain controls which functions. On another tablet, she scrolls through a number of memory disorders: amnesia, hyperthysemia, Korsakoff's syndrome. With each, a part of the first image grows red. On a third tablet, a newscaster drones through the catalog of daily updates on Alabast: the upcoming graduation ceremony for the latest class of students at the Institute and the preparations being made on the street level, the rising rate of homeownership given the recent influx of Colonists from the Nordic bloc Colonies. A small blip of news about an attack involving a recent immigrant from one of the outposts that served as home to fourth- and fifth-generation Earthland refugees from what was once Southeast Asia on Earth. It bothers Ify how the descendants of some Earthland refugees tend to live only among their own, as though clinging to the memory of the tragedy that befell their ancient homes is some act of bloody solidarity. Wars, rising waters, invasions, nuclear disasters. Too many catastrophes to count. Carnage caused by other humans and by the Earth itself. *You've already left Earth behind,* Ify wants to tell them, *leave behind the past as well.* She thinks back to the people of Centrafrique and the half-built structures, how so much of the capital seemed under construction, all gilded in possibility. Glowing with potential. *Be like them,* she wants to say to them, to those other migrants from Earthland who insist on speaking Ixcatec or Mayan in honor of a homeland that's now nothing but deforested, irradiated desert. *Be like them,* she wants to tell those from the Russian Federation who insist on building monuments in their Colonial enclaves to heroes that, in Ify's mind, should remain lost and forgotten.

Be like me, she realizes she's saying.

Memories of her own transformation, those moments in which her past and the trauma in it fell away like weights from her ankles, flicker in her mind: her departure from the Refugee Intake Facility to the rooming house that held other unaccompanied minors like herself, others who refused to answer the questions about their past that aid workers insisted on asking them; her insistence on speaking English anytime a fellow Nigerian refugee, seeing her tribal scars, tried to converse with her in Hausa or Yoruba; letting her prayer rug collect dust after her first time accompanying Céline to chapel, where Christian refugees from all over Earthland could worship alongside white Alabastrine citizens; taking the medicine prescribed to her by her doctor, medicine that purged her mind of Daren, who had loved her and cared for her and betrayed her, medicine that quieted her mind and helped her focus and kept the nightmares at bay. It had all seemed so easy, remaking herself, as though her course were already set. Why dwell on the horrible things people did to you? Or the horrible things you had done? Who would choose nightmares over freedom from them? Let the bodies stay buried.

No one in Alabast could call Ify a war criminal.

Only on what must be the third or fourth chime does she hear her Whistle. She sees the name flash across the digital retinal display her Whistle calls up before her eyes. She lets out a sigh of relief. Amy.

With her Whistle wirelessly connected to her tablets, she clicks a few buttons on the surface of the closest, and up pops the face of the woman who, over the course of four years, helped raise Ify from the mute, shivering West African refugee she had arrived as into the nineteen-year-old woman she is today. The woman who delivered baked goods to Ify's dorm, poking her awake whenever she found her asleep at her tiny desk, drooling all over her study materials. The woman who tirelessly coached Ify out of her bush accent and into the proper Colonial English she speaks today.

The display switches from draft to full color, and Amy's skin turns from holographic blue to the color of old parchment. Gray threads her coarse black hair. Wrinkles line the once-smooth skin by her eyes. But those hazel eyes have that same melting glow they did when Amy first set them on Ify. Like she is always just on the verge of crying.

"Mrs. Reed," Ify says, instantly at ease.

Amy frowns. "After *all* this time, Ify, and you still insist on calling me *Mrs.* Reed. You should know better." The frown twists into a smile.

"Fine. Dr. Reed."

Amy's frown returns, then they both burst into laughter.

Every time Amy calls, they begin with this dance. They'd done it whenever Amy called to offer encouragement before Ify's exams, whenever Amy called to summon her from the library for meals, whenever Amy called to deliver bad news about Ify's early immigration struggles. Whenever Amy called to vent about something her wife, Paige, had done or tell Ify far too much about their struggles having a child. Whenever she'd managed to find Ify at just the right time to console her over a bad test result or something her classmates had said or done to highlight the fact that she was nothing like them. Despite the changes that had raged around Ify like a maelstrom over the past four years, Amy had stood in the calm eye with her, holding her close.

"How was your trip?" Amy asks.

"It went very well. Céline is perfect for the job. You remember Céline, don't you?"

"Ah, yes! Your friend from school." To put it lightly.

"Yes. She will begin her post as a Colonial administrator after graduation. Among the youngest in the history of the Colonies."

Amy chuckles. "The Colonies aren't *that* old, babe. Some of us are older than the Colonies, in fact."

Life-preservation tech in the Colonies still flummoxes Ify. It means constant upgrades for your cyberization, constant maintenance, sometimes debilitating illnesses that only grow prolonged and never end. Eyes or legs or organs that cease working because they cannot adapt to the advancement of the rest of your body. All so you can take a few more breaths of recycled air.

"But I'm glad you were able to see her. How is it out there? Paige and I rarely get any time away from Alabast these days—it's such a shame—but we've been planning a vacation. And if you have any ideas of places to go in Centrafrique, maybe a safari or something of the like, do let us know. We haven't been on an adventure—a *true* adventure—in so long. And, if I'm being honest"—she lowers her voice into a conspiratorial mumble—"our marriage could use a little seasoning, if you know what I mean." She launches into a fit of giggles.

Ify chuckles nervously. "I will, Dr. Reed. I will." Normally, she'd let Amy drone on and on and make the conversation about herself—she does this more the older she gets—but the memory of Centrafrique and its vibrancy and its uniqueness still burns fresh in Ify's memory. *There are no lions in Centrafrique,* she wants to tell Amy. *No elephants. No safaris.* "What's new with you?"

"Oh, nothing." Amy pauses, bites her lip. "Well, actually, there's something I was hoping you could help me with. Us, actually. It's something Paige and I have been dealing with."

Ify stiffens, expecting more marital troubles.

"We've adopted a child."

"What?"

"A young boy seeking asylum. He'd been living in that dreadful camp everyone's always calling the Jungle. Absolutely filthy conditions. Alabast thinks they can just cram every refugee they don't want into that tiny island outpost and hope they get so sick of it they just go back to whatever war they came from. Well, some of them have no country to go back to! Hello! It's underwater!" Amy takes a moment, then goes through her breathing cycle. "I'm sorry, Ify. It's just . . . it's so difficult not to feel outraged these days. That's why I'm so happy you're doing what you're doing. All grown up and being a medical doctor, helping these refugees to adjust." She smiles at Ify, and it looks once again like tears are pooling in her eyes. "Get past their trauma. It's good work."

"So you adopted a child?" Ify can barely push past the shock.

"Well, we're sponsoring him. His asylum paperwork is being processed, but you of all people know how arduous that process is. All we can do is try to make him as comfortable as possible while we battle it out."

"What do you need me to do?" Ify knows there's too much bite in her voice. But she can't entirely mask how annoyed she is with Amy, always making these impulsive decisions. Upending a person's entire life, thinking only of herself and her supposed good intentions. She probably just did this to *add seasoning* to her marriage with Paige.

"Well, we were hoping you could help him adjust. You know, relate to him. Maybe bond with him. He's . . . he's been having problems. Acting out. His temper's all over the place. One minute, he's practically snuggling, then the next minute, he's shrieking at us that we've destroyed his life. He won't eat any meat, which I can understand—"

No, you can't, Ify almost tells her.

"—but the other stuff. Ify, I just don't know what to do. You're the only person I could think to come to. Especially since . . ."

"Since what?"

"He's . . . well, in his entrance interview, he said the reason he was seeking asylum was that he was fleeing the Biafran War."

Ify allows herself precisely two seconds of shock before she makes a determined frown. She will do what she needs to do. If not for Amy, then at least for this poor boy. But no more. She will not build this boy's future for him. Only point him in the right direction. Still, she can't fully push past her anger, so she only nods perfunctorily. When Amy says, "Thank you," Ify replies with a curt "Sure, Amy," then shuts off the transmission.

CHAPTER 4

When I am being refreshed by one of the robots, I am watching the other robots chop chop at the ground. They are standing in straight rows, and every hole they are making in the ground is the same. Same long, same wide. And I am noticing the bodies that once were covering me so much that I could not breathe. The memory is fresh in my mind and in my body, so that when I close my eyes, I still am seeing the darkness I am seeing when I first wake up and the robots pull me free. Some robots are standing in the distance, farther than I am seeing with my regular eye, but I am being able to be zooming in, and I am seeing them standing by caravan of trailers that is being made out of dirty metal.

One of the robots that is close to me is having hose with needle poking into my arm, and a different kind of water is flowing like river into me. Not river that is just water, but river with stones and sticks and other tiny things in it. It is feeding me.

This one robot is feeding me, and it is speaking to me at the same time. It is not moving its mouth, but I am still hearing words.

You're a child of war, the robot is telling me, and when the robot is telling me that I am child of war, I am remembering all kind of things.

I am running through the rain in a too-big shirt and my face is angling to the sky and I am feeling fast and I am smiling.

I am walking on a dirt road to church, and Mama is holding my hand as we are walking, and everywhere is light and bright colors—the leaves on the trees, the red clay of the earth, the colors on Mama's gown. And we are sitting in a church pew, and the pastor is speaking in loud voice, and Mama is smiling.

I am sitting on the ground in a home, and my legs are being crossed, and I am wearing green shorts. I am talking to my brother—I am not knowing how I am knowing he is my brother—and there is a bowl of chin-chin between us, and I am reaching into it, and I am eating it, and it is being crunchy and sweet in my mouth. I am trying to say something to my brother but I am not being able to say words, and he is laughing and holding his stomach and laughing and I am laughing too.

"Stop that-oh!" someone is shouting in another room. "Are you trying to choke on your food? Stop laughing with your mouth full before you fall down and die."

And my brother is saying, "Fall down and die" in funny accent like our father, and it is making me to be laughing even more.

None of these thing is feeling like war in my body.

You're a child of war, the robot is saying into my mind again.

When the robot is saying this, I am remembering a time when there is being blood everywhere on the road, shining in the light the sun is giving it in front of a military outpost. The outpost is messy because me and other soldiers who are looking like me with too-big helmet and too-big gun and too-big knife are running through it and burning thing and breaking table and collecting enemy items. And we are making circle—me and the soldier who is looking like me—and there is a man in the middle of the circle, and water is falling from his eye, and he is saying thing but it is not English. It is not any language I am understanding. And one soldier who is looking like me is taking the man's arm and dragging him to tree stump and laying arm on tree stump and holding it still. And I am having big stick in my hand. It is being as thick as my arm but I am not having problem holding it. And the soldier who is looking like me—small small child like me—is looking at me and even though his lip is not moving, he is telling me things and I am understanding. And because I am understanding, I am raising stick high above my head and I am swinging it down on the man's hand. Up and down, up and down, up and down, and man is screaming so big it is thundering in my head but I am swinging stick up and down, up and down, up and down until hand is gone and the sun is making the blood to shine everywhere.

I am remembering holding gun as big as me. I am remembering how the butt of the gun is feeling against the inside of my shoulder and how it is a comforting thing. I am remembering how the feeling starts out cold but after you are shooting it is feeling warm and my whole body is feeling warm like it will always be feeling warm.

We are in jungle and it is being dark outside and machete is slapping my back like it is angry with me while we are walking. My body is feeling like electricity is running all through it, and the man I am calling Commandant is ahead of us in jungle and he is being like second father to me because my first father is lying in hole in ground with many holes in his body and many cuts, so he is no longer looking like man.

I am remembering both of these things—eating sweet chin-chin with my father and watching him lying in ground with many cuts—and I am sadding.

The robot is pulling back the cord from my arm. And putting bandage on it, and I am remembering wearing soiled bandage when I am being child of war, but this bandage is like the color of my skin and smelling like hospital. I am trusting the robot will not hurt me.

Buzz buzz is sounding all around me. It is the robots plugging their cords into some of the dead bodies on the ground. Some of the bodies are having hole made of machete metal at back of their necks, and the robots are putting their cords into these holes and standing still, and light is pulsing like river from bodies to the robots, and I am asking the robot who is feeding me what they are doing, and the robot is telling me they are remembering. But when it is saying *remembering* it is also saying *downloading the digital information stored in the braincases of the dead and restoring the sensory data that has not been damaged beyond repair; we are collecting all of the data encapsulating their memories from their earliest moments until the time of their death.* And, at the same time as it is saying these other thing, it is also saying, *We are gathering their names.*

"What is my name?" I am asking the robot, even though I am not moving my lip.

Uzo, it is telling me.

"What is your name?"

Enyemaka, it is telling me, then it is making me to be looking at all the other robot that is hunching over body and gathering names. *We are all Enyemaka.*

CHAPTER 5

It is always quiet in the residential cul-de-sac in which Amy and Paige live. Automated bots sweep over carefully manicured front lawns. Flaxen-haired young kids have their bot move a magnetic ramp back and forth so they can practice flips with their hoverboards, not caring about the havoc the ramp's magnetism is wreaking on the bot's insides. Some of the two-story houses have balconies facing their backyards, and some of them have pools in the front. Some people hang birdboxes in their verandas facing the street, while wind chimes sing on the front porches of others. Some would look at this and see paradise, but, as more time passes, Ify tries to find less and less reason to come here. The automated cleaners, the birdsong she can hear from somewhere overhead—it's all fake. Even the bees or flies or whatever monster insect was concocted in a lab to mimic the summertime hum. Ify sets a small charge in the gold rings on her braids to emit a constant, near-silent buzz that zaps the insects when they get near enough to her, short-circuiting them and leaving them twitching on the ground. By the time she reaches Amy and Paige's front porch, a ribbon of dead bees trails behind her.

Ify notices a new plaque above the front door. Emblazoned on the raised wood is the phrase *Wir schaffen das*.

Just as she's about to press her palm to the scanner, the front door slides open and Paige spreads her arms and shrieks her welcome. "Ify!" Instantly, she swallows Ify in her embrace, smushing Ify's face into the loosely tied once-gold, now-silver ponytail draped over her shoulder. "Oh, so glad you could make it. Come, come, come." And she nearly drags Ify by the arm over the threshold. "IFY'S IN!" Paige shouts up the front steps all the way to the second floor, even though a biometric scan would have announced Ify by now. Paige turns to Ify. "You're just in time, dinner's just about ready."

Paige still hasn't let go of Ify's arm as they pass through the living room with its hand-knitted pillows and blankets, past a music room where untouched instruments have been collecting dust for at least a year and a half now, and into the joint dining room/kitchen.

Steam fills the room, billowing in clouds so thick Ify coughs. Paige waves some of it away to reveal Amy in a loose pink sleeveless gown bent over a boiling pot of red sauce. She scoops some out with a wooden spoon.

Paige nudges Ify forward, and Ify skids to a halt just far enough away that Amy, without pausing, can turn and put the spoon right to Ify's lips.

"Too hot! Too hot!" Ify leaps away and flaps at her tongue and lips. "Mrs. Reed!"

Paige puts her fists to her hips. "Oh, there she goes with that *Mrs. Reed* nonsense again! Well, Ify, if Amy's Mrs. Reed, then what am I, huh?"

Ify instinctively ducks her head amid the chaos of their playful shouting. "Can I at least sit down?"

Amy shoos Ify away with her dripping spoon, and Ify takes

a seat in one of the faux-wooden antique bistro chairs by the rectangular table. Paige sits at the head and gazes lovingly at Amy as her wife cooks.

Ify snatches the woven basket of warm bread rolls from beside Paige's elbow and stuffs one into her mouth. "What's with the sign?"

"The sign?" Paige asks.

"Yeah, out front." She rests her hand on the table, and up from her gloved palm floats a holographic snapshot of the sign above the front door. *"Wir schaffen das?"*

"Oh, that was Amy's idea. It's German. Right, Amy?"

Amy, back turned to them, nods.

"It means *We will do it*, or something like that."

Ify swallows the rest of the first roll but takes her time with the second. "Do what? Is it like in a football game? Or getting high marks on an exam?"

"No, more like . . ." Paige considers the ceiling.

"Like doing your homework," Amy says, gliding to the table and placing a steaming plate of pasta covered in marinara sauce before Ify. "Or finishing your plate." She winks at Ify in that annoying and obvious way that, Ify has realized, is Amy's way of being charming. "It's sort of like a duty. What you're supposed to do. Like how Paige is supposed to go upstairs and tell Peter that dinner's ready."

Paige lets out a loving purr-growl, then smirks and gets up from her chair. She lights a soft kiss into Amy's hair before vanishing around the corner.

Amy sets places for the rest of the table, then crouches by Ify. "The words on that plaque? They were spoken by a woman named Angela Merkel. Long ago, back when there was a

Europe to speak of, she was what they called the chancellor of Germany. Their leader. Near the beginning of the previous century, in 2015, there was a massive refugee crisis. Because of war, many people had to flee the countries they were born in, countries they'd spent their entire lives in. Many of these people came from countries in Africa and the Middle East."

"I know about the migrant crisis, Amy." She makes sure her voice is soft so it doesn't sound like too much of a chastisement.

"Well, when most of the countries with means were refusing refugees or trying to make life as difficult as possible for them, Chancellor Merkel said those words you see on that plaque. *We will do it.* You know what else she said? '*Wenn wir uns jetzt noch entschuldigen müssen dafür, dass wir in Notsituationen ein freundliches Gesicht zeigen, dann ist das nicht mein Land.*'"

"*If we must now begin to apologize for having, in dire circumstances, shown a friendly face, then this is not my country.*"

"Exactly. She was a real leader. She was kind when everyone around her thought it was better not to be. It didn't matter where these people came from, what color they were. They were in distress, and she had the power to help them." She lowers her voice, grows serious. "It means a lot to me that you would help us with Peter. He's . . . broken."

Like I was . . .

Ify's heart softens. She puts her hand on top of Amy's. Their fingers intertwine. "I am happy to help. *Wir schaffen das,*" she says, which gets Amy giggling.

"Oh, there he is!" Amy scurries off into the hallway, and Ify rises to her feet.

The smoke is nearly gone. Tendrils steam from every plate,

but the air is clear. So clear that once Peter steps into the light, Ify can take in all his features at once.

Her heart stops. *It can't be . . .*

Paige looks down at Peter, as dark as Ify, with a small single scar on each cheek and what looks like a sewn bullet hole near the top of his head. But those eyes. Ify has seen those eyes before.

In a detention center, on the other side of an invisible electric field. His hands were bound by metal restraints and rested in his lap. A collar ringed his neck, and Ify stood on the other side of the electric field, dressed as a Nigerian official with Nigeria's best mech pilot beside her, deciding whether or not those eyes deserved to see more grief because of the war the boy was caught fighting.

Five years ago, that boy had been Ify's prisoner.

Paige, her hands on Peter's shoulders, grins at Ify. "Peter, meet Ify. Ify, this is Peter."

CHAPTER

6

After the robots are finished downloading and their cords go back into their necks, they begin burying the bodies in the holes in the ground that they are making earlier. I am asking Enyemaka if they are doing this often, and Enyemaka is saying, *It is our task. It is our programming.*

You are being made to do this thing? I am asking it.

I was made to protect. But I failed that mission, so I have given myself new programming. We have made our own purpose.

You are saying I am child of war. Is this possible for me? To make new purpose?

Enyemaka is staring at me for long time, and light is moving in its eyes, and then Enyemaka is saying, in voice of woman, "Yes." And even though Enyemaka is having no mouth, I am thinking she is smiling.

So that is how I am helping Enyemaka to bury the bodies. I am smaller than them, but I am able to carry many bodies on my back so that when they are done downloading, I am picking up the bodies and laying them in front of the graves the other Enyemakas are digging for them. And we are doing this for many days. And one day, when the sun is bright in the sky and

I am having pack for water and for fruit that we are picking by river the day before, I am asking Enyemaka how they are locating these graves.

Enyemaka is hunching in front of me so that our eye is on same level. Then, in front of me is hologram map the same color of blue that is sometimes shading my rememberings. And it is showing map with squiggle lines that are supposed to be mountains and valleys, and there are red dots that are pulsing, and I am knowing that these are being people like I am seeing in my rememberings. And around every red dot is pulsing like waves of circles coming out then vanishing, and I am remembering a stone skipping on the water of a pond, and someone is throwing it to be doing this thing, and that someone is me.

We discern the location of the graves from the speech of nearby humans residing in villages not far from the burial grounds. And the map is zooming in on one of the red dots, and the squiggle lines are turning into buildings and huts and gardens, and the red dot is turning into a man who is having water falling from his eye and who is sadding.

"When are you talking to these people to be knowing where the graves are being?" I am asking Enyemaka.

And Enyemaka's map zooms out so that I see the red dots gathered in clusters, and I am knowing now that where there are many red dots to be sadding, that is where bodies are being buried or left outside for rotting. Then Enyemaka is showing me hologram of satellite photo, and in the photo is upturned dirt like scab, and it is awkward and without order and sometimes it is just one square that has not been flattened properly. Or it is like someone is wounding the earth and then being messy when sewing the wound back together.

That is how the Enyemakas are finding the graves.

One time, an old woman is coming from village to watch us work, and there is water brimming in her eyes, and no one is making sound, except for the digging. And then she is seeing me carrying body and she is screaming that this is no work for a child, and this is the first time that someone is calling me fifteen-year-old girl, and I am looking to Enyemaka, and she is looking at me like, yes, I am fifteen years old, but I am feeling older and younger at the same time, so I am moving the bodies I am carrying to their graves and then I am walking to the old woman who has red dirt on the hem of her gown.

When I stand in front of old woman with water in her eyes, she is not saying anything but her lip is trembling like she is holding something in her face but she is still sadding. So I reach my hand and touch her arm, and she is shaking with holding back sobs.

And I am asking her, "Is there someone you are knowing who is being killed here?" And my voice is scratching like knife in my throat because I am not speaking too much with Enyemakas and I am not used to using my voice like this, but, for some reason, this woman is not being able to speak to my brain the way Enyemaka is, or she is not wanting to. Maybe she is wanting to think that I am human being and not child of war. As I am speaking to her, I am scanning with the metal that is being inside my head and I am seeing that she is having metal in her head too, and Enyemaka is calling this a braincase, and I scan and I am knowing where to look to see her rememberings, and I am seeing that she is thinking of gold tooth and brown slippers, and I am walking back to bodies in front of Enyemakas and I am looking and looking and looking until I am finding one with gold tooth and brown slippers. I am bringing this body to old woman and she is falling to her knees and beating the earth and making it dark with the water from her eyes. And I am just standing there without smile or frown, just face like stone with body of person she is loving in my arms.

When she is finished beating the earth, she is trying to smile and say thank you but no word is coming out. But I am looking down where she is coming from. And then she is walking and I am following her and we are arriving at her home and in backyard of her hut with blue dome around it to protect from poison red air. I am digging with my hands and digging and digging until skin is peeling away, and she is seeing that my fingers and my hands are made of metal. And I know she is thinking me disgusting, but I am not caring. I am only caring about my duty, and my duty is to help with the rememberings. So I dig hole and I look to woman, and she is nodding to me like she has forgotten that I am disgusting thing, and I put the body in hole and fill it back up again.

Then I am walking back to Enyemakas, and they have finished downloading the rememberings and have buried the bodies in neat rows.

It is good that I am able to be bringing the woman the whole body. Sometimes, when we dig, there is only a bag with pieces in it. Just a mess of clothings and blankets and hair pressed into strange shapes all with no smell. And the skull is only two pieces: the jaw and everything else. And sometimes the teeth are clean inside the bag but there is no outlet on the skull so we see no braincase. Sometimes there is braincase inside the skull and the Enyemakas are plugging into it to download the rememberings but it is difficult to bury the body again because it is already in many pieces.

At the end of a day of work, we are all walking back to the workstation. It is a few trailers linked together, and they follow the Enyemakas like a caravan. In the beginning, they were all always moving moving never stopping, but the caravan is needing to rest, so the Enyemakas make to rest as well, but I know it is just pretending like how I am pretending.

I am learning with this work that I am not needing rest like normal people.

Enyemaka are following me to the first trailer, where light is glowing, and they are walking in one at a time and passing few moments, sometimes whole minute, then walking back out and the next one is going in, and so on and so on. Every time Enyemaka is going inside, they duck their head so they are not banging it on doorway, and this is making me giggle for some reason.

Then when they finish, I am walking up the metal steps to the inside of the trailer, and everything is metal, and the door is sliding shut behind me like whoosh, and the air is cool in here and not paining me with fire like outside.

I am closing my eyes when I am suddenly smelling sulfur like rotten egg, and then my head is paining me and I am falling to the ground like the woman I am giving dead body to and I am seeing nothing, then all I am seeing is white, then I am seeing little girl with pigtail on both side of her head and barrettes in pigtails and I am crouched over girl, then I am seeing girl covered in blood but still alive and looking at me with blank face like face carved from stone, then I am back in trailer and I am shivering but not from cool air.

When this is happening before, Enyemaka are telling me that I am having what is called temporal lobe epilepsy and that it is wounding in my brain from when I was child of war. Most times but not always, I am waking in trailer and I am receiving medicine in my arm, then I am better. But they still come and my body is shaking shaking.

And I am trying to remember the mission. I am trying to be remembering why we are downloading all these rememberings, and I am seeing the hard drives that the Enyemakas are transferring the information to, and it is these hard drives that we will give to people when we return to the city, and I am trying to think of my duty, but then Xifeng is holding me and not letting me move.

I am wanting to tell Xifeng thank you, but my tongue is not moving in my mouth, so I am just letting her hold me until my head is no longer paining me.

CHAPTER

7

"In the beginning," Peter says around a mouthful of spaghetti, slurping a noodle so that it smacks his nose with sauce, "we were on the side of the government, and we were against the rebels. I was a child, so I didn't know sides, but we had government stations broadcast on our BoTas and iFlexes."

Amy sits to Ify's left and twirls pasta around her fork. She leans toward Ify as though to whisper some conspiracy and says, quite loudly, "Peter's father worked in the mining industry and was apparently very high up in the food chain." She looks at Peter, and Ify worries she will wink at the poor boy. "On a first-name basis with the president, right?" When Peter nods, Amy nods too, satisfied with herself. "Tell Ify about the bakery."

Peter turns his eyes to Ify. "When you're a child, you don't know what revolution is or what a regime is. You only know who puts suya in your wrapper on the street or who turns off the light to your room when you go to sleep." He talks of these things to Ify as though she were oyinbo just like Amy and Paige. Like she hadn't spent so much of her life in exactly the same place he is describing. But she grits her teeth because something is strange about this boy. "I had everything I could ask for. I wanted for nothing." Where did this boy learn his English? His accent is gone. "Electronics, trips into town by rail or bus. We were wealthy. So wealthy that I would be brought to the front of the line when I went to the bakery to collect bread for my family. But then fighting came closer and closer to our village and we couldn't go out and play as far as we would before."

Both Paige and Amy have furrowed brows focused on Peter, like he is both an equation to solve and a fascination, some strange and exotic animal from another planet that they've come across. Ify has seen that look before, and every time, she's struggled to find the words for what boils in her chest, what she wants to say to get them to stop. He is not a shiny foreign object. He is a boy and quite possibly a liar. But she just remains silent, twirling sauce-drenched spaghetti around her fork and trying to look as though she's enjoying the meal while listening to Peter's story.

"There was one rebel group, they were called Angels of Heaven, and they were inching closer into the countryside. And getting closer and closer to where we lived. The morning they came, I was asleep in the guest room at a cousin's house. It is tradition for us to—how do I put it—swap relatives from time to time. Our houses have many stories, and cousins come to live with you or you go to live with them. For a while, my grandmother stayed with us, and I had to give her English lessons because she was too old to be cyberized, and she only spoke the kind of Igbo that I couldn't use my software to translate. But the heart knows." He smiles, and charm sparkles in his eyes. It repulses Ify. The manipulation is so blatant. She can tell immediately that he is doing everything he can to take advantage of them. But why? What is his agenda? "Anyway, I was in my cousin's house's guest room when we hear this huge BOOM!" He leaps from his chair and Amy and Paige shriek in unison, so that when he sits down again, he's fighting back a grin. "Glass everywhere. Pshhhhhh! Imagine how the ground would be shaking beneath you. It would be terrifying, right? I wasn't terrified. Maybe I was numb. Maybe I knew I was protected. The sound of the explosion told me that it had been a vehicle bomb. Maybe a car. More likely a truck. There's a very particular sound to a truck bomb. Once you hear it, you never forget."

Ify's frown deepens.

"So, I went outside. And everywhere, pieces of building were falling down. It was like weather, the way stones and shrapnel and pieces of metal fell from the sky. That is what the violence became in my country during the war. It was like the weather." He doesn't look to Ify for confirmation. Indeed, this whole time, it seems as though he's been making a conscious effort to ignore her, to pretend she doesn't even exist at this table. "I walked past a building that had been cut in half by the bomb. There was shooting. Katakata. Katakata. Everywhere, bullets flying. Even pinging the walls around me.

"Then I hear this poor man moaning. I look around, and that's when I see him. Lying on the ground in a government uniform. He'd been shot in the stomach. Soft moans. That's what he's letting out. Very soft moans, but I can hear very well, and I hear him. As soon as he sees that I am not the enemy, he begs for my help. Not in sewing up his wound, but in escaping. And I tell him it is absolute foolishness to try crossing this main street wearing a government uniform when there are rebels shooting katakata everywhere." Peter leans in toward Paige and Amy and lowers his voice. "So I tell him I have an idea. And I go back into what's left of my cousin's home, and I open the dresser in my aam and aamee's room, and it is just as I have hoped. The clothes are untouched. Not even a speck of dust on them. So I take one of her dresses and return to the soldier, and I say, 'Hey, put this on, it will be very helpful.'" He bursts into laughter.

After a nervous beat, Paige and Amy join in. Ify can't even bring herself to pretend. But when the table calms down, Paige asks, "Well, did he?"

"He refused at first, but eventually, he realized he wanted to live, so he wore the dress." Peter takes generous sips of his water, then loudly smacks his lips.

"Where was your village again?" Ify asks.

All heads turn to her.

After a moment's pause, Peter's expression changes from one of surprise to one of smirking understanding. "Kaduna State."

"An Igbo-speaking family that far north? Among the Muslims?"

Peter holds Ify's gaze for long enough that sweat begins to bead Amy's forehead. Then he looks away. "Everyone loved our family. Before the war, no problems."

Ify lets out a quiet "Hmm."

"Back then," Peter continues, turning his attention to his more sympathetic audience, "it was possible to be a young man without joining a militia. Even though they would leave bodies to rot in the street, they would leave you alone if it was clear to them that you were not on the side of the government. The Angels of Heaven didn't steal anything. They weren't the reason we lost everything. That happened when another group, the Popular Front for Justice in Biafra, came in to take their territory. They were truly vicious. This group didn't just want a

Biafran state in southeast Nigeria. They wanted all of Nigeria to belong to Biafra. What is the expression? 'Scorched earth'? That was them. Burn everything in their path, and as they left, they would salt the ground so nothing good could grow there."

Amy gasps.

"Not literally. I mean that as a figure of speech. But, yes, that is what they did. They claimed to install hospitals and places where you could get an ID card. They claimed to have a police force and all these things that governments were supposed to have, and they claimed to represent the Igbo minority in the Muslim north. We should have welcomed them with open arms, right? They were here to rescue us from a government that cared not at all for my tribe. But when the Biafrans came, it was nothing but blood and thunder." He turns to Ify. "You spent time with the Biafrans, yes?"

The only sound, other than Peter's voice, had been the scraping of forks and knives and spoons against plates, but now even that stops. Ify doesn't feel surprise. She doesn't *let* herself feel surprise. All this time, this boy has been building toward something, and while Ify still doesn't quite see the game he is playing, she can tell what type of person he is, and she is prepared for this. So, when her shoulders tense, it is not from being caught off guard. It is from what she wants Paige and Amy to see as her visceral, roiling anger. Just barely contained in the pulse of her jaw and the trembling of her utensils in her hands.

Amy puts her hand on Ify's, and Ify knows she too is manipulating the woman—getting her to believe that Ify is in more distress than she really is—but if Amy were to ask, Ify would tell her that it's for her own good. For a long time, Amy stares at Ify until Ify looks up and the two meet each other's gaze. Amy gives her a soft, understanding smile, then turns to Peter. "We don't really talk about Biafra or Nigeria with Ify here."

"Oh," Peter says, then leans back in his chair, his face blank.

"And your parents?" Ify asks. When she sees Peter thrown off balance, she knows she's hit on something. "Did they die in the rebel attack?"

"I don't know."

"You don't know?" Ify makes sure it sounds like an accusation when she says it.

Peter frowns. "I don't know, because one day my cousin went missing, and when I went to look for him, I was captured. The Popular Front called me a spy, and they arrested me. Before I could look for my parents, I was thrown into prison."

Ify fights to keep her frown from turning into a scowl. But her suspicions have been confirmed. Peter has been lying. Maybe about part of his story, maybe about all of it. There's no way he could have known that Ify was once a high-ranking Nigerian official, that Ify had had access to all of the data collected on rebel movements during the Biafran War. There's no way he could have known that Ify knew the names and military capabilities of every recorded rebel group in the country. Because, if he did, he would have changed his story.

■ ■ ■ ■ ■

The box is hidden under the floorboards of Ify's living room, beneath a rug and in a place where the grooves of panel hiding it are invisible to the naked eye. She's buried it in the only portion of her apartment where the cameras cannot angle to see her. The one blind spot in her apartment's surveillance system. She could have turned the cameras off and even blocked the auxiliary cameras. She could have found blankets to put up. She could have kept this box somewhere else. But this is what she does. She keeps it close, so that every time she walks over this space, she's reminded of what she's put here. What she's carried with her.

With the removed panel next to her, she sits cross-legged in front of the space and reaches in and pulls out a black box large enough to fit in her lap but far too heavy for it. So she sets it beside her, careful to keep within the blind spot.

For several minutes she simply stares at the thing. Laying her eyes upon it sets her mind ablaze with memories, images colored with fire, coated in blood: she stands at the threshold of an apartment, the door slides open, she raises her arm and pulls the trigger on the gun in her hand; explosions rip through the city of Enugu, and she runs and runs and runs through the chaos and destruction as civilians cry and weep and die around her; a boy sits on the other side of an invisible electric fence, shadows cutting across his body in this cage, hands limp in his lap, evil smile sparkling in his eyes, and Ify on the other side of that fence, staring, analyzing, inspecting.

She puts her fingers to her neck, presses her index and middle fingers against the skin of her bodysuit, and immediately, chemicals flood her system with pleasure and relief and fill her with just the perfect amount of vertigo to wash away the memories.

Her hands stop shaking enough for her to lift the lid on the box, revealing row after row after row of mini drives. Small, almost obsolete micro SD cards on which are stored evidence. She pulls one out and fits it into an external device she's pulled from a pocket and which she fits to her Bonder, a visor-shaped device whose edges she slips over her ears. A cord slithers out of an outlet by her temple, and she connects it to the external device.

A vision splashes to life before her, first in the faded blue of a holographic projection, then in the technicolor of a proper memory.

A tablet screen, held in gloved hands Ify recognizes as hers as a maglev jeep spirits her away from what she knows is a detention facility. Across from her sits a man who rescued her from rebels, who took her in and taught her about herself, a man who would then destroy her life. Daren. Ify has angered him—she remembers this much. But the version of her in the memory keeps her gaze focused on the tablet as she scrolls down a list.

Angels of Heaven.

Asawana Avengers.

Niger Delta Water Lions.

The list of terrorist groups—Igbo, Yoruba, Christian, Muslim, even Hausa—goes on and on. Ify scrolls with the regular speed of intense focus. Ify outside the memory knows what Ify inside the memory will find. Or, rather, will not find. She disengages from the memory, thrown back into her body with an intensity so strong it forces her to take several deep breaths. She is right.

The Popular Front for Justice in Biafra, the group Peter claims raided his village and arrested him, never existed.

CHAPTER
8

Xifeng is showing me that I am having hole in the back of my neck. She is holding mirror to the back of my neck and making me watch in other mirror, and I am seeing hole and I am feeling it, and it is metal like gun or like Enyemaka. It is not shining. It is being covered in dust from the desert, and every night after our working, Xifeng is cleaning it for me, and it is like taking bath. I know what taking bath is like because I am downloading rememberings too, just like Enyemaka.

Because I am downloading rememberings, I am remembering what it is being like to be child of peace, not child of war, and to be sitting in tub with soap like clouds on the water and to be feeling mother's hands in my hair. I am remembering what it is like to be laughing and splashing the water and maybe mother is sometimes talking soft to me and sometimes mother is splashing with me. I am remembering water is warm, and I am also remembering that mother is changing dial on wall in washroom to make water colder or warmer, so I can always be giggling. Some of the rememberings are being washed in blue like hologram, and some of them are coming in flashes with static, but some of them are whole and I am not just seeing thing, I am smelling and feeling it too. All of this I am remembering when Xifeng is cleaning the hole at the back of my neck. She is calling it outlet. *Outlet* is strange name to me, because I am using it to bring rememberings into me, so I am wanting to call it *inlet*, because I am letting things into me.

"An inlet is something else," Xifeng is saying to me. "English is a strange language." She is speaking in soft soft voice like her mind is being somewhere else.

"It is not what you are speaking when you are child?" I am asking her, and my throat is not paining me so much when I am speaking to her, though I am wishing I am speaking to her like I am speaking to Enyemakas. Our speaking is being full with sound and color, like what is being trapped in word is being released. I am feeling like Enyemaka is knowing all of what I am meaning when I am saying thing. But Xifeng is only knowing piece of it.

"What makes you say that, Uzo?"

"You are being Han Chinese. You are mostly speaking Mandarin, but you are wishing to be speaking Cantonese, because you are coming from Guangzhou. You are knowing people who are speaking Taishanese, and when you are not noticing you are sometimes moving from Cantonese to Taishanese, and I am thinking it is because you are wanting to be near to someone who is not being here."

Xifeng is looking at me with wide eyes, and water is brimming in them, and she is not moving. Her hand is hovering over my neck. I am knowing that all of this is happening even though my back is to her, because I am feeling it, and thing is happening in my brain to be mapping where I am sitting and calculating her heart rate and diagramming the movement of her muscles and the ways in which her brain is sparking. Even though Xifeng is behind me, I am seeing all of her vital sign and numbers and the map of her body with some parts glowing red and other parts glowing blue. Retinal display is showing me diagram of her brain and which neuron is firing where. I am sensing these thing like how Enyemaka is sometime knowing when I am needing water to cool down or oil for my joints. Xifeng's body is telling me these thing, and I am not knowing why it is doing this, because all I am doing is saying thing to her.

"H-how did you . . ." Her body is moving like the other woman when I am burying person she is loving who is dead. And I am expecting water to be falling from Xifeng's eyes to my neck. Then Xifeng's body is stilling like water after stone is kissing its surface. "Were you rummaging through my recordings?"

I am wanting to tell Xifeng that I am knowing these thing because I am hearing traces of where she is coming from in how she is speaking, and I am sometime seeing her writing and I am seeing how she is moving and what she is looking at and how she is walking and the way she is breathing when she is talking or when she is even just smiling, and all of these thing is telling me that she is wanting to be speaking Taishanese. I am wanting to be telling her that she is carrying rememberings inside her body and inside her bones and inside her skin and her body is speaking with rememberings every time I am looking at her. I am wanting to tell Xifeng that I am knowing all these thing from watching her, but I am not knowing how to say the full thing the way I am saying it to Enyemaka. And what I am wanting to tell her is crashing inside my head and trying to force itself into word. But then I give up. "Are you wanting to be speaking Taishanese to me?"

For a long time, Xifeng is not moving, and I am not moving. Then Xifeng is wrapping her arms around me and holding me close to her chest and water is falling from her face and landing on my neck and washing the dirt from my outlet.

"Oh, child," she is saying to me in Taishanese.

And I am wondering if I am making her to be sadding. Then I am wondering if this is making me to be bad person. But I am not knowing how to be asking Xifeng if I am bad person because I am shooting gun and breaking hand and making there to be dead bodies, so I am not asking her. I am just letting her hold me until water is no longer coming from her eyes.

Then I am listening to her body. It is saying to me that it is happy.

I am making Xifeng to be happy, and it is making me to be happy too.

■ ■ ■ ■ ■

Outside, the sun is shining bright and red on us again. Enyemaka are telling us that the next grave site is not far, and I am hearing the buzzing from what Xifeng is calling nanobots. To get the rememberings from the dead bodies, we are sometimes plugging into them directly. But sometimes, we are getting to a grave site and it is covered in nanobots that is swarming like flies. I am seeing that they are different from flies because they are being made out of metal like the gun or the outlet at the back of my neck. Xifeng is not seeing the nanobots because they are small small, but I am seeing them and Enyemaka are seeing them too. And when we get to grave site, Enyemaka are standing still while nanobots fly to them like mosquito, and they are taking the nanobots inside them and their eyes are glowing because they are receiving the rememberings through the nanobots, and the same is happening to me. The nanobots fly into my ears and are buzzing into my blood, and I am collecting the rememberings like this too.

When I am asking Enyemaka where they are coming from, they are telling me that they are being built and that they are being given life by nanobots. They are telling me that person made out of metal but still person with flesh and blood is having nanobots inside her and she is spitting on Enyemaka's ear, and I am thinking that spitting is bad thing because Xifeng is telling me not to do this when there is much saliva in my mouth, but Enyemaka are telling me that this is what this girl did and that it was to put nanobots inside them. And then when Enyemaka met the other robots, Enyemaka did the same thing to them, and that is how they are being given life.

When Enyemaka are telling me these thing, they are sending image into my brain and I am seeing girl with hair in braids down her back and rough fingers and dirt smudged on her face and who is cleaning Enyemaka with hand that is made of metal, and I am seeing that her whole arm is being made of metal, and something is shaking in me when I am seeing this person. I am not knowing this feeling, but it is taking all of me and shaking the inside of me, then the image is gone, but the feeling is still there, then the feeling is gone too.

Who is that? I am asking Enyemaka.

Our maker, Enyemaka are telling me.

Why am I feeling like this when I am seeing picture of her?

But Enyemaka is not answering me. I am asking them again, but Enyemaka is still not answering me.

So I am finding dead things in the desert like lizard or animal with two heads or giant boar and I am spitting on its ear, but it is not working. And I am thinking there is problem with me, but Enyemaka are telling me that there is no problem with me. Some things are dead and are staying dead. And I am thinking that Xifeng is having Enyemaka telling me these thing so that when I am finding dead body I am not spitting on them to give them life.

We are not far from grave site when I am hearing buzzing. But this buzzing is different. It is lower like rumbling, and we are all looking to where the ground is meeting the sky in the east, and I am seeing dust rising like clouds from the ground where the air is so hot it is looking like water.

The first gunshot is like a really fast bee. It is just buzzing by my ear. Then there are being many of them and they are just pinging the sides of the trailers, and Xifeng is running inside while the Enyemakas stand guard around her trailer. Nobody is having gun, so there is nothing we can be doing while Xifeng is driving the trailer away and searching for shelter.

But my body is moving without me thinking. The Enyemakas are making line to protect the trailer and I am behind them, but suddenly I am running and running and running and there is only desert in front of me and there is dust behind me rising from my running, and it is like everything is blurring around me, but I see them coming toward us fast fast.

Bullets whistle at me. FEWN FEWN FEWN. But my body is moving to dodge them. They are shooting with pistol, and it is easy to hop to left, to right, to duck, to jump where they are striking the ground at my feet. From far away, I am hearing CLICK-CLACK of rifle, and I am running faster toward the sound and timing my moving perfectly so that when I hear RATATATATATATA I am flipping and hopping and always moving forward. I am not knowing how I am able to do these thing. I am not remembering this doing in the rememberings I am downloading. I am just moving. Like this remembering is deep in my body. Like it is not being in my braincase, but it is instead being in my bones. In my legs and in my arms and in my fingers. It is like electricity but it is also cool, and I am feeling like I am being washed in cold water that is feeling nice under the desert sun. And maybe this is how I am knowing that Xifeng is wanting to speak Taishanese. Her body is remembering.

In front of my face, I am seeing target reticle and I am seeing enemies outlined in red. And I am hearing beeping as each one appears to me and my brain is being told what guns they are carrying and how many bullets they are having left after wasting them on me. And my brain is being told what they are riding and how many of them there are, and suddenly they are close enough for me to smell.

They are riding hoverbikes and trucks and are in a staggered line, all jagga-jagga. And they are wearing masks and bandanas over their faces to keep from breathing the red dust. This is how I am knowing that many of them are weak.

The first one is speeding his bike toward me. He is steering it while another sits behind him with a shotgun balanced on the driver's shoulder.

As I am running, I am picking up stone and throwing it with all of my strength. It is hitting boy with shotgun straight in his forehead, and he is falling backward and landing on the ground. Driver is swerving and losing control and turning too fast so that his bike is flipping over and crashing and flipping and crashing, and he is dying when it lands on top of him. I am jumping over the bike and running to boy with shotgun who is not moving, and I am picking up shotgun and shooting through cloud of dust at a man on another motorbike. He is flipping and crashing and dying too.

The buzzing of their vehicles is now a roar around me as some of them pass me, then turn around. I know I must destroy their vehicles so they cannot move fast fast to Xifeng and Enyemaka.

I hear RATATATATATA fast fast and duck behind first bike that I am causing to flip and crash. It is man on another bike who is shooting at me. I am peeking my head out to see him and ducking again when he is shooting.

He drives past me, and I am aiming and shooting, and his partner with gun is falling over and crushing the driver and causing him to swerve back and forth until he is stopping.

I am running and bullets are chomping at my feet, and at moment when driver is reaching for his partner's rifle, I am shooting him and his face is exploding. I grab rifle so I am holding shotgun in one hand and rifle in the other.

And I am turning and shooting and turning and shooting until all around me is explosion and dying. I am jumping and taking cover behind overturned bikes and I am hearing rumbling of truck getting closer. It is the last vehicle left.

There is dust making clouds everywhere, but I am seeing through the dust, and my brain is locating the target, so I sling shotgun over my back and fall to one knee, and I am aiming the rifle and shooting, and the front tires of the truck are making loud POP and truck is skidding until it too is falling over.

I am hearing screaming and I am seeing blood splashing on front window, and that is how I am knowing that driver is dead.

But I am seeing shapes move behind the truck. There are more attackers coming out, and they are wearing dirty bandana over their nose and mouth, and they are shooting and I am shooting, but I am only having two guns and I am quickly running out of bullets.

Small bikes and larger bikes are lying like dead animals almost in semicircle around truck. So I am moving fast fast from one to the other and dodging bullets until I am getting to behind truck and the attackers are not seeing me.

I am holding my rifle by its neck, and I am swinging at the back of the first bandit's head, and he is falling like sack of yams. I am dropping my gun and picking up his and shooting the second bandit, and there are three left and one of them is holding knife and running at me.

I am shooting at him but he is moving fast fast like me, left right left right, until he is in front of me and knocks gun away from me.

He is slashing at me and I am raising my arms to keep knife away from my head and my chest. He is raising arm and bringing it down, and I block and twist his wrist, but he is dropping knife and catching it with other hand and stabbing, and I am moving out of the way, but he is cutting my shirt. I turn behind him and twist his arm, and it is making snapping sound. But snapping sound is also CLICK-CLACK of rifle behind me, and I know other bandit is going to shoot. So I spin around again, and bandit with knife is catching bullets with his body, and I am running using his body as shield and taking knife from him. And I am crashing into bandit with gun and raising knife and cutting his neck.

I am rolling to the side when new bullets are cutting line

through ground straight for the bodies. And I am coming up to one knee and throwing knife at another bandit, and he is dropping and everything is being quiet again, not even mosquito or nanobot is buzzing.

Slowly, I am standing again and I am walking to pick up knife and take rifle and put it over my shoulder so it is hanging with shotgun, and I am picking through pockets for bullets and shells and putting them in my own pocket, and I am taking vests and other clothes and putting them on so I can hold more bullets and shells, and just as I am turning to go, I am seeing him.

He is boy. Vest is hanging off his bare chest that is all skin and bones. He is so small that gun he is holding is as big as him. And he is standing so still that not even my mind's eye is detecting him. He is not glowing red like living things. When smoke clears, he is just boy covered in dust.

Even though he is not shooting at me or throwing knife, I know he is like me. He is child of war.

"You are not having to be like this," I am telling him. And I am saying this out loud because Xifeng is saying I should practice talking but also because I am sometimes missing the sound of my own voice. So I am saying, "You are not just child of war."

But the boy is silent.

"You are not needing gun to live." I am looking for more words, because I know I am supposed to be saying more to this boy. "I am once being child of war, but I am learning of more way of being. Different way of being. Only killing and fighting when I must. To protect people. Some days, no killing and no fighting. I think before I am killing and fighting all the time, but I am not doing these thing all the time anymore."

He is looking at me and not saying words, and there is small

small hair on his head and I am wanting to shave his head so that his hair is not trapping sun-heat on his scalp, and I am wanting to give him headscarf and protect him from sunburn. And I am wanting these things because I have remembering in me that I am doing this thing before for someone who is making my heart happy. And I am wanting to make this boy happy, but he is saying nothing.

"Come with us. Come with me."

"You're one of us," he is saying in quiet quiet voice.

Blood-covered fist is clenching at my sides. "I am not bad person."

But boy is saying no more thing and is just looking at me with nothing in his eye, not even water. Then he is walking away with gun in his arms and machete slapping his leg softly like it is walking with him.

I am collecting gun and bullet from dead bodies, and I am walking and walking and walking until I see Enyemakas and Xifeng's trailer. And while I am walking, I am telling myself I am not bad person.

And I am trying to believe it.

CHAPTER

9

To wash the away the memories of terrorist groups and detention of militants and Peter, like oil from her skin, Ify wanders past the Viewer, that giant glass-encased observation deck where she has spent countless hours staring out at the stars and the Refuse Ring that circles the colony of Alabast. She continues past the school dorms where she and Céline had lived as students, then past the streets where, as a young refugee, she had been stopped by bots and other authorities and asked for her papers. She wanders and wanders and would have no way to gauge the passage of time were it not for the information that her bodysuit, connected to her Augment, beams into her brain. But it disturbs her that it always seems to be daylight here. Meandering without direction, she finds herself back in Amy and Paige's cul-de-sac. This is how she will spend the end of her dwindling time off from work, worrying about whether or not the foolishness of these well-meaning white women will result in tragedy.

It always grates on Ify how the synthetic sunlight never properly mimics the days and nights she remembers. When people should be readying for bed, it still looks outside as though it is the middle of the day. Sometimes, she thinks this is a malfunction of this particular neighborhood or this corner of the Colony. But it is really that the people who live here like it this way. They like long days, even if it means that children grow up not knowing when they should go to sleep to get proper rest and be ready for school. Or teenagers will play their music too loudly for too long while others are trying to sleep. Remove the rules, and you might as well prepare for chaos. That is what she feels, sitting on the front porch of Paige and Amy's home. Whenever she is in Alabast, this is what's waiting for her: messed-up sleep cycles and unseasoned spaghetti.

"Not enough spices," says a voice from behind her, as though reading her mind.

She's halfway to her feet when Peter shuffles down the steps to sit next to her. They're close, but he leaves enough space to be respectful.

"I should say something, shouldn't I?"

Ify doesn't disguise her skepticism.

"Don't worry, they're busy cleaning right now. And saying loving things to each other. I am happy to give them their space."

Ify lets him sit in silence long enough for it to become uncomfortable, but Peter seems unfazed, focusing his gaze on the starless simulated sky. "What really happened?" She hopes he hears the low threat in her voice.

"What do you mean?"

Ify's frown deepens.

"Oh. Well, I was captured by the Popular Front. I wasn't tortured or anything. There were others in my prison. One of them was a journalist who kept going on and on about what a beautiful country Nigeria was. I thought maybe he was a spy with the Popular Front. They maybe put him in prison to see if any of us was with another group or with the government. Maybe they put him there to trick us. If he was a spy, he wasn't a good one. They even tortured him a little bit, but perhaps this was just part of their plan to make it convincing. Anyway, after my release, they took me to the local chief for that area, a big oga draped in golden robes and jewels, and he apologized for jailing me and asked for my forgiveness. Then he gave me many naira and sent me on my way."

"This is what you told them?" Ify asks.

Peter shrugs. "It is what I tell everyone who asks." He shifts closer to Ify. "And when I know I have their attention, I tell them that, while I was in prison, I would ask my guards for photographs of people hugging, and I would say that I asked for this because I'd forgotten what hugging looked and felt like because I had been in prison for so long. Sometimes, in front of the other prisoners, I would take off my clothes and snuggle with them to pretend I was being held in my sleep. That makes them cry every time."

"But none of that is true," Ify says, no trace of a question in her voice. "It's not true, because no rebel group ever captured you. The Popular Front for Justice in Biafra never existed. And you were not an innocent boy."

A tremor runs through Peter's shoulders, then is gone.

"You were a militant. A soldier in a secessionist group that used children to blow up crowded buildings." Ify says this all in a low drone. "You were captured as an enemy of the state and held in detention for your crimes. And, if my guess is correct, you were released as a result of the ceasefire." She refuses to look at him, not because he very likely did horrible things during the war but because he dared to lie to people Ify loves. "I'm sure you endured trauma during those years, but you have no right to lie to these people. When they discover the truth—"

Peter jumps to his feet and kneels on the steps before Ify. Suddenly, there are tears in his eyes, and he has his hands clasped together as in prayer. For a panicked moment, Ify looks behind her to see if, through the open door, either Paige or Amy can see this, but they're gone. Out of sight. "Please," Peter hisses through his teeth. "Please do not be telling them where I am really coming from."

"Your accent."

"You are correct. You are correct. I . . . I am not being entirely truthful. But—but I am trying to save my life. I am desperate, and I am needing help, and they—they are helping me. Please."

Options war within Ify. Expose him and maybe limit the damage. But how to tell Paige and Amy without breaking their hearts? Maybe try to push him toward other sponsors. Let him deceive other oyinbo with his fanciful stories.

A mask comes over his face. Like a shadow. "If you tell them, I will hurt them. Deeply." He clenches his fists and stands like something spring-loaded, like a bullet ready to be fired from a gun. "I have learned ways of making people suffer. I know they are dear to you. All the time, they are talking about you. So if you want nothing bad to be happening to them, you will be keeping my secret."

Ify's heart leaps into her throat. She can't move. The thought of anything happening to Paige or Amy roots her where she sits, as though each word from Peter is another pour from a barrel of concrete.

"Now that I am seeing your face, I am wondering another

thing. I am wondering how much they know about you. There is only one way you can be knowing that I am lying. That is because you are being soldier as well. For Naija Army. And you are knowing who is rebel and where they are being rebel. And now I am recognizing your face." A smile splits his lips. "I am wanting to kill you once. I know because I am sitting in cell and you are standing on the other side of it wearing army gown, and you are standing with fancy army pilot, and you are writing things about me in your tablet, but you are not writing that I am being tortured by government and being held in my cell for almost every hour of the day. And you are not even changing your name when you come here." He shakes his head, smiling wryly.

"They would never believe you."

But Peter's smile doesn't fade. He knows. He knows that Ify is not certain. He knows that when the time comes, Ify would be unable to bring herself to lie. "I am thinking that for now, they are looking at you like daughter."

Ify grits her teeth.

"But when they are finding out you are war criminal, maybe this change." He shrugs, then walks back up the stoop and into the house. The door whisks open and shut behind him.

And Ify is left to the sunlight and the birdsong and the buzzing of insects, all of it a façade. A flimsy, horrible façade.

■ ■ ■ ■ ■

The refugee ward sprawls before her. Her bodysuit tells her she has arrived just as the night shift is beginning. Even though she is off duty, Ify wears her lab coat with her nameplate on it. Over her bodysuit, it feels like a proper uniform, a thing this new Ify has grown comfortable in. The cavernous space, with its high, rounded ceiling and its silver walls, is filled with synthetic light. But the light here doesn't bother Ify. Everything—the light, the temperature, the softly antiseptic smell—has been calibrated to allow for maximum comfort of the patients whose beds extend in row after row before her.

Ify is only here to watch. She's not on duty, and she's loath to disrupt the rotation of nurse attendants, red-blood and bot, who make their rounds, checking vitals and having quiet, smiling conversations.

She sees her assistant at a patient's bed, which is elevated to a sitting position. Ify's assistant, brown hair tied back in a messy bun with strands falling over her face, fingers folded to keep her fingers from twitching, probably bubbling from the caffeine streaming into her from the patches on her skin beneath her top and lab coat, is smiling. Grace.

Ify taps her temple to activate the Augment in her neck and enhances her audio input to better hear what Grace is saying. She tells herself it's to observe and critique her assistant's work, but she sees something human in the connection between Grace and the Chinese woman with blanched skin and fading black hair, and a part of her longs for that. So, she enhances and listens and starts when she realizes Grace isn't speaking English.

A frown creases her brow. Grace isn't cyberized, not even partially. She has no language translation software downloaded into her, and Ify spies no Augment on Grace's body, nothing in her hair, nothing on her temple, no small half-sphere attached to the back of her neck. Ify scrolls through her languages and alights on Cantonese. Then it all comes through clearly.

"You've never had durian?" the patient asks Grace, shocked.

Grace chuckles. "No, ma'am, I have not. My grandfather says it is popular on Earthland and is always complaining that he can never find it in the markets here."

"Does he not live on Earthland?"

"No, we brought him to the Colonies several years ago. He's getting older, and my parents wanted him to be near family."

"That is so sweet. Well, when you see him again, tell him I know where he can get good durian. I know where the good Hong Kong market is."

Grace laughs. "But where will he eat it?" she exclaims. "The whites will complain about the smell before it even leaves the bag!"

Which gets both of them laughing loud enough for Ify to hear without her enhanced audio. She wants to chastise Grace for displaying such boisterous mirth in a place where people are suffering, where people will look to her and see joy and be plunged even deeper into their own despair—*Ask the patient about her medical condition! Ask her about her sleep patterns or her food intake or her stool!*—but she can't bring herself to stay angry at her assistant.

"Come close, child," the woman says, when they're done laughing.

Grace leans in, and the woman whispers something Ify can't catch. Grace slowly breaks away, and the woman puts a hand to Grace's face, smiling. The urge bubbles in Ify to ask Peter about gari and pepper soup, to tell him where to find the best jollof in Alabast, to connect him to Nigeria here and be reconnected with Nigeria on Earthland. Then she realizes where her thoughts have taken her, and suddenly the lights in the refugee ward are too bright, the scent of antiseptic too strong, the temperature too warm and too cold at the same time. Ify doesn't see the rest of Grace's interaction with the patient, because she has rushed out of the ward, shedding her lab coat and badge and thoughts of Peter along the way.

■ ■ ■ ■ ■

The walls of Ify's bedroom glimmer with soft blue light.

Her tablets glow with readings of patients she has been studying and their various medical conditions. The physical ailments are easy enough to treat. Sometimes, it is simply a matter of seeing how the body and the brain are interacting, how they are learning from and about each other. At first, Ify thought it would be different when working on cyberized or partially cyberized patients. The braincase or the false organs, they were supposed to work on a pre-regulated rhythm or operate on a predetermined schedule, something that could be tweaked or adjusted or changed in a laboratory. She thought it would be like tinkering with the inside of a watch. But, just like with red-bloods, it is all about harmony. If she's learned nothing else, it is that disharmony in one part of the body will lead to disharmony elsewhere. And that sometimes, to aid someone suffering physical pain, you needed to treat a disharmonious mind.

She knows she should be asleep, but her mind is working the main problem before her, and she cannot let herself rest until she finds a solution. Peter.

It takes all her effort to keep from cursing herself for underestimating him. But how could she have known he would piece things together so quickly? She still can't figure out what he's after. But what if it's as simple as a place in Alabast? It's an attractive enough life. She looks around at her room and thinks about the rest of her apartment: the spacious living room with its high-backed sofas and minimalist-patterned cushions, the kitchen connected to it, and the bathroom large enough to do a cartwheel in. It would be attractive to any migrant, especially one fleeing war. But she has tried to chase him away, and rather than look for easier marks, he has dug his heels in. And why lie about his origins? Why not just say that he is fleeing conflict? Maybe he is worried that, because the war is ended, his application for asylum will be denied and he will have to languish in the Jungle before being deported. She feels as though she is on the cusp of figuring out his motive, figuring out what he is trying to get and what he's willing to do to get it, but that moment when it all clicks is just out of reach. Whenever she tries to grab it, it slips further and further away. So she stares at the ceiling and waits and hopes it will fall into her head.

Answers come to prepared spirits, a professor told her.

Her wallpaper TV flashes with a broadcast from the main Colony news station. A light-skinned woman in a blazer and red blouse is talking while a chyron rolls by below: NEW IMMIGRATION POLICY PASSED BY LEGISLATIVE COUNCIL TO GO INTO EFFECT TOMORROW. EXPERTS PREDICTING RISE IN DEPORTATION ORDERS.

Is this the answer Ify's been looking for?

Her Whistle chirps with an incoming call.

She activates it, and before her appears Grace. All the poise and tenderness from earlier is gone, replaced by a jittery, barely restrained urgency. "Doctor, there is an emergency. Your presence is needed in the east wing immediately."

If Ify is honest with herself, she needs this. Work can distract her from these other worries. It can cocoon her in purpose. Already, she is changing into her hospital outfit. "What's the emergency? And you don't have to call me Doctor . . . yet. My licensing exam isn't until three months after graduation."

"Well, Doct—I mean, Ms. Diallo. We . . . we're not quite sure. It's the refugees. They're not responding."

Ify freezes in the act of putting on her hospital coat. "What do you mean not responding?"

"Please come immediately. I will keep this comms channel open as you make your way to the hospital. In the meantime, I'm uploading all the information we have at the moment. But I think it's best if you see this in person."

Ify receives the documents with a ping before Grace has even finished talking. Patient diagnostic after patient diagnostic. Hundreds of documents she reviews as she leaves her apartment, takes the elevator down to her street, and hurries to the ward. All of them children. She looks at the FOUR scores, the measure grading their Full Outline of UnResponsiveness. Nearly all of them are at zeroes. Those with higher scores start to decline right before Ify's very eyes, so that by the time she arrives at the hospital, all of them have reached zero. Eyelids closed. No response to pain. Absent pupil, corneal, and cough reflexes. Their breathing steady with the ventilator rate. But what worries Ify is what may happen if the comas persist. The longer they stay like this, the greater their risk of catching things like pneumonia. And dying.

All thoughts of clinical diagnosis fall away, however, when she arrives at the ward and sees them. Hundreds upon hundreds of beds holding children strapped to cerebral monitors. All of them beeping in unison. All of those sounds telling her that these children are just barely alive.

CHAPTER 10

In the trailer, Xifeng is swabbing my wounds and putting together the skin of my arms where it is ripping. I am thinking backward to attack and not remembering feeling any pain. And when I am sitting on stool with my arm in Xifeng's hands soft as beachsand, I am not feeling any pain either. I am only feeling pain from sun and from poison in the air when I am being pulled from mountain of bodies, like I am being born, and when I am baby and everything is new. I am feeling thing like pain, but then that is going away and I am not feeling any thing. And I am wondering if it is because something is broken inside me.

For a long time, Xifeng is working without saying any words. I am thinking that this is the first time she is seeing me fighting and killing, but I am remembering that I am running away from caravan to keep her safe but also to be keeping her from seeing me fighting and killing.

"Do you know why we are doing this work, Uzo?" she is asking me in Taishanese.

I am looking at Xifeng's face when she is saying this softly. She is not looking at me. She is focusing on my arm and on repairing my wound and spraying chemical on it that will be binding the skin back together and hiding the metal underneath that is my skeleton.

"We are preserving memory of a painful time in your country's history. We are making sure that people don't forget. It is important to remember these things, even if they hurt to remember."

When she is saying these thing, I am thinking of the old woman and when I am carrying dead body to her and water is leaking from her eyes. She is sadding, but it is feeling like good thing to be doing this thing for her.

"The government in this country is forcing people to forget."

It is the first time I am hearing Xifeng talking about government. Every time I am hearing or seeing government it is when people are wearing soldier uniform or people are shooting at people wearing soldier uniform. Always in rememberings. This is the first time I am hearing it with my ears.

"The government is using their powers to erase the memories of everyone in the country. Everyone is connected by way of their braincases like the one you have in your head. They are all linked to their net, which helps them live their lives. It helps them buy groceries, listen to music, study in school. But it is also a tool of surveillance for the government, and the government is peeking into the minds of every citizen and erasing their memories of the war. Do you know why this is bad, Uzo?"

I am watching Xifeng lifting my shirt and dabbing with antiseptic at the cuts on my side. And I am thinking of woman who is sadding over body I am bringing her. But I am also thinking of rememberings I am downloading into my braincase and things I am seeing in my mind, and sometimes seeing those things is making me angry and is making me to be sadding. Air conditioning in the trailer is chilling my skin. "It is hurting," I say.

Xifeng is looking at me and stopping with my medicine, and I am thinking that she is thinking I want her to stop healing me, but I like it when she is touching me like this.

"The rememberings, I mean," I am saying to her, and I am making sure to be speaking Taishanese too, because even though she is sadding at first when she is hearing it, she is then smiling, and I am thinking that this is a thing that is making her to be happy.

Xifeng is smiling and going back to fixing me. Cotton and gauze that is red-black with the oil that was spilling out of me is all over the floor where Xifeng and I are sitting. "The government thinks that if they erase all memory of the civil war, then they will have peace. If your neighbor kills your family, how will you be able to live next to them when the war is over? You will be consumed with anger and rage. You will want vengeance."

"You will not be wanting to be living next to this person." I am looking at the hard drives on the shelves at the far end of the trailer, and I am beginning to be understanding what vengeance is. And that there is being war here and maybe war is why I am at bottom of pile of bodies when Enyemaka are finding me. Maybe war is what I am doing in my rememberings when I am hurting people or killing them.

"So if you forget that this happened to you, then you can live next to your neighbor again," says Xifeng.

"But you are also forgetting that you are having family. You are forgetting that you are having mother and that she is loving you. Maybe you are forgetting you are having brother who is mean to you also. But maybe you are also forgetting that brother is protecting you from bullies and pulling blanket over your head when it is raining in your home."

Xifeng is looking at my face, and I am understanding that she is proud of me for saying these thing.

"We are bringing these memories to the people." Xifeng is finishing with the woundings on my stomach and on my ribs, and she is pulling my shirt back down. She is putting her hand on my knee and kneeling in front of me and looking in my face. "Do you see those hard drives over there?" And her finger is pointing to the black boxes piled on top of each other against the walls of her trailer. And I am nodding my head yes, and Xifeng is saying, "Those contain the memories of people who died in the war. People who left behind loved ones. And those loved ones don't know what happened to these people. We will be going back to those loved ones, and we will show them what happened to the people they lost. We will be restoring memories."

"It is good that we are doing this." It is question in my mind, but it comes out as answer when I am speaking.

We are smiling at each other's faces when I am smelling rotten egg, and before I am telling to Xifeng what is happening, my eyes are rolling up into my head and I am on the ground shaking shaking.

I am seeing little girl sitting on side of bed and she is having tablet computer on her knees and I am saying something to her about needing to wake up and go to school and she is dragging her feet and I am saying, "Come on, now! Chop chop-oh!" and I am hurrying her out of tent and into humid air filled with mosquitoes. Then there is static like I am seeing when I am downloading into my braincase broken memories, and I am on side of a small hill and I am looking out over water and this same little girl is sitting next to me and we are saying something but it is mumbling in my ears, but I am calling her Ify.

Then I am waking up again in Xifeng's trailer. She is holding me in her arms and rocking me back and forth to be calming me and she is humming a song, and even though there are many many question in my head buzzing like mosquito I am happy and I feel safe and I am thinking that Xifeng is only this way with good person. Never with bad person.

This is how she is telling me that I am good person.

■ ■ ■ ■ ■

The city of Lagos is giving me too much information in my brain. Too much information about too many people is fighting inside my braincase, and I am breathing regularly again when Xifeng and I and a smaller Enyemaka are finding passage on small boat into Makoko shantytown.

The moon is shining on the water, and the water is shimmering and making quiet sounds that is making me to feel like smiling. Small small drone is hovering over the water and spraying chemical over the surface that is shimmering, and I am knowing that this is to be killing the mosquitoes that are carrying diseases. The drones are sometime looking like mosquito themselves, but they are not stinging people, and I am seeing that they are metal and safe.

As we are moving through the water by the Third Mainland Bridge that is connecting Lagos to the outer islands, we are passing under smaller bridges that are so skinny only one person is walking up or down at a time. But some people are walking fast fast like they are not worrying about falling into the water. I dip my hand, and the water is cold to touch, and Xifeng is watching me and smiling, and I am taking my hand out because I am shy suddenly. And she is trying to hide a giggle by pressing her lips tight together.

She is holding hard drive in her lap with tiny squirming Enyemaka who will be standing guard, and I am holding rememberings in my head. We are soon arriving at a home on stilts that are being driven deep into the water of the lagoon. There is a ladder leading up to the edge of the platform the house is sitting on, and even though the person inside is knowing that we are coming (Xifeng is telling me this), we move quiet quiet. Xifeng is paying boatman, and we are climbing until we get to the platform, and then Xifeng is knocking softly and wooden door is opening slowly and old man with beard like his chin is covered in dandelion seedheads is standing in the darkness. Xifeng puts down tiny Enyemaka, and it is standing outside door to keep watch for trouble. It is linking to me through my braincase, so I am seeing what it is seeing while seeing what I am seeing.

Xifeng and I are walking into the darkness, and I am detecting another person here. An old woman who is looking like she is all wrinkles and who is not moving but who is appearing on my screen as alive. She is having heartbeat and pulse and she is having breath in her lungs.

The man with dandelion beard is speaking to the woman, who is just saying nothing, then. He is walking to Xifeng, and they are speaking quietly. Xifeng is making sure that they are the right people and that she is bringing them what they are asking for.

Then Xifeng is making hand signal for me to come to her. "It is time," she is telling me.

Cord is coming out of the back of my neck and I am plugging into hard drive, and I am sending rememberings into it. Before we are arriving here, I am sectioning off these rememberings and placing them in mental folder for when I will be needing to upload them. When I am finished, I unplug my cord and it is slithering like snake back into my neck.

Then I am stepping away while Xifeng is finding projector and plugging hard drive into it. Suddenly whole room is filling with blue light, and in the center of the room is a young man and he is wearing soldier's coat, but it is open and loose on his shoulders. He is eating yams on a plate and he is being with other soldiers like him, relaxing under tent, and I am hearing them speaking and telling joke on each other and laughing with mouth full. Then I am seeing all of the soldiers facing commander and looking to right and seeing soldier and looking to the left and seeing soldier, and I am seeing commander giving them commands and saying they should be proud of what they are doing, and commander is putting hand on person's shoulder so it is looking like he is putting hand on our shoulder and he is pinning medal onto person's chest.

Old woman in the room we are standing in is moving. Small small. So small I am not knowing that Xifeng is seeing, but old woman moves and small small river is running from her eyes. I am thinking that maybe the remembering is belonging to her grandson.

There is another part of the remembering. We are seeing from the person's eyes that they are piloting mech and zoom zooming through the air, and there is much shouting and katakata, then explosion and static and nothing.

The remembering stops, and the room is being like night again.

The man with dandelion beard is being quiet for long time and water is coming from his eye too, and then he is telling Xifeng thank you in small small voice, and then he is hugging her and he is making hand sign to old woman, who is slow slow turning to Xifeng and smile is crossing her lips.

My head is beeping, and I am seeing with small Enyemaka's eyes that boat is disturbing the water outside. Police.

"We must go," I am warning Xifeng in quiet voice. I am speaking in Xifeng's language so that man and older woman who is smiling through the water on her face are not understanding what we are saying.

Xifeng is wanting to linger and spend more time with family but I am pulling her through door and wishing I am having pistol with me. But Xifeng is telling me that it is bad for me to be walking with gun on me, even though I am telling her it is to protect her and I am not bad person.

We are leaving the home, and I am careful not to just throw Xifeng into water. She is picking up small Enyemaka and holding her in her arms, and I am looking down to see that boatman who bring us here is gone. He is leaving with all of our money.

I am pulling Xifeng with me, and we find bridge connecting to another house, and we are walking fast over it.

"Uzo, please slow down," Xifeng is whispering to me. I am wanting her to not be speaking at all. We cannot be slowing down now. Bridge is bending too far beneath our weight.

We arrive at another platform and we run to another bridge, but it is just plank of wood and Xifeng slips, and the only thing that is keeping her from falling in water with small Enyemaka is my hand wrapped around her wrist. Bridge is bending beneath me and almost snapping. Creaking, creaking, and creaking. I am swinging Xifeng back and forth.

"Wait, wait," Xifeng is hissing, scared.

But I am ignoring her as I use all my strength to throw her onto next platform as plank is snapping beneath me and I am falling into water with loud splash.

Lights are moving over me like circles, and at first I am thinking this is moonlight, then I am realizing there are too many circles and it is police on boats, and I am staying underwater hoping Xifeng is not looking over ledge trying to find me.

When the circles pass, I swim up and poke my head above water.

They are stopped at the house where Xifeng is crouched. They will be finding her.

I swim fast, and when I get to the stilts holding up the house's platform, I climb. Xifeng is hiding at the back of the house, and when she is seeing me dripping with lagoon water, she is nearly making sound but I am putting my hand over her mouth and telling her shush.

Then I am going around house and finding first police, and I am seeing the skin of his neck where it is showing beneath his helmet, and I am not knowing why this is important or what it means but I am fast fast putting my fingers there hard, and he is crumpling like he is losing his legs.

I drag him back to where Xifeng is sitting, and I am taking his gun and I am feeling good with gun in my pants again. Then I am taking Xifeng and saying, "Climb on my back."

And she is doing this, then I am sliding over the edge of the platform but hanging by my fingertips. And like this, I am moving along the edge of the platform, and when I need to, I am moving to underside of platform and clinging to it while Xifeng is having her arms and legs wrapped around me.

Like this, we move from house to house, platform to platform, until we get to Third Mainland Bridge and I am climbing over and we are blending into crowd again.

I am dripping, and my shoes are making squishing sound when I am walking, and Xifeng is breathing heavy, then she is looking at me and she is giggling and I am giggling too, and I am wondering if it will be like this every time we are delivering rememberings to families.

■ ■ ■ ■ ■

It is nighting outside and I am sitting on the steps to Xifeng's trailer. We are on an empty span of shoreline, and some of the Enyemakas are coming with us to make sure to be keeping people away from us. I am not sure if this is to be protecting us or to be giving Xifeng privacy and a chance to be being alone. But I am sitting on the steps to the trailer, and I am drawing in the dirt with a stick I am finding on the beach. Stars are making the water shimmer, and I am drawing and stick is making scritch scritch sound until door is opening behind me and splashing light on what I am drawing, and I am actually seeing it for the first time when before I am not even paying attention to what I am doing.

And Xifeng is standing in doorway and staring at thing I am drawing in the sand, and I am looking at it too and I am seeing face. It is meaning something to Xifeng. Maybe Xifeng is having rememberings.

"Are you knowing this girl?" I am asking Xifeng. I am thinking maybe there was being one like me before me. A someone who Xifeng is holding and who she is telling you are good person.

"Where did you see that face?" Xifeng is asking me, ignoring my question. She is not speaking her language to me anymore, so I am switching to my own language too.

"When I am having epileptic attack. I am smelling sulfur and I am tasting metal and I am seeing her face. Not all of the time but many times. My body is telling me I am loving this girl. In my dreams, I am calling this girl Ify." I am not knowing why, but air is choking in my lungs and my arms and legs are feeling heavy and I am wanting to know if this person is real. It is want that is deep deep inside me. "Are you knowing Ify?"

After long silence, Xifeng is nodding her head. "I did. Once upon a time." There is softness in her face, but then the light is changing and she is being lit from behind and is only silhouette in the night and I cannot see her face and what expression it is making. "But she died in the war. You should rest. We have more work to do tomorrow."

She is closing the door and taking the trailer's light with her. I think she is wanting to hear me cry at news that Ify is dead, like what red-blood human is doing. Like woman whose loved one I am burying or like man and old woman who are seeing remembering of person who they are loving who is dead. She is wanting me to cry, but it is wasteful to cry for this. I am remembering how Xifeng is standing and holding herself when she is telling me about Ify, and I am remembering what my brain is telling me about how her body is talking to me when she is telling me words, and I am knowing that when Xifeng is telling me that Ify is dead, Xifeng is telling lies to me.

CHAPTER
11

Ify walks up and down the rows of children, checking for the same thing—vital signs—while Grace strides at her side. "Have they shown any trace of plague? Or disease? If necessary, we will need to quarantine them."

Grace has her tablet out in front of her and clicks through tab after tab. "No sign, Doctor."

Ify doesn't have the time or energy to correct her.

"The first few cases were staggered. Some of them were children who had been living in Alabast or adjoining Colonies for several years. They were students at local primary and secondary schools. Their parents were employed locally, although many of them had jobs as unskilled labor. There is no sign in any of the scans of underlying neurological conditions."

Ify stops in her tracks. "Are they all red-blood?"

Grace nearly runs into her. "Um, Doctor. By law, we are forbidden to check. I had just assumed . . ."

"If they have brought a disease with them, perhaps it is something with a delayed fuse. Or worse, like cholera." Ify stops at the bed of a boy who looks like he has just begun high school. Hair comes in patches above his lip and on his chin. He has a cleft lip, and his hair—grown long—is like a pool of ink on his pillow. She picks up his wrist, raises it a few inches over his forehead, pauses, looking for any reaction, then drops it.

It lands with a smack on the boy's face, and Grace winces. When she recovers, she returns to her tablet and says, "They are totally passive. Mute, unable to eat or drink, incontinent, and"—looking down at the boy while Ify leaves his arm draped across his forehead—"unreactive to physical stimuli or pain."

"When was the first case?" Ify asks, her voice devoid of emotion. She now has a puzzle in front of her to focus on. She's been looking for this.

Grace taps a sequence into her tablet. "Someone with similar symptoms appears in the system from six years ago."

"Is that the first?"

"The first that matches up, Doctor."

"Let me see." Ify snatches the tablet from Grace and scrolls through the information. There is a video file attached, and Ify opens it to a holographic projection of news camera footage. The camera follows a team of medical professionals around something on a stretcher as they hurry across tarmac to load it onto a shuttle craft. People dressed in worn-down clothes—the family?—crowd around the stretcher and follow it into the craft, some of them falling onto the tarmac in tears. The stretcher is loaded onto the shuttle and vanishes as the lid closes. "What is happening?"

"Deportation," Grace says, quietly. "The child was deported. His father's asylum application had been denied, as had his brother's. The three of them were sent back to Vanuatu."

Ify looks up in surprise. "Vanuatu? But there is no Vanuatu. That country has been underwater for . . ." The implications all hit Ify at once. She looks around her at row after row of beds and gulps. "Grace?"

"Yes, Doctor."

"Pull up the immigration status of the patients' families. And mark those who have received deportation notices within the past three months." As she says this, she recalls the news broadcast of the government's new stance on the migrants. And she recalls the feeling that had enveloped her, the idea that she'd solved a puzzle, that she'd found a way to get rid of a problem. And guilt grips her heart.

■ ■ ■ ■ ■

After Grace leaves to do more research, Ify wanders the rows of hospital beds alone. Or almost alone. A few beds have family members crowded around them. Their clothes seem to reflect all manner of success or lack thereof. Some of the people attending to the comatose children or hovering over them wear slim-fitting patterned tunics with pleated pants. Others hold battered workers' caps in grease-stained fingers. Some have small vacuum-sealed containers of food with them, aromatic scents wafting over to Ify and speaking to her of places filled with brown people, black people, on a floor crowded around a massive dish or a table and eating and talking and complaining and laughing. Food is forbidden in this part of the east wing, but Ify doesn't stop them. Maybe that family is hoping the smell of home will waken their child. At one bed stands a child who looks only a few years older than the one in the hospital bed. They wear the school uniform of one of Alabast's most prestigious secondary schools, and they are speaking in hushed whispers to the comatose child. It is not English. Ify scrolls through the options in her translator and finds it: Gujarati.

They really are from all parts of Earth. From the scattered whispering and murmurs and prayers and quiet pleadings, Ify hears Tamil, Persian, Pashto, Javanese, Tongan, and half a dozen other languages. Including Igbo.

She turns, and almost by the far wall, far enough to appear as a speck to the unaided eye, there he is. She uses the embedded camera on the Whistle attached to her temple to zoom in, and he appears in high definition before her eyes. Lanky limbs awkward, like he's folded in on himself in the chair next to the hospital bed. She knows it's him because of the bullet scar on the side of his head. There's no one else it can be.

Peter.

A gasp catches in her throat. A cord snakes from the back of his neck into the cerebral monitor by the patient's bed. How could she have not seen that outlet before? Ify thinks back to that time on Paige and Amy's porch with him sitting next to her, then him jumping down a few steps and pleading, face to face, that she not reveal his lies, then him threatening to expose her past as a war criminal. Had he somehow managed to disguise it? There was no hair to hide it. Ify squints, then realizes her foolishness and zooms in further with her Whistle's camera.

The cord isn't connected to a cerebral monitor. It vanishes beneath the bed. Ify's jaw tightens.

It's connected directly to the patient.

The patchy skin. The outlet. She's sure that were she to cut open the skin of his forearm, she would see gears and pistons and oil.

She's seen a boy like him once before.

Lying in a rattling truckbed, part of a caravan passing through dark and heavy jungle, refugees either sleeping in one of the trailers or walking alongside, children playing bulubu by moonlight. She has a tablet in her lap and a pistol in her messenger bag, and she's on her way to kill the woman who murdered her family. And sitting across from her is a boy with a touchboard clutched close to his chest, patchy skin on his arms, voice hoarse with disuse, rifle in his lap. A boy she has seen kill an entire group of marauders and show no remorse because he claimed he was doing it to protect the caravan as it wound its way to the refugee intake center near Enugu. The boy's vitiligo, the way he only spoke in the present tense, as though everything that had happened or would happen to him were always happening to him, as though the war was simultaneously a memory and a thing still raging in his mind, as though he saw the ceasefire as a thing that could never last, as though he knew war was returning. His name had been Agu, and he had saved the woman whom Ify had tried to kill, the same woman who had then abandoned Ify to a lonely future in the Colonies. Agu, who had loved to make music with his touchboard. Agu, who had been forged out of other people's parts and made a killer.

Ify sees it now.

Peter is a synth.

■ ■ ■ ■ ■

"He's not human." Ify has to keep herself from shouting. Still, the projection of Céline hovering by the window overlooking the refugee ward winces.

In her office, Ify has a number of documents glowing at her

in the form of holographic projections: Colonial human rights statutes defining enemy combatants and refugees, medical files for several of the most recent cases of patient coma, and the information page for immigration authorities.

"I could call the number right now, Céline. I could tell them where to find Peter, that that's the name he gave his sponsors, even though it may not be his real name. I could tell them that everything he's said to them is a lie. Céline, he's an enemy combatant."

Céline's face has none of its usual sly frolic. There's no joke at the edge of her lips, no mischief twinkling in her eye. She has her arms folded and frowns, an expression somewhere between disapproval and concern. "Ify."

"He's a synth."

"Ify. *Mais t'es pas sûre.*" Céline swings her arm wide as though to indicate the vast number of questions awaiting Ify if she were to go through with this. "That's what the deportation authorities will ask. They'll ask, 'How do you know this?'"

"It won't matter." Desperation forces Ify to pace back and forth in a small orbit behind her desk. "When they see . . . when they see what he is, they'll be forced to act. Céline, you don't understand. He was built specifically for war. His body—his organs, his skeleton, his tendons, his muscle—all of it is entirely false. Manufactured. They made him in a lab, Céline. If I were to scan him, I'd see that his memories are nothing more than mnemonic and sensory data taken from other people and inserted into his braincase. Specifically to simulate human feeling!"

"Ify, *calme-toi. S'il te plaît.*" She pauses. "You saw him plug into a patient. Maybe he's only a partially cyberized boy—"

"We have to stop him," Ify cuts her off, lost in thought. Knuckle to chin, she resumes her pacing. "He's clearly on some mission. Just masquerading as a human." She looks up at Céline but doesn't see her, sees only the completion of her own mission. "Maybe he's even had a hand in the illness affecting the refugees. He was plugged into a refugee. I could pull the security footage from that hospital ward and show him plugged into the refugee in the bed he's sitting next to. There. Done." She wipes her hands of invisible blood. "There's the problem, wrapped up in an airtight package and fired off into space to sit alongside the Refuse Ring circling Alabast."

"Ify, that's not what they would do to him." The tone in Céline's voice stops Ify where she stands. "They'd send him to the Jungle to suffer until he self-deports back to Nigeria." Céline takes a step toward Ify, but because it is a hologram projected by her Whistle, it looks only like more of Céline's body has vanished off-frame. "You see what color he is. You know what they do to les noirs." And Ify sees in a separate hologram what Céline encounters every day in real life because of her position as a Colonial administrator. Children playing in glass-studded mud, malnourished and with faulty Augments, weaving their way around crudely built zinc trailers and huts that stand no chance against the freezing temperatures when the Alabastrine administrators of the Jungle choose to open the vents and clear the waste that accumulates in the slum. Trailers slashed with yellow or blue or purple paint depending on which aid agency they represent, refugees waiting in lines that go on forever for a vaccination or treatment for whatever disease is rampaging through the population at any given time. Families wrapped in bubble coats; when they speak, their breath clouds before their faces and frost tips their eyebrows. Large pools of wastewater dotting the landscape. Drones ever circling, looking for crimes, whether committed out of malice or desperation, they don't care. They swoop in and fire electric bolts at the target, then their claws retract and they drag the victim away, on the ground and through the wastewater, then into the air, where a jail transport van hovers. Or Augmented police, towering twice as tall as any human and muscled with steroids and gear oil, stomping through the tent cities, crushing homes, beating men and women. Hammering, always hammering, as people try to build their makeshift homes or legal aid clinics or mosques or churches or art therapy centers. Discarded sleeping bags, rotten food, broken shoes half-buried in faulty, recently re-poured concrete.

The place Céline tries to rescue refugees from. The place too many of them don't escape. The Jungle.

"You would send him to this place?" Céline asks.

Ify clenches her fists at her side, fighting the guilt that rises like bile in her throat. "But Paige and Amy. He could hurt them. I could have him sent away, and they would be none the wiser. They'd think it was simply the luck of the draw." She waves away the concern. "Besides, Nigeria is safe now. It's not like Vanuatu. It hasn't been swallowed by waters. It is still there." And she realizes then that she's thinking of the deportation Grace had shown her, the child who had fallen into a coma, the family weeping in the aftermath of receiving their deportation orders, the unconscious child wheeled onto that aircraft to be spirited to a home that no longer existed. "The economy is rebounding," she says, her voice faltering. "There's peace. It's a familiar place for him." As she speaks, her voice loses conviction. "The rebel groups have been put down." When she says, "There is peace," one last time, she can't bring herself to believe it.

"They all deserve your help." Then Céline ends the call.

Ify tries to speak, but a sob catches in her throat. She remembers when she and Céline would walk to school and get stopped by the Alabastrine immigration authorities, and they would have to wait on the sidewalk, standing by the large, intimidating police vans while their classmates walked by and snickered. She remembers the aid workers who fed her in the dorm and those moments she would spend with Céline at the Viewer, looking out at the stars and seeing their futures plotted in them. She fights and fights for the resolve to move against Peter. To condemn him.

Until she gives up, closes all the tabs, and powers down her devices.

"What am I going to do?" Ify asks, not knowing if she means the unknown medical condition that has afflicted an entire hospital ward or the fifteen-year-old child soldier named Peter.

CHAPTER
12

Like this, we are bringing rememberings to people.

I am uploading copy of rememberings from hard drives into my brain and carrying them with me while I am walking with Xifeng and Enyemakas through streets of Lagos and down small small alleys, and sometimes we are walking up to the second level or third level of some houses and Xifeng is pulling out second drive and I am downloading rememberings into it. Sometimes we are carrying small projector with us and sometimes house is having own projector. We are connecting drive to projector, and family or sometimes man or sometimes woman or sometimes person who is not calling themself man or woman is watching. Sometimes there is water in their eyes because they are watching remembering of someone who is dead, someone who we are burying in desert. So they are sadding because they will never see this person again. And sometimes they are thanking me and Xifeng, and sometimes they are quiet and not saying any thing, and sometimes they are angry and breaking many thing.

Xifeng is always ending projection with last moment of

remembering. Sometimes is soldier crashing or being shot with bullet. Sometimes is person lying on ground who is moaning in pain and who is getting shot with bullet, and sometimes it is someone getting chop with machete. Sometimes person with remembering is not even soldier. Sometimes they are just being person in home or at school and they are being chop with machete or being shot with bullet. Sometimes there is loud boom and suddenly that is being the end of the remembering because there is bombing and person is too near. But many time, because we are finding so many rememberings in desert where battle and war is being fought, we are seeing soldier.

On face of people watching the rememberings is many thing. Sometimes their face is like carving from stone or wood. Sometimes their face is like fast-changing weather. There is meadow, then is rain, then is thundering and lightning and katakata, and sometimes there is earth cracking and groaning and lava is shooting out. Many times in remembering, you are seeing face of someone who is doing the killing. You are seeing person who is shooting you or stabbing you with knife or chopping you with machete. You are seeing person who is walking by after planting bomb. You are seeing someone who is killing, and I am looking at the people in this room and I am thinking that they are seeing someone who is killing them.

And then I am looking to Xifeng and seeing something that is looking like almost-smile on her face. Like this is thing that she is wanting. And it is making me to be feeling not-good.

One time, man is asking us what we are doing when we are coming to his house. It is close to street in Lagos that is never sleeping and there is always thing happening and there is stealing and cooking and laughing and fighting and selling and buying and noise from all these thing come muffled through the walls of this man's home.

"Ms. Adebayo asked for us," Xifeng is telling the man. "She reached out to me and my group, she gave us the information we asked for, and when we had gathered what she asked for, we returned." She is taking a step to the man. "We interviewed her for details. And we spent a lot of time out there learning what happened to her son." She is patting the sack that is holding her hard drive. "It was very important to her that she have this. Where is she?"

For a long time, the man is saying nothing, just shaking. Then he is saying in quiet voice between teeth that is clenching, "My wife is dead. She has been dead for one year, three months, and eighteen days." He inhales deeply, bringing so much air into his chest like it is being courage that he is gathering. "Whatever you've brought, I don't want. I don't want it." He is shaking more, and I am thinking that he is losing control and soon he will be trying to attack Xifeng. I am readying to be hurting him.

"Sir," Xifeng says, but I am wanting to tell her that we must be leaving. Something bad is soon happening. I am smelling badness in the air and feeling it on my skin. The air is moving in way that is making me to feel like I will soon be fighting and killing, and I am not liking it.

"She told me nothing of this," the man says. "She did not speak a word of this! She never would have done this thing. Involve you . . . you Chinese! How dare you come into my house like this! Odoodo! You know nothing about my son!" He is taking table and he is flipping it, and lamp and bowl is falling off and breaking on the floor, and he is taking small thing and throwing it against the wall over and over while he is shouting at us. "She's dead! And she told me nothing of this! You know nothing of my son! And you never spoke to my wife! You are lying! Odoodo, get out of my house!"

I am moving to protect Xifeng, but even as I am doing this thing, I am seeing that he is not mad at us but he is being mad at his wife who is dying without telling him she is doing this, and maybe he is mad at son too for dying.

"That's it," he is saying, and it is looking like he is calming down, but I am seeing his vital signs and heart rate, and I know that he is still dangerous, and I am seeing him reach for his temple as he is saying, "I'm calling the police," and I am rushing fast fast to him, and I am crossing the whole room in one step, and my fingers are wrapping around his wrist and holding him still, and he is fearing me with his eyes and looking at me like I am monster who is trapping his wrist like this.

Blood is rushing in my ears, then I am hearing Xifeng saying soft soft, "Uzo." Then, again, "Uzo, it's okay. We're leaving." She looks to the man and says, with firmer voice, "We're leaving. We're going. We're sorry to bother you."

But I am knowing this man and how he is. I am knowing that as soon as I am letting him go, he is calling police on us. And I know this is being dangerous for us because before we get to Lagos, Xifeng is telling me that nobody is to be knowing what we are doing. It is against the law to be speaking of the war. In fact, it is against the law to even be remembering it. She is telling me of people who are having their rememberings of the war emptied out by the virus the government is feeding into their brains. And it is being our mission to be freeing them. To be helping them to remember what is happening, that war is happening, and that killing and dying is happening, and she is telling me that it is important to be remembering these thing because it is helping it not to happen again. And government is being wrong and we are being right and, like this, I am being soldier but in bigger and better war.

"Uzo," Xifeng saying to me. "Uzo, let go of the man's wrist."

But I am not wanting to. I am wanting him to be quiet. I am wanting to snap his neck so he is not shouting and making much noise. I am wanting to bury his body and be erasing him from the world so no one is even knowing he is existing. But Xifeng is telling me to let go, and she is saying it soft soft like she is speaking to me when I am having epileptic fit and wanting to be held by her.

So I am letting go, and man is falling to the floor and holding his wrist, and he is sadding and telling us, "Please leave me, please, please go away from here," and Xifeng and I are walking out and we are walking fast, but when we are getting to mouth of alleyway where it is leaking into main street, we are stopping because police are gathering, dressed in all black like beetle walking on two legs.

People are scattering out of street like water as ground mech is stomping through and is turning its head left and right and scanning buildings with red light. Police like beetle is scurrying all over the place. Some people are shouting but most are quiet quiet, like this is thing that happens every day. Like this is weather.

Enyemakas are standing in different places in city center, and I am communicating with them and they are telling me where police is blocking off road and where police is entering building and where police is leaving, and I am seeing map of city in my head and this is how I am figuring out where to go.

I pull Xifeng behind me, and we are running up metal staircase next to building on other side of alley until we are getting to final level, then I am saying to Xifeng, *Get on my back*, and she is climbing on but is spending too much time fitting hard drive into her bag, but I am carrying her onto rooftop then letting her stand by herself.

Everywhere is roof made of corrugated steel or red brick. On some, there is glass stuck along edge of rooftop to cut hands of people grabbing. I am seeing all of this instantly. I am also seeing police in street with big gun noticing us.

I am grabbing Xifeng's arm and pulling her just as bullets are hitting near us PING PING, and we are running and jumping to other rooftop and our footstep is bang DHUM DHUM DHUM on roofs as we run and jump, run and jump, run and jump.

Bullet is following us as we turn away from street and run and jump from roof to roof. Ahead is glass on one ledge, so I am grabbing Xifeng's arm and bracing myself and throwing her over, then running, and putting my hands to the glass and jumping over. And before Xifeng is catching her breath, we are running again and bullet is finding us and then I am hearing bootstep beneath us and there is big jump ahead because houses are on lower slope and we are jumping, and as we are jumping I am hearing large crash of brick and metal coming open. Xifeng is rolling on roof and I am rolling on roof, and when I am looking up large metal soldier that they are calling juggernaut is running toward us. Stomping stomping stomping like giant made of metal.

"Mogwai," Xifeng whispers, and I know that she is seeing

vision of demon from ancient Chinese myth, but I am seeing only machine that is trying to kill us and that is why fear is making Xifeng not to be moving but I am feeling no such thing. My retinal display is telling me what metal it is being made out of and where it is being organic and human and how it is using energy and motion to propel itself and where its weapon is being stored, and I am learning all of this in less than one second. We must run.

I am grabbing Xifeng and putting her on my back just as she is grabbing bag with hard drive, and we are running while juggernaut is chasing us.

Light is shining us from above, and I am seeing in my mind's eye that drone is following us and is readying guns to be firing on us. So we go right, and I am jumping and we are crashing through window of home and Xifeng is flying off of my back and my legs are paining me and my hands are bleeding from the glass. I am hearing crying, and baby is nearby. Then something large is hitting my side, and I am flying through the air and hitting wood and glass with my back.

When I am looking up, I am seeing police looking at me with rifle pointed and finger on trigger. Before I am knowing what I am doing, I have sharp piece of wood in my hand and I am rolling to avoid bullets pinging like THWIP THWIP into ground, then rushing forward and knocking gun away and kicking leg of police and ripping off helmet and stabbing him with wood in neck.

Before other police are coming, I am looking for Xifeng and I am seeing her across hallway in other room and I am walking to her when wall is exploding and juggernaut is standing in front of me. It is smacking me all the way into other room, and I am crashing through wall and flying through air. At last minute, I am flipping myself and holding on to metal railing, but metal is bad and creaking from my heaviness and breaking and breaking. And my back and my side and my legs—all of these is paining me. But I am pulling myself up and jumping into room just before balcony is falling into street. I am walking bad and there is being blood on me, but I am noticing rifle and I am hearing Xifeng screaming from far away and I am trying to find other Enyemakas with my mind but am hearing nothing, and this is how I am knowing that they are dead.

I am picking up rifle and then walking to hallway and seeing juggernaut, and just in front of him is Xifeng lying on ground and shaking. And I am aiming rifle and I am shooting and shooting. But bullet is going ping ping ping and is doing nothing to him.

But he is stopping and turning to me and he is running STOMP STOMP STOMP. And I am running too, but I am sliding under his legs, and then I am seeing Xifeng and I am grabbing her and putting her over my shoulder and I am running to window and jumping through onto other balcony, then I am seeing line of balconies in direction of end of city and I am running and jumping hop hop hop from one to the next and the next. Drone is appearing beside to me and shooting at my feet. Then I am seeing maglev cars in traffic below and I am jumping down onto them and I am running and jumping and people are shouting at me but I am not hearing them, just BUDUDUDUDU from drone shooting at me, and I am sending signal out for any Enyemaka and hearing nothing and sending signal and hearing nothing and sending signal and BOOM—

■ ■ ■ ■ ■

I am wishing to be telling you that I am knowing what is happening right after, but I am spending many hours searching my memory, and there is being only darkness. I am not knowing what is happening to me after explosion. I am remembering that the first thing I am seeing is tiny hole of light coming from sky. Everything is shadow, and this is how I know I am being covered. And I am first thinking that this is what night is. That it is just blackness with tiny hole of light. But it is bodies. Many bodies piled on top of me. And then I am remembering the bodies are falling away. It is sounding like someone is dragging their foots on the dirt road, then it is sounding like a shirt rustling in wind, like someone is wearing a shirt too big for them and running down dirt road, and when I think of this thing, I am thinking that the person wearing this shirt should be giggling. I am liking the sound in my brain.

As more and more bodies are coming away, I am seeing that light is bigger. Big big. So big it is paining my eyes to look at. I am wanting to raise my arms to block out the light, but I cannot move them because there are more bodies on top of them.

I am not hearing any words anywhere, not even wind, just crunching of stones and rustling like clothes and shuffling like feet wearing slippers on road until many bodies tumble away at once and I am seeing blue and white and gold and red, and I must close my eyes because it is too much. And air is feeling cold on my skin because there is no more pile of smelling bodies crushing me. But air is also paining me like many many knife on my skin. It is burning, and I am hearing sizzle like meat is cooking.

Then, I am waking up. Is no body on top of me. Just metal. Many many pieces of metal, and it is burning. I am not sure why I am thinking of when Enyemaka are pulling me from pile of bodies and finding me and I am joining them and meeting Xifeng and finding purpose. But my body is shaking shaking.

I am trying to see with my mind's eye but it is broken and I am not being able to access maps or reach out to Enyemakas. I am alone.

If I am closing my eyes tight, I am making my body to stop shaking and I am being able to pull myself out from under pile of metal that is trapping me. I am not able to be standing straight because one leg is being twisted wrongly, but it is not paining me so I am dragging it while fire burns around me.

It is still night, but smoke is blocking the stars. There is still some people in street taking picture of car wreckage with their phones, and I am hurrying away and taking cover behind other burning car and moving from shadow to shadow and hoping no one and nothing is seeing me.

And I am stumbling into darkness until I am finding forest and rain is hitting me through the leaves. It is making the ground soft soft and I am falling many time, and one time I am falling and letting myself lie still and hoping that the mud will rise and drink me entirely so my body is not paining me anymore. I am thinking that maybe this is what it is meaning to be sadding. You are wanting the earth to be consuming you.

I am thinking of Xifeng and how I am not looking for her, I am just thinking of running away. And I am thinking that I am coward and bad person to be doing this. Xifeng is protecting me and giving me purpose and telling me that I am not child of war and that I am good person and I am just leaving her behind.

I am trying to reach her with my mind's eye, but I am hearing nothing. I am sending signal and hearing nothing and sending signal and hearing nothing and water is falling from my eyes.

CHAPTER
13

Ify watches the pro-immigration demonstration from the window of her office, arms folded, brow furrowed. Among the marchers are Black and brown protestors, and sprinkled throughout are cadres of Japanese protestors with banners bearing slogans in kanji. At the head of the march are mestizos and descendants of the First Nation tribes, alternating verses of a song they chant at full volume, their arms linked together. Many protestors wear traditional garb from their cultures, but many more wear the dress of those who've acclimated to Alabast, simple-colored loose-fitting shirts and blouses and suit jackets. Red and blue and white and green and pink and orange, but throughout the procession, a shimmer. Many of these people can afford to take the day off from work to protest the government's new hardline immigration policy. Among them is Grace, holding a placard of her own with slogans in Alabastrine English, French, Dutch, and Traditional Chinese characters.

You care too much, Ify wants to tell the girl, who, were she in Ify's position, would be risking not just her job but her medical license as well. If Grace wants to be the best medical care provider she can be, she should focus on her studies. Focus on actual patient care: the checking of vital signs, conducting the right tests, offering the correct prognoses. She shouldn't be waving a poster in the air and shouting like some rabble-rouser. But Ify hears them call for shutting down the Jungle, and the images return to Ify. The horror and the squalor.

She turns away from the window and finds herself thinking of the boy whose hand she'd picked up and dropped at the hospital the other day. Completely unresponsive. Afterward, she and Grace had overseen the insertion of a feeding tube through his nose. No reaction whatsoever.

Projected on the screen behind her from her tablet is page after page of the recent report from the Alabast Psychiatric Association done in collaboration with a number of political scientists hired by the government. It is a mess of hypothesis and conjecture, so much guesswork with no concrete proof, and no throughline or central argument. The medical epidemic that has overtaken the refugee children isn't yet widespread knowledge. So far, it has only made noise in the government and medical communities. Ify shudders to think of what form popular feeling might take. Before she can arrest the visions, she sees white Alabastrines shouting that this is what those migrants deserve, that they should have never come here, and so on and so on.

"Focus," she hisses to herself.

One theory explaining the epidemic is that what is happening is specific to the cultures of the afflicted children, that it is the body hacking the mind or the mind hacking the body or both. Some physiological mystery. But a quick scan of medical documentation from each of those countries—whether the Babylonian Republic or Australia—shows no widespread occurrence of these symptoms. There is no indication in these lands of origin that this is a problem. Not a Babylonian problem, not an Australian problem, not a specifically Pacific problem, not an indigenous American problem.

Another theory, related to the first, is that the affected children were raised in cultures that prioritized community over the individual. These children, this theory says, are sacrificing themselves for their families. By now, it has been concluded that the majority of cases are from families that have received deportation notices. The children are literally throwing their bodies on the gears of an immigration machine bent on getting rid of them.

"The solution is simple-ah," Céline says from the other end of their connection. Ify has activated the camera function in her Whistle, and Céline's face hovers in holographic projection next to hers so it looks as though they are both watching the anti-government demonstration below. At first, it looks as though there are only hundreds in the streets of Alabast's main city, maglev cars ascending into higher levels of traffic to fly over them. But if Ify cranes her neck, she can see that the protesters may perhaps number in the thousands. Even in the distance, banners are being waved by people sitting on the shoulders of taller marchers. It is perhaps the sound-canceling coating of her walls that muffles the chanting and the singing, disguising their true volume. "Cancel the deportation orders."

Ify knows that her friend is trying to adopt a joking tone, but an electric current of concern runs through her words. And fatigue? "It's not that simple," Ify catches herself saying, and she knows it's just another meaningless jumble of words, a sentence that people say to keep progress from happening or to keep from having to explain why a good thing can't be done. Is this a medical issue or a political issue? She is a doctor. She is not trained in the workings of government. "I am not a politician-oh."

"Ify, *arrête*. You are already a high-ranking medical professional. *Ne fais pas comme une bébé.* You have a responsibility to these people." Céline calms down. The more excited or agitated she gets, the more her native French starts to saturate her sentences. "They need security. It is not difficult to see. I am sure many of the children were already being treated for other things when this began to happen. But the news is saying that many of the new cases are from children who had integrated well into Alabast. They were pretty much Alabastrine." When she says it, she makes it sound more refined than what it is. Alabastrine means sameness. It means being swallowed up by the bland majority culture. It means whiteness. But maybe that is security. "Freedom from danger," Céline says, completing Ify's thought.

"So what are you saying I do? Secure residency permits for every patient in my ward?"

"*Précisement!* In one month, they will all be cured." Céline grins.

Ify frowns at the procession. In her mind is a series of obstacles she would face were she to try something like that. Still, there seem to be too many missing pieces. Why now, when refugees were being deported since before she even arrived in Alabast? Why certain refugees and not others? Were refugees who had come alone to receive the same treatment as refugees with healthy families? Why weren't adults being treated for this? What about Peter?

Her Whistle chirps angrily. It's Amy. The last person Ify wants to talk to. She cancels the call, but the Whistle chirps again. And chirps and chirps. "I'm sorry, Céline, I have to take this. It's Amy. She won't leave me alone."

"That's fine. Family first."

"She's not my fa—" But Céline has hung up, her projection gone with the suddenness of a wink or a thunderclap.

Before Ify can get out a tired "Hello Amy," the frantic voice on the other line bursts into her head. "It's—it's Peter," Amy stutters. "He . . . he tried to hurt himself and we found him in his bedroom and the knife was on the floor and there was just blood all over the sheets and oh my God, what is going to happen? I'm so scared, why would he do this, Ify, please please please come home."

The rest of Amy's words turn into a dull hum, a buzz, as though Ify's ears have been stuffed with gauze. She knows it is foolish to think this, knows that she doesn't possess this degree of power, knows that she wouldn't have been as malicious in handling it even if she did, but she cannot help but whisper to herself, "What have I done?"

CHAPTER
14

Every day I am returning to Lagos to look for Xifeng.

I am moving like thing that can only live in shadows. I am hiding in alleys between buildings, and is tough sometime because buildings in Lagos too close together. And there is being no order to the streets, so it is being easy to be lost. But in my head, I am mapping my way so I am knowing what streets I have search before. But is difficult because I am thinking that tomorrow Xifeng is standing on street I am walking on today, so I am looking and looking.

I am thinking the best time to see her is being in daytime because one time I am looking for her at night and man is looking at me like something to eat, like suya wrapped in old piece of paper. And he is licking his lip and coming to me, and I am breaking his arm but I am not killing him because Xifeng is not wanting that and I am not child of war anymore. I am only doing bad thing to protect people. Sometime I am doing bad thing to protect me, but I am never killing to protect me because I am not as important as Xifeng. I am knowing that she is leader of army of rememberings and I am soldier, and something in my brain is telling me that soldier must do everything to finish mission even if everything is meaning I am dying.

Sometime when I am thinking of Xifeng, I am also thinking of man who we are calling Commandant and who is being like father to us and who, when he is first giving me helmet and gun and making me to be carrying ammo crate, is knocking on it and saying, "I saved your life. I saved your life. I saved your life." And, when we are preparing to storm bridge, me and other child of war, he is making us to be singing and dancing before, and as we are singing and dancing, he is pressing his ear to our chest to be hearing our heartbeat, and if he is liking what he is hearing he is choosing you to fight that day. And I am thinking of how he is always making me to be looking into his eyes and how there is silent pledge happening between us. I am making promise that I will be protecting him and killing enemy. So when I am looking in Xifeng eyes, I am making promise that I will be protecting her and killing enemy.

I am also looking for Xifeng in daytime because police come at night and they cause bad thing to happen. They are stopping people for no reason and sometime they are shooting and sometime there are drone in sky watching all thing and is too many thing looking for me. So I am spending night under bridge where no police come.

Under bridge is all shadow and people moving like me, from shadow to shadow. If there is drone, it is drone that is spraying the water with thing that is killing mosquito, then leaving. It is not drone that is shooting us.

Many people here are sleeping in tent, and there is being drug in the air that they are putting in their face, and they are walking like thing that is dead and alive at the same time. I am not liking this because dead thing is supposed to be dead and alive thing is supposed to be being alive. But even though people are sometime being mean to each other, they are also being kind to each other. They are sharing blanket sometime and they are sharing tent sometime and sometime they are coming back wet because they are going to beach and splashing in water and laughing.

I am seeing people leaning against pillar under bridge and closing eye to sleep, and I am doing the same and it is feeling familiar to me. In my brain I am seeing Enyemaka, and she is showing me how she is being given life and how it is because someone is spitting nanobots into her ear, and when I am seeing people who are looking dead, I am wanting to spit in their ear, but then I am remembering Xifeng telling me that this is not what I am supposed to be doing with people, and she is laughing when she is telling me this.

I am remembering time when I am sleeping standing up, and when I am remembering that I am remembering crawling under razorwire and I am remembering holding gun as big as me and I am remembering climbing wall and running and saying *YES, SAH* very loudly to Big Man and this is me being soldier, I know.

When I am pretending to be sleeping even though I am still standing, my mind is walking other places like it is finding rememberings on its own. And I am inside a mech that is rattling jagga-jagga all around me, because I am flying fast fast through the sky and this mech is old and is being rusty because of radiation in the air around me, and I am pulling trigger and bullet is coming from my mech's gun like BUDUBUDUBUDUBUDU and stitching enemy mech I am chasing like TKTKTKTKTKTK. And is all katakata, but it is like

I am not really seeing or hearing or smelling. My body is moving without me. It is pressing button on console and it is pulling gearshift, and it is like my mind is vanishing. It is feeling like lying in warm sand and letting water wash me, and it is feeling like being in womb and I am remembering Xifeng hugging me. That is what it is being like when I am remembering flying. It is feeling like I am being hugged by someone who is loving me.

But I am remembering other thing too. I am remembering riding in jeep hovering above the ground like a bird flying low, and big leaf—too big—is poking through the windows SWISH SWISH against my face, and it is annoying the man driving and the man next to him but I am child and I am liking the feel of big leaf SWISH SWISH on my face. And I am remembering that I can make hologram out of my rememberings, and when other people under the bridge are sleeping, I am making hologram and I am watching and it is glowing blue and sometime red and sometime it is full of color, and I am knowing that this is my life. Leaf making SWISH SWISH against my face. Smelling beans and okra that commander is eating at table in command tent. Learning that I am not needing to eat or to sleep because I am not like normal child.

Then, I am seeing white ceiling, and when I am getting up in vision I am seeing that I am lying on bed and I am asking what am I and I am being told that I am having all of her gifts and none of her pain and I am not knowing who "her" is, but I am seeing camp and I am seeing other girl who is looking like me and I am seeing one smiling at me and she is having small thing like bee come out of her hair and swim around her head like cloud of mosquito and she is smiling at me and I am thinking that I am smiling at her too, and then I am in spacecraft and

I am floating and this girl is floating and we are touching and we are putting lip together and she is humming against me her whole body is humming against me and I am seeing camp again and I am seeing beach and I am seeing sun touch water and turn all around me to gold and I am looking down and I am seeing girl sitting next to me and she is pointing at tiny shiny things in the sky and I am following her finger and I think I am smiling again and I am calling her Ify.

I am calling her Ify.

CHAPTER 15

In the hall outside the operating room, Paige and Amy sit, Amy with her arm wrapped around Paige's shoulder and Paige with her face buried in her hands. Amy looks up at Ify as she approaches. Her eyes are redder than Ify has ever seen them. Amy tries to get up from her seat to hug Ify, but Paige has fallen onto Amy's lap. Her weeping has grown quieter, but her body shakes even more. So Amy just gives Ify a look of soft pleading. A look that says, *Please help us. However you can, please help us.*

Ify's resolve stiffens, and she looks through the window and into Peter's hospital room. All white, even the cyberized nurse who attends to him. The door slides open, and the nurse looks up, golden hair in a bob framing an angular face that ends in a pointed chin. She looks like a cartoon drawing of a nurse.

"May I help you?" The voice is too robotic for Ify's tastes, like the voices announcing a rail line stop. *Please mind the gap while descending from the train.*

"I am visiting the patient." She presses a button at her waist, and out of her eyes beams a holographic projection of her name and medical credentials.

"This is the trauma ward, not the neurology wing." Rudeness

or a mechanical lack of decorum, Ify can't tell. The nurse stands before Ify and doesn't move. It doesn't help Ify give her the benefit of the doubt that this half-droid is coded as white. "Your pass does not permit you access to this patient."

"My pass?" Ify grits her teeth, clenches her fists. In that moment, she doesn't want to dress down the cyberized nurse who's refusing her, she wants to hit her in the face. But she calms herself. The last thing she needs prior to her graduation and official appointment as assistant director of neurology and chief of the Refugee Program at this very hospital is documentation of a physical altercation with a half-droid who doesn't merit the effort. "I'm family," Ify says at last with a sigh. And it sounds like a concession. Like admitting defeat. She calls up her biographical information, and the nurse's eyes go blank as she, undoubtedly, scans a list of permitted visitors behind her retinas.

"Very well," the nurse says, before walking past Ify and leaving the room.

Ify swallows the anger. It burns her throat and stomach on the way down. A younger, less acclimated Ify might have looked into how to get that nurse fired or transferred to more odious work or might even have attempted to hack the nurse herself, enter her braincase and wreak havoc in direct violation of not only hospital protocol but Alabastrine law. But now, she gives herself several deep, long breaths and lets her shoulders settle. Her fists unclench. She has already forgotten the nurse.

When she gets to Peter's bedside, she sees a boy without any visible wounds. MeTro sealant has healed the incisions running along his wrists. The blood has been cleaned from his body. Ify knows that were she to run her fingers through Peter's hair, she wouldn't even find red flecks along his scalp. The bullet scar remains, however. Like it is as natural a part of him as his fingers and toes and the hair under his armpits.

There's a chair beside his bed, but Ify refuses to take it. Nor does she sit on the ledge where visitors are supposed to put their gifts for patients. Ify imagines every room on this floor has one, as though it's expected that patients here will have loving family and friends showering them with presents and well wishes. As though everyone on this floor has someone who cares for them. Ify doesn't know why the assumption annoys her. Maybe it's lingering anger at the nurse's racism, algorithm-powered or not. Maybe it's how much the problem of the refugee patients is needling the back of her mind. Maybe it's that whenever she thinks of Peter, she's assaulted by a basketful of emotions: anger at his attempts at manipulating Amy and Paige, anger at her own hesitation in getting rid of him, guilt at whatever role she's played in putting him here. Still, she can't quite get rid of the feeling that this too is part of his plan, that this is what he's willing to do to stay in their home and on this Colony. That this is checkmate in the game between him and Ify.

Her cramps have started again. She closes her eyes against the pain, then exhales slowly until it shrinks into something she can handle.

She pulls her Bonder from her coat pocket. Maybe if she can see what dreams he is dreaming while sedated, she can get a clue as to his motivations. Unlock more of the mystery of him. Were she cyberized, she'd be able to plug directly into Peter, but this visor-shaped device whose edges she slips over her ears has to do the job of an external link. She presses the button that lifts Peter's bed into a slight incline, then searches the back of his bed for the opening that circles his outlet. When she finds it, she plugs her loose cord in, Bonding with him, and the world around her pixelates then falls apart block by block until darkness surrounds her.

She hears murmurs. Faraway voices, then static, then they become clearer. Words. She can hear their words.

"He says that when the militants came to his village, they took hostages. He also told us that his little sister was standing next to him and offered them five naira to let their mother go." A snicker. "Apparently, it was all that she had."

Another voice: "What is a child from the bush doing with five naira? An Efik family north of the Redlands? Probably stolen."

The first voice drones as though the speaker is reading from a report. "During his initial interrogation, he claims the men were led to a room farther down the hall in a"—a pause while he scrolls through his notes—"a school building. The men were brought to the math room. Subject claims his father was led there with thirteen other men and shot. Allegedly, their bodies were dumped out of the window." The speaker lets out a bureaucratic sigh. "This boy is the village's only survivor."

"Unlucky for him," the second voice says, chuckling. "I am betting that he claims that God spared him because he only spared those with a higher purpose. Well, we will show him his higher purpose."

Static distorts the voice for a second. Then a brief image of jungle, then a sunbathed road filled with pedestrians and vendors shouting their wares from their stalls. Then static.

Ify's vision becomes clearer, and she sees that she is in a dark, dank room. Somewhere underground. Maybe abandoned. Water drips into a puddle somewhere outside of her vision.

When she looks down, she sees that she's bound to a metal chair. She's in Peter's body. Sounds echo, but she believes this is the type of place where sounds are made that aren't supposed to be heard aboveground.

"Well, let's get this over with, and we can bring him back to his cell upstairs."

Two men, the speakers, walk into the room, and Ify feels Peter's fingers clench into fists, where they're bound behind his chair. They wear all black and don't bother hiding their faces. Their hands are gloved. One of them is older, his face like it was carved from obsidian it's so expressionless. The other is already grinning, and Ify, in Peter's body, feels their heart race. Their jaw clenches. Tears spring to their eyes. Even though their legs are bound to those of the metal chair, their feet scuffle madly against the ground.

Static. A kitchen. Stew is cooking over a pot. A woman stirs with a massive wooden spoon. A hand—Ify-Peter's hand—reaches over. The woman smacks it. Static.

"So," says the first man, pulling at the gloves on his hands. "Let's talk about that higher purpose of yours." He walks to a side wall and comes back with something buzzing and sizzling in the palm of one hand.

Ify-Peter squirms in their seat, then thrashes as the interrogator comes near. When the interrogator is close enough, they see that there are bees buzzing in the man's hand, their metal carapaces glistening with light from a source they can't find. "Please." More thrashing. "Please, please no more."

Static blitzes out the vision, then everything comes back.

"We don't believe your story," the second interrogator says.

The first kneels before Ify-Peter. "If this group massacred

your village, then why would you join them? Why did we find you in their camp?" His voice is low and almost playful. "It doesn't make any sense. A proper victim would seek revenge against those who wronged him. Like a man. Are you a man?"

Ify-Peter chokes back a sob.

"I asked you a question. Are you a man?"

More wordless weeping.

"Very well then." The interrogator pulls a knife out of a pocket on his vest and cuts away Ify-Peter's pant legs, exposing their thighs to the cold. Then the interrogator upends the swarm of metallic bees onto their legs, where they burrow beneath the skin, and pain sears through their entire body, spiking at the base of their brain, turning everything to gray static, and suddenly—

Ify is back in the hospital room, gasping. The other end of her cord lies on the floor. She staggers into the chair and forces herself to take several deep breaths. She presses her palms to her eyes, trying to block out the vision and the experience she's just had, racked by sobs that shake her shoulders. She should have been prepared. She curses herself, for not expecting to intrude into a painful memory. Then she straightens. That memory could belong to anyone. Peter is a synth, a combination of other people's neural data cobbled together to generate enough information to simulate humanness. It's all fake. That couldn't have been Peter. With this, she's able to take the pain she experienced and box it and stuff that box deep in her mind. She puts her fingers to her nose, and they come back red. Hurriedly, she snatches tissues from the dispenser above Peter's bedstand and dabs at the nosebleed.

Then she takes off her Bonder, folds it, and stuffs it back into her pocket.

When she looks down, Peter is staring straight at her. His eyes didn't flutter open. One moment, they're closed; the next, they're not. The more she observes him, the more like a machine he seems. "You lied," she says, trying to make her voice as hard as possible. "Your family is not Igbo. You are Efik. Or you would be if you weren't a synth. But you were a synth, made for war and aligned with rebels. Then you were captured. Who's to say that you were actually tortured?"

He says nothing. His face doesn't move.

"Because you are a synth, you are not subject to human rights protections under Alabastrine law. Your very existence is a danger to everyone here." She searches his face for a reaction. "You are not human. Once the authorities are notified of your presence, you will be arrested and deported."

"Please," he says, and his voice sounds just like it did in the memory of his torture.

Ify steels her heart against him.

"You made them torture me."

"What?"

His words are weightless. Breathy things that a strong wind could blow away, yet Ify feels as though each one could pulverize her. "It was beneath the cell where I was being held where I saw you." He licks cracked lips. "I remember. I know it was you."

"You don't know—"

"Please." He raises a hand limply, as though to stop her. It immediately falls back onto the bed. "I know it was you. The men obeyed you and the pilot you were with. If they are torturing me, it is because you are making them." His words don't match his tone. The words should be coming from someone angry, someone threatening vengeance. But his voice is one of resignation and soft certainty, the type of voice with which the elderly speak when they know they don't have much longer to live. Tears brim in his eyes. "But I am not hating you. I should be hating you, but I am not. I should be wanting to kill you, but I am not. Even while others that I am with are wanting to be killing you and doing horrible thing to you, I am not." He holds her gaze. As weak as he looks in that bed, he refuses to break her gaze. "You are leaving the war. You are surviving and leaving. And you are coming here. Why am I not able to do the same? You are doing horrible thing during war, just like I am doing horrible thing during war."

"We are *not* the same."

A tear slides down his face, drops from his chin. "But I survived. And I left. And I came here."

"You are a weapon. You will always be a weapon. You can't change. And this?" She gestures at the entirety of the hospital room. "You doing what you did? It changes nothing. I know what you're doing. You're trying to manipulate them into caring for you. You want them to hold on to you even tighter, so you do something like this." She's getting angrier than she intended, and tears spring anew to her eyes. *This isn't my fault*, she tells herself. "But it's not going to work. Because I"—she jabs a finger into her chest—"I am here to protect them. I know what you are, and I won't let you hurt them."

She leaves before she can say any more, stomping to the door and waiting frustratedly for it to slide open. When she stops outside, she remembers that Paige and Amy are on the bench right next to her. She wipes the wetness from her eyes and stuffs her bloodstained tissue in her pocket.

"Oh, Ify," Amy says, rising to hug her.

She thinks I'm in mourning over Peter, Ify realizes. A part of her wants to tell her the truth, that she just lived through what may be Peter's very real trauma, that she was transported back to a time she's done everything in her power to forget, when she was complicit in exactly those same acts of torture. She wants to tell Amy that she believes a part of her, however small, is responsible for the boy in that hospital bed, for turning him into what he is, for creating him in the first place. War does that. It is the pot and it is all the ingredients for the stew, and what gets spooned out and put on the plate is Peter. But she says nothing. Instead, she accepts Amy's hug in silence.

It is not her fault.

■ ■ ■ ■ ■

Except for a few attendants making their rounds up and down the rows of beds, Ify is alone in the ward housing the refugee children. The lights have dimmed. Ify figures it's part of a power-saving measure now that the kids have been marked down as unresponsive to light. She makes sure that the attendants are far enough away that they won't see what it is she's about to do.

It's against all protocol to perform an invasive procedure without the patient's consent. But curiosity has taken hold of Ify like never before. She must know the answer to the questions stirring inside her: What happened between her and Peter? Is there something in there that can help Ify figure out what's been going on with these children?

When she's certain she's in the clear, she takes a seat next to the child she'd seen Peter with earlier, the one she now knows for certain is cyberized. She pulls her Bonder out of her pocket and checks to make sure it's in working order. She dares not put it on, but she calibrates it to download instead of stream. And like that, she plugs her cord into the outlet at the base of the child's neck. There's no way to know what memories she's downloading, whether they're peaceful or painful, whether they're of family or torturers, whether they'll provide coherent snapshots of an episode or whether they'll be a chaos of disparate puzzle pieces.

Satisfied with the data she's downloaded, she disconnects and stands up. Just before she leaves, she smooths out a wrinkle in the motionless child's bedsheet.

■ ■ ■ ■ ■

She knows, even as she's cleaning her room, that she's avoiding her device. The Bonder sits like an accusation on her desk. It's even connected to a projector so she won't have to actually live through the recorded moments. If she closes her eyes, she can still imagine, in her entire body, the suffering that Peter remembers. Whether or not the memory was false, it still rattles her bones.

For several minutes, she stands in the center of her now-pristine workroom, staring at the device. Finally, before the urge leaves her, she rushes to her desk and inputs the set of keys on her tablet to fire up the Bonder.

It hums, then prepares to send the data to the projector when, suddenly, sparks pop out of it. The projector shuts down and the Bonder goes dark. Ify frowns, then tries to turn the projector back on, but nothing changes. She disconnects the Bonder, and nothing she does will bring it back to life. She turns the thing over in her hands, and, before she knows it, she's got her tools out to repair it. Her desk is festooned with all shapes of pins and chips and pliers and scalpels, pruning shears and tiny torches. And above it all hovers a small group of nanobots to help hold parts of the metal open while she works.

By the time she looks back up, the false light from the Colony's lighting system has started to spill through her windows. Wisps of smoke still curl from the device. Her rotation starts in two hours. She's close—she can taste it like the beginnings of blood on her tongue from chewing through her cheek.

Finally, she's got it. She lets out a sigh. The next instant, her fingers blaze over the table to put the thing back together.

With her Bonder reassembled, she takes a moment. Then she plugs it into her tablet to read its data and perform a system diagnosis.

Her tablet registers the device. Victory.

Its internal data unfurls down the system monitor. The scroll continues, down and down and down, until it stops. The cursor blinks, then starts to move in the opposite direction, gobbling line after line of code.

It's erasing its own data, eating its own organs. Frantic, Ify inputs recovery protocols, trying to revert the Bonder to an earlier version of itself and regain what was lost. But nothing. The massacre continues.

She pulls the cord out and forces closed both the tablet and the Bonder. But the damage is done. Almost all of that data, gone.

What just happened?

CHAPTER
16

Surveillance drone that is having police markings is passing under broken stone bridge, but people who are living here are sending their own drones that they are making, and they are attacking the surveillance drone and beating it into pieces then picking at its corpse like they are vultures. While the people are laughing and cheering at this, I am pretending to be sleeping. But I am always sensing thing that is happening, even if my eye is not being open. I am knowing how people are coming together to protect themself from enemies like the police or bandits. I am knowing that this is being called community.

When I am pretending to be sleeping, I am leaning against pillar like someone who is sleeping or doing drug or both, but I am not sleeping. I am watching. When I am watching, I am seeing what people are bringing into this home where we are living under the bridge. One night after water is coming in from lagoon and washing over everything like big big flood and breaking tent and sometime grabbing people and pulling them back out, we are bringing up sandbag and people are digging and building wall to keep lagoon out when it is rising and becoming big big and trying to eat us. Sometime they are bringing stick, but sometime they are bringing metal. Small piece of metal to help making stronger the wall but also bigger piece of metal like shield. One night I am recognizing piece. It is like chestpiece of Enyemaka. It *is* chestpiece of Enyemaka.

Man with chestpiece is bringing it into shadow under bridge, and I am walking fast to him.

"Sah, what are you using this for?" I ask him, pointing at the chestpiece.

"Child, how you dey?" the man asks, smiling.

"I dey fine, sah." And I am trying to be nice and polite and learning that it is not good to be speaking like robot to people. They are liking when you are speaking like human, and when they are liking you, they are doing what you want. "Wetin dey?" I am asking him and pointing to the chestpiece.

He is looking at it and scratching his chin and looking at me like he is trying to decide how much to tell me. "Ah make boat am." He is nodding his head, and his afro is bouncing when he is doing this. "Part of my boat. For when water fi eat us again." And this time, he point to the lagoon, and I know he is talking about flooding and how every time the lagoon comes in, it is coming closer and closer, and the water is rising even though we are building wall for protection. Eventually, the water will eat us.

"Where de rest of de boat, sah?"

He is quiet one moment, then he is looking at me different. He is looking at me like I am no longer little girl or friend but like I am stranger or wild animal. "You be wayo?"

"No wahala," I am telling him, and I am holding my hands out, palm up like saying, *Please, sah, my hands are empty, I have no weapon.* "I wan no vex you. Just where are you getting metal from. I no wan take it, I just wan know where it is coming from."

He is looking at me with wild eye, then he is calming and he is pointing to Lagos proper. My heart is thumping in my chest and I am feeling blood rise in my face because I am not wanting to go to Lagos even though I am going every day and looking for Xifeng and not finding her. But I am thinking, then I am asking him, "Where in Lagos?" because Lagos is big big city as big as many jungles.

He is looking at me like man with secret, and then he is dropping to ground and he is drawing map in the sand and moving stone to make building. And like this he is making noise and moving thing without speaking. Then he is looking at me and pointing and saying that this is Falomo Bridge. He is saying Falomo Bridge again and pointing above our head, and I am seeing what he is saying: that we are eating and sleeping and making bathroom under Falomo Bridge. And he is drawing Falomo Bridge long and long then he is stopping, and I am asking him why he stop and he is saying that there is nothing but water.

Then he is drawing rest of map and he is telling me what is Ikoyi in eastern part of Lagos Island, and I am seeing map in my head and suddenly I am knowing what is Ikoyi and what is Lagos Island and even Victoria Island and Iddo and Mainland Lagos. I am seeing it all. Like light that is flashing in my head. Man is showing me that he is getting chestpiece from man in Ikoyi and, too loud, I am asking him man's name, and I need to know but other people is turning and seeing us and maybe thinking I am attacking him, so I am lowering my voice.

For many seconds he is looking at me silent and not saying

anything, like he is doing calculation in his brain, then he is telling me, "It is very dangerous where I am get the metal from."

"I am feeling no fear."

And he is telling me that close to military barracks is yard of abandoned scrap metal. It is place like rubbish bin for broken things. They are putting broken weapons there like gun and tank and mech, and that is where he is finding this piece of metal he is using for boat. And I am thinking of Enyemaka in that pile of garbage, and I am thinking that she is at bottom of pile and maybe she is already broken in many pieces and they are just putting more and more metal on top of her. They are maybe burying her beneath old carcass of ground mech or drone or juggernaut, and I am remembering what it is like to be buried under bodies and I am remembering not breathing and seeing small hole of light like single star in the sky and I am wishing to be there with Enyemaka, and suddenly I am remembering where I am and man is looking at me like he is scared and sadding at the same time. And I am thinking that he is knowing that someone or something is dead that I am not wanting to be dead, and maybe he is wanting to tell me words to make me not sadding but he is saying nothing. He is only continuing to be drawing in the sand and make arrow from where we are to where I need to be, and I am saying thank you. I am making note in my mind and I am saying thank you and I am following arrow.

CHAPTER
17

"Time of death?" Ify says, trying to sound as clinical as she can. She shouldn't be this rattled. But the sight of the woman in the hospital bed—unconnected from the machines monitoring her vital signs, and with the helmet monitoring her cerebral activity settled on a pillow behind her—has unsettled her.

The attending nurse says in an even voice, "Nineteen hours, forty-one minutes." She's been looking at Ify the whole time, and Grace has been at Ify's side, alternating her gaze between the woman and the tablet clutched to her chest. Grace has seen the deceased before. She's certainly worked in this hospital long enough. Some of the patients she's seen have even died of violent wounds. Blunt force trauma to the head or gangrenous limbs. Some of them came in with internal bleeding too far along to stop, or their internal organs had been so damaged they would not have withstood replacement. Even people who had died during the cyberization—Ify is sure Grace must have witnessed those as well. But for reasons Ify can guess, Grace can't look at this Cantonese woman and muster the clinical distance she's had to build in this occupation.

This is what happens when you care too much, Ify wants to

tell her. All those conversations Grace had with her—about food, about grandfathers, about Earthland—gone. Wherever the Cantonese woman's mind and spirit has gone in death, she has taken all those things with her. And left Grace with the grief that is surely shaking in her bones. None of what Grace did could save this woman. *Now look at you*, Ify wants to say, then wonders where this cruelty is coming from.

"There was a spike in brain activity just prior to her flatlining," the nurse continues.

Ify had expected to find relief in treating patients other than the children who had fallen even deeper into their comas, but there is no deliverance waiting for her here. Not for the first time, she wonders if she is the right person to direct the Refugee Program. Something has cracked inside her. "How was her sleep cycling in the week prior?"

"Irregular. She was also being treated for sleep paralysis and obstructed airways disease."

"Sleep apnea?"

"No. A lung disorder."

Ify makes a note of that. They should have seen this coming. Still, so many of their patients had come in with irregular sleep cycles and damaged respiratory function. Hospital protocol and Alabastrine law prevented cyberization without the consent of the patient or the patient's guardian. But what to do with those patients who could not understand the language Ify or the others spoke? Ify and the rest of her staff had the electronic capabilities to immediately translate whatever language they heard, but they could not speak it back to those who lacked that technology. And so many of the refugees had been unaccompanied minors. No guardian to give permission for them. No guardian to guide them through this new, terrifying, sterile world.

Grace has long since stopped taking notes; she only stares blankly at the deceased.

"Preparations had been made to treat her post-traumatic stress disorder," the nurse droned, nodding at Grace. "But after her latest sleep, she never awakened. And it is against office protocol to perform mind-altering operations without the patient's consent."

Ify's frown deepens.

"Immediately prior to flatlining, she screamed."

"What?" This from Grace, awoken from her stupor.

"Her first vocal effort since she had fallen unconscious. It was a single scream, sustained for approximately two and a half seconds. Then her vital functions ceased."

A moment of grief pierces Ify's heart. "Nightmares. Her nightmares scared her to death." When she raises her head, new resolve stiffens her spine. "Have a record made of her brain function since her arrival in our ward. When did she first come in again?"

"Last month, Doctor. Before entry, she had been in excellent health."

"Grace, let's go." Ify leaves the room without bothering to correct the android nurse. She has never felt less a doctor than she does walking away from the woman she could not save. The woman whose trauma none of her medical knowledge could help her heal. A familiar fear fogs her mind: *I'm just some bush girl pretending to be a doctor.*

As they walk down the sterile, too-bright, ivory-colored hallway, Grace swipes at her tablet to bring up information on the next patient. "Mr. de Freitas," she says in a hard voice after clearing her throat. "Angolan. Six feet, two inches. He began hospitalization at a weight of 172 pounds." She continues with his physical state, but Ify stops her. "Yes, Doctor?"

Why is everyone calling her Doctor? "Tell me. His story. What . . . what difficulty did he suffer before arriving in Alabast?" It sounds so trite and simple to put it that way, but it is the only language Ify can find for what she wants to know.

Grace's words stumble over themselves as she tries to find an answer. Then her expression changes. From one of confusion to one of gratitude. Finally understanding what Ify is asking, she says, "He witnessed his family's torture at the hands of the regime. He is one of several patients from that village who have suffered the same condition."

"And who have endured the same trauma," Ify finishes.

"Yes, Doctor."

They arrive at the door to the man's room. "Thank you, Grace."

After a stunned moment, Grace permits a small, embarrassed smile. "Certainly, Doctor."

As they walk in, an aerial drone assistant hovers before the man's face, adjusting the wires connected to his temples.

Mr. de Freitas sits up in his bed. "Doctor?"

Ify surprises herself by smiling. "Yes, Mr. de Freitas."

"I can see!" he shouts. "I can see! My eyes!" He puts his fingers to his face, touches his cheeks and his chin, his eyelids. "I can see again." He can't stop touching his face, even his ears and his small afro. "They gave me new eyes! I can see!"

Ify notes the small scars by his temple, the mark of recent cyberization. "And your adjustment to light sensitivity? Is the light too bright?"

"Light? Oh my God." He laughs. "Light. I can see light!"

"Careful!" She rushes out to touch his arm. "Please do not stare directly at it. You may damage your new retinas. They are made to be more durable than natural eyes, but that does not mean they are indestructible."

He stares at Ify for a dazed second before letting out a full-bellied chuckle. "Yes. Of course. Not indestructible." His chuckle turns into a string of cackles. "Of course. Of course." His voice grows softer, filled with awe. "I thought I would never see again. After the things I had seen, I thought I never wanted to see anything, but I can see. Thank God, I can see. God is good all the time!"

Ify smiles, even as tears fill her eyes. "And all the time, God is good."

Tears spill down the man's cheeks. "Will . . . will crying damage the retinas too?"

Ify takes the man's hand in hers. "No, Mr. de Freitas. It is okay to cry," she says, as though she's giving herself permission as well.

Maybe Grace was right. Maybe this thing happening right now—the same thing Ify witnessed when the Cantonese woman had motioned Grace close and whispered lovingly into her ear about the food market—maybe this thing is important too.

■ ■ ■ ■ ■

The bot sits unactivated in its slot on the wall of the bathroom stall as Ify removes her menstrual cup and deposits it into the bin that sterilizes them. Most have the bot conduct the entire process automatically while they recline and read or let their mind wander. But Ify prefers to do it herself.

When she's finished, she leaves and heads to the sink to wash her hands. But just as the water begins to sluice through her fingers, she hears whimpering. The water stops, and Ify listens for a moment to whoever is crying in the stall two down from her own. Then she moves her hands, and the water pours from the faucet again, drowning out the sound.

A few seconds later, Grace appears at the sink next to her, checking her face in the mirror, wiping away tear streaks, tucking loose strands of hair behind her ears. She gives Ify a perfunctory nod and a swift "Doctor" before she begins washing her hands.

Ify moves her hands to the air dryer next to the sink, then wipes the remaining water away. She should leave, but she doesn't. Something keeps her there as Grace works to put herself together.

"Doctor?" Grace asks, her hands clean and dried.

"Yes, Grace?"

Grace looks Ify in the eye, and the grief is still there, despite her efforts to wash it away. "Why did you choose this work? Why this?"

Ify folds her arms and leans against the sink, staring off into the middle distance. "Before I arrived here, I wanted to be a pilot." The instinct rises in her to crush the memories bubbling to the surface—memories of a refugee camp in Nigeria, memories of the sister who abandoned her smiling at her and telling her to hurry up and get to school on time, memories of mechs and enemy soldiers raining fire and death on that camp—but she lets them come. "I would look into the night sky and see the Colonies winking at me like stars, and I would tell myself that, when I was older, I'd go there to study orbital physics and flight. My . . ." The word catches in her throat. "My sister was a pilot. During the war."

Grace's eyes go wide. "You had a sister?"

The last time Ify saw Onyii's face, it had been a blur. Ify had just undergone a surgery. Onyii had removed a tracker from inside her body. Then a haze had blanketed Ify, cocooned her. The next thing she knew, she was in the complete darkness of a cargo hold and wouldn't see light until the shuttle she'd been put on had docked in Alabast.

"What happened to her?"

For a long time, Ify is silent. She moves past Grace's question. "Whenever I think of piloting, I think of her. And whenever I think of her, I think of killing." She turns to Grace and hopes that Grace can see the new brightness in her face. The warmth she's trying to put there. "So I decided to study medicine. I wanted a job where I didn't have to break things. I could fix them instead."

Grace sniffs against a sob and smiles.

Ify takes a step and is close enough to see the shards of morning in her assistant's eyes. With her thumb, she wipes the still-shining tearstains from Grace's cheeks. "Take the rest of the day off."

"But, Doctor!"

Ify raises a hand to stop any further objection. "Physician, heal thyself." At the question in Grace's eyes, Ify says, "I attended chapel when I was recently arrived. I would go with a very dear friend of mine while we were students. That's where I heard that passage from Luke 4:23. 'Physician, heal thyself.'"

Grace's smile broadens. "Thank you, Doctor." Then she's off.

Ify lets out a heavy sigh after several seconds of watching the door Grace has just passed through. Then her Whistle trills. She sees the number for a mechanic and answers, "Hello?"

"Hi," says the young voice on the other end. "You dropped off a Bonder earlier this week?"

Her heart races. The comatose girl's neural data. "Yes. Is it ready? Were you able to recover the data?"

"Err . . . you should probably come by."

■ ■ ■ ■ ■

The mechanic's shop is a pristine collection of glass surfaces. External connecting devices and custom-made cases for them, encased in glass boxes, hang from hooks in the wall. Customers mill around, attended to by aerial service bots. Light just bright enough to make everyone feel comfortable, filling the air with soft chatter, shines over everything.

Behind the front counter leans a young man whose eyes glisten with the sheen of cyberization. When Ify draws near, she hears none of the humming and whirring of the gears and machinery at work inside of him and figures his central processing unit must be state-of-the-art. The twinkling nameplate on his chest says VIKRAM.

"You called me with an update?" Ify asks.

A goatee makes his otherwise shaven face more angular. There's an agelessness about him. He could be fifty years old or just a few years older than Ify. Or he could be a fifty-year-old man in the body of someone who looks only a few years older than Ify. He holds up her Bonder with one hand, elbow pressed to the glass counter. Tattoo ink swims in designs over his forearm. "The update is there is no update. You have a minute?"

Ify surprises herself with an exasperated sigh. "Sure."

Vikram leads her behind the desk and into a back room with the complete opposite ambiance of the store floor. In here, lamps illuminate small, seemingly random circles of a space otherwise smothered in shadows. Tools litter workspaces, and Ify finds herself stepping awkwardly over Bubble Wrap and empty boxes and glass cases strewn all over the floor. Nimbly, he makes his way to his desk, where mini projectors and tablets and small, cube-like data processors lie in a neat semicircle. He sits in a hoverchair and seems too preoccupied to offer Ify a seat until he extends his arm and a chair speeds out of the shadows and lands close enough for Ify to fall into beside him.

He connects the Bonder to one of the data processors, then connects that to a larger device and enables a wireless connection that Ify can feel in her temple, connecting the Bonder to half a dozen devices on the desk. It powers up, and up from one of the tablets pops a holographic projection of its screen. The fingers of Vikram's right hand break apart, and his wired fingertips blaze across a separate touchboard. Down scrolls the text of the Bonder's data. A swirl of letters, symbols, and numbers.

"I wasn't able to recover the lost data, but I was able to stop the virus from eating any more of it."

"Virus?"

"Yeah. Once you connected the Bonder to an outside device, whatever was in there just went nuts and started eating all your data." He shifts in his seat. "You sure it didn't contract a virus from any of your other devices?"

"I regularly have every piece of tech in my home checked. It couldn't have come from them. I would have noticed data loss earlier." She only half believes herself. Worry settles in the pit of her stomach that the virus had been hiding in one of her devices all along, devices that she has connected to in the past. What if the virus is inside her? The urge creeps into her to remove her Whistle from her temple and put it in a garbage disposal unit to be jettisoned into space.

He turns in his chair to face her fully. "Can I ask what you were doing when this happened?" He holds up the Bonder when he speaks, even though wires still hang from it.

Ify resists the urge to squirm. How can she confess to breaking office protocol and performing an invasive search of a patient without their consent? Even if this man doesn't know the full extent of Alabastrine law, he'd know she was up to something suspect.

"I was inspecting materials I'd downloaded."

Vikram frowns. "What kind of materials?"

The word *memories* almost slips out of Ify's mouth. "Cerebral data. I work in a hospital."

He holds his frown for a moment, then his face loosens. "Possibly a damaged braincase, then. Either way, the virus has crept into the Bonder's other functionalities. It's useless at this point. Most of its projection capabilities have been corrupted beyond repair. And if you were to connect to it, you'd be in for a world of pain. And you'd risk corruption yourself. You're not connected, are you?" It sounds like a statement coming from him.

"No. Red-blood." She pauses. "I do use Augments, however." She points to her temple. "My Whistle. Here. It activates an implant at the base of my neck, connecting to my central nervous system." She pulls back the collar of her shirt to show him the scar that will never heal. "It is removable. But that is what I use." She lets go of her collar and straightens in her chair. "The Augment is for heightening my sensory perception—seeing farther, hearing more clearly—and it's connected to my bodysuit for information transfer. It also enables remote connection to wireless devices. The Whistle is just for communication. Making and receiving calls, translation, that sort of thing."

"Like a phone," he says absently.

"A what?"

Vikram waves the Bonder in the air like it's just some disposable piece of tech. "Well, whatever you downloaded is likely the source of the virus. I'd recommend a clean sweep of whatever devices you used to connect with this. And I'd suggest having it decommissioned and put in a steel box to prevent accidental remote connection with anything—or anyone—else."

"That bad?" Ify says, trying to joke.

"It might try to connect on its own."

"What? Without my turning it on?"

"Yeah. Without you even turning it on."

Fear settles in Ify's stomach. The cyberized girl's memories: a poison. A virus. Her eyes grow wide with the question that rings between her ears.

How many of those refugee children are cyberized?

■　■　■　■　■

Paige and Amy take Peter to an artificial lake a brief walk from their cul-de-sac where teenagers wearing waterskates glide and twirl and leap as though they were skating on ice. Amy has Peter in a hoverchair with a blanket over his legs.

Upon his return from the hospital, his arms had been leaden and he'd had to be fed his liquids with a spoon. Paige had felt too nervous to feed him intravenously. He still has a listlessness about him, a lack of reaction to most stimuli. But it is a relief to Ify that he still squints when lights shine too brightly and that he will shrink away at something that might cause him pain. And now with an artificial wind blowing in his face to simulate springtime, the slightest of smiles crawls across his lips.

A pair of white, middle-aged neighbors waves to Amy. Amy lets out a loud squeal and beckons Ify to Peter's hoverchair. Then Amy and Paige hurry over to join their neighbors and huddle in the mirthful buzz of excited conversation sprinkled throughout with cannon bursts of laughter.

Ify walks slowly to Peter's side, and for a long time, they watch the kids skating in silence.

"I won't remember this," Peter says, at last.

"What?" Ify looks down at him, this unmoving boy who suddenly contains a sadness so unbearable it can't possibly be false. She wants to believe that every word out of his mouth is an attempt at controlling her, steering her in the direction he wants. But the stillness in his voice, its lack of tremor, rings too true in her chest.

"I don't remember being a child." He squints at the kids skating on water. One of them splashes a large wave on a little boy whose hair is the color of wheat grain. "I know that before, I am little, and I am reaching up to take things from kitchen table. And I am standing on my toes to do it. But I am not remembering it."

Ify wants to tell him this is because he's a synth and those memories weren't his to begin with. But she restrains herself. Let him speak. Maybe this is part of his therapy.

"I am singing song that I am hearing long long ago. But I am not remembering I am singing it. The only reason I know I've sung that song is that my sponsor recorded me singing it when I was newly adopted. It was soon after I'd arrived here. When I was in bed, I am hearing my own voice. It is Paige playing back my recorded voice. I am not remembering singing it. I am not remembering those words. But I know I sang them, because there is that recording." His speech patterns are changing. Maybe more evidence of trauma exerting itself. Is he reverting?

Ify watches him lift one arm and consider his wrist.

"I know I was in the hospital, because Paige and Amy told me. And they've been taking care of me more than usual. And my body feels it. My body is telling me that I have been lying down for long long time." He shakes his head. "But I am not remembering any of it."

Something niggles at the back of Ify's brain. A hypothesis. A light shining a path to an answer. "Do you remember . . . do you remember being captured? And . . ." She heaves a large, nervous sigh. "And tortured?"

He inclines his head toward Ify. "Did that happen to me?"

She breaks his gaze and focuses on the teenagers playing on the water. "I . . . I don't know." An idea occurs to her. "Do you remember ever holding a gun?"

He furrows his brow in concentration. "No."

"Do you remember my name?"

When he looks up at her again, tears well in his eyes. "No." His bottom lip quivers. He turns his gaze to his lap. "I am remembering that my name is Peter because that is what they are calling me." He gestures with his head at Paige and Amy, still chatting with their neighbors. "But I don't remember who is calling me that first. Who is giving me that name." He sniffles. "I will never remember." Something shifts in his jaw, and he stops crying. Tear streaks glisten on his cheeks. He looks at the teenagers laughing and playing. "I will not remember this either."

Ify wants to ask him about the girl in the refugee ward, whether he remembers connecting with her. She wants to ask if they were having a silent conversation, about food and family and where they came from.

Whatever you downloaded is likely the source of the virus, she thinks.

It might try to connect on its own.

Breath catches in Ify's throat. An entire ward filled with children. Hundreds upon hundreds of them, any number of whom could be cyberized. Any number of whom might even be synths. Any number of whom might have the entirety of their memories wiped away.

CHAPTER
18

It is not difficult for me to be finding hole in fence that is surrounding junkyard. There is footprint of many many people going through here so that when I am seeing it, it is looking like single groove in ground like mark made by tire.

I am slipping through and everything is smelling bad, like humans doing all of their living here. It is smelling like under Falomo Bridge but worse. And I am wondering if people are dying here too and they are being buried under metal.

Some things are tall tall above me and are blocking out light from moon, but I am still seeing everything. And some pieces of metal are crunching beneath my feet and I am thinking these are maybe small computers or hard drives, and then I am seeing on the ground and hanging from windows sometimes arm or leg, and they are metal like mine are when I am peeling back the skin.

I am searching and searching and I am hearing beep in my brain and I am seeing with camera in my mind certain pieces of metal and other pieces of metal and I am knowing what they are made of, what alloy they are being and what is their previous use. I am knowing this is being part of carbine rifle and I am knowing make and model and I am knowing this is part of undercarriage of spider mech and I am knowing this is piece of Bonder and this is arm and this is leg and this is broken braincase and—

I freeze. It is like root from tree is coming from ground and wrapping around my ankles, then my legs and my whole body.

I see it. It is being guarded by four soldier, and I am knowing their pattern of walking, and I am knowing how far each is going in each direction and where they are looking, and cone of light is forming in front of their face and I am knowing that this is their range of vision. I am thinking that I am knowing these thing because I am soldier once. But they are standing with their back to it, and even though it is night and even though moon is not shining on it, I am seeing it like it is daytime.

Xifeng's trailer.

I am seeing the trailer and the four soldier guarding it, then my mind is emptying, and when I am waking up again, I am waking up covered in blood, and arm and leg and head is covering the grass like rubbish. I am not taking time to think about what happen or why I am covered in blood and there are no more soldier just pieces of them. I am just breaking the lock to the trailer with my elbow and hurrying inside and feeling the fresh cool air of the inside and closing my eyes because it is like feeling Xifeng whenever she is holding me during my epileptic shaking.

I am sitting on metal floor and hugging my knees to my chest and blood is on my face and my fingers and covering my knees, and my fingers are slipping on my pants where they are holding them but I am sitting and rocking back and forth and closing my eyes and thinking of Xifeng and thinking it is being long long time since I am hearing her voice.

When I am opening my eyes again, I am seeing around me stack and stack of hard drives.

I am not sure how I am knowing but I am knowing that police or soldier or both is going to destroy all of this and I must save it. So I am taking cord from my neck and putting it in hard drive after hard drive and downloading the rememberings so that they are pouring like water into my brain. My brain is never filling, but I am sometime hearing voice many voice and sometime if I am closing my eye I am feeling sand between my toes or I am feeling big leaf SWISH SWISH on my face or I am putting my lips to lips of other girl or I am riding on the shoulder of man I am calling father.

My eyes are opening fast fast when I hear voice outside.

There is window and I am wiping it but it is making blood on it so I am using shirt and wiping blood and dust off window, and I am seeing far away soldier bringing out children who is looking like me and making them to fall on their knee and is lining them up. And these children are having collar around their neck and having restraint over their hands and their forearm. And I am looking closely and my mind is scanning them without me telling it to and I am seeing that they are having outlet like me at the back of their neck. And I am seeing under their skin that their bones glow blue like mine when I am looking inside myself sometime.

Soldier behind them is raising their gun at the back of the child head and not waiting a moment or even speaking before pulling trigger and all of the child are falling dead.

Then soldier are standing around and facing each other and

joking behind their helmet and I am pressing my ear to window to hear them, and I am hearing them tell about child they are executing and calling them Ceasefire Children, then they are calling them synth and saying they are rubbish and I am hearing that they are looking for more of them. I am hearing them say *extermination* and *Biafra* and *memory*.

And then, they are seeing me.

CHAPTER
19

The Medical Committee sits before Ify like judges at a tribunal. The vaulted ceilings are painted with depictions from the Bible of moments of healing. Lazarus raised from the dead, someone's hand reaching out to touch the hem of the Christ's garment, even the beginnings of the universe. The floor's tiles glisten as though, every second, nanobots are hard at work giving them their extra sheen. The benches behind Ify are largely unoccupied, which seems odd to her, given what is at stake. If there were any sense of justice or concern beyond the very clinical, the committee members would have allowed the families of those affected by the widespread coma epidemic to this hearing. They would have publicized it. They would have distributed the reports—report after report—written by scientists, medical professionals, and political thinkers on why, all of a sudden, thousands of children have suddenly become unresponsive to treatment and seem to have cast themselves to death's edge.

But no. In the benches behind her sit Grace and a few other medical professionals, most of them Ify's contemporaries and subordinates. Many of them are native Alabastrines, scattered fallen snowflakes amid the steel pews with wood overlay. And some of them, Ify knows, have resented her rise, how she has surpassed them in rank, how she already has *assistant director* in her title. How people are already calling her Doctor even though she has yet to take her licensing exam.

The man at the center of the five committee members has the face of a stately middle-aged white man. He could pass for a legislator. Remove a few of the wrinkles from around his mouth and he could be any billionaire whose name is stamped on the side of a small Colony. This is the hospital director, Dr. Jacob Towne. Perhaps the only administrator who has ever looked favorably on Ify's career. Ify replays her interactions with him in her head, him noticing her high marks early on, as well as her aptitude for science and technology, noting the fact that she spent her extracurricular time away from those kids who played around or got in trouble neglecting their studies and instead worked on ways to make computers smaller and smaller while maintaining their processing power and then integrating them into larger systems of computing, something that could revolutionize the medical industry. Then, armed with Towne's letters of recommendation, there were the internships, the formal mentorship, then her choosing the medical track in school with his guidance.

But, looking at him now, he has the demeanor of neither a mentor nor a father figure. He has the look of a judge willing to hand down a life sentence for what one would call a crime but others would call a mistake.

One of the judges to the left of Towne, a man the lower half of whose face is swallowed by a gray beard, leans forward. His information pops up on Ify's retinal display. Dr. Mar, head of neurology. "So. Internist Diallo. I'm sure you have read through the reports." He makes a face like he is scrolling through them himself. And scrolling. And scrolling. "All of them."

"Yes, Dr. Mar."

"Any initial conclusions you'd like to share with the rest of the class?" The slight joking in his voice grates on Ify.

She pulls up the report she prepared for this hearing. "We began our treatment by tracking down the earliest case of a patient displaying these symptoms." She transmits a video file to the committee members, all of whom are cyberized. "Six years ago, a patient with these symptoms was deported to the island nation of Vanuatu." At the raised eyebrows of several members in the committee, Ify continues. "At the time of that patient's deportation, there was no island to go back to."

"So, what then? What happened?" Dr. Mar asks. "Did we just drop the patient in the ocean?"

"There is no record of the patient after they left Alabastrine jurisdiction. Their whereabouts are unknown."

"Hmm." Dr. Mar strokes his chin.

A committee member to Director Towne's right, whose face is fashioned to look unreasonably young, taps a stylus against the wooden bench in front of him. Dr. Langrishe, head of genetics. "I assume you have studied the country-of-origin data with regard to the affected patients? Is there any correlation between falling into a coma and your country no longer existing?"

Ify does her best to maintain an even temper. What a basic question. Of course, this was one of the first questions she researched. "The initial outbreak of the disease seemed indiscriminate with regard to country of origin. One commonality regarding country of origin is that all of the affected

141

seem to have come from countries that have experienced political turmoil within the past five years. War, violent change in leadership, government-sponsored repression, or some other sort of violent upheaval. Many of those countries of origin are still, in fact, experiencing these upheavals."

The one man not wearing a medical doctor's uniform and instead wearing a boxy suit jacket leans back in his plush chair. With the fingernail of his pinky, he scratches the side of his nose. "Well, that's rather the point of their being refugees, isn't it."

Ify can't tell if the comment is addressed to her or to Dr. Langrishe.

"People tend not to swim for shore if their boat isn't sinking." He leans on his elbows. "Tell me, Internist." An accent. French? "Do you believe that political turmoil in the countries of origin is the cause of this medical epidemic?"

"I believe it is a proximate cause, yes. But not the trigger."

The man—he must be some sort of academic—raises his eyebrows. "Oh? Do continue."

"While there have been sporadic cases over the past five years, the epidemic started in earnest a month ago with the announcement of the government's changed stance on migrants. Immediately following announcement of the policy, a number of families—many of whom had long been residents of Alabast—received notices of deportation. It is at this time that the disease became more widespread."

"Is this a hunger strike, then?"

There are too many missing pieces for Ify to call it that or even something akin to that. How to tell this group of old white men that many among the population—an unknown number, in fact—might be synths and not human beings at all? How to tell them that many of the children in her care are not even subject to a single human rights protection under Alabastrine law? And where does the virus affecting Peter and the girl he connected to come into play?

"I'm not sure, sir."

The academic glances at the others, as though to finally include them in the dialogue. "Do we know if this is a virus? It seems contagious, does it not?"

"Well," says Dr. Langrishe. "We've all been in Alabast for how long now? I see no reason to suspect we haven't been inoculated against whatever disease has taken these people."

Ify nearly sneers at the racism she hears in his words. Her fists clench at her side. "Among the patients are several from the icelands of the Caucasus on Old Earth. They are white as well."

Langrishe turns in his chair to look at Ify, one eyebrow raised, like he has just witnessed a dog trying to assemble a watch. "I was referring, Internist Diallo, to the palliative powers of citizenship."

Of course you were, Ify says to herself. "With your permission, sirs, I would like to continue treatment of the patients while investigating a potential solution to the epidemic. Before it spreads even further."

"I have some ideas on that front." Towne's voice doesn't boom, but it reverberates throughout the entire room. Everyone hears it. Ify senses Grace startle behind her. "From my own research, I have noticed a preponderance of cases among recent African migrants. Specifically Nigerians." His gaze grows sharp, as though he knows Ify is holding within her a secret to mysteries he wishes he could unlock. "There was war in your home country, yes?"

Ify struggles not to show any emotion, any indication that the invocation of where she came from has as much effect on her as it does. "The war has ended, Director Towne."

"Indeed. But you know as well as I that wounds persist."

"Psychological trauma does necessitate treatment following the advent of the initial traumatic incident. And untreated, it can result in grave psychological and physiological harm to the patient. Yes, Director. I know this."

"And I am sure you can imagine the trauma of growing up during war, coming of age during a ceasefire, then having your life adversely impacted when that ceasefire ends."

Adversely impacted. Director Towne *would* go for such understatement. Ify knows, however, that there's no malice in it. Still, resentment builds in her that the director has so directly confronted her about her past. But it takes her a moment to realize his point. When she does, her breath catches. The ceasefire. The ceasefire that Ify played a direct role in ending. The ceasefire she broke by—

"Internist!" This from Langrishe.

Ify snaps out of her trance. "Yes. Yes, sorry. Um." She pinches the bridge of her nose. *Get it together, get it together. Think about what's in front of you.* She raises her head, her eyes cleared, her heart rate slowed. "Yes, Director. I . . . it's still rather fresh for me. My homeland." *Play into his stereotypes and the racism he thinks is so subtle*, she tells herself. "Please. Continue."

"Well," continues Langrishe. "What Director Towne was saying was that you would be the perfect candidate for such a mission."

"Mission?"

Langrishe sighs loudly.

Director Towne silently rebukes him, then turns to Ify. "Many of the afflicted refugees have come from Nigeria or the area immediately surrounding it. What we're suggesting is a fact-finding mission. If the disease is coming from Nigeria—"

"Director Towne," she growls. Regret swims through her. The rest of the committee leans back in their chairs. Towne pauses. There isn't the slightest hint of a smile on his face, no recognition of Ify's moment of courage, no approval. But then he doesn't look affronted either. Sheer expressionlessness.

"If information on the epidemic can be found, we are confident that it can be found there. As director of the Refugee Program, you have the deepest knowledge and first-hand experience of this crisis. And, as a Nigerian refugee yourself, you understand what has been happening in your country."

She wants to tell him that she hasn't been back in almost five years. That she has left that part of her behind. Completely. The way she talks, the way she carries herself. All of it an effort to put Nigeria squarely where it belongs: in the past. Everything she did, everything she loved, everything she was. It's supposed to be gone now.

But she can't tell him any of that. So, instead, she says, "I think that is a prudent course of action."

Still that lack of expression from Director Towne. "Great. Details will be forwarded to you shortly. You can leave now. Oh, and your assistant will be accompanying you."

Angry shock rips through Ify. She resists the impulse to look behind her to see Grace's face. She has no idea why Towne would issue this order, nor does she have time to puzzle it out, because he nods at her—swift, perfunctory—to dismiss her.

Grace follows Ify out. It's not until the doors to the committee chamber have closed behind Ify that she realizes her hands have been shaking.

■ ■ ■ ■ ■

While Grace packs, Ify keeps the lights off in her office. Her Bonder sits in a steel box on her desk. The blinds are drawn. Not a single device in the room blinks to indicate it's been turned on. She still hasn't been able to stop shaking. But the tremors running through her have lessened. The first few times she'd tried to hold a stylus, she'd dropped the thing and it had clattered on her table like an accusation.

Puzzle pieces swim inside her head. Clues. Hints. Theories. Hypotheses. But flickering in bright red like a broken neon sign are the words *It's your fault.* She closes her eyes and sees it all in flashes. She's standing at the threshold of a door with a bag at her side and a gun in her hand, and on the other side of that door is the woman she's traveled across a country to kill. On the other side of that door is the woman who murdered her entire family. Onyii. Then she sees the city of Enugu, the city to which she'd tracked this woman. And she sees the people ambling through it, buying jewelry, cooking ogbono soup on the side of the street, selling their wares, flirting, joking, all in a burst of colors and light glinting off shining surfaces. She closes her eyes tighter, trying to force away the memory, but then, as though it were happening right around her, she hears the explosions, thunder that surrounds her, that takes the ground out from beneath her. Thunder going on for what seems like forever. Then screams and weeping and a city covered in blood. No.

No.

She refuses to believe it. There is something else. There has to be. Something else has caused the influx of refugees from Nigeria. Something else brought Peter here. She tells herself this over and over again. There is something else. And after several minutes, she can bring herself to believe it. There is something more to the mystery of the comatose children. It's not her fault.

She says this to herself—*it's not my fault*—as she takes a few deep breaths, then rises from her chair to, with a thought, raise the blinds in her office.

She pulls up surveillance of the refugee ward so that it broadcasts over her floor-to-ceiling window. Like this, she can monitor the comings and goings without having to actually set foot among her patients. When the contact with them becomes too much—the antiseptic smell, the too-fine detail in their faces, the sounds of their machines' monotonous beeping and humming and droning—she can watch them like this. It gives her an odd sense of peace, gazing down at them from above. Surveilling them. She dares not call it godlike. But it is like that—the part of God that's supposed to be caring and loving and watchful—protective, even.

And that's when she sees them. Two women sitting next to a bed. She sees their hair, their hands, and the way they fold over the patient's hands like layers of soil. Or beach sand. She zooms in, and one of them looks up, her eyes closed, her mouth moving in prayer Ify can't hear. Paige. And beside her, with head bowed, is Amy. They're praying over Peter.

■ ■ ■ ■ ■

Ify gets to the ward floor and stands by the entrance. As much as she tries to will her body forward, it won't move. So Paige and Amy are two shivering specks in the distance. A primal fear chills Ify. She feels as though her bones are vibrating inside her. She grits her teeth against it and closes her hands in fists and waits for tears, but they never come. She's too scared even to cry.

In all the time she's known Amy and Paige, she has never seen them so helpless. Even when they had no idea how to care for Ify or how to make her feel at home or how to help her build her future, they'd moved with confidence. They'd blundered out of love for her. And with every fumbling move, Ify had known that they did this or that thing, made this or that mistake, committed this or that error, all out of love for her. They knew, or felt they knew, that they were doing right by her. And whether or not things turned out the way they'd wanted, their love would carry them through. Ify stands now as living testament to their efforts. They had indeed made her the woman who stands today on the precipice of being a licensed Colony doctor, already assistant director of her own ward.

And now they cling, helpless, to a hospital bed. Helpless.

It's not my fault, Ify tells herself.

She repeats the mantra as she returns to her apartment and packs for her trip. She repeats it during the rail ride to the shuttle transit station. Even as droids load her luggage and Grace's and usher the two of them to the plush cabins afforded to Colony officials, she says it over and over again.

She repeats it as the shuttle hurtles through the ejection column and, once it settles into its flight pattern toward

Earthland, she continues to say it. She's forgotten the young Cantonese woman sitting across from her, dutifully organizing her notes and studying her materials and preparing her research plan. *It's not my fault. It's not my fault.*

By the time the shuttle touches down in Abuja and the doors open to Nnamdi Azikiwe International Shuttle Station and she has gathered her things and, blanketed by light, proceeded through the busy but efficiently run terminals to the exit where her and Grace's minders wait for her to bring Ify and Grace to Ify's apartment, she has said it a thousand times.

And each and every time, it has felt like a lie.

As the jeep flies through the well-ordered streets of Abuja, a message beeps through Ify's Whistle. A lone envelope icon. Sender: Céline Hayatou.

> Dear Ify,
>
> I've only just now received news of your deployment. Do you remember when we used to attend chapel together? I was always running late, and I would ask you to save me a seat. And, without fail, by the time I arrived, you would have cleared a whole pew for me. I once thought you contained magic. If there were someone near and dear to you, you would move heaven and earth for them. You were younger than me, newer to Alabast, and yet you seemed so certain of yourself and your powers. Eventually, you told me why you were able to guard so much space for me. You told me it was because whenever you would sit in a pew where the whites sat,

they would see you and move away. You always
had a logical, scientific explanation for things.
Even if they didn't make sense, they contained
logic. I still believed there was magic in you. I
still do. I encourage you to let go of logic as you
return home. Fear does not contain logic. Our
sense of home does not contain logic. There
is magic in both of these things. I am learning
these things as a colonial administrator. You
can pave streets and make them ordered. You
can introduce ordinances for waste disposal
and educational requirements. You can create
a proper protocol for migrant resettlement. You
can do all of these things, but at the center of
our work is people. People and the hope they
bring with them. People and the memories
they bring with them. Please don't walk away
from your memories. There is magic in them.
Be well, ma copine.

Take care of yourself.

Je t'aime.

Your chapel seatmate,
Céline

Ify closes the message to find Grace sitting across from her,
hands folded in her lap, a concerned look on her face.

"Home," Ify says to the question in Grace's eyes. "I haven't
been back in a very long time." She looks out the window at the
once-familiar streets and whispers to herself, *Home.*

Lagos, Nigeria:
2181

I am running. Always it is feeling like I am running.

When I am in Xifeng's trailer and the police are first seeing me, I am running and they are chasing me and I am losing myself in Lagos. But then drone is sighting me and more police are hunting me. So I am living in jungle and finding cave and I am watching other people be wandering and thinking maybe they are like me. Maybe they are running too. And some of them have burned skin like jollof at the bottom of a pot, like Xifeng used to make. And some of them have metal inside them like me, but it is on the outside and their metal is having rust on it.

I am seeing what is looking like family, and little boy is hugging flying drone to his chest. There is being deadness in his eyes. Mother is holding his hand and they are walking behind father, who is carrying machete to be cutting through jungle where it is too thick to pass.

I am sitting on fallen tree trunk when they are seeing me, and small flecks of radiation, like flakes of snow, is hanging in the air and making parts of their bodies to be glowing. They are walking by me, but little boy is stopping and staring at me. My clothes are being ripped, and much of my body is showing, and it is the first time that I am wanting to be hiding my nakedness. Boy with broken drone is stopping and looking at me, then mother is stopping and looking at me, then father is stopping and noticing his family and then he is looking at me. And for a long time, they are all looking at me and saying nothing, and I am not moving.

Boy is taking step toward me, but mother is pulling him back, and I am thinking that they are thinking me dangerous. Then he is reaching into his pocket and pulling out fruit that is having black marks from radiation on it, and he is holding it out to me.

"No," I am saying and shaking my head.

Mother is seeing her child, and softening is happening in her face. When she is looking at me, she is not seeing synth. She is not seeing child of war. She is seeing lost girl who is alone and without food or proper clothes. "We have a purifier," she is telling me. "You can still eat it, child."

But I am shaking my head again. "I am not needing to eat."

Mother is frowning, then she is making boy to be putting fruit away.

"Where are you coming from?" I am asking, and I am hearing loneliness in my voice.

Father is stepping forward, and I am noticing that he is not putting his machete away. I am not wanting to be killing him, and I am wanting him to be putting his machete away. "The Redlands," he is saying. "We are Hausa. When we lived in Lagos, we were attacked and our home was burned. Bandits chased us and the people we lived with wherever we went. Before the government began its memory program, we were chased into the wasteland. But we hear that things are safer now. People have forgotten the war."

"The Redlands?" I am saying, because I am not knowing what he is meaning when he is saying this.

"It's very dangerous there," the mother is saying. "Please tell me that is not where you are going."

The boy is breaking away from his mother and running to me with drone that is looking more and more like toy in his arms. "There are monsters there!" he is saying, and it is sounding like thing he is excited about, not scared about, and he is holding drone out to me.

I am having drone in my hands, and my brain is telling me exactly where drone is being broken. Without speaking, I am taking it apart. My fingers is breaking apart into many pieces and going inside drone to repair circuitry and to fix wires, then I am sealing it, then I am spitting on it because that is how I am remembering to send nanobot into it to give it life.

Wire is coming out of the back of my neck, and I am plugging it in, and then vision is coming to me.

Land is flat and red everywhere, and the air is sizzling like food boiling in pot. And big bull with horns that are curling out of its head is with many other bull like it, and herd is moving fast over the land, and their hoof is making thunder in the earth. They are being beautiful to watch as they are stampeding past. Then I am seeing forest, and everything—leaf, fruit, tree—is too big, because radiation is making thing to be misshapen. And wolf with two heads—what they are calling wulfu—is staring at drone and snarling, and drone is showing family trying to hide while wulfu is getting closer, and father is having gun with him that he is trying to aim at wulfu, and he is shaking and shaking. I am seeing more large red plain with mountain range over them, and I am seeing small small hut with blue dome over it and man pulling water from nearby river and putting it through purifier before bringing it back to his hut. Then I am unplugging from drone.

When I am unplugging, family is looking at me strange. They are seeing now that I am machine and not lost little girl. And I am holding out drone for boy to take back.

Father is holding machete like he is ready to attack, and part of me is sadding because they are now knowing that I am maybe dangerous thing. "Lagos is dangerous," I am telling them. I am thinking of other thing drone showed me: father walking through Redlands with breathing mask but is moving like air is boiling his insides and cooking them so that he is coughing up blood, and drone is showing me little boy trying to make bathroom but blood is coming out. "Lagos is still dangerous," I am telling them again, before I am leaving fallen tree and walking away from them and hoping that what I am doing is helping them to feel safe.

■ ■ ■ ■ ■

Bird is twittering and leaf is making SWISH SWISH sound and when it is raining I am taking bath because river is too open and there are maybe police there. I am wishing I am back under Falomo Bridge because I am knowing people there. Maybe I am even calling them friend. And they are looking like they are running too, but they are finding safe space where no one is hunting them like animal. And they are building tent to live in and wall to hold back the water that is trying to be eating them. And even though they are doing drug and sometime dying and even though they are not looking like they are eating sometime, there are being many of them and many body together is making me feel warm. I am not needing blanket in jungle, but I am liking to be feeling warm.

I am walking and I am arriving at place where grass is tall as my chest and thick, and I am knowing that it is not grass that can be cut by machine. I am hearing people nearby, but I am knowing that they are really far away and it is only my good hearing that is making me to hear them. But I am settling because I am liking to be hearing their voices in this quiet place that is not noisy like Lagos. They are chatting and laughing and they are not angering or sadding. I am thinking that they are friend and friend.

Night passes then day then night again, and it is day when one of them is complaining about tall grass, and I am knowing that it is tall grass that I am sitting in. So I am walking and I am finding strange animal—geese—and memory is telling me that this is animal that will cut grass. And I am bringing them to the edge of tall grass where there is clear field then house and man sitting in plastic chair writing with stylus on tablet, and he is wearing sandal and hat is covering his face with shadow and he is smiling and frowning, but I know he is looking like peace if peace was being person.

I am finding two gander and one goose, and they are pure white with orange beak but dirt is staining their white feather so before I am putting them down, I am brushing dirt from their feather because I am wanting them to be clean.

Goose and one gander are pairing like family, and one gander is liking to be staying with me but they are all chewing grass with soft chawp-chawp sound. And day and night and day and night and day is passing. Then one morning I am hearing shriek from one gander, and goose is sounding like it is in pain and honking and honking and dying. When I am coming to edge of grass, I am seeing goose and one gander lying on ground and they are all wet with blood, and dog that is big with fur in patches on his skin is snarling at me, and I am feeling strange because I am hearing dog's thoughts and I am wondering if there is metal inside dog like inside me. But I am not caring because dog is saying I am hungry and I am saying back to dog I will kill you. Then I am never seeing dog again.

Then I am going back deep into jungle and am finding duck egg but no duck. But then I am seeing nearby little squirming ball of yellow, and I am walking to it and picking it up and holding it in my hand, and I am seeing it and it is opening eye at me and I am thinking with my heart that I am first living thing that it is seeing.

I am bringing more geese to chawp-chawp on grass belonging to human, but little yellow gosling is staying with me. Even when I am telling it to be going, it is not leaving me. When other geese are returning to me, gosling is sticking neck out and is making small-small squawk sound like squeak, and it is driving away other geese, and I am laughing quiet because I am thinking little yellow gosling is wanting to be with me and is not wanting anyone else to be with me.

They are sleeping at night. Or, rather, they are not moving and I am thinking that they are sleeping. And when it is daytime, they are making chawp-chawp with the grass and moving and sometime sleeping and they are forming gaggle and they are making like family, and some geese are slow and behind the rest. And when they are leaving person's yard and I am feeding them, they are chasing away gosling and making gosling to be sadding, and I am holding gosling and feeling its feathers and it is soft like nothing I have ever felt and I am even rubbing gosling against my cheek and it is making soft thrum against my face.

Then one day gosling is coming back to me and it is walking like it is liking one leg more than the other. I am knowing that it is fighting with gander but I am never seeing it wounded like this. So I am bathing it and feeding it alone. Then I am seeing that it is going to bathroom and making strange color. Green but not like grass. Green like acid. And I am wishing to speak to it but there is no metal in it, and I hear humans talking about their yard and how they like it now when it is trim and how they are using chemical to keep it that way, and I am sadding because gosling is maybe eating grass with poison on it.

It is moving slow and sometime not moving. It is not eating, then one morning I am finding it on its side and it is beating its wings trying to be standing right but it is not being able to stand. And it is trying and trying but nothing is working. And then I am picking up gosling in my arm and its head is making wild movement, then it is staring at me, then it is staring at nothing and I am knowing it is dead.

I am digging grave for it and I am sadding and then I am walking away. Because it is paining me to be remembering him.

It is paining me a lot.

■ ■ ■ ■ ■

One day, I am climbing tree in the forest to be able to see better where I am, and I am climbing branch and branch and setting my foot, and I am moving fast and I am almost at the top when

I am smelling metal and sulfur, then I am not seeing anything and I am waking up in the grass and face is staring at me.

It is boy crouching over me. Before, I am wanting to be fighting person who is sneaking up on me, but I am not having the same feeling now. I am not wanting to be fighting and hurting this person. He is looking like me. He is having skin like mine, and I am knowing there is metal inside of him. And my brain is scanning him and seeing that he is made of different pieces. He is having one arm that is different from other arm, and he is having legs but they are not coming from same place as his arms, and he is having face but that is coming from somewhere else too. He is looking like regular boy but I am telling to myself that he is having seams like someone is sewing him together and making him.

"Who are you?" I am asking him.

He is not saying anything for a long time. Then I am scanning him again and I am looking for his story. His history. I am trying to find out where he is coming from and if he is needing help. Is he needing to eat? Is he trying to be eating me?

Then he is looking up at tree, and I am thinking that he is wondering how I am opening up my eye after I am falling from big big tree. And I am wanting to tell him but I am coughing once twice, and black thing is coming out from my mouth.

He is turning and he is seeing this, then he is touching me and he is feeling my face and my hair that I am keeping to cut because when it is big things are hiding in it. And then he is feeling my neck and then he is touching my outlet. Cord is coming from his neck, and he is taking it in his hand and he is putting it in back of my neck.

He is not saying anything while he is doing this, but suddenly

I am feeling thing swimming inside me. I am feeling it hum-ming in my blood and I am feeling it crawling on my inside organ, and suddenly my heart is feeling faster. Stronger. And I am wondering what he is doing, but then I am feeling lighter and suddenly pain is leaving me and I am startling because I am not knowing until now that I am being in pain constantly. I am thinking how I am feeling is being normal and I am not knowing that I am hurting even though I am having bandage wrapped around my wrists and chemical from leaves inside the scars on my back and I am pulling my shoulder after arm is hanging loose when police and drone and juggernaut are chasing me and Xifeng through Lagos. But now all of that is just memory and my body is no longer paining me and I am starting to know that this is what nanobot is doing to me and then I am starting to know that boy is giving me nanobot.

His cord is leaving me, and I am sitting up in leaves and grass. "What are they calling you?" I am asking him.

"They are calling me Uzodinma," he is saying in little boy voice.

"Who is calling you that?"

He looks to the forest, and many many boy and girl come out, and even though they are looking different and having different arm and leg and face and some are having scar on their face and some are having metal showing in their arm and some are not I am starting to know that they are same like him.

They are same like me.

■ ■ ■ ■ ■

As we are walking, I am wondering why Xifeng is giving me name like boy if I am girl, and Uzodinma is telling me that my name is Uzoamaka. Even though we are both being Uzo, we are different. And I am thinking that he is telling me this about our name but I am thinking he is also telling me this about something bigger. About who we are being.

About what we are being.

We are walking and I am finding myself asking why we are walking.

One of the boys looks at me, even though I am not saying my question out loud. "We are walking because it is what we are doing."

"But why?"

Then boy is shrugging.

A girl next to him who is having scar on her face running from forehead to the opposite side of her mouth is saying, "In all of my rememberings, I am walking. Sometime, I am doing other thing, but mostly I am walking."

None of this is answer to my question.

We are never eating or drinking or needing to bathe or make bathroom, but sometime one of us is sitting down and staring into space and I am wondering if this is how I am looking when I am dreaming. And I am wondering if *dreaming* is the word for this thing. I am thinking that they are remembering and maybe they are wondering if their remembering is belonging to them or if it is coming from someone else. I am thinking that all of us is searching for clue. We are being like puzzle or mystery. We are being question, and we are looking for the answer to ourself.

I am missing Enyemaka because when I am thinking on me

being question and not knowing who I am being, Enyemaka is telling me thing to make me feel peace. Enyemaka is telling me about purpose and about machine and what machine can do, and Enyemaka is making me not to feel strange in my body. Enyemaka is making me not to feel strange for being child of war.

Boy who is being named Oluwale is sitting and looking at nothing, and no part of his face is moving. He is just sitting and crossing his leg like his body is being here but his brain is being elsewhere.

When he is waking up, I am standing over him and watching him. "Where are you going when you do that?"

He is looking up at me with no expression.

"It is looking like you are leaving your body, and when you are doing this, there is peace on your face. I am wanting peace."

"I am remembering," he is telling me in voice that is like song.

"What are you remembering?"

He is showing me holograph video of him being on hoverboard with other boys who look like him, and they are riding over water and twisting and turning and laughing, and there is being no expression on Oluwale's face. Then he is turning it off. "Watching this thing gives me peace." Then he is showing me other remembering: he is looking in direction of sun as it is sitting on the edge of the earth, and grass is tall up to his waist, and he is looking down and his hand is running through it slowly. And it is the same again where I am looking at him and seeing no smile on his face but I am knowing that he is feeling peace, and I am remembering that Enyemaka is not having mouth to smile but Enyemaka is still smiling. So it is with Oluwale. He is having mouth to smile but he is not using it to smile. But I am feeling him smiling still.

"How . . . how are you doing this?"

And he is knowing without my saying that I am meaning how is he calling specific remembering? Because when I am trying to find specific remembering it is all jumble in my head and I am not knowing what is new and what is old and I am seeing myself in place I have never been and I am remembering people I have never seen. Some remembering are from graves I find with Enyemaka and some are from after I am joining Xifeng and the Enyemakas and we are walking through desert and some are from before they are finding me at bottom of pile of bodies, but I am only feeling like everything from there is truth and the rest is mystery. Some days I am feeling like the rest is lie.

Oluwale points to the grass in front of him. "Sit." And I am coming in front of him and facing him and doing like he is doing.

Then he is telling me to raise one finger to my face, and he is raising finger of left hand and I am raising finger of right hand. Then he is telling me to raise opposite hand higher, and I am doing this. Then he is telling me to take finger and move it across my chest, and I am doing this. He is telling me to poke under my raised arm, and I am doing it. Then he is telling me to put finger under my nose and inhale. I am thinking this is strange, but I am doing it. Then he is putting finger to his nose, and I am following him, and he is digging into his nose, and I am doing it. And then when he is watching me, he is laughing. He is falling back laughing and kicking his feet in the air. And I am getting ready to fall onto my back and do as he is doing, but then I am thinking that he is playing joke. He is laughing and laughing and I am angering, but I am not wanting to hurt him so all I am doing is to be kicking dirt on him while I am angering. And I am angering but I am also smiling. I am not feeling smile on my face, but I am feeling it inside me. And when Oluwale is finishing laughing he is looking at me like I am new creature.

Like I am gosling that is coming from egg.

■ ■ ■ ■ ■

When it is being night, I am going away from group of boy and girl like me and I am finding quiet place in jungle and I am sitting like I am seeing Oluwale sitting. And I am looking in front of me but trying to look how he is looking when he is finding peace, and I am thinking and thinking, then I am moving past thinking and feeling. And I am hearing thing move inside of me. Between my ear and behind my eye. And I am worrying that I am breaking something but I am then not caring because I am feeling like I am close to something.

Then, I am seeing it. It is not blue like holograph. It is all colors. I am seeing geese and gander in field making chawp-chawp at grass.

Then, I am seeing Xifeng's face while she is holding me after I am having epileptic shaking. And I am seeing how she is putting finger to my face and caressing.

I am controlling. I am guiding myself into rememberings. I am looking and I am finding them. I am making order.

Then, I am seeing inside of tent where it is being dark. Memory is glowing blue at the edges but also green. I am seeing this color before but only with certain rememberings.

And I am seeing shape moving softly in bed, up and down, up and down, under blanket that is having red splotch on it like coin but I am knowing it is from blood and radiation. And I am seeing my hand move and lie on bundle in bed, and I am moving forward and blowing on its forehead, and it is blinking eye at me and it is waking up and its eye is being so beautiful, like I am looking at two mornings.

"Ify, it's time to wake up. You will be late for school." And it is sounding like my voice.

CHAPTER
21

It's been almost a month, and every time Ify walks through the streets of Abuja, she wonders if anyone will recognize her. They are all strangers, but she had once been a high-ranking student at the nation's most prestigious academy. She had been an aide to Shehu Daren Suleiman Sékou Diallo, the Nigerian army's most skilled and decorated mech pilot, the man who had given Ify his family name. She had overseen countless council meetings where policy that would affect the hundreds of millions of people in the nation was debated and enacted. She had been a Sentinel, charged with sitting in any number of watchtowers sprinkled throughout the capital city and conducting surveillance via the orb drones that lazily hovered over everyone's heads. Now she looks around and there are no orbs. No drones. No watchtowers. Only hyperloop rail lines overhead, framed by walls of glimmering flexiglas, and giant advertisements for clothes and streaming football matches reflected on the shining surfaces of skyscrapers, and citizens whose silver-threaded outfits glisten in the sunlight.

Beside her, Grace has her gaze inclined upward, taking in sign after sign after sign in Mandarin.

Ify sees the frown developing on her face and says, "China was instrumental in the rebuilding effort during the ceasefire. Though they did not recognize Biafra as a country, they aided in the resettlement effort." She knows that, if she were to close her eyes, she would see that refugee convoy again and the trailers around which walked or played little children and the little boy, the synth named Agu, who guarded them, and Xifeng. In so many of her memories, Xifeng is there waiting for her. Even now, with her eyes open, Ify finds herself glancing at the faces of those they walk past, and in so many faces, she sees Xifeng's.

Grace doesn't ask where they're going, and if she did, Ify would have no answer for her. Maybe she would tell her that this was some African part of the research process, getting in touch with the land before studying it, feeling it with one's feet as a way of detecting illness, some juju to play into stereotypes. How to explain that, at the root of everything, is a desire to be caught? For someone to recognize her and declare her crimes for all the world to hear, then arrest her? How to explain that since she woke up this morning, she's wanted that more than anything?

I'm walking until the guilt goes away, she wants to tell Grace, but can't.

Ify cranes her neck and does not see a sky festooned with digitized Nigerian flags like she expected. Maybe her memory of that is false. Nor does she see the Nigerian president's face projected onto the giant façades of glass-and-steel business centers. There are no soldiers patrolling the streets. When they arrive at Aso Rock and Ify sees the outcrop of granite rock, almost one thousand meters high, on the city's outskirts, she expects to see a parade of military vehicles and parliamentarians surrounded by their bodyguards. She expects to see soldiers acting as leaders, generals assuming their places in government, but everyone wears suits, some of them more slim-fitting than others. They all look like businessmen. They all look alike.

Using the Augment embedded in her neck, Ify scans them and notes on her holographic retinal display what districts they represent. This one represents Abia State and this one Bayelsa. Those three there are from Katsina State, and the two standing next to them are from Oyo and Delta. But were she looking at them with an unaided eye, she would see clones. Nothing but clones. Perhaps they are all cyberized and all outfitted with similar facial features and similar body structures. Maybe this is simply what is fashionable. And they are all shaking hands and joking. Some of the legislators who do not look older but talk as though their insides are older than their outsides speak in patronizing whimsy to the younger ones. But there is no military. Not a single bar denoting rank. Not a single soldier stiff at attention. She adjusts her scanner to see if perhaps the vehicles are cloaked. It could be that the air is swarming with drones, clouds of them thick enough to blot out the sun. All it would take is the right calibration for the massive ground mechs she's sure are there to materialize out of thin air. To have the sky shimmer around them, then to have them revealed in all their violent, militaristic glory. If she squints hard enough, maybe she can even detect the outline of high-powered minimechs hiding in the shadows or strapped to the bottom of the maglev Land Rovers, ready to detach and fire at whatever needs killing.

But nothing. The air is still. The chatter is soft; then, as the parliamentarians walk into the halls of the National Assembly to begin the session, the chatter is gone. And nowhere in this area is there a statue or monument or plaque—anything—to indicate that she had once been here, that Daren had once fought a war for this place, that millions had died. At the very hall of government, no markers of sacrifice. No sign of the vanquishing of villains.

No indication, even, that there had been heroes.

"Were there this many Chinese during the war?" Grace asks.

Ify turns to consider Grace for a moment before leading them back the way they had come. Enough walking for today. "No," she says quietly, too harshly.

There is no more war, Ify tells herself. Even as she can't quite bring herself to believe it.

■ ■ ■ ■ ■

Ify finds an isolated stretch of gilded fencing along Jabi Lake and rests on her forearms. Jabi Lake Commercial Center is a hive of activity, and Ify turns and leans back on the railing to watch all the life happening in front of her. So much of her experience of the world can be filtered: by way of her external Augments, she can lower the murmur of voices and raise the volume of the lake lapping against stone behind her; she can increase the intensity of the new-grass smell, even as she knows how false this grass is beneath her feet. She can watch the setting sun splash colors like oil paint across the sky and twist the dialings on her settings to filter the colors, making them sickly or blurring the lines between the golds and the blues and the purples.

It's as she's playing with the colors in the sky and as couples glide by with small silver balls strapped to their ankles, allowing them to hover above the ground, that Ify hears Céline's reply.

"You sound disappointed," she says in her Francophone accent. "'It's not completely destroyed,' so *il doit y avoir un problème*." She clicks her tongue. "Something must be wrong, that is what you're thinking."

"It doesn't feel right." Ify is grateful she doesn't have to move her mouth to have her words beamed straight through space off three satellites and directly into Céline's Whistle. Still, paranoia expands and contracts like a second set of lungs inside her chest. Something's not right. And others could be listening. Her very next thought is that this is precisely what she used to do to others. During the war.

"Maybe this is you adopting the colonizer mentality. You expect Nigeria to be a"—Céline chuckles—"what is that old phrase . . . 'shithole country'?" Her chuckle turns into a full-throated laugh. "Even when you lived there, the technology far surpassed much of what was in the Colonies. You said it yourself. Those few times you did speak about where you came from, you showed me pieces of what was maybe the most advanced country on the planet. I mean, you were developing technology to simulate regional spacetime phenomena with the gravitational pull of a black hole and using that to combat forest fires! Your country is in the process of terraforming land that *les blancs* had said would be uninhabitable for at least another century. And you come back now, after four, five years away and expect to see bullet holes in the buildings and craters from shelling in the roads. There can be such a thing as peace, Ifeoma."

"You're just saying that because you're going to be a colonial administrator and you want your job to be easy."

"Perhaps. Or perhaps I am right because I am right." There's an edge of fatigue to Céline's voice that wasn't there before.

Ify smirks, then turns her back to the youth outside the mall and stares out over the darkening water. Fireflies dance over it, winking in and out of sight. Ify resists the temptation to light up their entire trajectories and track their movements. Let this natural wonder, at least, be preserved. "Is that what I am supposed to tell the committee, then? When they ask me how to cure these refugee children of their mysterious disease, I will tell them I couldn't find a cure because there was too much peace?"

"Well, where are they coming from? The children."

Ify squints. Although many state functions happen in Abuja, this isn't where most refugee applications are processed. Preliminary research told Ify that. No, that happens further south. She walks herself through the intake process at the hospital. First, she receives the refugees from the shuttle, then she records their background information—as much as they can bear to remember—then she sets them up with treatment. Some of the cyberized will have been damaged either prior to or during their travel, some of the Augments as well. As a result, extracting information from them by way of download is difficult—in some instances, impossible. So they had developed the consent protocol to allow for a deeper dive into the braincases of cyberized refugees and those with Augments. Once permission is given, then technicians and doctors can get all the information they need, create a record in the government database, and move on to the next. For those red-bloods among them who had managed, against all odds, to flee war and devastation and make their way to the Space

Colonies in one piece, bureaucracy and mystery await them. No matter how pressing their needs, they don't have an outlet anywhere on their person, nor do they have a router in their brain that outside devices can connect to. There is no easy way to know them. So they have to wait.

Looking back at the process now, Ify lets herself feel a pinch of pain in her heart. So much of how she has designed her program has been with efficiency as the guiding principle. Get those who have been harmed in the care of the galaxy's best hospital as quickly and securely as possible. And every quarter, she's been asked for her numbers: number of admissions, number of discharges. And always, it has been the numbers. With the refugees, always the numbers. Maybe if she'd paid more attention, she could have stopped this. Could have prevented it.

"Are you avoiding a solution because you have to walk through some pain to get there?"

Ify knows Céline doesn't mean to be flippant about it, but she asks herself how Céline could possibly know what Ify's been through, what she's done. What she would have to face if she were to do exactly what Céline is suggesting.

The wind blows softly on her back, and she closes her eyes. And there she is again.

A dark, dank room. Two men walk in from around a corner. Her fingers clench into fists where they're bound to a chair. The men wear all black and don't bother hiding their faces. Their hands are gloved.

Static.

The first is stretching his gloves on his hands. "Let's talk about that higher purpose of yours."

Static.

The man is holding bees buzzing in his hand, their metal shells gleaming.

Static.

Hissing through her teeth, "Please, please, please no more."

Static.

A knife comes out of a man's vest pocket, cuts away her pant legs. And the bees swarm her legs and burrow beneath her skin and—

She gasps when she returns to the lake. It takes her several moments to realize where she is, that she's not in an underground chamber being tortured, that she's not Peter, that she's not being strapped to a chair while another version of herself—another Ify—waltzes through the aboveground facility with a government official at her side. She dashes away tears. No. No, there has to be another way. She can't go back to that facility.

She can't.

■ ■ ■ ■ ■

The thoroughfares of Abuja glow with neon light. It still startles Ify how much Mandarin there is in the signage, like it is gobbling up the English. The signs of Chinese investment in the recovery of this place are evident, but there's a further penetration. Foreign smells wafting from roadside restaurants, foreign chatter overheard in the streets and alleyways. A mixture of fashion trends she doesn't remember: kaftans tailored to look like tangzhuang jackets with straight Mandarin collars, cheongsam in bright multicolored prints.

A shout rises above the music. Ify dismisses it, part of the chaos of urban nightlife, until she hears it again, followed by an unbroken string of Cantonese. Suddenly, she hears English mixed in, then she recognizes that voice: Grace.

She breaks off into a sprint, crashing through people on the side of the road, not bothering to apologize, nearly tripping over a sizzling hot dish outside a restaurant stall. Grace. As she gets closer, she looks for the crowd that will have inevitably gathered, but nothing has broken the steady stream of Abujans. The shouting is getting louder, less insistent, more frightened. Ify hurries until she sees large men on either side of Grace, one holding her arm in a vise grip while the other has his finger pressed against his temple, face angled to the sky. Like he's talking with a commanding officer. They wear all black, black visors over their eyes, and stand a full head taller than the tallest person for miles. Their boxy, muscled frames tell Ify that they are Augments, if not fully cyberized. They don't carry guns but have shocksticks and wrist restraints hanging from their hips.

"What's going on?"

Grace sees Ify, and Ify's heart drops at the bottomless fear in her assistant's eyes.

"Let her go! What's the meaning of this?"

The officers, with the pattern of the Nigerian flag emblazoned on their shoulders, ignore Ify. One of them slips wrist restraints from his hip. All thought leaves Ify as she smacks them away. In one swift motion, she puts herself between Grace and the arresting officer, forcing him to look down at her. For a long second, he's silent.

"I am an Alabastrine official on diplomatic business, and this is my assistant, and you will unhand her *now*." She can feel herself being scanned, both officers instantly pulling up her credentials on their retinal displays. For several moments, no one moves. Not Ify, not Grace, not the police officers made of steel.

Then the officer holding Grace lets her go, and she falls onto the ground. "Grace Leung was found in violation of Article 263, subsection 10, of the penal code, relating to violations of memorial integrity—"

"Memorial integrity? What?"

"According to witness and surveillance reports. Punishment to comprise a fine of 250,000 naira or five years' imprisonment—"

Grace lets out a whimper, and Ify shouts, "What?!"

"Subject to the ultimate judgment of the state magistrate."

Outrage overpowers any fear Ify feels, and she raises herself up to the machine. "As Alabastrine officials, we are outside your jurisdiction and therefore not subject to your *penal code*." She spits the words out, hating herself even as she does. What does she look like, using her status as an outsider to trample on her own country's laws? Still, she looks around for anyone to stop and at least pay attention to the commotion. Someone to lend a hand or to record the encounter on a device in case anything were to happen. Someone to leap in and help. But it is as though she and Grace are invisible. As though there is no one but them and the police. Them and these machines.

The second officer, who has so far been quiet, puts a hand on the shoulder of the first, and the two exchange a wordless gaze, no doubt communicating an entire conversation between them. It shocks Ify to see so human a moment happen between the men, snapping the illusion that they are nothing more than chunks of unthinking metal.

When the first officer looks back, he seems to relax. "Enjoy your stay in Nigeria, Ms. Leung." They turn, almost in unison, to walk away.

"My ID!" Grace shouts.

The first officer turns back around, fishes a card out of his pocket, and holds it out to Ify. By now, Grace is standing, if hunched over and brushing the dust off herself.

Ify snatches it out of the man's hand and glares at him, unblinking, until the two officers vanish into the crowd.

When Ify is certain they're out of earshot, she whirls around. "What were you *thinking*? Are you stupid? Are you trying to get us killed? Do you have *any* idea what could have happened to you?" It's as though so much of the anger she's tried to suppress is now spilling out of her. She catches herself when Grace's composure breaks and her bottom lip begins trembling.

"I'm sorry, Doctor," she manages through the beginning of sobs.

Then Ify sees it. The terror shaking Grace's bones against each other. The resolve and clinical discipline washed away by fear. And she brings Grace into her arms. "It's okay."

Grace cries into Ify's shoulder, and they stand there for several minutes, Ify smoothing Grace's hair, an island of quiet in the sea of people rushing around them. "I thought I could conduct some research."

"Shh. It's okay."

Grace looks up at Ify. "I didn't do anything, Doctor. I swear."

"It's okay. I'm . . . I'm sorry for losing it. I just . . . it's been a long time since . . . well, I'm not used to being back is all."

"But, Doctor, all I was doing was collecting stories of the war."

"We don't have to do any more work tonight. Let's just go home and rest."

"But wait!" She breaks away from Ify, and that resolve is back.

Ify moves closer so that they can speak in whispers. "It's normal for people not to want to talk about their trauma."

"That's the thing. I'd done all my research previously. When I asked them about the war, they had no idea what I was talking about."

"Maybe some of them were far from the worst of it. There's an explanation, Grace. Let's go."

"But, Doctor, no one *knew* about the war. I spoke with over a dozen people before the police came."

Ify frowns. "Where were these people?"

Grace steps out of the mouth of the alley where they've stood and points up and down the street. Ify looks up into the sky, and as the maglev cars pass by, ambling up and down their flightlines, she sees them. The orbital surveillance drones. There are surely more embedded in the buildings and perhaps more strung throughout the air, too small to see with the naked eye. And they all would have seen Grace.

They all might have heard her too.

"Come on," Ify says, grabbing Grace's arm and pulling them back into the rush of crowds, zigzagging a path the long way back to the apartment. Ify knows it's foolish to hope, but maybe they will have spent at least a moment or two outside the sightlines of the surveillance drones thickening the air above Abuja.

CHAPTER
22

Sometime when we are walking, I am seeing what is in front of me and sometime I am not.

Sometime, there is being forest with heavy leaf that is blocking us from the sun and there is being chirping and growling and rumbling of bird and animal and even there is being slow stomping of shorthorn, and baby wulfu is playing and we are climbing over root that is sticking up from ground or we are crawling under low branches or tree trunk that has fallen. And sometime, I am seeing boy and girl in front of me with dirty shirt that is being inside out and there is being gun over their shoulder. And I am seeing big man we are calling Commandant at front of the line and we are stopping in some place and creating hologram to trick people who are coming so that we are later killing them and stealing from them. Then I am seeing forest again with Oluwale and Uzodinma and the others who are walking with us.

In the beginning, there is no pattern to when we are stopping and sitting down and finding our peace.

But when we are sitting down, I am practicing looking for rememberings and sorting them. I am practicing organizing them, and it is becoming easier for me to be finding which I am having after Enyemaka are rescuing me from pile of corpses and which are coming from before then. I am knowing now that some of these rememberings are not mine. They are belonging to other people and being given to me. Some of these remembering is colored with red and others with yellow. But the ones with the girl I am calling Ify are blue-green. There is sometime being full color to them, but always there is blue-green at the edge. Like hologram but fuller. Maybe realer.

Sometime, it is early in the morning while grass is still wet with dew and insect buzzing is not yet as loud as it is going to be, and this is when we are sitting and finding peace. Sometime, the sun is already shot up into the sky fast fast before we are stopping to sit and look at our rememberings to find our peace. And sometime, it is when the sky is dark and the stars have come and maybe there is moon and maybe there is not that we are sitting down and looking through our memories and learning and finding our peace. Even when I am finding thing that is paining me or making me to be sadding, I am feeling like I am finding my peace. I am thinking this is what Xifeng is wanting. I am also knowing that I am having remembering I am downloading from her trailer inside my braincase, and I am knowing that it is living in me. If they are destroying trailer and burning everything inside, then I am only evidence that the people we are burying ever died. I am only evidence that people we are burying ever lived. We are observer or history writer. This is being data. These are being people, but this is being data.

Because of what Oluwale is teaching me about finding specific rememberings, I am learning how to be separating and organizing them in my brain. It is like making rows of graves and putting data into each and marking each grave to tell me what is inside it. And I am organizing by person, so this person is getting this row, and this person is getting the next row, and I am learning that I am even having inside me rememberings from people in same family, brother and sister, mother and son, father and father's sister, so I am grouping them together as well.

"Like this," Oluwale is telling me one day, and he is drawing spiral in the mud with his finger. It is spiraling outward and outward and outward, and he is then pressing his finger into points in the lines. "This is how people know each other in my memories. They are connected. Everyone is connected to each other. Sometime, it is not being evident how they are connected, so I put them over here." He digs his finger into spot in the mud far from spiral. "But it is my project, seeing how everyone in my rememberings is connected. Sometime, it is because they are family. Sometime, it is because they are warring with each other. Sometime, it is because they are walking by in the street, and they see each other, and they are falling in love, but they are never seeing each other again. It is small small connection, but it is still connection, so they are going here." And he draws a line from the faraway point to the spiral, then continues making the spiral until it touches the faraway point.

I am crouching and wrapping my arms around my knees when I am watching him do this.

"Uzodinma does it differently," he is telling me.

"How?"

"He has made a spiderweb." Oluwale takes his hand out of the mud and his fingers break apart at the joints into tinier connected pieces. These are scrambling fast fast in the mud so that where there was being spiral there is now complicated spiderweb. Pattern. "Each person is connected to a number of people. And each moment in that person's life is connected to all these other moments."

I am staring at the drawing Oluwale is making, and I am feeling wonder blow up like balloon in my chest. I am having picture of spiderweb in my head and thinking of point and how point is getting smaller and smaller and smaller and more and more specific, so that when you are seeing it from far away it is like a star in the sky and every point where spiderweb is connected is like star in the sky. This is what I am thinking when it is nighting in the forest and I am looking at the sky. I am thinking I am looking at data. At rememberings.

It is being night and I am sitting next to Uzodinma and he is just finishing finding his peace and I am looking at his eyes change as he returns here from wherever he was being before. I am wanting to ask *Where are you coming from?* but I am knowing that we are the same in a very important way so I am asking *Where are we coming from?*

He knows that I am not using my voice, so he is knowing everything that I am meaning when I am asking this. There is being no expression on his face when he is saying, "I do not know."

And then he is showing me holographic video of him being child of war and shooting and killing and being small small but pointing gun and killing, then there is explosion, and then he is showing me other holographic video of him being in what is looking like hospital. And I am knowing it is hospital because I am seeing place like it in other rememberings, and there is no blood but there is being nothing but air where his legs are being. And we are turning in the remembering to see the doctor's face and the doctor is saying things, but I am thinking that there is so much pain in the remembering that the person is not being able to hear the doctor's words. Then I am seeing other holographic video where Uzodinma is holding himself up on two metal bars and he is looking down and his legs are metal and there is no skin on them, they are just gears and pistons and rods, and they are moving slow slow and Uzo is gritting his teeth and moaning and sweating much, then nurse is coming to hold him up before he falls to floor. Uzodinma is fast-forwarding through other memories. He is receiving new arm and he is returning to one room over and over again and he is being put into chair, and we are both feeling cord plugging into outlet at the base of our neck and then there is darkness until he is waking up.

"I don't know what happens to me when they put me in that chair," Uzodinma is telling me. "There is only darkness. I don't know if I'm dreaming or if I am dying and coming back to life. But I am needing to know what is happening in that time, because that's the secret to who I am." He is looking at his hands and the different color skin all over them. "What I am."

"Is that where we're walking to?"

Uzodinma nods.

"What about the others? Do they want to go to different places?"

Uzo is looking up at the sky where it is showing between the tree leaves, and I am looking up with him and thinking that maybe he is seeing in the sky the same thing that is being inside his head. "Some of them might. But some of them want to know what they are, just like me. If I can find an answer, maybe they can as well." Then he is looking at me. "We are the same," he is telling me. "We are sharing mystery."

It is taking me a long time to speak because I am feeling like he is seeing me. Not how Xifeng or Enyemaka are seeing me and not how drone is seeing me and not how people under Falomo Bridge are seeing me, even though I am calling all of these people friend. He is seeing inside me and outside me at the same time. He is seeing all of me. He is seeing the question I am asking and he is seeing the question underneath that and the question underneath that. He is seeing that I am worried and scared and that I am sadding and that I am learning new thing every day and it is filling me with fear, and I am thinking he is seeing all of these thing because he is once feeling them too. I am feeling like he is seeing me, and it is making me to want to be thanking him. "How are you knowing where to go to find this place or this person you are looking for?"

"I am retracing my steps," he is telling me. "I am remembering that one time when I am being child of war I am walking this path, but I am going in other direction and I am leaving many dead body. So I am walking this path again and I am seeing what I am doing in my head when I am being younger and more foolish. And this is how I am knowing where to go. When the killing and the bleeding in my head is stopping, I will know that I have arrived. I will know that I've found what I am looking for."

And I am thinking that maybe when he is finding what he is looking for, I will be finding it too.

When he is first saying we are sharing mystery, I am thinking he means we are both having something wrong with us or we are both having disease inside our body or our leg or arm is broken the same way, but now I am thinking that he is saying it more like we are sibling. We are brother and sister.

We share mystery. We are being family.

CHAPTER
23

The head of radiology at Nizamiye Hospital wears a shimmering white changshan with mauve magua jacket and traditional chieftain's kufi. His pant legs whisper against each other as he leads Ify and Grace through the open ward where patients, who look the absolute picture of health, are being attended to by hovering drones and the occasional nurse. Small conversations and occasional laughter fill the room. Ify notices that every patient has bandages wrapped around their head and neck. A few have bandages swathing their arms, and through the gauze, the copper-red markings indicating a healing circular incision. An outlet.

"Many of our patients," Dr. Ezirike says, "are farmers from the borderlands just outside the Redlands." With a wave of his hand, he indicates the patients lining both walls. They don't look like farmers, but then Ify wonders what she expected farmers to look like. "Proximity to radiation has adversely affected their internal organs, so they are prime candidates for the government's mass cyberization initiative. Our target is to achieve full cyberization within the year."

"There were quite a few empty beds in the room before this one," Grace remarks.

Without looking back, Dr. Ezirike tells her, "A year or two ago, we were at full capacity. And before that, every hospital was strained almost to breaking. But the establishment of regional clinics throughout every state, as well as an extensive training program—thanks to the Chinese—has helped stem the flow quite a bit. Only those in most dire need of care are sent here. As you can see, our facility is more than equipped to meet their needs."

They double back and reenter the hallway they had walked down earlier. Internists and doctors and nurse attendants hurry past, some of them making idle conversation, others with their eyes filmed over, no doubt reading reports or preparing to meet patients. A woman pushes a patient forward in a hoverchair that covers her legs, occasionally bending down to whisper something in the patient's ear. Though the patient's catatonic expression never changes, the woman smiles as though the patient were smiling too. As though the patient were laughing at a joke she'd just heard. There's a levity here that Ify never noticed in Alabast. Everyone is about their work, and it is difficult work, but they don't seem burdened by the seriousness of their tasks. There is joy in caring for the sick. Ify wonders if Grace sees the same thing, if she would see herself at home in a place like this, where it wouldn't be out of the ordinary to speak with a patient about food and family and where to find the good markets.

Down another corridor, they stop at a door. Dr. Ezirike puts his hand to the pad. It beeps, and the door slides open, revealing a warmly lit anteroom with a carpet at its center and old-fashioned leather-bound books lining the walls. Instead of a wall at the far end of the room is a window, opening out to a room where children and a few young adolescents play or sit or stare into space. Before some of them sits an easel at which they paint with their styluses, some with their fingers. Others arrange blocks into increasingly complex patterns.

Dr. Ezirike pauses in front of the window before turning and indicating the two hovering armchairs for Ify and Grace. "Don't worry, it's a one-way mirror. They cannot see us."

Grace sits, stylus poised over the tablet she has in her lap, ever the dutiful notetaker.

Ify can't take her eyes off the children.

On the other side of the glass, adults walk around the room, but they don't wear any armor. Just robes with green and white stripes at the ends of each sleeve. Here, the kids cluster in groups, some young enough to barely be walking. A few of them rest against the wall; these ones seem older. But through the flexiglass, Ify can see movement. She can see children talking to each other. Some of them are animated, others withdrawn. But they all seem . . . alive.

Once inside the room, she sees the drawings that line the wall. She walks to one of the pictures and sees a compound sketched out, seen at an angle from above with soldiers toward the center of the page around what she realizes is an explosion. The captured moment finds the limbs frozen in mid-flight. A shaheed. A suicide bomber. Someone in a military vest stands at the bottom right corner of the page, looking both at the scene and at Ify.

Then an explosion outside the building, and Ify, held down

by the guards protecting her, staring at one of the children, who is giggling and saying "Roses" over and over again, and Ify realizing he means the new blood on the walls outside the compound from the suicide bomber who has just detonated himself.

"Doctor?" Dr. Ezirike's voice snaps Ify out of her reverie.

Ify closes her eyes, pinches the bridge of her nose, then shakes herself out of her stupor. Her bodysuit tells her where she is, beams into her brain their location, the time of day, the year. *We are not at war*, she says to herself, turning to smile at Dr. Ezirike, then taking her seat in the hoverchair next to Grace.

"I was just telling your colleague," the doctor says, "that some of our most important advances have been in the field of child cyberization. It was common wisdom that children should reach a certain age before undergoing any such operations, but with our technology and growing expertise, we are able to push that age further and further back."

"Machines from the cradle to the grave," Ify says before she can stop herself.

The doctor frowns at her, then opens his face again for the both of them. "Some will look at these children and see the future best and brightest of Nigeria, able to attend and succeed at the best schools anywhere. Some will see future scientists able to accumulate data at hitherto unknown rates and assimilate them and conduct incredible analyses. And in a way, we are breeding future environmentalists. I'm sure the government is trying to get all the help it can in its efforts to combat climate change. But we are also building people more able to survive in this world. Their organs don't deteriorate at the same rate.

They have automatic immunity from any number of diseases that may have devastated previous populations. Can you believe there was a time when a thing like malaria could kill you?" He chuckles softly.

Grace pauses in her note-taking. "Doctor, you said earlier that the government's goal was widespread cyberization?"

"Yes. For a number of reasons. The health of the population, but also increased productivity. It opens the space for remote workers. We have high-speed rail from Borno State to Enugu, but for some, the trip is still not feasible. That shouldn't keep them from having the good job they qualify for."

"Aren't there security concerns?" Something is niggling at the back of Ify's mind, but she can't quite pin down her worry. "Mass connectivity. The government can watch everything you do."

Grace stiffens in her seat, as though a thought has just occurred to her.

Dr. Ezirike shrugs. "Would you rather the government carry your data or a private corporation? At least this way, your wallet is safer. The Ministry of Health certainly isn't trying to bully you into buying that sweater." He chuckles.

"No, it isn't," Ify says quietly to herself.

"After the cataclysm that ended five years ago, the people have been more than eager to protect against such widespread catastrophe."

Ify's eyes spring open. "Cataclysm?"

"Yes. The Climate Cataclysm, the Nine-Year Storm that ravaged the country for nearly a decade. It set fire to almost everything, devastated the southeast. The Igbo were hit hardest. It saw the expansion of the Redlands, rising sea levels. Almost every imaginable horror." He doesn't speak like someone affected by the calamity. He speaks as though this were a thing that happened somewhere far away, that killed people he can only barely bring himself to care about.

"Is that what happened?" Ify asks, trying to keep the edge out of her voice. Grace has stopped taking notes and now stares intently at the both of them.

"What? Of course that's what happened." The doctor laughs. "Millions died and millions more were displaced by the Nine-Year Storm. It wasn't until 2176 that the worst was over. And that's when the mass cyberization initiative got under way in earnest."

"But the war—"

"Tell us more about the regional clinics, Doctor," Grace interjects.

For less than a second, a dark expression washes over Dr. Ezirike's face, but he continues, explaining the intake process and the local efforts to combat the worst effects of the Climate Cataclysm while caring for the climate refugees most adversely affected. But, to Ify, his voice has turned into the buzzing of a distant insect. Her gaze returns to the children, some of whom would have been alive in 2176. Some of whom would have been alive before then. Alive to have witnessed the end of the war. A war no one seems to want to talk about.

A war, it seems, that didn't even happen.

■ ■ ■ ■ ■

Grace waits until the driver has taken her and Ify some distance from the hospital before speaking.

A wave of relief moved through Ify at the sight of their two new guards. Since the night of Grace's encounter with the police, Ify has insisted that the two guards, smartly dressed and thankfully taciturn, accompany them on every trip. She was foolish to think that simply having come from here meant that she was safe from whatever dangers lurked in this place. It took Grace's near-arrest to show her that.

"You don't have to worry about a robot taking your job if you're the robot," Grace says, a hint of a smirk at the edge of her lips.

Ify raises an eyebrow. Grace doesn't make jokes. Ify sees the nervousness in her again, the way she grips her stylus, on the verge of breaking it. She should send her home. Even though Director Towne had ordered Grace to come along, maybe to spy on her, this is too taxing a mission. Ify knows this place, as strange as it appears to her. The newness for Grace must be overwhelming. And layered on top of that unease is the stress that comes with having to uncover a medical mystery imperiling the lives of over a thousand children in Alabast. That's what Ify will do. She'll send her back. As soon as they're back at the apartment, she'll begin drafting the paperwork.

A thought strikes Ify.

"Grace."

"Yes, Doctor?"

"Why did you interrupt me? In the doctor's office."

Grace looks behind her. The driver and the other minder sit in silence as the jeep glides down the city flightlines. Then she presses a button on the console beside her, and the partition rises. She waits until it's closed and, even then, leans forward in a whisper. "There were no security cameras in that hospital."

"What?"

"I thought I was being paranoid. But when I started looking, I saw that there were none. Not a single room we walked into had cameras."

"But surveillance drones."

Grace shakes her head. "I had my tablet set to detect drone activity once we entered."

Ify remembers that Grace had held her tablet to her chest almost the whole time . . . to mask the readings. "What are you saying? We weren't being watched?"

"We were being watched. Everyone in that hospital was either cyberized or undergoing cyberization, permitting the government access to their braincases."

Ify's eyes widen in horror.

"Everyone was watching us."

They've been watching her. Ever since she set foot in this country, they've been watching her.

"That's how the police knew to come after me. They heard me asking about the . . ."

Breath leaves Ify's lungs so that she can only speak in a whisper. "And if the government can control what people see, it can block their sight too." Grace nods. Ify shakes her head in disbelief. "No one helped us, because they didn't see us."

"Couldn't see us." Grace glances behind her, as though unsure that the partition is still in place, then turns back to Ify. "There was no Nine-Year Storm, was there?"

A maelstrom rages in Ify's head. Too many questions, too many clues, none of them joining together, just flotsam and detritus hurled about against the walls of her skull. "No," she breathes. "There was no storm."

The lack of memorials around Aso Rock. The attack on Grace

in Abuja. This story about a massive decade-long climate event that never happened. They're erasing every trace of the war. But there has to be something left.

The coordinates must have been buried somewhere deep in Ify's subconscious, somewhere beneath conscious thought, beneath language acquisition, beneath her bloody childhood memories, buried in her bones and in the thick of her muscle. Because when she presses the button by her armrest that unveils a console with a digital map, her fingers blaze over the glowing keys, the map's target reticle zeroing in on a point near the border between Enugu State and Benue State.

Things will be different in the southeast, she tells herself. There will be at least some remnant of the war. They may have scrubbed all trace of it from the capital, but where the fighting was thickest, the land must bear some scars that remain.

She doesn't realize how tightly she's holding on to her hope until after the maglev jeep has veered into new flightlines, taking them a few silent hours through part of Nasarawa State and Kogi State before bringing them to near-empty country roads, flanked occasionally by villages or a single solar-paneled dwelling. Their jeep then soars over the treetops of nearby jungle, and memory of the journey returns to Ify. Riding in the back of a jeep with Agu, Xifeng's trailer behind them. Refugees either on or beside the caravan, walking with it, dancing with it, clinging to it. Ify presses herself against the window to witness the changing of the landscape, to see the snaking road the caravan had taken five years earlier. They continue, and she angles her face to see if they'll be coming up on the converted remains of the refugee intake center she had passed through all those years ago.

"Take us down," Ify says. "Take us down now." She doesn't care how urgent she sounds, how unhinged. She doesn't care that she's forcing the driver to break several traffic laws in descending as swiftly and as directly as he's doing. But soon, the jeep is hovering only a foot over a patch of empty grass before lowering onto its absorbers.

Ify struggles against the door, then bursts out and runs into what she sees now is an empty field. Wind turbines spin lazily before her, well in the distance. She runs forward until she's in the midst of them and whirls around. This has to be some illusion. This was where she and the other refugees had passed through. This was the spot. She is certain. But she looks, and everywhere she looks, she sees a lie. Clean air and soft breeze and verdant plain and clear sky. All of it a lie.

"No," she whispers, over and over, looking desperately for something to tell her she's right. "No. No, no, no, no." Rage fills her. "WHERE IS IT?" she screams to the sky, before collapsing.

She feels Grace at her side, face close to hers, hand on her back, trying to soothe her rage away.

"It was here" is all Ify can say. "It was right here." The rage collapses. Only numbness is left. "I was a refugee, and there was an intake station right here. All of us, we went through it. They gave us blankets, processed us, put us in the database so that we could be reunited with any living family. They . . . they gave us food. And showers and . . ." A sob catches in her throat. "It was right here." The fingers of her right hand fumble for the button on the neck of her bodysuit, which she presses, sending chemicals into her bloodstream, slowing her heart rate, dulling the pain constricting her chest. Fog clears from her mind.

Are you avoiding a solution because you have to walk through some pain to get there?

Céline's words ring like a proverb through her head. Like an alarm. Like a command.

She knows where she has to go.

■　■　■　■　■

Open field greets Ify.

Her minders wait by their jeep. Initially, Grace waits with them. In moments like this, Ify finds herself reverting to her old thinking. Familiar suspicions arise. Grace, so meticulous with her note-taking, ostensibly there to provide documentation of their progress and assist in Ify's research, but probably there to spy on her. Her minders are probably beaming their reports to Alabast as she stands here. Searching for any misstep, cataloging any mistake, and gathering all the details so they can be sent in a post straight to her superiors. Ify turns her thinking elsewhere. She thinks about the fact that where there had once been concrete buildings with unpaved roads between them and cells with electrified openings designed to sizzle into amputation anything that touched them and where there had once been young boys in those cells with collars around their necks, bodies limp from having given up on fighting back, there is now field. Nothing but open field and the biomech animals that graze on it.

Grace materializes at her side, a little behind her, tentative. Unsure. Ify knows that Grace wants to ask what they're doing here, what this place is or, rather, was. But Ify wants just a few more moments to herself here. Just a few more moments of her private grief.

She wants to walk through. Feel the grass against her ankles, make sure it's not all a ruse. She almost reaches out a hand to touch the air where one wall had been. And in her mind, she hears the boom of a loud explosion and feels the wash of imaginary dust on her face, all from the memory of a suicide bomber's detonation just outside another building. And she then sees in her mind a boy, even younger, who had, just before, been playing with blocks and telling Ify about his dreams of becoming an engineer. And this boy is telling her about the roses painted on the wall, and Ify is hearing him and realizing that he is talking about blood from the boy who's just detonated the bomb he'd been carrying inside him.

She wants to put one foot in front of the other and see if she actually passes through air or walks straight into a wall or a room or an entrance or the end of a hallway. She squints and wonders again if maybe it's just a trick of the air that is hiding the phalanx of black-suited guards from her. They have to be here somewhere. There had been so many of them before, and now there are only horses and small bulls and a few deer, none of them completely natural, all of them false. All of them lies. Big or small, all lies.

"Doctor?" Grace's voice, fire melting the ice encasing her.

Ify opens eyes she had not realized were closed. "Yes?"

Grace pauses before speaking, as though she is testing potential sentences out in her head, trying to match words in increasingly complex and sensitive combinations. When she does speak, the words halt and start back up again and tumble over each other. "At the hospital . . . when we were in the doctor's office . . . did you . . . what—"

"This was a detention center," Ify says, cutting Grace off

and, Ify imagines, answering half of the dozens of questions swimming behind her assistant's eyes. Something in Ify has broken. She knows what she's doing, and she recognizes the desperation driving it. If every remnant of the war, every trace of the carnage and trauma, is being washed away, she will plant her flag, be a living testament to the fact of the horrors that happened. They will not erase her experiences. It was not all a dream. It happened. She happened. "In a section of the compound was a room holding children only a little older than the ones in Dr. Ezirike's office. They were enemy combatants."

A sharp intake of breath from Grace at what Ify is implying.

"They were held here after their capture. Some of them fought with militia forces. Some of them fought directly for the Biafran rebels. But here is where we held them."

"And . . . what did you do to them?"

Ify says nothing. Instead, she steps forward, then forward again, then forward again, and stops. When she looks down, she feels she's arrived at the center of the thing. Certainly the center of something. And she wonders if she is standing above the spot where Peter had been tortured. She wants to close her eyes but can't bring herself to relive those moments. So instead she stands in that spot and turns and turns and turns.

She's reminded of visiting Aso Rock and the sight of those parliamentarians, those government leaders, completely devoid of conflict, not even arguing. She's reminded of how pristine and stainless all the buildings had been: the presidential complex, the National Assembly, the Supreme Court building. How she'd been expecting a statue, something large and hulking and made out of marble or obsidian, some massive, tragic thing to commemorate the unfortunate deaths Nigerians had suffered or to make reference to the unfortunate necessity of killing during wartime. Or a plaque with names on it, even just one name. A hero. Thinking back on that now, she knows what she was looking for.

She was looking for the man who had taken her from a Biafran camp and brought her to Abuja and raised her as his little sister. She was looking for the man who had taken her with him through the ranks of Nigerian society, dressed her in the finest robes, enrolled her in the finest schools, made sure she had a front row seat to the workings of government.

She was looking for the man who had killed and killed and killed and had taken her—a little bush girl—in as his own. Her adoptive brother. The man responsible for so much that was good in her life.

Who then became the man who took all of that away. Who let her rot in a Nigerian prison, who was too weak to save her.

The man she'd abandoned. The man who'd let her abandon him. Daren.

It all comes washing back over her.

She remembers walking the corridors of this facility with Daren at her side and strolling down a hallway to look in through a large window at an aid worker trying to coax adolescent child soldiers out of their trauma with toys and colored styluses. She remembers walking past cells where older boys, collars glowing around their necks with deadly red lights, would hiss at her. She remembers feeling nothing but a clinical distance. They were puzzle pieces in a larger project to be figured out. Puzzle pieces that screamed and bled and fought and cried out for their loved ones. But still just puzzle pieces.

Please don't walk away from your memories.

You don't know my memories, Ify wants to tell Céline.

What does she do now? She doesn't know exactly what she was expecting, but perhaps what was waiting for her, she hoped, was completion. Or absolution. Or something to take the guilt growing in the pit of her stomach and scoop it out of her. This is what she ran away from. This is what she has tried so hard to forget. And if the past month has proven nothing else, it's that everyone else has forgotten it too.

Except Peter. Who is still in a hospital bed in a Colony high above her head, comatose and trapped in dreams whose horrors Ify can very well imagine.

Around her is pasture. Animals too mechanized to know that she should be feared walk by and sniff her and chew grass and process it in their multiple stomachs. Mechanized bees flit from flower to flower around her ankles. The night sky's blue has deepened into black. Stars hang above her, and Ify even starts to doubt those. How does she know a giant dome doesn't hang over this rural patch of Kaduna State, over all of Kaduna State, maybe over all of Nigeria? Who is to say that someone hasn't built a false sky and painted false stars on it to watch over false animals in a false field at the center of which stands . . . a false doctor?

Who is to say that anything she looks at now is anything other than a lie?

Including the dark thing, like a moving shadow the size of a small boar, coming straight for her in the distance.

CHAPTER
24

It is feeling strange to me when we are leaving forest. Good thing is happening to me in forest. I am finding gosling, and Uzodinma is finding me. It is like I am wishing to be spending the rest of my life under ceiling made of leaves that is blocking out the sun when it is being too hot and I am wishing to spend the rest of my life being able to lie down in the cooling mud when it is raining and thing is crawling and slithering all over me but I am not minding because it is feeling like I am hugging the earth and the earth is hugging me. When I am seeing red-blood, it is reminding me that there is metal inside me and that I am killing and that I am doing bad thing.

In forest, I am not doing bad thing. In forest, I am not bad person.

So I am standing at the edge of the forest while others are going on ahead of me, but Oluwale stops and turns to me and waves me to him, and even though I am not saying any thing to him, I am thinking that he is knowing that question lives inside me, so much question it is feeling sometime that I am made of question, that if you peel my skin, you will find question spilling out. So I am walking with him.

Very quickly, land is flat and turning to pasture. It is easy to be seeing where they are having home made out of clay that is built and government building that is stone and clay and glass and plaster. It is looking like this is older place than rest of country. Like it is being left behind. I am seeing, in the distance, farmer sitting on chair beneath *Piliostigma thonningii* tree, which is also being called camel's foot tree and monkey biscuit tree, while he is having droid machine picking his rows of plants, and the rows are not all straight or even but some are crooked like the grave me and Enyemaka and Xifeng are sometime finding before we are fixing them. But farmer is far away and he is not seeing us.

Is this where you are from? I am asking Uzodinma, who stands next to me. When I am asking like this, it is being more than words. It is being images of laboratory where he is being plugged into machine and made to lift big thing and fire weapon and they are scanning his brain. It is being images of hospital where he is waking up with no leg and they are giving him leg but it is first belonging to someone else. It is being images of him seeing new arm and new leg for the first time and looking in mirror and seeing face and him saying to himself, "This is my body." It is being *Is this where you are from?* but also *Is this where you are learning that you are mystery?*

I don't know, but when Uzo is telling me this, it is like his word is being colored with hope. *I don't know, but I'm getting closer.* And *I don't know, but there are answers here.* And *I don't know, but I am glad that you are here with me.* All of these thing he is saying to me when he is saying *I don't know.*

Sound is beeping and clicking inside my head and suddenly I am knowing that we are in Zaria, in Kaduna State. Suddenly, map is filling my head and I am knowing where is Ahmadu Bello University and the palace of the emir. I am knowing where is the old city and the adobe houses where people are living and I am knowing where is being mosque and mass graves. I am seeing all of these thing at once.

Against the darkening sky, I am seeing Kufena Hills. My brain is telling me the geological formation is being made out of metamorphic rock, that it is looming tall and is wide too and is having old wall built around it that is crumbling now but that is telling me that people are living there once. I am also hearing faraway splashing sound of waterfall, and I am knowing it is Matsirga waterfall, and I am seeing in satellite photo that is being beamed into my brain that the land around it is green and it is supposed to be impossible that the land there is green with all the radiation that has been happening in the world, but they are saying it is because this land, this country, is being blessed.

And I am feeling like all of these thing around me is beautiful, and it is like it is all being untouch by people, and I am wondering if maybe this is what people are calling paradise. Then, I am turning off all these thing in my brain that is showing me what everything is called and where it is, and I am just letting earth and night sky talk to me, and I am closing my eyes and smiling.

When I am lowering my head, I am seeing ahead of me specks moving along the base of Kufena Hills. They are being deeper pieces of black against the larger black of the mountain. The stars make light on the ground so that the grass is silver and glowing, and it is like this with some of the tree and some of the animal that is roaming and making chawp-chawp on the grass. And one of the speck is walking and it is not seeing me, I don't think, but it is moving to me and it is walking and it is passing beneath a beam of light and I am seeing its face and I am gasping like someone is reaching down my throat and squeezing my lungs tight so there is being no air in them.

I am standing still, not being able to move, and others are spreading out around me, and they are exploring and learning the land, and some of them are walking ahead of me but my eye is frozen on the face I am seeing, and it is like face is jumping straight from my dream, from my remembering, and sitting right in front of me. I am saying, *It can't be, it can't be.* Even as I am turning my braincase back on and being able to hear the beeps and the whirrs and know the name of all things, I am saying to myself, *It can't be, it can't be.*

Because now I am shivering and I am running and I am not paying attention to anything because there she is ahead of me at the base of the mountain, walking back and forth, then standing still like she is waiting for me, like she has been waiting for me my entire life.

Ify.

The ground is exploding with light. Something shining from above us. Then grass is being whipped around me. It is blinding my regular eye, but I am seeing with my other eye helicopter and drone, and my heart is thump-thumping in my chest because I am not needing to strain my ear to hear stomp-stomp of juggernaut. And I am turning back to Ify and I am wanting to scream at her to get away and I am running fast fast.

My brother and sister are running out of the way, and some are being captured in electrified net that is short-circuiting them and making them to lie still, and some of them is vanishing back into the forest. But I am the only one running to Ify because she is real and I must tell her that I have been looking for her all my life. And I am thinking that she is in danger and I am coming here just in time to save her.

CHAPTER
25

Everything happens at once.

A series of small shapes breaks free of the forest behind them. Then helicopters and large drones burst out from over the tops of the trees. Police vehicles zoom into view out of nowhere. And lights shine from the aerial assault vehicles to show that the moving shapes on the ground aren't animals at all but children. Children moving unnaturally fast.

Ify's minders grab her and Grace by the arms and try to hustle them into the back seat of their jeep. Grace, too stunned to resist, is swept into the vehicle, but Ify breaks free and stares at one of the children, who bounds straight for her, heedless of the bullets that have started zipping around her, heedless of the way the earth explodes into columns around her with each detonation. Slipping through the legs of the police that try to capture her, vaulting over another officer, wrapping her legs around its neck, and twisting on the way down. Rolling into a sprint. Flicking a knife from out of nowhere into her palm and slicing and stabbing at whatever comes for her, never once taking her eyes off of Ify.

Ify should be scared, should be terrified that this is coming for her, this thing so efficient at killing, but it is a child. A girl no older than fourteen or fifteen. And there is something about her that compels Ify to stand still.

"Madame!" one of her guards is screaming. One of the guards she'd insisted on having at her side at almost all times. One of the guards she'd hoped would keep her safe. Whom she's now refusing. "Madame! We must go! This is a police operation."

But Ify is entranced. "The children," she murmurs to herself. Time has slowed down for her, so she can watch it all unfold like paint splashed onto a canvas: the aerial vehicles spilling over the treeline, the children scattering, some of them being caught by ground forces, the one girl charging, barreling, like a faultline in the earth, straight for her.

The child is close enough for Ify to see her face, then the girl leaps from an impossibly far distance. Arms outstretched, as though there are claws on her fingers. One of Ify's minders sticks his arm out to bat the child away, but Ify, acting before thinking, pushes the man aside and walks straight into the child's embrace.

The child wraps her arms and legs around Ify like a restraint, like something made out of metal, and is shaking. The thought occurs to Ify that maybe she is being targeted. Maybe this is some odd assassination attempt and this child is carrying a bomb inside her body.

She tosses away the thought. No, this is peacetime. No one would want to blow up a Colonial official in peacetime.

The girl shivers against Ify even as the tableau of violence plays out before Ify and the children scurry, some of them vanishing into the forest, others unlucky enough to be caught in the electrified netting or shot down by paralyzing bullets.

The minders grip the girl by her shoulders and arms and try to pry her loose, then the girl cries out in pain as electrical currents sizzle along her skin and she falls to the ground.

"What did you do?" Ify shouts at one of the men as the girl writhes, then comes up onto her hands and knees. Ify sees a shockstick raised to strike the girl down and grabs the man's arm to stop him. "What are you doing? Stop it."

The girl coughs, and a spattering of oil stains the grass. She comes up and stands too close to Ify, and there is beseeching in her eyes, and joy and fear and wonder. "Ify."

"What?" How does this girl know her name? Suddenly, the girl's hands grip Ify's face and pull it down and close so that her head is bowed before the girl's. A small breeze, like a breath exhaled slowly, whispers against her forehead. Ify's eyes shoot open. What is this? What is happening? Flashes of Onyii flit through her mind. She breaks free and can't help but stare in horror at the child.

"Ify, it's me."

She backs away. "I . . . I don't know you." What just happened to her still rattles her, loosens every thought in her brain until she can't think clearly anymore. "I don't know you."

"But, Ify, it's me! Telling you to get ready for school. It is me! Watching sunset with you and carrying you in my arm and waking you when you are sleeping, it is me! You are knowing me." Then, strangely enough, the girl begins to cry. "Ify, please."

Police dressed in full black riot gear snatch the girl off the ground. She stretches her arms out to Ify, begging to be let back, begging Ify to take her, to hold her, screaming, "Ify! Ify, please! It is me!" She writhes and bites one of the hands holding her, falls into a crouch, then, just as she's about to burst at Ify, a net appears from nowhere, wrapping around her and pressing her into the ground and sizzling her into submission.

As volts of electricity run through her and sparks fly from the skin of her exposed legs, she keeps her gaze locked on Ify. Never looking away until her eyes go blank. Even then, it seems as though the girl sees Ify and nothing else.

"Please," says one of her minders, "we must get you to safety."

Too stunned to resist, Ify climbs back into the jeep and lets the door slam shut. Then they are moving again. The fog in her brain is too thick. She doesn't even know where she is going.

The driver is complaining about police operations and how there is never enough warning, about how much noise is made during these things, and something breaks through the mist clouding Ify's thoughts.

"Where are they being taken?" she asks.

Grace is still catatonic.

After a pause, the driver offers, "The police station, I think. There were military present, but it seems as though it was a state police operation. Yes, the police station is most likely."

The man in the passenger's seat nods in agreement.

"Take me there," Ify says, with as much sternness as she can muster.

"What? Are you mad?" asks the driver.

"Take me there. I want to go to the police station, and you will take me there."

The passenger snorts. "She is not serious-oh," he jokes to the driver.

Ify leans forward, past Grace, sticking her head through the partition space. "Do you think you are irreplaceable? Both of you? It will not be an anonymous communiqué to your employer that you were derelict in your duty. It will be a report directly from me. So you will know it was me that ejected you from your place of employment like a space dinghy from a shuttle station. I am a Colonial official. You will take me where I say you will take me. Are we understood?"

The driver and the other minder both look at each other before nodding. The driver takes the jeep into gear, and it hovers off the ground. Ify consults her tablet to give her hands something to do, though her fingers tremble too much to be of much use. The passenger mutters a joke beneath his breath.

Without looking up from her tablet, Ify says, "I think I prefer you both silent." After a beat to confirm their obedience, she says, "Thank you."

She stares sternly at Grace, sending in her direction as steely an expression as possible, so that when Grace does finally look up from her lap, she sees in Ify's face the silent command to pull herself together.

They have work to do.

■ ■ ■ ■ ■

"Grace, stay here," Ify says as they pull up before the police compound.

The officers who stand in the parking lot by their maglev jeeps and their hoverbikes, watching Ify walk straight for the front entrance with purpose and the confidence of an oyinbo, don't have to know who she is to see that she has the bearing of someone with authority. One or two of them might snicker at the sight of that woman striding so far ahead of her minders, but others see her minders and the bulge of weapons beneath their jackets and the way every single door opens for Ify and their quiet laughter dies down. Whatever badge she wears or title she holds or uniform she has on, it has imbued her with power. She has spent nearly half a decade in the Space Colonies perfecting the use of that power, getting accustomed to wearing it, to wielding it, especially as someone who does not look like how many think the powerful should look. She has grown used to the tenor of her voice when she's addressing authorities she needs something from, the way she must braid together compassion and command when speaking with her subordinates, the fact that she must treat every encounter as though she is talking to an equal or an inferior. She moves with the walk of someone who owns the land she sets foot on. She has to.

There is something she wants ahead of her. Possible answers to questions she's been asking herself ever since she landed in this country over a month ago. In the form of a girl whom she never recognized but who seemed to know who Ify was. With a certainty that unnerves her.

So it is with the demeanor of an entitled Colonial oyinbo that she passes through the gated entrance, immediately traveling through the massive gray walls that surround the compound, then walking up the broad stone staircase to the front doors, on each side of which stand gendarmes with submachine guns in their hands, the metal of their wrists showing clearly that they are Augments.

She pays them no mind as she nearly charges through the doors that whisk open and shut for her, a gust of air-conditioned breeze rushing straight into her face. Immediately, she notes a front desk, behind which sits a man in a short-sleeved officer's uniform and a beret. The others who walk up and down halls wear the same thing, minus the golden rope over this man's left shoulder. Ify strides directly to him.

"Please take a ticket," the man drones without looking up from his touchboard. "And fill out our online form describing your query or complaint, and we will be with you shortly." He pops a piece of chin-chin into his mouth.

"My name is—"

His mouth full, he says, "Please take a ticket and fill out our online form describing your query or complaint—"

"I am here on an urgent matter!"

"—and we will be with you shortly."

"I don't think you understand! I am a Colonial official representing Alabast. You will see to my matter immediately!"

Most of the work in the police station continues. The officers walk by, the hum from videos projected from tablets continues. But more than a few officers and administrative personnel stop what they're doing to look at this woman who has turned herself into the center of their universe. Color rises in Ify's cheeks, and she struggles to maintain her posture of authority. When they all see that it is a nineteen-year-old woman dressed like some oyinbo from space, they return to their tasks. By now, the desk attendant has his chin resting in the palm of his hand. He finishes chewing his chin-chin and makes a show of swallowing. The bored expression has not left his face.

"I just need you to look someone up. I need to know where they're being held."

"Please take a ti—"

"Please, they've just arrived." She lowers her voice. "I just need this one thing." She realizes now that she has no idea how big or how small this compound is. Is there a jail attached, or do they merely process the people the police arrest here and transport them elsewhere? Ify doesn't recall seeing transport vans in the parking lot, but that doesn't mean they aren't somewhere on these premises. So many things would have been prudent to know before making this play, and yet she has let emotion drive her. She has let herself be guided by the face of that girl. That girl they snatched away from her. That girl who would not stop staring at her. That girl whom Ify had refused.

What will Ify say to the girl when she sees her again? Will she apologize? Will she tell her that, yes, she is the Ify the girl has been looking for? Even though she has never seen the girl before? Will she ask the girl where she learned to blow on Ify's forehead like that? Or will she say nothing and let the child hold her, cling to her as though she's the answer to whatever questions might have gripped her?

"Do you have identification?" the man asks loudly, and, Ify realizes, for the second time.

Ify scrambles to call up her information in a holographic projection on her palm.

"No, not your identification. The detainee's."

"Oh. Um." Ify looks about, trying to figure out what to say, what to do. An idea occurs to her. She uses her Whistle to replay the last moments she spent with the girl, rewinding from the girl's capture to the girl standing in front of her, just before she pulls Ify's face down to blow on her forehead. The image freezes, and in the girl's face is that mixture of emotions Ify remembers so clearly: gratitude and sorrow and fear and hope and love. Ify downloads that still and slips the image file into the projector that shoots the image in three dimensions from her palm.

Surprise flickers over the attendant's face, before that familiar expression of boredom returns. He looks up from time to time as he taps a key sequence into his touchboard. His fingers don't detach, and Ify wonders if he's a red-blood or if he's merely being slow on purpose. It is beginning to irk her that she can no longer tell the difference.

"I am cross-referencing the image you have sent me with every portrait that has been taken here within the past week."

"Oh, I don't need the past week. It will have been within the past twelve hours."

He raises an eyebrow at Ify, perhaps on the verge of asking about matters he has no business asking about. But he thinks better of it and returns to his task. "Okay. The past twelve hours." He stares at his monitor, then squints. "Hmm." He inputs the same key sequence as last time, waits a moment, then lets out a quiet "Huh."

"What's wrong?"

"Are you sure this person was arrested within the past twelve hours?"

Ify resists the temptation to lean over the counter and look at his screen. "Maybe they were brought to a different facility? In a different state? What if you checked with all the holding facilities in the country?"

"That is the problem," the attendant says, looking up at Ify. "I just did."

It is the last thing Ify hears before an explosion rips through the walls around her and brings the ceiling right down on top of her and the attendant.

CHAPTER
26

We are sitting with our hands being bound in front of us between our legs. And there is chain looping through to connect to metal that is wrapping around our ankles. It is being wound tight so that we are always hunching over. We are being six of us in this van and there are being collars around our necks and they are being connected by thin glowing wire and I am feeling as they are putting this thing on me that my brain is shutting down and I am not hearing noise in it anymore and light is leaking out of the world like water from a lake or blood from the hole made by bullet. It is like they are putting shadow over everything when they are putting collar around my neck. And it is being impossible to talk to Oluwale or any of the other like I am wanting to be talking to them. I am not hearing them in my braincase and I don't think they are hearing me either. Some of them are looking like they are trying to be finding peace but they are fidgeting and itching like ant is biting them all over their skin, and it is the first time I am seeing many of them like this and it is sadding me.

I am hearing engine and moving, and I am knowing that we are rising and we are to be moving somewhere, and I am hoping that the others who are not being in this van with us are being in a van that is going to the same place because even though we are being many, like thirteen, we are all of us being close from so much time together sharing mind and sharing mystery.

With collar that is squeezing my neck and with cord that is attaching all of us, I am not able to be seeing map in my head, so I am not knowing where we are going. I am just knowing that it is being small time between when we are moving and when there is explosion that is throwing all of us all over the place like shaking pepper on jollof rice.

Instantly, I am hearing gunshot and everything is sounding like war again like in my rememberings. Part of me is wanting to move and be joining and my hand is aching for gun, but part of me is seeing cord connecting us and collar and knowing that if we are doing this thing something bad is happening to us. But then I am hearing sound like something is sticking to back door, then sparking and sizzling like something is burning, then all light inside van is shutting down with popping sound and everything is dark, and I am seeing that there is no longer cord connecting all of us. Our collar is no longer beeping.

Back door is blowing open like someone is ripping it away, then someone is climbing in fast fast with light in one hand and shockblade in other hand and they are going up and down line and putting blade to the metal thing covering our hands and it is falling away and we are moving our fingers again.

Now with door open I am hearing katakatakatakata of gunfire with puhBOOM of grenade, and as soon as I am no longer having metal on my hand or collar on my neck, I am running out of van where everything is smoke and there is being blood on the ground and it is wet under my feet and some people is coughing but I am not because all of this is feeling familiar to me. Like I am being here before. The world is coming to me again in lights and I am seeing everything, even map in my head of compound, and I am seeing even more than that. I am seeing from every camera in police station that is being behind me, and even though it is far away and there is long road between us and it and we are near to pathway in forest, I am seeing it clearly.

Without looking, I am picking up gun that is being on the ground and I am taking cord from my neck and I am plugging it into police that is at my feet but who is being cut in half and his legs are being far away. Even as policeman is dying, I am hearing through his comms network everything his comrade is saying and shouting, and there is many shouting shouting and puhBOOM and katakata. I am disconnecting, and when I am looking up I am seeing all of my sibling but I am also seeing other girl. Some are being older and taller and they are having bandana wrapping around their faces and some are wearing masks and some are having painting on them, and they are looking at us with gun in their hand and not saying anything until one is stepping forward.

"Go into the forest. There is a rescue vehicle waiting for you there. To take you to safety," this girl is saying.

"Where is Ify?" I am asking, and some of my sibling is looking at me strange because they are never hearing me speak like red-blood before.

"Come with us," the first girl is saying.

But another girl is stepping forward and pulling the bandana down from her face and saying, "I think who you are looking for is back at the compound, but—"

"Shut up!" is screaming the first one. Then she is turning to me, but before she is saying any more thing, I am moving from corpse to corpse and picking up gun and knife and ammunition clips and putting them in my pocket. And this girl is saying thing like more people are coming to get us and that police compound is many kilometers away, but none of this is meaning anything to me.

Then Uzodinma is seeing me, and I am stopping collecting weapons.

I have to go back, I am telling him, and he is seeing not just Ify as I last saw her, at Kufena Hills, but Ify as she is always appearing in my rememberings. Ify as little girl, Ify as older girl, so many different Ifys, and I am feeling in my body that I am loving all of them, and I need to know why. All of this, I am saying to Uzo when I am saying, *I have to go back.*

Instead of Uzodinma saying word to me, he is showing me image and recording of all of us being together in the forest. He is showing footage of some of us sitting down and finding peace or climbing tree or playing game and giggling or teaching each other thing. It is taking me several second before I am understanding what he is saying. *I have to protect them*, he is telling me. And it is not until now that I am looking at him like leader. But they are not calling him Commandant. They are calling him Uzo and sometime they are calling him Commandant, and I am wishing that when I am being child of war, I am having Uzodinma with me, because then maybe I am feeling less alone.

But I am saying, *Protect them*, and then I am realizing that this might be the last time I am seeing Uzodinma. I am having rememberings in me of people when they are to be parting and they are hugging, so I am going to Uzodinma and even though there is rifle and knife in my hands, I am hugging him. I am not caring that we are looking strange to the people watching, because I am feeling love for Uzodinma and I am wanting him to know I am feeling this thing.

Then I am running away.

■ ■ ■ ■ ■

I am running, and while I am running I am aiming and shooting. And I am hitting tires of jeeps, and they are swerving back and forth and skidding and making screeching noise, and as they are toppling, I am leaping over them and climbing over them and running back to the police station. And in the beginning I am not knowing why I am doing this, but then I am seeing in my mind eye the last face I am seeing before they are putting me in van. I am seeing face of Ify.

I am running into cloud of smoke that is covering everything and I am shooting and shooting and jumping, and immediately after I am jumping through hole in wall, I am falling falling falling onto railing and I am seeing that there is being prison underneath top floor of police station.

There is being chaos all around me and I am hearing alarm bell wailing and there is being smoke everywhere and people are coughing but there is fighting so much fighting. All of the cell are being open, and the prisoner is fighting with the soldier and police who is guarding them, and there is water flooding into place because building is trying to put out fire inside itself.

Rock is falling from above, and I am seeing hole in ceiling that is showing upper level of police station.

I am finding soldier and police behind me and they are chasing me, but I am running to them and jumping and climbing on them so I am reaching up to catch wire that is hanging down from ceiling, and I am climbing fast fast because ceiling is cracking and piece are falling. I am swinging myself up onto main floor and is more blood and bodies here but there is light from sun, and I am in hallway and down hallway I am seeing pile of rubble, and under the rubble is being Ify. She is being covered in dust like snow and is not moving but I am seeing that her vital sign are still showing themself to me, even though they are being lower than normal.

As I am beginning to be running to her, something is grabbing my arm and twirling me around. It is girl from forest with bandana wrapping around her face.

"Come with me," she is hissing.

"No!" I try to break free, but she is not letting me, so I am hitting her wrist and trying to break it, then I am shifting my feet to be with my back to her, and I am flipping her over me and slamming her on the ground. Then I am leaping over her and running, but I am not getting far before something is wrapping around my leg, and I am flipping myself so rope is not catching both of my leg, and I am flinging elastic rope away from me and spinning and running to Ify, who is being trapped under big big stone.

Just as I am reaching her, girl is landing in front of me. Same as last time.

She is striking me, but I am blocking and escaping her striking and she is holding collar in her hand, and I am thinking that she is enemy who is pretending to be being friend because she was not waving collar before but now she is flicking wrist trying to get it onto me as I am hitting her and she is hitting me. Whenever I am nearly escaping her and running to Ify, she is grabbing me and twisting or throwing me away. I try to hit her, but she is grabbing me by my throat and she is too strong to be red-blood and she is raising me in the air then slamming me on the ground and I am seeing static, then Ify's face, then static. And I am trying to move but something in me is broken. Then I am feeling cold metal of collar around my neck and I am angering and sadding more than I am ever doing in my life, and I am wanting to be killing this person who is disabling me and who is now tying my ankles and wrists with electric rope and is carrying me on her shoulder away from the police station and the katakata and the girl who is knowing the answer to every question inside me.

"Ify!" I am screaming. My throat is paining me because I am not often using it, but I am not caring for how words and sounds are scratching like knives inside of it. "Ify!" I scream and it is paining me and I am screaming and screaming and water is falling from my eye.

■ ■ ■ ■ ■

When I am waking up, there is bag over my head. I am knowing that is darkness surrounding me but it is not darkness of room without light or darkness of night sky with few few star. I know this is different darkness because I am seeing through the cloth even though there is still being collar around my neck and it is keeping me from seeing with all of my eye.

Then bag is coming off my face and I am seeing we are in cave and I am the only one that is being bound with metal.

I am looking for my siblings and I am seeing them sitting or standing and some of them are crouching at the mouth of the cave we are in. And it is raining outside so that waterfall is coming over cave's mouth, and I am blinking and trying to learn this place.

What is happening?

Girl who is kidnapping me and keeping me from Ify is appearing in front of me and kneeling and undoing the restraint on my wrist. Before I am even thinking, I am wrapping my fingers around her throat. Her leg is buckling beneath me, and she is going limp and she is not resisting me and blood is pumping in my ears so loud I am not hearing anything else.

Until I am hearing footstep that is being soft and heavy at the same time. Like thing that is made of metal but is also light and playing in the grass and giggling sometime like child. I am turning and the others are coming through with girl from the forest who is telling girl I am now choking to shut up.

They are passing through the water that is falling at the mouth of the cave so that when they are stepping inside the cave the sound is even more real to me. I forget the girl in my hands when I see Oluwale in the group. I count them and it is almost all of us. Then I see him.

Uzodinma.

But then I am seeing behind him another person. And I am saying no because I am not believing it. And water curtain is parting, and they walk in until they are filling much of the space near the cave's mouth.

"Xifeng," I am saying.

She is looking up at me. Her hair is being longer and it is shining more silver and it is coming in waves over her face, but when she is looking at me, her eyes thin with joy. "Uzo." Then she is saying to me in Taishanese, "Welcome back, my daughter."

And I am running and jumping into Xifeng's arms, and I am holding her with arms strong enough to crush her, but she is not worrying. She is holding me and knowing that even though I am once being child of war I am being gentle, and she is bringing me close and squeezing her arms around my neck, and I am wanting to tell her everything that is happening to me.

I am wanting to tell her that Ify is alive.

CHAPTER
27

Beeping. It seems as though that is the only sound in Ify's universe. Like there was always beeping and there always will be beeping. The exact same note beating a metronome. Like background noise. The beeping is what she notices first. When her eyes open, they take in the pristine white ceiling, then the end of her bed, which, with tech she can only guess at, rests suspended above the ground. To her left is a bag filled with torn and dusty and burnt clothing. Including the bodysuit Ify had worn from space. Raising her arm reveals another black bodysuit beneath her hospital gown. It doesn't have the familiar feel of her own, and it certainly won't connect to her Augment and link with wireless networks so that her entire body is connected without her being cyberized, but it's better than being naked. Barely.

She tries to connect to the building's network, out of habit, but finds her way blocked. This thing is just another piece of clothing. She feels her temple. Her Whistle is gone. It's probably somewhere in the bag. Or maybe there's a tabletop somewhere in this room with a tiny bag on it containing her Augment. When she tries to turn her body onto her side, she feels the helmet on her head. It holds her head in place for the most part, and when she feels around it with her hand, she can find no groove or button to disengage it. Which means she's stuck until a nurse can come to free her.

She relaxes, lets her muscles loosen and her body melt further into the depths of the mattress. If her clothing isn't customized for her, then at least this bed seems to listen to her body.

When she tries to remember what happened before she woke up here, she catches only snatches of memory. Like bursts of static. But each shard of memory reveals only chaos. Shouting, an explosion of colors . . .

Explosion.

She sees it in her head, the desk with its attendant and his bowl of chin-chin. She remembers him being rude. Or maybe she was simply impatient with him. She remembers they spoke and Ify had made a commotion. Everyone stops. That's why she remembers that moment. Almost like the hush of calm before the storm hits. She'd embarrassed herself, everyone had turned to watch, then the sounds of warfare.

Feeling her arms, her wrists, fingers, chest, ribs, she can find no holes. Even her face is without scars, from what her fingers tell her. They must have put her in a healing bath.

Bit by bit, she pieces together what led her to here.

But why was she in that police station? What was she doing there?

Panic starts to rise like ocean water sweeping her under, but she closes her eyes tight and tries to reclaim that looseness she'd felt earlier, that calm, that assurance that wherever she was headed, she was facing the right direction. Panic won't help her now.

The door to her near-featureless room whisks open. Two men

in slim black kaftans enter, moving with the efficient grace of cyberized law enforcement. Ify sees no weapons on them, but that likely means that their bodies have been outfitted for whatever they would need to do should they encounter a threat. Their faces aren't too wrinkled or too smooth. Ify judges them safely middle-aged at first, but they carry an agelessness about them in the smoothness of their movements combined with the learned stare of practiced interrogators—so that Ify is no longer sure. They could be just a few years older than her. They could be almost a century older. In those bodies, wearing those uniforms with those manufactured faces, she can hardly tell the difference.

They arrive at her bedside but stand in such a way that they block her view of the door. Hardly a mistake on their part. Certainly not an innocuous maneuver. They know what they're doing.

Ify remains alert, even as she settles deeper into the bed and adopts a pose of comfort. She fights to keep the wry grin from her face.

First the police who came for Grace, now this. They always seem to come in twos. *Grace!* Ify's heart rate spikes at the thought of her missing assistant. A man's voice, however, snatches her back to the present.

"Madame Diallo," the first officer says in a deep, melodic voice. "We are pleased to see your recovery proceeding."

Ify arches an eyebrow at him, as though to say, *Get on with it*.

"Your body was recovered at a police station in Kaduna State, the site of the terrorist attack. Your business at the police station in Zaria Local Government Area?"

"Excuse me?"

"We would like to know what you were doing at the Zaria Local Government Area police station at the time of the explosion."

Ify snorts and looks away, pretending to be annoyed. Explosion. Terrorist attack. A few more puzzle pieces fit into place. "I was speaking with a desk attendant."

"We have attempted to recover the logs containing your conversation, but the material was damaged during the initial explosion. The contents of the desk attendant's braincase have proven to be . . . irretrievable."

"He's dead, then." The weight of what Ify has survived begins to seep into her, begins to make her feel heavier in her bed. Questions swarm. Was she a target? What did this have to do with the little girl? The little girl she was looking for, the one who had called her Ify, who had been so sure that Ify was who she had been looking for. Even though Ify had never seen her before in her entire life. "And you could not recover the information from my logs?"

The first officer speaks again. "You are not sufficiently cyberized for such an operation. And your Augments were damaged in the blast."

The second rushes in, more polite. "We would have needed your permission to access the logs, madame. Were we able to recover them in the first place."

After a beat, Ify says, "Certainly."

"Now," continues the first, "your business at the police station in Zaria Local Government Area?"

She searches for an answer until one lands squarely in her lap. "Part of my investigation."

When she doesn't continue, they stare, both of them, with unrelenting expressionlessness.

"I am on a fact-finding mission launched by Alabast Central Space Colony. Much of our refugee population is afflicted with an illness, and I am in the process of researching its causes and, hopefully, its potential cure. I was in the course of this investigation when the police station was attacked." She realizes something. Her minders. Her eyes shoot open, and she looks to the men standing over her bed.

They do not open their mouths, but Ify can tell from the expression on their faces that her minders are dead. They must have been standing right by the entrance when the bomb went off. They would have been caught in it immediately. Torn to shreds. No part of their form recoverable. She wishes she hadn't been so dismissive of them, so intent on reminding them at every opportunity that she was their superior.

"I was conducting field research in Kaduna State and thought I might find some of the information I was looking for at the police station. Perhaps there was someone there who could offer some insight into . . . into the problem I was facing."

"Did you speak to anyone other than the desk attendant?" the first asks.

Ify shakes her head. "No. Only him."

A moment of silence passes between them before the second one says, "When you are released, please come and contact us regarding your stay in Nigeria. We want to make sure it is as smooth and pleasing as possible." His words do not match his tone. He sounds like a tree trying to give a hug. Then they turn to leave.

Ify is about to ask how she is to contact them, then thinks better of it. They have probably been following her since her arrival in Abuja. Every set of eyes in this country is capable of telling the government where she is at any given moment. If they need to find her, they will.

It's only now that she begins to let misgivings fill her. It was easy, when she was a Sentinel in another life and part of Nigeria's security apparatus, to let herself be part of the country's extensive surveillance network, to let herself be watched. Everyone was always being watched. If you were connected, your every thought or conversation or purchase was seen. The surveillance orbs that hung overhead tracked every citizen's movements. At the time, Ify thought nothing of it. It had simply been a part of the world. It was understood that this meant peace. But as Ify sits in her hospital bed, thinking over this encounter with the Nigerian security service, she can't help but think that all of this didn't mean peace; it meant order— something else entirely.

With the men gone, she turns her gaze to the ceiling. Her arms begin to tremble. Her bottom lip quivers. Only now that she has let her guard down does the severity of it all come crashing into her. The concussive wave from the explosion, the fear that had enveloped her, the pain that had wrapped itself around her entire body just before her world had gone black. All of it comes rushing back into her in a tsunami of sensation. She closes her eyes, but that just makes her see it all more clearly. The wood paneling of the desk in front of her, the scuff marks of boots on the tiled floor, the spiderweb in the arch above a hallway, the face of the desk attendant in that moment when he was just starting to come out of his boredom. Then bedlam.

Suddenly, she's a little girl again. A refugee child in a new, faraway place, a glistening white Space Colony where she knows no one and the only thing she wants is to see her sister, Onyii, again. Tears stream down the sides of her face. She grips the bedsheet in her fists. This feeling she's kept at bay for so long, smothered and bottled up and stored in a dark corner of her mind, out of sight, out of reach, it's all back, and she lets herself swim in it because she knows that she can only build a wall so high. Eventually, the floodwaters will beat her and break the dam. She finds small comfort in the fact that she was able to hold out until the men left before shock from the attack melted away.

The sobs slow and become softer. She sniffles. A mechanical arm from above descends, holding a bouquet of wipes, and she cleans her face, then tosses the tissues into a wastebucket that rises from the floor next to her.

The door swings open, and a blur of white rushes to Ify's bedside, burying her face in Ify's bedsheets. "Ify, I found you!" says the muffled voice. Grace's voice. "Thank God." When Grace breaks away, Ify sees tears and snot over Grace's face, and the mechanical arm descends from above Ify's head to dangle wipes between them, insistent. To which both Ify and Grace laugh.

Grace cleans her face but keeps her body close to Ify's, as though to let any more distance come between them is to risk separation like the one they just endured. "I saw from the car. I saw you walk in. Then, when it seemed like you were taking a long time, the guards went in after you. Then the explosion, and . . ."

"I'm all right," Ify says quietly, smoothing the wrinkles out of Grace's sleeves. She notes that her assistant's face and part of her clothes are still marred with soot. And her eyes are bloodshot.

Her hands tremble from adrenaline. She hasn't slept. "When I get out of here—"

A shadow passes by her door, then it slides open.

Ify frowns at the nurse who walks in. The uniform doesn't fit. The pantlegs are too long. The sleeves cling to muscled arms. Loose braids are poorly stuffed into the cap that sits on her head. And she moves too fast. The look she gives Grace is almost a glare.

"You have to leave."

Ify raises a hand to the nurse. "No, she stays. She's my—"

"I don't care if she is your shadow. She must leave. Now."

Ify rises on her elbows to protest further, but Grace stands to her full height and nods reassurance at Ify, a nod that tells her she'll be back.

"It's okay," Grace says before leaving. The door whispers shut behind her.

Without a word, the nurse is behind Ify, out of her line of sight, and Ify can hear fingers fast at work, disconnecting the wires from her helmet.

"Wait, what are you do—" The helmet comes loose. She tries to sit up, but dizziness pins her back into the mattress. "What's going on?"

The nurse has her head bowed as she works, first settling the helmet in place behind Ify, then pulling something out from under Ify's bed that folds out into a hovering stretcher. "We don't have much time. I need you to do exactly as I say."

"No. Tell me what's happening."

The nurse looks Ify in the face, and that's when Ify notices the scars. Tribal marks but also other brandings. There's no order to them; those came at a later date. The doctor in Ify notes the way the tissue has reformed, the jagged edges. Their shapes speak to her. They tell her that these scars didn't come from marking ceremonies. They came from bullets and knives and shrapnel. Ify realizes with a start that this is the very first face she's seen since arriving that feels like it belongs to a previous time, a period in Nigeria when there was war, a period in time that holds the secrets she's been looking for. This nurse is a veteran.

"Who are you?"

The nurse raises the stretcher. "My name is Ngozi. I don't have time to tell you more. The secret police will be back, and when they return, there will be nothing I can do to save you."

"Save me? Save me from what?"

"From having your memories erased."

Ify shakes her head and instantly regrets it. "What? Why? What are you talking about?"

"Your name is Ifeoma Diallo. You served as an aide to mobile pilot Shehu Daren Suleiman Sékou Diallo of the Nigerian Armed Forces Mobile Defense Unit. Before that, you lived with the Biafrans in the secessionist republic. And after the ceasefire was broken, you were sent to the Space Colonies, where you were successfully granted asylum."

Shock paralyzes Ify. "How do you . . ."

"I served in the war with your sister, Onyii. That is all I can say for now. And if you don't get on this stretcher right this instant and let me get you out of here, the men who came here earlier will return and remove every single memory of Onyii that you possess."

CHAPTER
28

We are all of us sitting in semicircle while Xifeng is in front of us with large cave wall behind her. There are some of the girls who attacked the police station with us and they are sprinkling themself throughout us so that red-blood and Augment and child of war is all sitting together. And some of the red-blood is drinking palm wine to be staying warm but also because they are thinking it is tasting good. But we are all looking to Xifeng like she is leader of us all. Something inside me is wanting to be calling her Commandant, then I remember that Commandant is making me to be killing and maiming and shooting gun, and Xifeng is making me to be doing none of these thing. I am wanting to be calling her Father, but person I am calling Father is also making me to be killing and maiming and shooting gun. Xifeng is making me to be doing none of these thing. So I am searching in my rememberings and looking for someone who is doing what Xifeng is doing now, which is tell story in soft voice almost like she is singing. It is story of her family, and she is saying it with thing in her voice that I am knowing is love. And I am looking in my remembering for other person who is doing this thing, and people are calling her Mother, so when I am looking to Xifeng, I am calling her Mother too.

"It started with an application on her phone," Xifeng is saying. "Long ago, in ancient times, before mass net connectivity, people used their mobile phones to communicate. They were devices the size of my palm." She holds up her left hand and points to her lined palm. "And everything that you can do"— she points to the children of war—"these phones could do. This woman's name was Meryem. On her phone were a number of applications, and what they allowed her to do was share. She loved to take pictures of her children"—Xifeng mimes using an old digital camera—"to send to her friends and family. She would send a picture, and next to the picture—or beneath it, depending on the phone—she would attach an emoji." Xifeng pushes a button on the Augment wrapped around her wrist and connected to the Bonder at her temples, and a blue hologram of a crude yellow face rises from her palm. First, it is smiling, then it is frowning, then it is winking, then it is winking and sticking its tongue out, then it is opening its mouth like it is scared, then it is sadding, and the face is changing and changing and Xifeng is showing us this thing, and some of the girl that is with us is laughing while other is having face like stone. Xifeng presses the button, and the hologram disappears. "She would send these pictures of her children most of all to her husband, who often traveled for work. They lived in Xinjiang, an oasis in the northwest of Earthland China, and theirs was a lovely and simple life.

"Then Meryem downloaded WeChat. It allowed her to send these pictures to even more people using her phone. Now she could show pictures of her children to all those relatives scattered across the globe.

"What people like Meryem all over the world did not realize was that these applications—these things on your phone—were watching you. So when Meryem downloaded WeChat, rumors began to circulate that the Earthland Chinese government was using the application to watch its citizens, specifically Uyghur Muslims like Meryem.

"Then the police began to visit the office of Meryem's husband. Then they began to visit the schools of her children and her friends' children. Then they came to visit Meryem's house. Her husband shaved his beard. Meryem stopped wearing her hijab when outside."

I am seeing among the girls that some of them are Hausa. None of them are hijabi, but I am seeing from the way their body is changing when Xifeng is telling this story that they are hearing a familiar story here.

"Their friends stopped communicating with them. She had no one to share pictures of her children with. Her children had grown withdrawn. They no longer wanted to leave the house, because police were always waiting for them outside their school. It continued like this until Meryem's husband decided to move the family to Turkey, where others like them, Uyghur Muslims, had made lives for themselves. He decided to send her first while he waited for their children's passports to be approved. On the day she left, he was arrested. When she arrived in Turkey, her phone stopped working." The hologram of a phone reappears, and the once-glowing screen snaps to black. Dead. "By the time she had the phone repaired, everyone had deleted her from their WeChat contacts. They feared she was contagious. Like a disease. If the government could do this to her, maybe it would punish them for communicating with her."

I am knowing that some of the girls here are red-bloods, but none of them is making to go to the bathroom or to eat something. All of their attention is focused on Xifeng and her story.

"Others like Meryem arrived in Turkey. Women who had escaped while their husbands were trapped in Xinjiang. They were called the Widows because they did not know if their husbands were dead, alive, still in prison. They had no way of knowing. So they banded together, to protect themselves." Xifeng is looking at all of us—child of war and red-blood—and smiling like she is talking about the women in her story but all of us too, and I am beginning to lose myself in the story, looking for pieces of myself in it. I am thinking this is how Xifeng is having power over us, how she is being able to tell us to do things. She is giving us purpose, but she is also showing how we are being connected. Not connected like knowing what the other person is thinking or being able to hack into satellite but connected like sharing heart. Like how I am feeling with other child of war. "The Widows shared apartments. They helped each other attain jobs as seamstresses and tailors, making clothes for other people.

"Some of the women still spoke with their families, but the messages became shorter and shorter. A brother would say, 'We're okay. Safe,' then the Widow would hear nothing for months. Others spoke in code. If someone was arrested, the other person would say that they had been 'admitted to the hospital.' Then they only spoke in emojis." And here, Xifeng presses a button on her wrist again, but instead of seeing changing faces, we are seeing rose. "A half-fallen rose for when someone was arrested. A dark moon to say that someone had been sent to the camps. A sun emoji meant 'I am alive.' A flower: 'I have been released.'

"The Widows used another app to stay in touch—WhatsApp—and they would share whatever information came through. One day, someone shared video of a group of children running around in a room and shouting, *Bizi! Bizi! Bizi!*" She is saying it like she is one of the children, and it is making some of us to be smiling. "Meryem's breath stopped in her chest. In the video, among the children, was her daughter, Nur. That video was the last time Meryem would hear her daughter's laugh. They never saw each other again."

For a long time, Xifeng is saying nothing. And we are stirring and wanting her to be continuing, and that is when I am seeing that she is shaking small small. She is keeping herself from crying. When she raises her head, there is being metal in her voice again.

"Nur and her siblings were scattered all over Earthland China. Nur was brought to the other end of her country: from the northwest to the southeast. She no longer spoke her native language. She no longer identified as Muslim. All of her past was stripped away. She began speaking Cantonese and Taishanese. And before long, she forgot her family altogether."

My heart is speeding up because I am suddenly knowing what Xifeng is going to be saying and it is like light is shining in my head. Xifeng is revealing herself to me. She is no longer being mystery. Xifeng stands, and now she is looking like leader. Now she is looking like commander of army. Looking at her, I know I will be doing everything I can for her.

"That girl grew up to be my grandmother. And what the Chinese government did to her and her family all those years ago, the Nigerian government is doing to families all over Nigeria right now." She is pointing into the distance, past the walls that are surrounding us. "In the north, in Borno State, is a facility where the government is forcing cyberization on its citizens. And it is using this process to erase all memory of the war. The war that each one of you"—now she is pointing at us, at me—"fought and bled in. The government is trying to erase all memory of you. But we cannot allow that to happen. We are going to take that facility. And we are going to spread this truth. This country will know who you are. They will remember us."

Xifeng is looking at me when she is saying this last thing. I am not understanding everything she is saying, but I am wanting to be following her everywhere and doing what she is telling me to do. Even hurting and killing.

CHAPTER
29

Ngozi is in the middle of helping Ify out of bed and into a hovering stretcher when the door slides open and Grace, face buried in her tablet, walks back in. She breaks off mid-sentence when she sees what's happening. But an instant later, Ngozi flicks a shockstick from out of the sleeve of her hospital blouse and cracks Grace across the face, knocking her unconscious.

Even though vertigo threatens to pitch her over, Ify is on her feet. "What did you do?" she shouts. It occurs to Ify that this woman is trying to kidnap her, not help her. She fishes around for anything she can use as a weapon. Finding nothing, she backs away. "Get out or I'll shout."

Suddenly, too fast for Ify to see, the woman is on her, hand clasped over Ify's nose and mouth, shockstick sizzling perilously close to Ify's eye. "Scream and I will blind you. I'm supposed to keep you alive, not in one piece. You are coming with me one way or another. You will not want to find out what happens when they come for you here." A pause. "I'm going to lift my hand now. Make a sound, and I will knock you out and haul you out of here on my shoulder. Understood?"

Ify manages a nod.

Slowly, Ngozi pulls her hand away. Ify exhales. The sight of Grace's prone form, with the wound on her head leaking onto the floor, pulls at Ify.

"We can't leave her."

"Why not." It is a statement, not a question.

"Don't leave her. Please."

Ngozi glares at Ify, then peeks her head out into the hallway and says something Ify can't hear. Another woman—this one dressed as some sort of lab technician in a blue jumpsuit—comes in and tosses Grace's body over her shoulder, then vanishes. Ngozi looks back to Ify as if to say, *Happy?* Then she gestures at the stretcher. "Get on."

Ify does as ordered, and a moment later, they're out in the hallway, Grace in a hoverchair behind them, pushed forward by an attendant.

As soon as they leave the room, Ify notices the differences in the atmosphere. She notices which nurses and hospital personnel only try to look the part, those who don't fit all the way into their disguises. She notices how they position themselves in the hallway, some of them ready to run interference should the need arise, some of them making sure every available entrance and exit is within their sightlines to take on enemies. There's an operation under way, and she's at the center of it.

Outside a back entrance, she and Grace are loaded into a MedTransport that only goes a short distance before, suddenly, the van stops and masked people with pistols at their hips snatch Ify from the stretcher. One of them fits cloth tightly around her eyes, then seals it with a tinted visor. Someone else attaches beads to her temple that instantly block out all sound. Another binds her wrists in front of her with zip ties that automatically slam her fists together. Then she's bundled into what she thinks is the back of another van. Though she can see and hear nothing, she feels every bump in the road, every sharp turn, every time something thwacks against the vehicle's frame. Unable to perceive her surroundings, she has no idea how much time has passed. A familiar feeling creeps into her, the claustrophobia that suffocated her when she was once a prisoner of war held in a cell she could walk across in three steps. She fights the feeling. These people aren't going to kill her. They've rescued her. There's the possibility that she's been lied to, that the men in the black kaftans and with the false faces were there to protect her from exactly the kind of people that have Ify trussed up in the back of a van. But Ify has no choice now. She's in the hands of this Ngozi. Who invoked Onyii's name. A name Ify hasn't heard in nearly five years. Once she'd adjusted and began her new life, Ify had hoped never to hear that name again. She realizes she still hasn't forgiven Onyii for abandoning her all those years ago. She's gone through every possible scenario in her head, tried to reason through every possible rationale that Onyii could have had for leaving her like that. And they've all failed in the face of Ify's logic. Back then, she'd wanted nothing more than to see her sister again, to hear her voice, to be held in her arms. When it became clear to Ify that Onyii was never going to come, Ify had done everything in her power to purge Onyii from her mind, to leave her behind, to craft a new self that would never need someone as desperately as she had once needed Onyii.

Is this what Céline had meant? *Are you avoiding a solution because you have to walk through some pain to get there?* Céline had asked.

That's when Ify determines that she will follow this path wherever it leads. If it means a cure for the refugee children in Alabast, then she will do this. Enough resisting. The detention center, that girl who had embraced her, Onyii. So far, Ify has been pushing all of these things apart in her mind, only willing to deal with each thing as it arose. But maybe they're all connected.

The van stops. No one removes the sound blockers or the glasses or the bag from Ify. Instead, they pull her out of the vehicle. She stumbles over roots and giant leaves and nearly runs into the person leading her when they stop.

Through the bag, a breeze brushes Ify's cheeks. Then, her wrists are freed. Bit by bit, her makeshift cage is dismantled. The sound blockers, the glasses, the bag.

When Ify's eyes adjust, she finds herself near a cliff's edge. Scrub dots the outcropping, which looks like a giant beak. Ngozi puts the retractable restraints in her knapsack, then turns to head toward the outcropping. Even from this distance, Ify can see a sniper rifle positioned near the cliff's edge, along with padding to provide comfort for someone who expects to occupy that post for a very long time. If Ify squints, she thinks she even spots the leftover wrappers of used steroid packets. She's about to ask where Grace is when her assistant emerges from the forest behind her.

"Bathroom," Grace says before gingerly touching the sealed forehead wound. It looks like someone applied defective MeTro sealant, because a trace of the wound still remains, and it's clear to Ify that the pain lingers too. "Where are we?"

Ify looks around, squinting. She feels her temple, but her Whistle isn't there. And she has no way of connecting to her bodysuit to activate any of its functionality. It's as though everything that allowed her contact with the outside world has been turned off. "I don't know."

Ngozi packs up her rifle, hefts the shortened thing against her shoulder, and heads back in their direction. "Follow me," she says, leading them deep into the forest. Fireflies blink their bodies at them. The sounds here have different texture. The crickets chirping, owls hooting, even the occasional faraway grunt of a shorthorn. Something subterranean in her stirs, and sensations swim back and forth behind her eyes: the smell of rain-turned soil, the lowing of half-mech beasts, the spray of water in a greenhouse. The camp. The camp where Onyii had raised her as a Biafran War Girl, where Onyii and the others had meticulously built the lie that Ify was one of them, that she belonged on their side of the war. *Why does this place remind me of that camp?*

"Watch out for the wulfu," Ngozi cautions without lowering her voice. "The babies may not have teeth, but their claws grow early. And they'll tear their food apart with their paws just to make it chewable."

Grace blanches, but then Ify realizes why the sounds and smells of this place are so evocative. They're real. She'd spent so long in Alabast, among false sounds and false light and false smells, that she'd forgotten what real animals sounded like, what real night felt like on your skin.

A rusted van awaits them. At first, Ify doesn't see it, blanketed as it is by giant red and dark green leaves. But Ngozi yanks open the back door and gestures for Ify and Grace to get in. Grace is first to head into the darkness, but she spares a tight, warning glance at Ngozi before climbing in. Ify follows. Then

Ngozi enters, pulling the doors closed behind them.

It feels like a different age, without the ever-present hum of always being connected. Without the hum against her body of her bodysuit at work, regulating her temperature, checking her vital signs, beaming her location to whoever needed to know. She winces at that last.

"Don't try connecting anywhere," Ngozi says, lying on a bed of pillows with her rifle draped across her body, as though she's reading Ify's thoughts, even though she's staring at Grace when she says it. "All your electronics have been deactivated. EMPs." Electromagnetic pulses. "Otherwise, the government's gonna be able to track you. Which gets us all in trouble."

A quick glance at Grace tells Ify that they're both trying to figure out which question to ask first.

Ngozi stares at Ify. Squints a little bit like she's measuring the face before her against some old, fuzzy holograph. "She never told us about you," Ngozi says suddenly.

Breath leaves Ify's lungs. "Sh-she?" Ify manages to say at last. But Ify knows there's only one person Ngozi could be talking about. Onyii.

Ngozi shakes her head. "Never told us a single thing. To be honest, I don't know what she'd make of you now." She gestures with her hand to indicate the entirety of Ify, not just her outfit, Ify feels, but her carriage, her voice, the way she takes up space. The fact that she is a Colonial official. "It's clear that you are just as smart as others have said."

"Why did you bring me here?" Her patience is running thin. She welcomes the new hardness in her voice.

"Like I told you in the hospital, they were going to erase your memory."

"Who's 'they'? And why would they perform an invasive operation on a Colonial official without consent?"

Ngozi snorts. "Is that how they talk up there?" She raises a finger lazily, pointing at a place worlds away. And Ify realizes in that moment just how far she is from home. She wants to tell this woman to answer the question, but the memory of her minders dying is still fresh and she can't bring herself to issue commands. So instead, she lets the emotion play on her face. *Please*, she asks with her eyes. So Ngozi says, "They deemed you a contagion risk. I'm sure they were tracking your movements as soon as you arrived in Nigeria. We found you only because they were looking. And they would have gotten to you had we not lucked into your location at that police station."

"You were there?"

Ngozi nods. Then she asks, "What are you doing here?"

Ify considers lying, but at this point she doesn't know what she should hold back, so she sighs. "I'm a medical professional in Alabast Central. I oversee the refugee ward. Recently, the children under my care have become ill. Each of them has fallen into a coma. Identical symptoms. We tried to figure out what was wrong, but we found no answers."

"And why does that bring you here?"

"The majority of those who took ill were Nigerian. My superiors thought it appropriate that I be sent to investigate."

Ngozi lets out another derisive snort. "Like we are bringing them plague."

No, not like that, Ify wants to tell her, but she knows Ngozi's not entirely wrong in thinking that this was the reasoning of her supervisors. "I just want to find out what's happening to them."

"It makes sense why the government is after you, then. You are breaking the law. Or you will be very soon."

"Why? What are you talking about?"

"It is against the law to speak openly about the war. It is against the law to document it, to write about it, to reference it, even to think about it." She pauses to let the notion sink into Ify and Grace.

Grace stares at her hands, then looks up at Ify. "The police attack."

Ify nods grimly.

"When you arrived, did you see any memorials? Any tombs or gravemarkers?"

Ify shakes her head. "No." Then she remembers how much it had unnerved her that she had seen no commemoration whatsoever of the war she had lived through. "No, there was . . ."

"There was nothing." Ngozi uses one bootheel to itch the other calf. "Just some story about a Nine-Year Storm, I bet."

"Yes," Ify says, her voice drained of energy.

Quiet fills the back of the van. Then the grunt of a large animal whose pelt fills the window, blocking their view of the fireflies and the leaves swaying in the night wind. The van rocks back and forth, and Grace scrambles for purchase, but Ngozi only closes her eyes like she's being lulled to sleep. Eventually, the large animal stops nudging the van and trudges onward. Ify looks at Grace and almost wants to chuckle at her assistant's terror. But she also wants to tell her it'll be okay. An almost overwhelming urge bubbles up in her to gently run her finger over Grace's wound and murmur something soft and loving into her hair.

She turns to Ngozi and is ready to ask her question, except

that when it finally comes to her lips, her throat closes up. Finally, she forces out, "How did you know her?"

Ngozi raises an eyebrow at Ify. "We served in the war, Onyii and I. You could call it her second tour." A morose smile spreads across Ngozi's lips. "A couple of the other sisters I served with knew Onyii from before. She'd lived in a camp that was attacked. Eventually, she made her way to us. That camp was where she raised you, wasn't it?"

It all seems too much to Ify. After so long of having first denied Onyii, then searching for any trace of her in this country she bled for and finding nothing—after all of that, to be confronted with so stark a reminder of her sister, to be told of the life she lived without Ify . . . her heart doesn't know what to do. "What was she like?" She has completely forgotten Grace.

Ngozi shrugs. "We didn't really like each other at first. She thought she'd lost more than anyone else in the war." Ngozi pauses to look at Ify and sees something that makes her face soften. "But we all loved. And the war took everything we loved away from us."

"There was someone you loved?"

Ngozi leans back, smiles at the memory. "A sister. Her name was Kesandu. Sacrificed herself so that the rest of us could escape at the end of an operation." She shifts, as though her mind is leaving the memory and returning to her body. "It was just before the ceasefire."

Ify flinches and fears that Ngozi notices. "What happened . . . after the war?"

Ngozi shifts her jaw like she's trying to stop tears. Then, for some reason, she glares at Grace before returning her gaze to Ify. "I tried to reconnect with my family. We tried to reintegrate, those of us who were left. Easier for some than for others. I was lucky. At least I had family left. But they were eager to move on. They thought they'd lost a daughter in the war. In some ways, they had. I couldn't move on. Everyone wanted to. The government, employment agencies, human rights commissions, my parents. Then the government started phasing in forced cyberization. My parents happily submitted. They couldn't wait to be a part of this new connected Nigeria."

"But you resisted." This from Grace, who has kept a posture of attention this whole time, like she's ready for Ngozi to attack her again at any moment.

"At first, we could chat by way of app. But the government used those apps to track our locations." Then a new deadness enters Ngozi's voice. "The police came to my parents multiple times. We learned quickly that it was because they were communicating with a veteran of the war everyone was in such a rush to forget. Eventually, everyone cut me off. Friends, acquaintances, cousins. By the end, the police were harassing my family so much that I left. I disconnected from everything, forced them to delete me from their contacts. All of it. I even had to delete my recordings because of the metadata." She turns her murderous look at Grace once again. "I haven't heard my mother's voice in almost five years." Ngozi's fingers curl around the barrel of her rifle. "All because of your Odoodo government."

Grace doesn't flinch. How often has she heard the slur since coming here? Odoodo. Odo odo. Yellow. Often enough to take it without showing any hurt.

"It wasn't like this before the war. Being watched all the time. Everywhere. The Chinese did this when they came with their"—she uses air quotes—"'foreign aid.'"

"I've never been to Earthland China," Grace says in a low, even voice. A voice Ify has never heard her use before.

"It was like this before the ceasefire," Ify tells Ngozi in an effort to relieve the tension. "Nigeria was already there. In Biafra, you had no clue."

Ngozi squints at Ify, as though a new piece of the puzzle has presented itself. But whatever it is that has occurred to her, she lets it go. "Because we were so backward in Biafra, of course." Before Ify can reply, Ngozi says, "You should get some rest." Without another word, she hefts the rifle, forces the back door open, then climbs out. The door slowly swings shut.

Ify pulls the blankets up to her chin and doesn't realize that she's been asleep until the muffled sound of voices reaches her. Reflexively, she reaches for her temple where her Whistle would be, but there's nothing but hair. She tries to grow as still as possible and listen.

"She would remove her leg," Ngozi is saying, her words gauzed by the van's metal walls, "because it was connected and the government could track her through it. But we would drive into the desert, and she would take off her leg and I would remove my own Augment, and we'd leave them behind in the car and I would carry her. I would carry her until we'd reached our spot, and then we would sit in the sand together and watch the sun set."

Ify strains her ears to hear what follows, then she realizes no one is speaking.

"Tell me what's happening outside." Ngozi again. "Do they know about us in the Colonies?"

Ify looks around her and sees that Grace is gone.

Then, Grace's voice. Low and soft on the other side of the

van's walls. Too quiet for Ify to know what she's saying, whether she's lying to Ngozi or not.

After a quarter of an hour, Grace climbs back in and buries herself beneath her own pile of blankets. Ify marvels at how easily her assistant is able to find sleep.

CHAPTER
30

Xifeng is making us all to wear clothing that is dampening our signal. When I am putting on this thing that is tight on my skin, it is like shadow is falling over the world. I am not being able to talk to my siblings. And I am not having so much information buzzing like one million mosquitoes in my brain. But it is giving me relief to be not always hearing and seeing everything that is happening around me. When I am putting on the signal-dampening suit, it is like someone is shutting down the noise in my head so I am hearing with ear like red-blood and seeing with eye like red-blood and even smelling with nose like red-blood.

"I am not liking this costume," Oluwale is saying next to me. "I don't like pretending to be a human."

One of the girls hears this and laughs, and this is the mood that everyone is having as Xifeng splits us into groups and sends us out on our mission. Before we are putting on suit, Xifeng sends us a map of the facility and its grid layout. There are also markings for where there is being crabtank and ground mech and even where aerial mech is patrolling. And we are having to memorize it because we cannot be accessing it in our braincases. But every child of war is being paired with one of the red-bloods who have more practice memorizing things. Girl in combat vest and with braids that is running down her back is moving close to me. My braincase is telling me that this girl is being named Binyelum, and I am knowing that this is Igbo for *stay with me*. Binyelum is fighting in war but only in later half after ceasefire and she is at first being separated from her family, but after war she is not reconnecting with them because she cannot forgive the people who ruined her family's life, the same people her family must share a neighborhood with. I am knowing these thing because of Augment that is making her eye to sometime be shining yellow, because Augment is being connected to her nervous system and other part of her body. She is connected, and she is patting me on my head like I am being her little sister.

Before we leave, Xifeng is giving us EMP and telling us where on map to go to place it, then to be moving far far from there.

And I am trying to remember this thing, even as we are going aboveground and going deep into nearby forest and climbing into our mechs and flying low over forest and abandoned countryside to Borno State, which is being far away but which we are getting to just as the sky is nighting. I am trying to remember where I am supposed to go as mech is dropping us so far from facility that it is dark shape like bug in the distance, but I am having gun in my hand, and it is feeling good to be having gun in my hand. I am seeing mech drop off other members of Xifeng's army far from us, but it is looking like we are all arriving safe, so when Binyelum is giving the signal, we are moving forward down cliff and into valley. And when we are getting closer, Binye is pulling small container from her packet and smearing cream on my face and on hers. We are doing this to be scrambling face-recognition technology. So that if cameras are seeing our faces or Augments or mechs are seeing our faces, they are not recognizing us. Our face is looking like someone else.

We are having to rest some time because Binye is red-blood and is not having legs of metal like mine and synthetic lungs like mine. And I am waiting patiently every time. But as we are getting closer, sun is beginning to rise. We are losing time.

Then I am hearing gunfire, and I am seeing one of our mech flying overhead, too close overhead, and it is taking bullet like PINGPINGPINGPING until it is bursting into flames. I am seeing it like it is moving in slow motion, and dread is building inside me until it crashes into building with curving glass ceiling and explodes, and suddenly everywhere is gunfire and explosion. Instantly, I am feeling more at home.

"Oh no," Binye murmurs next to me.

Suddenly, she is finding new energy and we are running. She is in front and directing me, and we are both crouching low and moving fast while ground mech is shooting in every direction. I am hearing FWOOMP and knowing from my rememberings that this grenade is coming. I am holding Binye by her belt and then tugging her to the side, and we are both falling against wall of other building just before ground where we are running before is exploding in big big cloud of dirt and fire.

I hold my hand out to her. "Give me the EMP."

"You know where to go?" she asks me.

I nod.

"Give me your gun," she tells me, smiling. There is blood coming down her face from wounding in her forehead, but she is smiling. "I'll cover you."

She jumps from shadow where we are both hiding and shoots at nearby soldier and is killing him instantly. Then she is moving forward and crabtank is turning toward her and firing big big bullet that is tearing apart the earth, and she is running fast fast until she is finding cover behind stone barrier.

"Go!" she is shouting.

And I am remembering that I am having EMP in my hands and then I am running. I am calling map up in my head, then remembering that I am wearing signal dampener. So I am trying to remember my step as I am tracing them on map. Left here, right. Down alley between big, long buildings with glass ceiling. But some thing is moved around and some of the mech are in different places because we are already attacking. And I am wishing that I could connect with my siblings so I can feel what they feel and see what they see and hear what they hear. I need to know where they are so I can be protecting.

Explosion is throwing me into the air, and I am angering because I am letting myself get distracted. When I land on the ground, something inside me is snapping but it is not paining me. I raise my hand and it is covered in oil, but EMP is gone. It is on a timed release, and if I am not getting to where I need to be in time, whole plan is failing.

I am turning and in front of me is stone barrier with dead guard draped over it and rifle hanging from his fingers. Behind me is pathway between two large building that is having special marking that I am recognizing from map. But on the other side is crabtank that is many many many times taller than me. I am glancing behind me and then hearing nothing but BUDUBUDUBUDUBUDUBUDUBUDU for long time until then I hear gun barrel rotating. Dead soldier is wearing helmet with visor, and I am quickly pulling body to me. But anytime I am making move, crabtank is shooting BUDUBUDUBUDUBUDU, but I am grabbing soldier and pulling visor off his helmet and wiping blood and soot and dirt from it so that it is shining my face back at me.

BUDUBUDUBUDUBUDUBUDU.

Stone barrier is falling apart behind me. Before long, I am having no cover.

Using helmet visor, I am seeing that EMP is halfway between me and alley that crabtank is guarding. Even though I am having gun in my hands, I am not knowing what to do because I am not moving fast enough to avoid big bullet from crabtank. Then I am seeing belt on dead soldier. Two grenades. Fast fast, I take them from the belt and activate them, then throw them over me. I hear BUDUBUDUBUDU then BOOOOOOOOOOOOOOM and ground shaking and glass breaking, and then I am running and through the smoke, I am snatching EMP from the ground, but then I am hearing gun barrel rotating like crabtank is getting ready to fire, and time is slowing and smoke is clearing and gun barrel is pointing at me and I am thinking this is how I am going to be dying and, for some reason, I am closing my eyes, then I am hearing AIYEEEEEEEE.

When I am opening my eyes again, I am seeing something so strange it is making me not to be moving.

Oluwale has two metal poles stuck in the crabtank's head and is steering it like it is shorthorn. And it is shooting all over the place while Oluwale is laughing and making battle-cry with his throat, and it is strange to me that he is doing this when he is barely using his voice before. He shouts an Igbo war song as he steers the crabtank away, against its own commands so that it trips over its own legs.

I run until I get to where I know I need to go. It is intersection of paths just like any other intersection, but I am knowing this one is special because Xifeng is marking it on map. Binyelum is waiting there for me and smiling, rifle resting against her shoulder.

A skinny black obelisk stands in the center of the intersection. It glows like blue lightning is rippling under its skin. I stick EMP to it, and Binye and I run for cover behind a building. There is all the noise and katakata of warfare, then I feel the wave from all the EMPs we put on the obelisks in the facility all at once. Like when the water under Falomo Bridge is trying to be eating us. Then there is no sound at all.

That is what Xifeng is telling us to wait for. "Wait for the silence," she is telling us before we are starting our mission. The silence of all the enemy's machines turning off at once. So when I am hearing the silence, I am taking off my signal dampener and suddenly my brain is open again and taking in all of the information and I am even hearing my brother and sister again and some of them is whooping and cheering, even as they are binding remaining guards. It is making me happy to be hearing the sound of my family again.

■ ■ ■ ■ ■

In front of me and Xifeng is wall full of pods, and in each pod is being a human being. It is like this in almost all of the buildings. Their insides are being like greenhouse where sunlight and water is being made for plants.

"This is where it happens," Xifeng is telling me.

While she is speaking, the other soldiers are going through the buildings and shutting off the pods and waking up the people that is being held in them.

"Forced cyberization." A snarl comes onto her face. "And then they wipe out the memories."

"Memories of the war," I say, to myself more than to Xifeng.

Something is stirring in me. Not a good feeling but a bad feeling like dizziness and nausea and then suddenly

metal is cold and wrapping around my wrists and my feet is dangling in the air. My neck is being stiff like tree trunk or like tree branch that is skinny because it is feeling like my head is going to be falling off of it and landing on the floor. I am turning back and forth slow, but that is the only way that my body is moving. Everything is feeling dry and stiff, even the blood that is coming from my nose and gash on my head.

It is feeling like I am waking up but I am not knowing if I am dreaming or not because when I am trying to be remembering what is happening before, I am just seeing black. Static is interrupting my seeing. It is just a moment and everything is gray and twisted and then I am seeing normal again, and I am thinking that something is broken. One of my eye is being swollen shut so even though my head is being bowed I am not really seeing what is happening to my leg that is just dangling like fruit from tree.

Light is coming into room, spilling like water. And I am hearing door opening. But it is old door because it is creaking and it is squeaking and light is suddenly everywhere and I am having to be closing my eyes against it. I am waiting to be hearing hard footstep but instead it is soft like swish swish and I am knowing this is the sound of sand. There is being sand in this room where I am hanging. And I am hearing sizzling too and knowing that something is burning even if I am not smelling it, and I am knowing that I am not smelling thing because my nose is being broken. Many thing in me is broken but I am not feeling pain. And I am remembering now that the person who is walking into this room is wanting me to be feeling pain.

That is why when he is walking in he is spitting on me and telling me I am not human and that I am rubbish to be thrown into ocean. I am wondering why he is keeping me here and as I am wondering this he is holding shockstick and he is hitting me in my stomach and chest and side with it and he is hitting me so hard on my back that he is breaking the shockstick.

I am thinking that I am supposed to be feeling thing. Big man that is with the one who is hitting me is telling him is not working. And I am knowing now that I am being tortured and then I am remembering that I am what they are calling enemy combatant.

Big man is telling boy that nothing is working because I am being made to not be feeling pain. He is saying that I am special soldier, I am synth, and I am not having pain receptor in my brain and it is this that is making me not to be feeling thing even though many thing inside me is broken. Boy is telling big man okay and big man is leaving, and I am thinking that boy is going to be leaving with big man but boy is staying and I am raising my head to be seeing his face and when he is looking at me he is smiling so his teeth are shining yellow like corn they are selling by the street, and I am seeing the way hair is over his face and the way the skin on his knuckles is broken, and I am seeing the vest he is wearing and the patches and I am knowing that he is soldier too and that he is with what I am knowing is a militia and they are small small army but they are killing just like soldier. And boy is looking at me like I am something to be eating, and then he is reaching behind him and pulling cord from his neck and he is walking close to me and he is putting cord in my neck and suddenly I am feeling everything. I am feeling the breaking in my ribs and in my back and in my crotch and in my arms and in my head, and he is smiling at me and saying now I will be feeling these thing and he is raising his stick and I

am waking up in Xifeng's arms, and she is whispering to me in Taishanese. It is taking me several second to be remembering where I am and what is happening, but then I am remembering raid and EMP and gunfight and red-bloods in pods, and I am relaxing in Xifeng's arms. But part of me is still not wanting to see her, so I am pushing myself to my feet and walking fast away from her and not caring where I am going until I am seeing Uzodinma in other room staring at what is looking like empty hospital bed in room of hospital beds. Bed is half-covered by cylindrical device, and I am knowing that this is being use to scan brains and braincases, and all the bed here is being like this, except that Uzodinma is standing at one bed in particular.

We are synths. He is telling me this and showing me hospital bed. Two bed. The one he is waking up in and the one he is looking at now, and he is showing me that they are the same. *This is where they are making me.*

When he is turning to face me, he is limping because I am seeing that one leg is standing badly. He is not showing pain on his face, but he is moving slowly and I am seeing that this is making him to be angering. Is not good for child of war to be moving slowly. That is how child of war is getting bullet or getting chopped.

I think I am expecting Uzodinma to be sadding, but his eye is not sadding. *We were created. We were never born.*

"What color is this remembering?" I am asking him. I do not know why it is important for me to be using my red-blood voice, but I am wanting him to hear me like we are both being red-blood. "Is it blue? Red?" Maybe if he is having rememberings like I am having rememberings, he is knowing that some of them is belonging to someone else.

You are wanting to tell me that you are having mother once and she is loving you. He does not sound like my friend when he is saying this. He is sounding like someone who is not caring if I am being happy or sad. *But I watch you fumble through your mind, trying to hold the right rememberings in your hands. They are still a mess in your head, no matter how you are sorting them. Scattered like pieces of metal on the shoreline beneath a bridge. You are looking for a woman and calling her Mother and seeing woman after woman after woman, but none of them have a face like yours. None of the women in your rememberings have done for you what you expect mothers to do. Because we never had mothers.*

When he is saying we never had mothers, he is also saying we are never having mothers.

But it is a lie, because when I am waking up from nightmare-remembering, Xifeng is holding me and talking to me softly and with love. And she is waiting for me in the other room. And I am calling her Mother.

■ ■ ■ ■ ■

In the mech, on the way home, Xifeng looks out the window. And I sit across from her. The other synths downloaded the memories from the external hard drives at the facility, the ones the government and the Chinese were preparing to eliminate upon completion of the mass cyberization, but Xifeng says that I don't have to. I think she is worried about me.

"What am I?" I ask her.

When she is looking at me, there is many thing in her eye and I am not wanting to sit in her silence, so I talk some more.

"Uzodinma is telling me that all child of war are being made in factory all over Nigeria. That we are machine and that they give us false memories that are belonging to other people. But I do not feel like machine." I am looking at my hands, because I am too scared and too angry to look at Xifeng's face. "I want him to be lying. But I know he is not lying. I am wanting him to shake me and I am wanting him to tell me I am right too and I am wanting all of these thing because it is easier to be pushing against him than to be sitting inside the doubt that is squeezing the air out of my lungs. If I am being made in factory, then why am I feeling this way? I am not robot! I am not android like Enyemaka! I am not simple machine! I am not machine. I am not machine." I'm crying.

"You are not a machine."

I am looking up from my hands when I am hearing Xifeng's voice. She is not smiling, but there are many thing happening on her face. Happiness, anger, sorrow, joy, regret. All of these thing is happening at once in her face.

"You're not a machine, but you're not human."

"We are something between these thing?"

For a long time, Xifeng is saying nothing, and I am only hearing the wind blowing by our mech as we fly over the forest trees. Then, she says, in Taishanese, "You are my daughter."

And it is calming the questions in my heart to be hearing this.

CHAPTER
31

Ngozi keeps the maglev jeep close to the ground whenever they move. And there's no rhyme or reason to their movements. Sometimes, Ngozi will bring Ify and Grace deep into forest, where they'll share a clearing with a pack of wulfu or a lumbering Agba bear. Sometimes, they will move at night, hugging cliffside roads even as the sun rises to gild them and the red mountain beneath them. Sometimes, they'll pull off the road in the middle of the day, lose themselves in off-road jungle, then Ngozi will vanish for hours on end, sometimes returning with food, sometimes returning with nothing. Then they will be off again.

It isn't until they find refuge on the ridge of a large, verdant bowl empty of people, of all sign of habitation, that Ify realizes where Ngozi's been taking them. The van is parked a ways off. Ngozi has left her rifle in there but has a pistol tucked into her pants. Grace brings up the rear and hangs back while Ify stands at Ngozi's side. Together, they survey the landscape: the rolling hillside, the mountains to either side of them, their clay sides red like open wounds. And Ify knows were she to dig deep enough into the ground here—anywhere here—she'd find Chukwu glowing blue right at her. The mineral over which a whole war was fought.

"We're in Biafra, aren't we?"

Ngozi sniffs and keeps playing with her chewing stick. "You didn't get to know Onyii the way I did, so I figured I would show you what she lived for."

"And what she died for," Ify says to herself, quietly. Then Ify looks back up at the land before her, and she recalls the winding journey they've taken, the forests they've passed through, the roads they've ridden down, the flightlines they've taken, the hillsides on which they've camped. This was her homeland. "I've never seen it like this."

"There used to be more people," Ngozi says casually. Ify knows the callousness of the statement is a mask for very real hurt. She's ridden enough with Ngozi to know that the war veteran still aches for the people she will never see again, for the life that once filled these places but that now leaves them desolate and too quiet. This land, not even the animals will touch.

"Ify," Grace says, insistent.

Ify realizes that Grace must have been calling her name for some time. She turns, and together the two of them walk out of Ngozi's earshot.

"What are we doing?" Grace hisses. "We have a mission."

Ify looks around, searching for an answer. If she is honest with herself, she wants to stay because Onyii, somehow, is here, in this place beneath her feet, in the air around her, in the lowing and growling and buzzing of the winged and feathered world around her. Dying children wait for her high in space, but doesn't she deserve her own brand of peace? "If we leave and are captured by the security services, what happens to us?" she asks Grace.

Grace smolders but takes the point. "We can't just do nothing. Are we going to sit in her van, driving around this country until she figures out what she wants to do with us?"

"That's exactly what you're going to do." Ngozi's heading toward them with a feline saunter. Her hand drifts behind her in case she needs to reach for her pistol. Ify knows now to keep her eye on it. "Come on, it's time to go."

Grace steps between Ify and Ngozi. "Go where?"

Ngozi looks Grace up and down, as though surprised by what she's seeing, then smirks. "Somewhere safe."

"How do we know you're not just going to drive us around until the end of time?"

Ngozi frowns at Grace and takes a step toward her so that their noses are nearly touching. "And if that's my plan, what will you do?"

"Ngozi," Ify calls out, warning. "Ngozi, please."

Grace backs away so that she can look at both Ify and Ngozi. "We have a job to do," she tells Ngozi, while never taking her eyes off of Ify. "There are lives at stake."

Ngozi stares without saying a word, her expression one of immovable cliffside rock.

"Ify, let's go."

"Where would we go?" Ify asks.

"She's right, you know." This from Ngozi, the pistol out from her waistband and firmly in her hand.

Grace notices it and stays still. "Ify. Please. Those children are dying." All the while, Grace has eyes for nothing but that gun. "Ify, what are you doing? Ify, please!" Her face changes, her spine straightens. "All right. Fine. I'll do it myself." She takes a step back, but that's when Ngozi raises her gun arm.

"What?" Grace asks, defiant but shaking. "Because I've seen your face I can't leave alive? After you shoot me, are you going to stuff me in your trunk, find somewhere quiet, and set it all on fire?" She looks to Ify, the accusation thick and dark in her eyes. "And you would let her?"

"You don't understand," Ify says, hating the weakness in her voice. "You've never had a country like Biafra."

Grace looks at Ify like someone she no longer recognizes. For a long time, her mouth forms around words but refuses to speak them. Then, she appears to give up. Her arms fall to her sides. "You have no idea what I have or haven't had."

Ngozi's arm hasn't wavered the whole time.

Ify steps forward and puts her hand on Ngozi's, pushing the gun to the floor. "Let her go. She can't harm us." The two Igbo women share a meaningful glance, then Ngozi relents and tucks the pistol back into her pants.

Grace runs back in the direction of the forest and vanishes.

"Think of the children, right?" Ngozi says, joking, as she and Ify head back into the van and set off.

Staring out the window at the country she feels she's seeing for the first time, Ify is surprised at how little guilt there is in her heart.

CHAPTER
32

We are sitting in cave and laughing at hologram projection Oluwale is making of when he is kneeling on crabtank and steering it with poles he is jamming into its head and screaming war cry. I am telling to the others how I am feeling fear in my chest like THU-THUMP of my heart over and over and some of them are having expression of marvel in their eyes because they are never knowing what fear is until I am telling them. Uzodinma is not with us. He is in other room, but I am wanting him to be hearing this—hearing my story and hearing Oluwale's story—because if he is seeing that we are feeling these thing and that we are telling story not like machine but like red-blood, then we are not being machine. We are being thing that is making family. I am wanting him to be seeing me and telling himself that we are being family. But he is in another room, and he is not seeing or hearing us.

While there is laughing and chat-chatting in the caves, I hear scuffling and someone trying to scream but hand is covering their mouth. I am telling from the sound that this person is being prisoner, then the sound is drifting away and Xifeng is coming to us. Some of the synths are standing at attention like little war child. Other is sitting down and smiling at her like she is big sister and not commander of army they are belonging to. And some of them are looking at her with love in their eyes and I am recognizing this as look that child is giving their mother when they are loving each other.

"Uzo, come with me?" Xifeng is asking me in English.

"Yes, Mother," I am saying in Taishanese, because, for some reason, I am wanting the others to know that I am special to Xifeng, that I am different. Favored.

We are walking down cave pathway, and orb is floating over our head all along the pathway, lighting our way. Xifeng is leading me past room filled with girls who are cleaning their guns and checking their ammo and other room where synth is connecting to external hard drives that Xifeng is collecting before we are being reunited, and synth is downloading rememberings onto hard drives, and I am thinking about how things used to be with me and Xifeng. I am thinking of how it was just us and the Enyemakas, and I am thinking of riding in a boat with Xifeng and how quiet the night is being in Lagos Lagoon when we are arriving in Makoko neighborhood to be delivering remembering. And I am remembering that we are small small group and even though there is no blue or red or other color shading the remembering like there is being with the ones that is not belonging to me, it is feeling like a different lifetime ago when I am doing these thing with Xifeng. Even though we are walking past that room fast fast, I am seeing that already external hard drive is filling entire walls.

"It makes me happy to see you with the children like this," Xifeng is saying suddenly.

My heart is heating when I am hearing her call us children.

"You are becoming your own people." Smile is spreading on her lips. "Growing from your memories."

"We are organizing them," I am telling her with excitement in my voice. I am truly feeling like child because word is moving from my mouth faster than I can think it. "Oluwale and Uzodinma are teaching me how to be organizing my memories based on what color they are being shaded in and who is appearing in them. And like this we are knowing which memories belong to us and which are being implanted and belonging first to others. And I am thinking that this is what is making us to be our own people."

Smile has faded from Xifeng's face, but I am telling from how she is walking that it is not because she is sadding or angering but that she is simply thinking.

"You're so special" is all she is saying to me as she puts her hand to the back of my head and draws me close to her.

As we are walking, I am hearing muffled sound even more, then we are getting to small small room branching off of hallway where girl I am not recognizing is bound to a chair with her arms being restrained behind her, so that I am knowing it is paining her. She is having plastic band over her mouth to be keeping her from shouting, and there is still marking on her face from where eye blanket is being stripped off. But I am also seeing cream that is smeared on her face, and it is the same cream that we are using when we are raiding the cyberization facility. The cream that is keeping camera and machine from recognizing our faces.

"Her name is Grace Leung," Xifeng is telling me, and when I am looking at the prisoner's face like a red-blood and not using the technology in my braincase, I am seeing that she is looking like Xifeng.

"She is Chinese," I tell Xifeng, like this is a thing we are both discovering at the same time. And I say it in Taishanese, because I am wanting even this person to know that Xifeng is treating me special. "Like you."

Xifeng smirks. "She's nothing like me." Then she steps closer to the prisoner who is having dried blood under her nose. Fear is shining in Grace's eyes, but there is also being defiance there like she is being ready to fight everyone she is seeing, especially Xifeng, who is walking close to her and is taking off plastic band that is covering her mouth and using her thumb to wipe off face-scrambling cream. "Are you?"

"Who are you?" Grace is asking through gritted teeth.

Xifeng rises to her full height, and it is looking like she is casting shadow over the prisoner. "I am your guardian," Xifeng is saying in Mandarin.

"Talk to me in Taishanese," Grace hisses in language I am understanding as language me and Xifeng are speaking when we are being proper mother and daughter.

Xifeng crouches on her haunches, so she is looking Grace in the face. "You grew up in the Colonies, didn't you? That's what you look like." She wrinkles her face. "That's what you smell like too. You smell like gweilo."

Grace is trying not to be crying, and it is making her to be shaking in her chair.

"Now, my children are telling me you are here from the Colonies on a medical mission. Is that correct?"

Grace is struggling not to be saying anything.

"That there is some epidemic sweeping through the refugee population and it has something to do with their memories. My children have also told me that the Nigerian Security Service is looking for you. Which means you've already broken the law."

Grace spits blood onto the floor next to her chair. "That's what you're doing here, isn't it? Breaking the law?"

Xifeng is looking at Grace with disappointment in her eyes, then she is standing to her feet. "You're all the same. You think the answer to your problems is here, so you come and you take what you want and then you leave. I have seen it with our people over and over and over again. But imperialism without yáng guǐzi is still imperialism." Xifeng is calming down. "I am here to actually help these people, and that's what I'm going to do. If you don't get in my way, you stay alive. It's as simple as that." Xifeng is then looking to me and nodding, then she is walking out of the room and it is being just me and Grace.

Then something is happening. Her eye is growing wide. She gasps. "You . . ." she says.

With less face-scrambling cream all over her features, I am seeing it too. I am knowing her. And I am knowing instantly from where I am knowing her. An open field. Leaving the forest. Police and army mech and helicopter and Augment that is chasing me and my family. Holding Ify's face in my hands. This girl, Grace, looking at me with wide eyes and not saying anything, just like she is doing now.

Without thinking, I am on top of her. I have knocked over her chair and I straddle her and my fingers are over her throat, squeezing, and I am angering and saying through my teeth, "Where is she?" When Grace is not saying a thing, I am slapping Grace hard across the face, and instantly it is beginning to swell and tears spring to her eyes. "Where is she?"

"I don't know," Grace is saying in soft soft voice.

But I am not liking what I am hearing, so I am slapping her again and wound on her forehead is reopening.

"Please, stop," she is saying as I am hitting and hitting and hitting her. And when I am doing this, she is vanishing and room is vanishing and I am suddenly hanging from chains over my head and evil boy is plugging into me and grinning and my body is feeling like someone is lighting it on fire and he is taking shockstick and beating me and beating me and beating me while I am hanging and beating me and beating me and . . . "Please." Then I am stopping and looking at Grace and glaring, and she is gritting her teeth and one eye is being swollen shut and she is telling me, "I'm never going to let you have her." Even though she is saying this, I am not angering. Instead, tear is coming to my eye, and I am not liking what I am doing. I am seeing her face and I am knowing it is like that because of me, then shame is washing over me like water under Falomo Bridge that is trying to be eating us.

Grace's eye moves from my face to room's entrance out into hallway, and she tries to push herself up but I am on top of her and she is still bound to chair, so she is only coming up halfway but she is shouting, "Ify? Ify! IFY!"

And I am turning around, and it is Ify with one of the girl that is rescuing us from police station. And Ify is seeing Grace's face and horror is coming to her eyes and she is saying, "Grace?" Then girl who is rescuing synths from police station is grabbing Ify and dragging her away. I run into the hallway and watch as more and more girl come to hold Ify while she tries to fight them and her shouting gets farther and farther away until I am no longer hearing her voice.

Xifeng is appearing in the hallway and she is looking at me, then she is walking away from me and Grace and in direction of Ify.

CHAPTER 33

They force Ify into a metal chair. She thrashes and struggles against them, but some of the people restraining her have the vitiligo and superhuman strength of synths, and it isn't long before her wrists are bound behind her, her ankles magnetized to the chair's metal legs. The sight of Grace's face, swollen and bleeding, fills Ify with a rage she can't remember ever feeling. But on the heels of that rage is desperation and an acknowledgment of her own powerlessness. But even as she knows she's only wearying herself with each jerk against her restraints, with each thrash, she cannot stop.

"Grace!" Ify calls out. "Grace! Grace, it's okay!" Someone smacks her hard across her face, and Ify looks up to see Ngozi staring back at her. "What is this, Ngozi? What's going on?" She jerks herself against her restraints. "What are you doing? Let me go. Let. Me. Go."

But Ngozi just walks away.

"Come back here!" Ify shouts. She's screaming more than she needs to, but it will do Grace some good to hear her voice, to know that she's still alive and kicking. Ify raises her voice as much for Grace as she does herself. She spaces out her movements and her shouting to conserve energy. Things had morphed so quickly. One minute Ngozi was leading her to a safe haven after all those days on the run from the Nigerian Security Service. Then Ify was manacled to a chair. A different Ify would have had her guard up, would have known how to read a body, would have detected the lie in how Ngozi walked and talked. "Grace?" Ify calls out, hoping Grace will hear her and, in hearing her, be put at peace.

Her captors spread out toward the wall of this room under orbs of light. Behind them sit shelves containing all sorts of foodstuffs and mechanical equipment. Bonders, Augments, EMPs. More synths start to file into the room. Ify recognizes them from that episode at Kufena Hills when the lot of them burst from the forest with half the Nigerian military chasing after them. That's when everything changed, Ify realizes. When that synth saw her face and gave her a glimpse of the sister who had abandoned her.

So lost in thought is Ify that it takes her a moment to register the new quiet. When she comes to and her vision focuses, she finds she can't breathe. *How . . .*

"Hello, Ify," says Xifeng, sitting in a chair right across from Ify.

Grace. "Let my friend go," Ify hisses after a moment's shock. "She can't hurt you."

Xifeng feigns surprise, then demurs, smiling. Her dark, gray-threaded hair comes down in waves to her shoulders. When she leans forward in her chair, forearms on her knees, her hair, coarse and thick, casts malicious shadows across her face. "I'm not worried about that, child," Xifeng says. Then she reaches out her hand, pulls back, then reaches out again to hold Ify's cheek in her hand. "I know she can't hurt us. I had her brought here for her own protection."

Ify grits her teeth. "She didn't look very protected."

Xifeng's hand falls away. She reclines in her chair. "You've grown." The smile that crosses her face chills Ify. "It feels like so long ago. When we first met, you were a little girl alone in the jungle. You'd been fending for yourself for I don't know how long. All alone. No family, no one to watch over you. And me, a simple VR filmmaker ferrying refugees to safety during the ceasefire." She pauses, takes Ify in with her gaze. "How much of that time do you remember? Do you remember our conversations? Do you remember the little boy named Agu? The child soldier who could play a touchboard like a master? Absolutely gifted. How much of that do you remember?"

Ify realizes her whole body has been coiled this entire time. "Xifeng, what are you doing here?"

"The same thing I was doing when we first met, Ify. I'm preserving memory."

"But . . ." Her throat has dried up. Words scratch against it. "But it's against the law."

The others watch in silence, but Ify finds herself wishing they'd intervene, wishing they'd take either her or Xifeng to another room, wishing they'd say something, do something, to put a stop to this. But Xifeng holds her gaze. So much of that face is as Ify remembers, but the hair has thinned a little, and gray threads through it. There are new wrinkles around her eyes and a new hardness in her cheeks and jawline. It is odd to Ify, seeing someone age, seeing someone who refuses to be frozen in amber, whose face isn't just the same cyberized

snapshot for the rest of their lives. Everything about Xifeng—
her posture, her naturally aging face, the look in her eyes—
suggests rebellion.

"Let me go," Ify says.

"No one's keeping you here." Xifeng looks around at the
young women standing guard. "You are absolutely free to leave
on your own. But should you make it out of here, know that the
security services will chase you." She pulls a small tablet the
size of her palm out of her breast pocket and swipes a few times
before holding the screen out to Ify. "You are a known fugitive."

Ify's fists clench against the chairback.

Xifeng puts the device back in her pocket. "You were asking
the wrong questions. Or, rather, the right ones. In these times,
that is enough to get you reprogrammed. We saved you, Ify.
If they find you, they will forcefully cyberize you and invade
your mind and rip your memories right out." She speaks with
her hands, and with each word, it's as though she loses more
control over herself until she takes a moment to breathe and
straighten herself.

"But I'm a Colonial official. They wouldn't . . ." The rest dies
in her throat.

A sigh escapes Xifeng. "Your country has changed so much
since you've last been here."

"I know my country," Ify growls. The sound surprises her.
Then she realizes how clenched her fists have been, how tight
her jaw feels. There's anger in her. "What do you know of
Nigeria?"

"You left and I stayed."

Ify lunges forward, hauling her chair off the ground. Instantly,
two guards are on her, twisting her arms behind her and holding

her in place. Despite her best efforts, they force her back down. "How dare you! You know nothing of this country!"

Xifeng considers her nails while Ify thrashes in the grip of her captors. "You're breaking the law! You're a criminal! Nothing more! When they catch you, they will bury you under the jail. You have no right to meddle in our affairs."

"Our?" The look she gives Ify fills Ify's stomach with fear. "Our affairs?" Xifeng rises from her chair and walks to Ify so their faces are inches apart. "I know what you did in Enugu."

Ify grows slack. "What?" It comes out as little more than a whisper.

Xifeng walks away, hands clasped behind her back, then makes a slow circuit of the room, as though to acknowledge every one of her soldiers. At the entrance to the room, that girl appears. That synth who moved so much like Onyii. Xifeng pauses in front of her, then, palming the back of her head, draws her near so that they both face Ify. The girl's expression is inscrutable.

"What are you talking about?" But Ify knows. Even as she can't bear to hear it, she knows.

"During the ceasefire. When you joined my caravan of refugees, you told me you were looking for a young woman and you showed me her face. I didn't know who she was at the time. Even when she brought you back to me, I didn't know quite what she had done. I hadn't known that this Onyii you were looking for was the so-called Demon of Biafra, that she was the most skilled mech pilot on both sides of the war, that she had killed hundreds, possibly thousands over the course of her service, and that she had raised you in a little camp in southeastern Nigeria when you were a child." Xifeng pauses to look lovingly at the synth clutching her leg, then continues. "You were going to Enugu to kill her because she had murdered your family. And in the process, Enugu was bombed. Hundreds wounded, dozens dead. Those were the initial tolls. Many more people would die by the time the rubble was cleared away. That is what you did. You led a group of suicide bombers into a civilian city where they proceeded to detonate themselves and kill as many people as possible." Around the room, several people—none of them synths—audibly gasp. The air thickens. Some of the girls clench their fists. Others shift their feet in the dirt like they're preparing to leap. Others tense, struggling to maintain composure in the face of the emotions roiling inside them. And at the center of this maelstrom sits Ify. And Xifeng. "There had been peace, but your quest for vengeance broke that peace. I remember, Ify, because I was there. I saw the waves of hatred you unleashed with that attack. But you left."

Ify starts when she realizes tears are running from her eyes. "It was a mistake," she says, but all she hears is a whimper. "It was a mistake."

Xifeng stops and steps forward, leaving behind the little synth girl. "What was the mistake?"

"I . . . I didn't know about the bombers. I . . ." She sags in the arms of her captors, her legs going limp beneath her. "I just wanted to kill Onyii." She has her head bowed and tears blur her vision, but she can feel the disdain Xifeng is staring at her. "I just wanted revenge." She lets herself go, and the sobs come rushing over her in waves. Her body convulses with each one. It feels as though she is being choked. "I didn't know. I didn't know." She says this over and over and over again, and she realizes this is the first time she's admitted this to herself. For so long, she has carried those two events—shooting Onyii and the bombing of Enugu—together in her mind, one single tragic episode, and it has been so much easier to believe she was responsible for both, that her thirst for vengeance had cost so many lives. She had even been prepared to die, to be executed by Biafran authorities after her capture. But Onyii had rescued her. Even as war was starting back up around them, Onyii had rescued her.

"Look at you now."

Ify looks up from her hands.

"Look at you now." There's no scorn in Xifeng's voice. In fact, there's wonder. And admiration. "You've grown and become successful and built an extraordinary life for yourself. All the while, you have been carrying these horrible memories inside you." She comes down to one knee before Ify. "Ify. Listen to me," she says as she undoes Ify's restraints and unhooks her ankle clasps from the chair legs. Her voice has grown soft. Recognizably soft. This is how she used to talk to that child soldier who played the touchboard when she was teaching that synth how to be a boy. "We have to keep these memories inside us. Or else there is nothing to push us forward. There's nothing to learn from. You grow nothing in a barren field."

Ify holds Xifeng's gaze and sniffles.

"Intentionally wiping away memories of our most important experiences is no way to live."

"It's so hard," Ify whimpers softly through her tears.

Xifeng brings her into an embrace that Ify is too weak to resist. "But we must, child," Xifeng whispers into her hair. "We must."

■ ■ ■ ■ ■

Ify watches several of the girls lay Grace on a stretcher and bring her to a medical tent.

"No harm will come to her."

Ify frowns at Xifeng.

"No more harm."

Xifeng walks on ahead and it's not until Grace disappears from Ify's view entirely that Ify follows Xifeng into the maze of caverns. Already, this place feels familiar. She no longer fears she'll fall into whatever puddle she steps into, not like when Ngozi had first brought her here. The guards have fully reactivated the bodysuit that had been damaged in the attack on the police station, and it feels good and secure to have it on again. Surrounded by so much strangeness, this is one familiar thing. Still, a part of her misses the mental and physical quiet that came with not being connected to anything.

"It wasn't this way in the beginning," Xifeng tells her as they walk. "The war ended, but there were still attacks. Militia that refused to give up, paramilitary still addicted to the high of war. I remember seeing it when I was running the caravans. Children with machetes at their waists and deadness in their eyes. There were still people who thought they could make their fortune off the illegal trade in certain goods, but for that to work, there needed to be a certain level of violence. But that?" Xifeng shrugs ahead of Ify. "That's easy enough to stop. It was when people started getting sick that the government began to think something was truly wrong."

"Sick?" Ify's thoughts race to the refugee children held in Alabast.

"The war was an open wound, but no one wanted to treat it. No one wanted to speak of it or deal with it. People went about their lives, living next to the people who had murdered their families. But containing that inside you with no outlet, it destroys a person." There's a faraway quality to Xifeng's voice, as though she's invoking the experiences of specific people, reliving the hurt they showed her in their faces. "The government tells you that there's peace and order and insists on rational dealings. But your mind, whether or not it has been fractured by trauma, knows there's more to life than this. So it protests. But you can't launch vigils or march in the streets, so these protests disappear into your body. They become kidney stones or trouble breathing. Backaches, migraines, neoplasms. Toothaches, depression, psychosis. They mushroom in your interpersonal relationships. Marriages fail, friendships disintegrate, the families left after the war are shattered." She looks over her shoulder at Ify without missing a step. "You're a doctor. Is *emotional constipation* a clinical enough term for that?"

Ify demurs. "I'm not a doctor yet." But everything Xifeng is saying is unspooling like thread in her mind, attaching to bits of driftwood, clue after clue after clue, and slowly pulling them together. She remembers the Cantonese woman who had died in her sleep, scared to death by her nightmares. Then there was the man who had gone blind after having witnessed his family's torture. His sight had been restored, but only after weeks of trying to figure out what was wrong with him. And now the children whose response to deportation orders was to fall into comas. Was that what it was? A response?

Xifeng stops in the empty cave corridor. The echoes of bustle and movement soften until the only noise either of them hears is the occasional drop of water from the ceiling, landing on a puddle at their feet. "It became an epidemic. And the only way the government could see fit to treat it was to wipe all trace of the war from the minds of its citizens."

"But how? How do you do that? How do you explain missing family members or a crater where a village used to be? How do you explain mechs that wash up on the shore in pieces? Or mines buried underground that haven't detonated yet? I . . . I saw Biafra. Like none of it ever happened."

Xifeng only shakes her head, then she resumes walking while Ify hurries to catch up. "I'm sure you've heard of the Nine-Year Storm." Xifeng can barely bring herself to snort derisively at the fiction. "The government was busy. The people were the easiest part. They just wanted peace. And they were willing to do whatever it took to feel it again. Imagine coming back to your neighborhood to find it reduced to ashes by the people you went to work with. Imagine your coworkers coming home to the poorly dug graves of their children whom you killed. Lie to them and tell them a tornado ruined their lives. A wildfire, a tsunami, radiation fallout." They stop at the threshold to another room. Outside the entrance stand two armed guards facing forward. Xifeng grows still, looks to the ceiling. "If you could be cured of any physical ailment, would you sacrifice nearly a decade of your past for it?"

The question is like nothing Ify has ever heard before. Faced with it now, she can't say what she would choose. So much of what and who she is now is not only because of what happened to her but what she remembers. And she knows for a fact that were her mind to be scraped of all those memories, her body would remember. She would carry those episodes, those experiences, in her ribs, in her heart, in her legs. In her eyes. Unless . . .

"Forced cyberization," Ify says in an awed whisper. "The government forced cyberization on . . . on everyone." The horror begins to sink in. When Ify looks up, Xifeng is facing her and only nods her head before passing through the beaded curtain that leads to the next room.

Ify can only stare, mouth open in shock. The government forced hundreds of millions of people to undergo cyberization. So it could catalog then delete their memories.

She pushes herself to move forward, and when she enters the next room, she's confronted by wall after wall of what appear to be, when she squints, hard drives. Piled from the floor to the ceiling. "What are these?"

Xifeng walks back to Ify and puts a hand to her shoulder. "Memories. Every memory I could find and download about the Biafran War. It's all here."

So much life, so much death. And to think, it can all fit in one room.

"Is this a library?" Ify asks. "What are you going to do with these?"

That hardness returns to Xifeng's face. "We're going to restore them. My team has already been delivering these to select households throughout the country. When people get enough clues, they realize where the holes are in their memory, and it is our job to fill them. People will remember."

Ify walks to one of the walls but feels as though she's outside of her body. "But doesn't it feel wrong?" She reaches up a hand to touch the ridged edges of the small devices, so many of them stacked together. "Making them relive their trauma?"

Xifeng watches her, hands clasped behind her back. "And yet you remain. You persist. You poke your head and your shoulders through the broken seam of the chrysalis, unsure even of your new form, having not yet seen it in its entirety. That was you when you first arrived in space, yes? You couldn't have had any idea what you would become. But what you went through. That breaking, that rending—that's where the pain is concentrated. Sometimes, what we are experiencing is simply our effort to reach forward. It's a protracted stretching, Ify. One reaches toward something, one stretches a bit farther and is freed, having left behind some rusted-over part of one's self, some shell that had clung to a familiar, safe tree but that is now an evacuated husk for which the butterfly has no more use." She arrives at Ify's side. "That's what I am going to do for this country. Will you join me?"

CHAPTER
34

War is raging inside of me.

When I watch Xifeng and Ify move through cave headquarters, a part of me is feeling joy that they are seeing each other after so long apart and that they are knowing that the other is alive after passing much time not knowing. But another part of me is jealousing because Xifeng is looking at Ify like she is special, almost like she is wanting to call her daughter, and I am wanting Xifeng all to myself. I am not wanting to share her. Then I am jealousing again because Xifeng is looking at Ify like Ify is having answer to question she is asking, even though I am not knowing what these question is. And I am wanting to be able to look at Ify and see the mystery of myself being solved, and it is not happening.

I walk into the medical chamber, and I see Grace Leung who I am beating before and then I am sadding when I am seeing her face, even though it is already healing from the chemicals and the small small surgery they are doing. But Grace is seeing me out of the corner of her eye, and her whole body is clenching like fist or like something preparing for blow. And it is making me to be hating myself that someone is looking at me and thinking this thing instantly. So I am running away and looking for empty room and finding small room that is branching off of one of the main pathways, and it is filled with cleaning products on the shelves and wiring that is bunching up in the corner. I am sitting on the floor and pulling my knees to my chest and hugging them there like this, because doing this is the only thing that is making me to be not crying, and I am wishing now that I never discovered feeling thing, never developing capacity for emotions or ability to do useless human thing like love and be jealousing.

Beaded curtain is rustling, and when I am looking up, girl is searching shelves on opposite wall for something. It is Binye, who is running with me during mission and shooting and patting my head like I am being her little sister. "Where is it?" And I am hearing thing rattling around until she says, "Aha!" and is turning around and seeing me and almost jumping into the air from shock. "You scared me. What are you doing here?"

But I am not knowing what I should be telling her.

She is seeing the look on my face, and I am not knowing what face I am making, but it is causing her to crouch down and touch my face. "Oh," she is saying like mother or elder sister. Then she says, "Oof," and opens bottle of painkillers in her hand, dumps a few out onto her palm, then swallows them. She makes a move to put the pill bottle back where she found it, but then puts it in her vest pocket instead. "Cramps," she tells me, and I am knowing she is talking about a thing that is happening with her body that is never happening with mine.

"May I ask you a question?" I say in small small voice.

Binye raises an eyebrow, then slides down the wall until she's sitting like I'm sitting but with her legs spread out and not hugging them to her chest. "Go ahead."

"When you are first cyberizing, what is it feeling like? Do you remember?"

Binye is considering the ceiling before she answers. "In the beginning? I felt . . . new. Like I'd been born a second time. There's darkness, then for a few moments, I see myself. My body. I'm lying in a hospital bed, not moving. My eyes are closed, and I think I'm asleep. Or dead. Then I wake up. But not like waking up from a dream. It's like waking up into the world for the very first time. And the lights are so bright it hurts. And the blankets are rough, and the noise makes my head feel like it's going to explode. And all I smell is antiseptic. It was as though I were a child experiencing all of this for the first time."

What she is saying is reminding me of thing, but the remembering is like sand that is running through my fingers. I am trying to make the remembering come, to be pulling it from Binye's words, but when I grab a piece of it—the smell of rain-wet soil, the sound of water lapping against shoreline—it is vanishing.

"Why do you ask?" Binye's voice is taking me out of my thoughts. Then she is squinting at me and saying, "Oh. You're a synth. I am not insulting you. I am just realizing why you must be wanting to know." She moves closer to me. "I see the way you all are. Like children. And you're different. If you were all the same child, it would be easier to think you're all machines, but . . ." She does not finish.

I am smiling, and then I am waking up on recliner chair that is also lowering itself to being bed or table. Cushion beneath me is blue and plastic and torn. Wall is hissing around me, fans whirring, spraying mist on me, cleaning radioactive dust from everywhere in here.

Around me, monitor is hanging at angles from the ceiling. A robot torso in the shape of a human leans forward from a wall, its arms limp in front of it, head bowed. Other Augmented parts is lying in neat rows arrayed by limb on counters opposite me, all the forearms in a row and, next to them, hands with their fingers separated and positioned in front of them.

On almost all of the tables lie blueprints. Random bits of gear litter the floor at the base of reclining chairs. Hornets buzz out from beneath the table I am on and spray misty alcohol onto me and I am wanting to be waving my arms, but I am seeing why I cannot.

I am having no legs and am having only one arm. But I am not being nervous, for some reason. This memory is in full colors. It has my colors, but it is sometime having blue-green on the edges. And it is having these edges when Chinese man with silver beard and doctor's cap is smiling in my face. The colored edges fade in and out, in and out when I say, "Am I alive," and he is chuckling.

"Yes, quite," he is telling me. "Though dinner won't be ready for a few hours. I don't think hunger will be an issue for you yet, however." He is looking at me like he is remembering something or reminding himself of something, like how to have proper manners, but I am reading the way his body is speaking and I am knowing that he is looking at me and he is seeing the rememberings I am holding in my head before I am winding up with one arm left on this table. He is seeing that I am inside mech that is being shot down because I am in battle, then mech is plummeting into lagoon. He is seeing that I had been a pilot in the war, and when he is first seeing my body in the lagoon, I am just a mangled mess of flesh and metal. But he is saving me somehow.

"Your name is Onyii, right?"

"How do you know my name?"

He smiles. "I'm your doctor. When we're finished, you can meet some of the boys." He looks at his hands, then up at me again. "I think they'll be happy to have a big sister."

CHAPTER
35

Ify's hand hovers over one of the drives. Small enough to fit into the palm of her hand. Large enough to contain most of the memories of an entire cyberized human being. Ify remembers once hearing in a lecture hall that all words ever spoken by human beings could be contained in forty-two zettabytes of data if recorded as ancient sixteen-kilohertz sixteen-bit audio. Of course, increasing the quality of that audio to today's standards would entail an order of magnitude in the thousands, but, looking at the drives before her, Ify marvels. Hundreds of zettabytes of storage in each one. And thousands of them lining the walls of this cave.

Xifeng's question rings in Ify's ears, the loudest echo she has ever heard. *Will you join me?*

Ify touches one of the drives, runs a finger along a ridged edge, then slowly pulls away. She turns to Xifeng and sees the look of expectant joy on her face, the look of someone already having made her plans. A pang of guilt stabs Ify's heart, but she smothers the hurt. This is bigger than them.

"No."

Disappointment pulls down Xifeng's features like Ify's words have deflated her. Then, for the briefest of moments, it curls her lips into a snarl before she schools her face into an aspect of calm and acceptance. "Why not?"

"You're forcing trauma on these people." Ify feels serenity radiate through her. She is right, and she knows it. Amid all the uncertainty and chaos surrounding her, all the things that have happened and been said to her to throw her mind into tumult, there is this certainty. She clings to it.

"I am showing them the truth. These piecemeal revelations are part of the solution, but they are not enough. You don't understand, Ify. I have the tools to reverse the virus the government has injected into the minds of its citizens. This virus of forgetting."

"What are you talking about?"

"A central data processing center. Everyone in Nigeria is connected. Everyone we will help is connected. Once I inject the right code into that center, it will flood the net with every forbidden memory. Everyone will remember. Only then will the country move forward."

"The country." That familiar contempt returns to Ify. She keeps her anger at bay. But she allows herself to feel pity. "The country that you know so well. You've lived here for less than a decade, and you know what is good for this country? You were not born here. You were not made here. You never knew this place before war. How could you possibly understand it after war?" She draws closer to Xifeng. "What you're doing is wrong." With a wide sweep of her arm, she indicates the walls of hard drives. "This will only bring war back."

"So the government is right? The only way to bring warring tribes back together, living side by side as neighbors, is to make them forget what they did to each other?" Venom drips from Xifeng's words.

"Warring tribes." This time, Ify lets a touch of anger infect her voice. "That's what we are to you. Just warring tribes who can't think for themselves. Who can't make decisions and govern their own lives. Just warring tribes who have no business running their own country."

Xifeng sneers.

"You're no different from the rest of the oyinbo. All throughout history, these people come in and try to tell us how to live, and all they do is create conflict. All they leave behind is death and destruction and dysfunction. What you're proposing will rip this country apart. Millions will die."

"And the country will move forward. Just like you did."

"I am not a country!" The exclamation rings throughout the room. Ify is sure it can be heard in every corridor and every chamber in this sequence of tunnels. She takes a moment to settle herself, to slow her heart's racing, to still her nerves. "I am a human being," she says with a lower voice, a kinder one. "I am one human being. I was lucky." As she speaks, she thinks of her patients. Their experiences fill her voice. "I've seen people who witnessed the torture of their family go blind. I've seen people so traumatized by their nightmares that they die in their sleep. Scared to death, Xifeng. Sacred. To. Death. So many others— deafness, impotence, suicidal ideations, children who take their own lives because they think it is the only relief from the trauma that haunts them every second of their day. That is not happening because people are holding it in. These people were seeking treatment. They were speaking to professionals. They were sharing their experiences. They were doing everything right, and they still didn't survive. Xifeng, you're going to kill these people."

"Would you sacrifice your memories of Onyii for peace?"

The question stops whatever words Ify had left in her throat.

"Everyone who remembers Onyii is in these caves. You can count them on one hand. And two of those people are standing here right now. Think about that, Ify. The only people who ever knew Onyii existed. After all she did for her people. We are all that's left of her. You would have us lose that."

Ngozi enters the room and hurries to Xifeng. She puts a hand to her arm to turn her, and whispers briefly to her. The two exchange a meaningful look. Then Ngozi leaves.

Rage floods through Ify, but she holds it in her shaking fists. "You're not doing this for Onyii. You're doing this for you. And I won't let you."

Xifeng smirks. "You're too late." She crosses her arms. "It has already started."

"No." Whatever hard drives Xifeng and her group have already distributed, whatever memories have already been reawakened, it's reached a critical mass. Enough people know of enough carnage that the reprisal attacks have begun.

"Yes, Ify. It's begun." Xifeng looks to two guards standing by one of the walls, and they reach Ify in three long strides.

Before Ify can fight back, they have her in restraints. "Stop this!"

Xifeng spreads her arms, as though to indicate the whole world and its burning. "This is the reckoning. This is how the healing happens." Then she turns and leaves. The little girl

Xifeng had held close to her side earlier has taken her place.

Ify lets out a wordless roar at Xifeng's back. Words fail her. Sentences fall apart on her tongue. And all she has to contain the emotions roiling inside her, the feelings and thoughts storming through every fiber of her being, is that roar. Long and loud until all breath has left her lungs.

CHAPTER
36

I am smiling at the Chinese man who is calling me Onyii, then I am hearing, *Get up! Get up!* and it is snatching me out of the remembering, the first remembering I am ever having that is feeling like it is mine and like it is before Enyemaka are finding me under pile of corpses. But I am not having time to be thinking about this because I am hearing rumbling overhead and, in storage closet, Binye is pulling me to my feet and we are both rushing to the entrance, where we are seeing girl and synth run in all directions to assume battle formations.

I am running in direction of where I know Xifeng and Ify are, and my heart is thrilling because I am knowing that I can be protecting Xifeng in way that Ify cannot, and I am not caring that I am feeling this way toward Ify, even though when I am younger and it is just me and Xifeng and Enyemakas, I am loving Ify with all of my heart and wanting her to love me too.

I arrive at the room where Ify is being held. I am standing by the room's only entrance and only moving so that some of the girls who remain can be bringing in Grace, who they are also binding to chair. That way, I am looking at the two of them. The swelling and bleeding is gone from Grace's face, but the fear is remaining. And I am seeing how Ify is noticing how her friend is changed, how she shrinks when she is touched, how it is like her entire body is being exposed nerve endings, how she is looking no one—not even Ify—in the eye.

"What'd you do to her?" Ify growls at me.

But I am saying nothing in reply. Now that I am knowing what I am and where I am coming from, I am not needing her. I am already having answer to the questions that is making storm inside me, and I am getting them when I am being with Xifeng.

Being connected with my siblings, I am seeing what is going on outside. I am seeing the synths and the girls guarding Xifeng as they are heading to their destination. And I am seeing some of the others fanning out into the city in battle formation to deal with the police and the army when they are coming. I think some are expecting me to be jealousing them because they are outside with Xifeng and I am here guarding prisoners, but I am knowing that this is important work and if Xifeng is entrusting me with important work, then that is meaning that I am special.

"What is your name?" Ify is asking me, and I am realizing that in the whole time we are seeing each other, this is the first time she is asking my name.

"Uzoamaka."

Ify is smiling. "That is a beautiful name."

"You are thinking that if you are flattering me and saying good thing about me, I am letting you go. Is this correct?" It is not like me to be asking rhetorical question, but I am angering a little bit still, and I am thinking it is because of remembering that is mine of hanging from ceiling while boy is beating me and delighting in it.

Ify's next words come out as a breath: "You speak like him too."

This time Grace looks at Ify and so do I. "Speak like who?" we both ask at the same time.

"A boy I knew." Ify bows her head. "He was a synth. His name was Agu. He had been militia before the ceasefire. Xifeng had rescued him. We met on a caravan heading toward a refugee intake station just outside of Enugu." Her voice chokes on the city name. Then a slow smile spreads across her lips. "He was kind to me. I didn't think a synth could be kind. But then . . . I'm sure many people said the same thing about Onyii. I'm sure there were people who didn't think my sister could ever be kind." She is talking to herself more than to me or Grace. "And I think you have her inside you." Then she is raising her head to be looking at me and maybe she is seeing what Chinese doctor is seeing when he is looking at me. "That's why we were drawn together."

"My name is not Onyii," I am telling her and trying to make my voice as hard as I can.

"I . . . I know. I just wonder." She squints at me. "You don't forget anything, do you?"

The question is surprising to me, and I am realizing I am never asking myself this question. "No," I say back.

"So many memories. And they are all just as vivid and immediate to you as if they had happened yesterday. Even if they never happened to you."

I am tensing, because she is speaking differently than before. She is speaking like doctor or scientist and not like prisoner.

"Your finger touches the floor and feels it. And it tells your brain that it is like that time your finger touched another surface, some experience your finger stores, then sends to your brain, and it gets tied up and cross-referenced to other experiences that you could have—holding a shovel or a gun or maybe the trunk of a tree—and that memory of the floor, of concrete, gets embedded there, so the two become linked. And there must be so much disorder. Without that human capacity for apophenia. For ordering these things, imposing a pattern on your memories, telling a story of self. I can't imagine what that must feel like."

"Is not your problem," I am telling Ify in a low voice. I am angering because I am knowing that she is trying to confuse me and this is somehow supposed to be resulting in me letting her go and disobeying Xifeng.

But Ify is still talking like she is never hearing me, and I am wondering if this is all something she has been wanting to say for a long time and is not finding chance to say until now. "The more I think about it, the more convinced I am that there are two kinds of memory in our heads. There's the one kind that debates with itself as to whether the sky had clouds in it or whether it was clear the afternoon of the drone strike. The kind where, by force of will, you're able to place the detail, to put the puzzle pieces together. Then there's the other kind. The kind that sneaks up on you. Or the kind that you stumble upon when you open an unfamiliar door in a hallway and find yourself in an open field, crouched before a hibiscus blossom." She pauses and looks as though she is remembering where she is. Her friend, Grace, is looking at her strangely, with sadness but also pride. "I thought you and Agu were only capable of one type of memory. But I know the other type lives in you as well." She is stopping, then closing her eyes, and I am feeling gratitude that she is finally shutting up. But then she is swaying back and forth in her seat, and I am squinting at her. Then I am seeing that her vital sign is changing and her body temperature is falling fast fast and her heart rate is slowing and slowing and if it is keeping like this, it will soon be stopping.

Ify falls over in her chair, and her body begins to shake. She spasms, then all the data in my retinal scan is telling me that her heart has stopped beating.

Grace is screaming, but I am not hearing it. It is like her mouth is being covered by gauze or like cotton is being stuffed into my ears. I am hearing no thing, but people are running past me to see what is happening to Ify, and I am not being able to move, and I am wondering why I am not moving because I am often seeing dead body, but none of them are being Ify.

CHAPTER
37

Even though they are underground, Ify swears she can hear it. The crash of glass breaking, the whoosh of fires climbing up through the floors of office buildings, the shouting, the people falling from windows, the crying, homes collapsing into rubble, the fighting, the dying. She closes her eyes, bound to her chair, and can hear it all even louder, feel the heat of the fire on her face, smell the soot in the air, feel it choking her lungs. No. She's remembering Enugu. The devastation that took that city hasn't happened here yet. If Ify understands Xifeng's plans properly, then the conflicts are in isolated pockets. Maybe specific neighborhoods, maybe in more than one city. But they should be small enough for the police to put down. But if Xifeng reaches the central nervous system running Nigeria's net, the entire country will go up in flames.

Her bodysuit. Linked to her neural network.

She commands it to increase in temperature, and immediately, she begins to sweat. Her handcuffs, twisting her arms behind her chairback, grow slick over her wrists. An idea occurs to her. It could kill her, but she needs to get out of here, and she needs to disarm as many of these guards as possible. They may be hardened war veterans, trained to kill and maim and survive deprivation, but they won't kill her. They can't. She contains some of the last remaining memories of the Biafran War, and she's not cyberized. If she dies, her memories die with her.

Her bodysuit's temperature drops, and her body temperature follows suit. The plummet is precipitous, sudden, and sharp. Her heartbeat slows, slows even more, grows sluggish and soft. Her eyes roll back into her head, she pitches forward in her seat and grows limp.

The timing is everything. If they take too long to notice that her heart has stopped, it could damage her beyond repair. If she stops breathing completely for too long, the damage to her brain may be permanent. She drifts in and out of consciousness and makes a choking noise to draw their attention. Then her body lists sideways, and she and her chair topple loudly onto the ground. Puddle water splashes onto her face.

Her memory drifts back to Enugu. The taste and sound and smell of the world ending.

Everywhere, collapsed buildings. Food stalls, shopping malls, school halls. Fires rage. Bots fight to extinguish the blazes. People run, and traffic bots try to steer them. The katakata has disrupted the flight paths so that maglev cars and buses crash into each other, their burning shells littering the streets of Enugu.

Gritting her teeth, Ify pushes herself to her feet, and that's when she notices her right arm hanging limp at her side.

A short distance down the way, flames lick the glass inside a fabrics store. The windows burst open. Ify skips into the front display and tears at a dress on a mannequin until she is able to rip off a long enough piece of cloth. Using her teeth, she ties a sling for her broken arm, then heads to the bus depot.

On the way, Ify sees the telltale marks of destruction. In open stretches of street, craters sit like perfectly formed half-circles in the concrete and metal. Towers stand with nearly entire spheres cut out of them. The bus depot is little more than shattered flexiglas and twisted metal.

Two guards rush over, and shouting fills the cave, but it reaches Ify's ears as a muffled series of barking argument. The world begins to turn black. Shadows encroach from the corners of her vision. *Hurry, hurry, hurry.* She feels as though she's swimming. It's almost too late. She'll lose control of her suit, and it will continue lowering her temperature until she's an immovable block of ice, until the suit itself freezes its own controls. Fires rage in Enugu, but she feel so cold. *Please hurry.*

Her arms spring loose. Her cuffs are off. That's it.

She lies on the ground, limp, tended to by the guards. One of them hauls her up by her shoulders, drapes one arm over her back, and begins to carry her forward while the other follows. Ify prays the guard won't feel Ify's body warming against her. Or that she'll think it's simply proximity to another person's flesh and not the result of Ify manipulating the temperature of her bodysuit. Her fingers twitch, at first from reflex, then with her actual willpower. Strength is coming back.

When she's ready, she slips from the grip of one of the guards, falls into a crouch, grabs the pistol at her waist, then shoots at one leg. When the guard screams and collapses, Ify pulls her body close, using it as a shield, then shooting the one behind her twice right in her bulletproof vest. The girl falls back, and Ify twists the girl she's been using as a shield around and hits her once across the temple with her pistol, knocking her out.

She crouches over the body, fishing through the pockets until she finds it: a small device, the size of her palm, like a bulubu ball cut in half. An EMP.

Just as she pulls it from the unconscious girl's pocket, her eyes catch Uzo's. Uzo, who has remained still this entire time. If Uzo hasn't attacked them by now, maybe she's willing to let them go. Maybe something Ify said made a difference, changed some of the synth's thinking. Ify can't take the chance. "I'm sorry," Ify murmurs, cracking the device's seal and slamming it onto the ground. The EMP detonates, and the blast hurls her and Grace backward, slams Uzo into the far wall, and sends the sound of frying circuits and breaking light bulbs echoing down each tunnel.

Lightning forks out of the ground, stitches up the walls, and strikes the ceiling overhead, then the sound of dozens of little puffs as machinery short-circuits and bursts apart. Cyberized shoulders, legs, eye sockets. Screams are cut off as quickly as they start. The rumbling and the popping and the screaming and the lightning's shriek carry on through the tunnels until Ify hears a single large thunderclap followed by a rumbling that tells her something has collapsed.

Her bodysuit sparks, and pain pops to life on parts of her body—her stomach, her lower back, her thigh, her calf—as the EMP short-circuits her own machinery as well. But it's a smaller hurt than what the others are going through. She's only wearing her tech. It's her clothing. But for the others—the synths and the rest of Xifeng's footsoldiers—their tech is what makes them. It's their bones and their organs. And suddenly those things are being turned off, all at once.

When the screams stop, their echoes bounce off the walls

and fade, and the only sound is the hiss of fried tech and the dull rumbling of whatever is collapsing far away.

She goes back and undoes Grace's restraints. Grace, who hasn't said a word since screaming her grief at Ify's faked death.

"I'm sorry," Ify says, softly and hurriedly. "I didn't have time to tell you what I had planned." Then she pulls a pistol out of her pants and hands it, butt-first, to Grace. "Can you handle this?"

"I'm not saying no, Doctor," Grace says, struggling to one knee. She keeps gently touching her face, and the memory of her wounding earlier hits Ify with enough force to leave her breathless. But then Grace's grimace turns into a grin, and she takes the pistol. "Lead the way."

As they head to the room's mouth, Ify stops at Uzo's motionless body. The girl's face is angled up toward the ceiling, gaze focused on a point past Ify, probably seeing nothing. Nothing in the girl's face moves, nothing signals reaction, notes the passing of Ify's shadow over her body. There's no snarl on the girl's face, no widening of the lips to signal a glimpse of the divine that the dying see before death. Ify wants to say something, to commemorate the life the synth was growing into, to apologize for killing her like this, but Grace tugs her away into the tunnels.

Ify heads down the first corridor, stepping over the bodies, picking up an assault rifle on the way, and makes her way through tunnel after tunnel, slowly and with Grace just behind her, sidestepping the downed guards where they lie. At first, she presses herself against walls and peeks around corners to see if anyone is going to jump out at her or begin firing from their perch or hiding place. But soon it becomes clear to her that she and Grace are the only things moving in this entire place.

So they break into a run, slowing down only when they get to a clearing through which fluorescent light shines.

The platform she descended on. It lies buried beneath a small mountain of stone. But there's an opening, and Ify spots the snapped ends of cables swaying overhead. Slinging her rifle over her shoulder and tucking her pistol into her waistband, she climbs up the rocks and leaps onto the rope. Sparks still occasionally shower in arcs from her suit, but they feel like small bug bites compared to earlier.

Grace scrabbles up the rocks, trying to follow Ify's path, but falls hard. Ify, holding on to her rope, swings to the wall to brace herself and rest while Grace tries again. Another leap, another fall.

She hears movement, then motions for Grace to stop moving. They wait, then Ify hears it again. More movement. People are getting up. They're coming for her. Now she can hear shouting. Commands being issued, weapons being distributed. They're fanning out. Tracking her.

"Hurry!" She motions for Grace to jump for her again. But Grace can't reach. Another leap, another fall. Another leap, desperate and flailing, another fall.

They're getting closer.

Ify lowers herself, swinging loose on the rope she's now tied around one forearm, and she stretches the other out for Grace. Grace jumps again. Their fingers brush. The voices get louder, the words clearer. Grace jumps. Just misses.

"I think they're in here!" Lights flicker back on nearby. Shadows dance farther down the corridor. They're coming.

Grace jumps, Ify extends herself, then grabs Grace's arm just as it looks like Grace will fall again. Without losing any time,

Ify pushes herself off the wall and swings Grace with all her might onto the other rope, to which Grace clings.

"Okay, Grace," Ify says in a hushed murmur, out of breath. "Listen to me. We don't have time, so I'm not going to repeat myself. Take your time. Pull yourself up by bending at the elbows. At the top of the lift, reach up to a higher part of the rope with the lower hand. Keep going like that. Keep the rope close to your nose. And just keep going. Okay?"

Grace nods nervously.

Ify is steady with her climb and tries to clear her mind. Anything to keep from looking down and seeing how deep the drop has already gotten. Anything to keep from worrying about how Grace is doing. She doesn't permit herself a single glance down the whole way up, hoping that if Grace were to look her way, Grace would feel empowered to climb the way Ify climbs. She would see Ify doing this impossible thing, and it would become just a little bit less impossible for her. It would anchor her when it begins to sound like their pursuers are right beneath them. Ify holds on to that hope all the way up.

Still, her arms and shoulders burn. It takes her forever, but eventually the light grows brighter, and she can hear sound. Shouting, cursing, crying.

The riots.

She pulls herself up, eventually reaching a ledge, and with her last remaining strength, she swings herself up and over, landing on her back in a field of grass. A moment later, Grace rolls onto the grass on the opposite side of the hole.

Trees tower over them. The air is cool against Ify's face, with a hint of moisture from nearby water. Then she smells it. Smoke.

After she catches her breath, she pushes herself up, first onto her elbows, then fully upright. Then she looks eastward, where fires rage.

"I can't move," Grace says to the smoke-filled sky.

An aerial mech streaks overhead. Ify closes her eyes against the memory of enemy mechs soaring over the camp where she was raised. When she opens them again, she climbs to her feet, takes her rifle in her hands, and tells Grace, "Hug the shadows."

Ify knows where they are. Unless Xifeng plans on going far to reach the core of Nigeria's net, they must be in Abuja. In or near Garki District, the city's principal business and administrative area. Headquarters of the Nigerian Armed Forces, the commercial broadcast networks, the Infrastructure Development Bureau, and the Federal Ministry of Information and Communications. Ify has walked through the halls of that building, ascended and descended in the glass elevators running along its exteriors, enjoyed the uniformity of its floors and office spaces. But she has never seen what lies beneath. No matter her access, she was never permitted there. She doesn't even think Daren had the security clearance to venture beneath that ground floor. That must be where the core of the net is located. But it would be heavily guarded, no doubt. Not just by armed guards, but likely by all type of mechanized droid, programmed for lethal engagement. How would Xifeng get past that?

As they head toward the city center, the sound of fighting has gotten louder. But there's another sound underneath it all. Ify would barely hear it were it not for her past among so many Augments and her constant proximity to tech. The soft whirr and buzz of highly powered cyberized people.

Ify and Grace press against the wall of an abandoned charred duplex and watch as an armored personnel carrier disgorges cyberized police officers in the middle of the street. As they fan out, aerial drones lift from their backs and, as they climb higher, unfurl the guns attached to their undercarriages. Ify motions for Grace to be quiet. They don't stand a chance against even this group, never mind the dozens—at least!—that have been deployed throughout the burning city. On top of everything else, they're still wanted fugitives, according to Xifeng. She wishes she'd had the foresight to steal some of that face-scrambling cream they'd worn earlier. As it stands, they're no match for the scanners.

Pretty quickly, the soldiers head away from them. Using the noise and commotion of the riots for cover, Ify and Grace stay as close to the buildings lining the roads as possible, skirting through alleys whenever possible, moving as fast as they can. The quiet is eerie here. It looks like the aftermath of a storm, like a Redlands wildfire has raged through here. But the buildings smolder, which gives Ify pause. There's been no rain. What could have put the fires out?

Too late, Ify detects the movement to her right.

Through an entire row of buildings crashes the largest humanoid machine Ify has ever seen. She and Grace dive out of the way of its charge but are separated when the hulking monstrosity comes to a stop between them. Its muscles bulge beneath its all-black bodysuit. A helmet fused to its steroidal shoulders reveals only its eyes. It looks like a thing out of a nightmare.

It scans Ify for just a millisecond before taking one too-fast step toward her and raising a fist.

It's going to kill me.

That's Ify's last thought before its comet-sized fist comes crashing down on her head.

She slowly opens her eyes and gasps. Onyii stands before her, trembling, knees bowed, muscles tensed to their limit, holding the juggernaut's fist in her hands. It presses down on her, digging her feet into the concrete. The ground cracks around her.

Onyii half turns to Ify. Ify blinks. Onyii's face becomes Uzo's. Tremors from the strain ripple through it.

"Run."

CHAPTER
38

I am pushing the fist away, but the juggernaut's other hand smacks into me, hurling me clear across the street, through the first floor of a department store and onto the next street. A maglev car swerves to avoid me and crashes into another storefront, bursting into flames.

My body is aching and it is feeling like metal is broken inside me, but I am not feeling fear when I struggle back to my feet and wipe oil from the side of my mouth.

Gunfire. It is pistol. Small-caliber, and bullet is pinging against too-strong surface. I am knowing just from the sound that it is Grace shooting at juggernaut, and I am running back and jumping though department store, over counters and through broken windows, and when I am coming back out onto first street, I am seeing juggernaut holding Grace in the air by her neck and her legs is flailing and she is soon not breathing. So I am running even faster and jumping and curling into ball that is hitting the back of juggernaut's knee. Juggernaut is falling to one knee. I am skidding to a stop on my feet, then I am running and leaping into the air and punching juggernaut in the helmet with all of my force. Helmet is not denting, but juggernaut is staggering backward and raising arm that is still holding Grace, and then I am kicking that arm at the elbow so that it is snapping and short-circuiting and finger is letting go.

Grace is falling into my arms and coughing and when she is seeing who is saving her, her body is tensing. But I am saying, "It is okay," and running away and scanning empty building that is burning on both sides of the street. And I am scanning and scanning and my brain is telling me how many floor each is having and where furniture is being and what it is being made out of. Then I am seeing building to my left with basement and I am running into it, even though upper three floors will soon be falling down. But basement is safe and empty and is having food and water in it. I am crashing through broken front door and running down first stairs, then I am running down underground stone hallway until I am getting to steel door with passcode scanner. Grace is climbing out of my arms to go to passcode scanner, but I am going straight to door and finding groove with my fingers and pulling and pulling and pulling, even until my arm is paining me, and pulling some more. And at first door is not moving, then slowly, it is groaning against the stone floor, and I pull it open just enough for Grace to get in. Then once she is inside, I am pushing it closed with my back. Then I am smashing my fist into passcode scanner so nobody else is opening door and bringing harm to Grace.

As I am going back upstairs, I am realizing that Grace and I are not speaking words to each other, but she is knowing to be letting me carry her to safety and I am knowing that I am to be keeping her safe, even though no one is telling me to do this thing and no one is telling her to be trusting me. And I am thinking that maybe it is like this when I am speaking to the synths and we are not moving our mouths but we are still speaking. Maybe this is how it is for the red-bloods when they are not moving their mouths but are still speaking. And understanding. I am glad that Grace is trusting me. And I am hoping that I am keeping her safe.

I am walking quiet quiet back to the street where is juggernaut, but I am not seeing it. Even with all the information that my braincase is sending to my retinal display, I am seeing no juggernaut. Then I am listening through the hiss and crackle and pop of building on fire and the faraway shouting and shooting and I am focusing. Then at the last moment, I am hearing the whirr that is telling me machine gun is soon firing. Then CHUDCHUDCHUDCHUD as bullet is chewing up the ground where I am standing. And I am running and running until I am jumping into abandoned home and leaping over furniture and finding cover behind wall while bullet is chewing chunk out of it.

In front of me is stairs, and I am hurrying up and up two floors until I am getting to attic. Through window, I am seeing where bullet is coming from. Then whatever is shooting is sighting me and bullet is crashing through window and I am flinging myself onto the floor and clinging to it. All this time, I am not seeing juggernaut but I am knowing that it is shooting at me. While bullet is firing, I am counting second, because I am knowing that it is needing to calm down soon to keep from overheating. Then I am hearing the slowdown and I am leaping through the window and sailing through the air. Wind is caressing me as I fly, and I hit the ground and roll forward in time to hear FWOOMP and see grenade speeding toward me. I roll away and it explodes, and ground around me is shooting up into the air like fountain water made of dirt.

I am still not seeing juggernaut, but I am knowing that it is near, and I am knowing too that if I am being too close, it is not firing because it is not wanting to injure itself. As dust and smoke is clearing, I hear FWOOMP. Another grenade is flying toward me. I jump to it, scoop it out of the air, and spin so I can throw it back at where I am knowing juggernaut is standing. Loud BOOM is crashing through the street, and building not far down the road is collapsing, and I am knowing that it is falling on juggernaut. But I am also knowing that it is not killing juggernaut, so I am crouching and making myself ready for when it is coming.

The rubble explodes outward and juggernaut stands, then charges toward me, STOMP STOMP STOMP so that the ground is shaking. It is winding up one fist and when it punches, I am moving to the side to dodge. But its torso swings all the way around. I catch the fist with my hands but it sends me flying into the air. I flip and land on my feet but when I look up, juggernaut is almost on top of me. It slams both fists down, but I scramble through its legs and climb onto its back. It is swinging and fighting and trying to shake me off, but I am clinging fast and beating its armored back with my fists and making small small dent but still making dent so making progress. I am banging and banging, but then it is reaching behind and grabbing my shirt and flinging me in a circle before throwing me so hard I crash through the window of an empty bus that is on fire.

It is taking me too long to get back up. I cough black oil onto the pieces of glass under me. The seats are black and torn from fire and violence. Before I can come all the way to my feet, bus is shifting underneath me. Juggernaut is picking it up and shaking it in the air like it is toy, then it is throwing it down the street, and my body is crashing back and forth and side to side as bus is rolling to a stop with me in it.

Many thing is broken inside me so that I am seeing static every three seconds and I am not being able to move. Giant hand crashes through the bus frame and wraps around my body, then pulls me out and I am not being able to move as juggernaut is pulling me close and squeezing and there is being static and static, but I am also seeing crack in its helmet and oil leaking from face that is having nose.

I am damaging it.

Pain is shooting through me as it is squeezing, and my legs is dangling, and it is squeezing and squeezing and I am knowing soon that I am going to be dying. It is raising its other fist to be crashing onto my head, and I am not being able to move. It is going to kill me.

I close my eyes, then squeeze my arms tighter to my body. It is causing my whole chest and stomach to feel on fire, and I am hearing many thing snapping, but I am sliding out of its grip just as other fist is coming down. I land on the ground in a crouch and tear open the skin over my ribs to pull out a broken metal rib bone, then, through the pain that is knifing my whole body, I run and slash at the armor over the juggernaut's stomach. It reaches for me and I slide behind it and slash the back of its heels to make it to be falling, then I am stabbing my rib bone into its spine and pulling it up and spark is flying and it is squirming and moaning and we are both being covered in oil as I slice open the back of its helmet that is coming away like calabash bowl that is breaking.

It rotates its torso too fast and I fall to the ground. I am too slow to get up because juggernaut is then palming my head and lifting me off the ground. It is on its knees because it is not being able to stand, and it is holding itself up with other hand, but it is squeezing my head and I am seeing and hearing nothing but static and I am knowing that thing is breaking in me that is not going to be fixed. But when I am not seeing static, I am seeing misshapen face and mouth that is opening, and I am knowing that this is where grenade is coming from.

In between bursts of static, I am hearing the sound it is making as it is preparing to fire grenade at me so close, and I am barely moving, but I am able to raise my arm that is holding my metal rib bone and I am jamming it into the juggernaut's mouth so that grenade is not firing at me.

I hear thunder and feel nothing but fire and the feeling of one million ocean waves breaking over my body.

I am not knowing where I am landing. Somewhere far away. But my face is on the ground, and no matter what my brain is telling my body, my body is not doing. So I am lying there as sound is fading and sight is fading and fire is raging all around me, and then I am seeing small small body trapped under burning building and body is not moving. And tear is coming to my eye, because I am knowing it is Uzodinma and I am saying to myself, *You are dying too,* and it is question and answer at the same time, like I am knowing that I will never be seeing him again and yet hoping that is a lie.

Then darkness.

CHAPTER
39

Ify grits her teeth as she fights her way through another mob. Fires rage all around them, roaring and devouring everything, burning so bright they turn the night into daytime. The flames loom so high, consuming market stalls and office towers and multistory adobe apartments, that they cast the people rioting in the streets as silhouettes, otherworldly spirits come from fable or from dreams to wreak havoc through a city.

A group of men caught in a brawl see Ify and lunge toward her at once. She has in one hand a shockstick and in the other a machete, and as they charge her, she parries each blow and slices and dodges and hits with her shockstick, electrocuting her attackers and disabling them. Soot and dried blood coat her face, and when she stalks past the shattered remnants of a storefront window, she sees in the shards of glass what she looks like.

It's the face of someone who has just watched national monuments burn, who has watched mobs form and lynch bystanders in Abuja National Stadium. It's the face of someone who has heard cries for help from countless people—innocent citizens, former combatants, people trapped while trying to flee—and been unable to save them. One perpetrator of an attack shouts out the reason for their vengeance and opens the wound, then others remember when they were attacked, and cries for revenge spread like a virus through the entire city. INCAR Plaza is ablaze. Dead bodies and weeping wanderers, some of them already shell-shocked, have turned Millennium Park into a graveyard. Abuja City Gate has become a macabre manifestation of the madness contained in the city. From its lowest arch hang half a dozen bodies.

The city is lost. Too many people already remember too much. And even now, new crimes are being committed, new wrongs that people will remember, despite the government's best efforts.

This is what will happen to the whole country if Xifeng is not stopped.

With her sleeve, Ify tries to wipe some of the soot and dried blood from her eyes. The resulting smudging only serves to make her look more demonic. She turns from the broken glass and heads away from the fires. She sneaks from shadow to shadow when she sees police coming, and increasingly they grow heavier in their use of force. What chills Ify is watching people be subdued, then bundled away into vans. It is like watching the wholesale emptying of a neighborhood.

As she gets farther and farther into Garki District and away from the worst of the chaos, she begins to feel as though some sort of natural disaster has struck where she stands. Nothing moves. Maybe the Nine-Year Storm is an appropriate name for what the Biafran War did to this country. No one can be seen. She can even still smell burning food that has been left to cook for too long. As though everyone has just vanished in

317

the middle of the business of living. There are some signs of chaos, but they're lighter here. The blood on the ground is patchier. People had enough time to barricade their storefronts and secure the windows to their apartments and hide in their basements before the warring began in earnest.

All the dead and maimed here are regular people, civilians. And yet Ify sees even these people being swept up in immediate cleanup operations. Massive land mechs with pouches attached to their fronts like kangaroos roam the streets, and mechanical arms unfurl from their sides to pick up the bodies or pieces of bodies that litter the ground, then drop them into the pouch that opens and closes with a soft hiss every time. Ify's eyes widen in terror. The erasure of trauma in real time. Like concrete paved over a pothole before the earthquake that created it is even over.

The tower she's looking for looms over collapsed and near-demolished apartment buildings and office headquarters ahead, and she moves dutifully toward it, slinking through alleys, wary of anything moving. But anywhere she goes, to her horror, she's the only thing breathing.

Empty plaza greets her before she gets to the tower.

She remembers the place teeming with life. She remembers the flood of workers spilling out wearing their djellabas and the women in their hijab as they met up and gathered in groups before heading to the nearby mosque for Friday prayer. Ify remembers Daren letting the both of them get swept up in the tide, being surrounded by all that industriousness. The city hummed with warm, thrilling life all around them. She remembers seeing young students flirt with each other on the benches on the first days of their internships, how pleasant the droids were in greeting people. Even the security droids seemed to have been programmed for maximum cordiality.

But now, before her, there's nothing but emptiness spotted occasionally with the bodies of dead Augments and security droids. For a moment, Ify wonders why security was so thin here for what is perhaps the most important device in the entire country. Then she remembers the riots and how thick the security presence seemed in some places, how much like a war zone it had felt. A diversion.

It had all been a diversion.

Ify turns off her shockstick and slips it into her belt. Then she pulls out her pistol and readies it. The glass doors lie in pieces, and she steps gingerly over the threshold, then slips under the security barrier just after it. Guards lie motionless in pools of their own dried blood before their stations.

There's been no attempt to clean up the carnage or to mask Xifeng's trail. Bullet casings litter the floor, and Ify follows the path they've made through the central circular clearing, where, when she looks up, she can see all fifty floors, each floor a ring, through the glass ceiling at the top of the tower. That same glass crunches beneath Ify's boots.

She's faced with a semicircle of elevator bays, but all it takes is a single button press on all five of them to confirm what she suspected. The elevators are locked. She heads back to the control panels in the main lobby, strewn around the blood-stained lobby furniture, but when she tries to connect, her bodysuit pops at her shoulder and pain pricks her spine at the base of her neck where her Augment sits. It's not worth it. Of course Xifeng would paralyze the building's comms system and disable access to the building's schematics.

Ify scans the walls and ceilings, and after some searching, she finds them. Orbs. Partly blackened from having been disabled, but there nonetheless. Xifeng and her group probably had them disabled remotely, which, Ify realizes, is how the orbs were able to remain suspended in place. She can't hack into them, and they won't have any of the recorded material she's really looking for, but if she can tell where they're turned, she can find the blind spot.

She looks from one to the other like she's threading them together, like each is a puzzle piece she's collecting. A pattern emerges, and she follows it with increasing speed until she finds herself at a far corner hidden behind the columns ringing the central lobby. A part of the wall has slid to the side, revealing an opening, and Ify steps through it to set foot on metal grating that clangs loudly. She's more careful with the next step, pausing to look around at the maze of walkways and piping around her.

When she's fully through, she surveys her surroundings. Islands of light reveal platforms at various levels and stairways or straight walkways connecting them. Through each island runs a pillar that disappears somewhere deep beneath Ify. When she looks down, all she sees is a golden glow. That's where she must go, she knows.

The islands and the consoles that artificial intelligence maintain there are a distraction. That some of the consoles are dark with inactivity tells Ify why parts of Abuja were suffering from blackouts during the riots. In other parts, she had overheard authorities talking about switching to remote communication because the net had gone down in certain districts. No, she can't think about that now. *Focus*.

She follows the walkways down and, after some time, finds

herself passing between two thick pillars. She's barely on the other side when a bullet rips through her shoulder. She hits the ground, pain tearing through her shoulder, then puts her back to the part of one pillar that eats into the walkway. The pain dizzies her, to the point where she nearly dips over the railing, but she steadies herself. *Focus*, she hisses at herself. *Focus, focus, focus.*

Wetness cools part of her shoulder around the burning wound. Were her bodysuit functioning properly, it would have worked to adjust her body temperature while locally numbing the affected area and cauterizing the wound, stopping the bleeding. But now, it's just polyurethane material growing darker and darker with her blood.

She chances a glimpse around the pillar, and a bullet pings by her face. A sound like a massive pipe being hit by a wrench reverberates through the entire space. Ify can almost see the waves of sound ripple outward. A headache begins at the base of her skull. And there was no time even to see if there were any other hiding spots between her and the shooter. Trapped. Then she realizes what she has to do. She wishes she could program her suit to shut off auditory input. But all she can do now is close her eyes and grit her teeth. With her shockstick, she strikes the pillar hard.

The gong ripples out like a concussive wave. Beneath it, she can just barely hear the clatter of a pistol. She squeezes through the gap between the pillars and instantly sights the shooter. Three shots and she's down. Ify continues in a hurried crouch and spots two more sentries, each on one knee with their rifles at the ready, just as they turn to see her run by overhead. Three shots for each of them and they're down. She rounds a corner down another staircase and dashes forward just as bullets snap at the walkway behind her. Someone below her.

She keeps running, then vaults over the railing and drops and drops and drops, trusting that she understands the patterning of the metal walkways. When she lands, she falls into a roll, but pain still snaps alive in her ankles. Through the hurt, she aims her pistol up and fires at the dark shapes above. Before they even have the chance to drop, she's on the move again. The glow she saw earlier begins to surround her. She's getting closer.

Her steps slow. Her left shoulder has gone numb. She keeps her pistol aimed with her right arm while her left hangs at her side, useless. Her heart is racing. The temperature around her is rising. The world starts to waver, as though she stands in the midst of a mirage.

She passes through what feels like a wall, then makes her way onto a platform. And when her steps echo loudly in her ears, she realizes just how much energy and electricity has been humming and buzzing around her in this basement. For some reason, none of that sound enters here. There's just the platform that rings what appears to Ify to be a large metal hemisphere towering over her, so wide she can't see its edges. Kneeling before it, almost in an aspect of prayer, is Xifeng.

Ify aims her pistol. "Get up," she growls. She sees Xifeng, and in her mind swim images of the destruction and death she witnessed, the mobs hurtling down streets setting fire to everything, the dead bodies left in their wake, the citizens wailing over those they had just lost in violent feuds whose origins they didn't even remember. Truly senseless violence. All because of the woman kneeling before the hermetically sealed vault in front of her. "Get. Up."

Still, Xifeng refuses to move.

Ify marches to her, grabs her by the scruff of her collar, then hauls her to her feet. Xifeng's face is twisted in determination. Ify knows where she's seen that expression before. Walking through the detention center, looking into the cells at the captured enemy combatants. The thought flits through Ify that any number of them could have been innocent children caught in a sweep or the object of some feud an officer or soldier had with someone. She's also seen that look on dying soldiers who clung to their weapons even as their life bled out of them. At one point, she had worn that same expression on her face: when she had been so absorbed in her mission of vengeance that she had helped bring about a terrorist attack that had killed over a hundred people and restarted a civil war. "Where is it?"

"Where's what, Ify?" Xifeng asks in a steely, knowing voice.

"The virus. Where is it?" She presses the pistol to Xifeng's forehead.

"You mean the antivirus."

"Xifeng, this stops. Now. You're beaten. Give up." She presses the pistol harder. "I stopped you." When Xifeng doesn't move, Ify grits her teeth. "Are you happy? Have you seen what you've done? There have got to be at least a hundred people dead above us right now. And counting. Tearing each other to pieces over nothing! Over things nobody cared about until you forced them to. You did this, Xifeng. You're oyinbo, and I will not let you destroy this country."

"I'm not destroying this country, child. I'm saving it." Her face softens. "Look at you. Look at what you've become." She says it without malice. Ify hears admiration in her voice.

Wonder. "The look on your face, the straightness of your limbs, the strength in your bearing. Walking through the fires of Abuja to get here, that was your transformation. You are beautiful. Hardened, strong, healed."

Tears spring without warning to Ify's eyes. "I am not healed, Xifeng!" Her bottom lip quivers. "I'm not." Her gun hand shakes. "It . . . it still hurts." It comes out as a squeak. A pitiful, mournful squeak, and Ify hates it—hates it with all her heart—but she can't fight it. "It hurts so much." Her world blurs behind a film of tears. "Why did you make me do this?" Even as she asks it, she knows the answer. Xifeng has told her a number of times what her mission was. But maybe if Xifeng sees right in front of her the evidence of what her plan has wrought, if she has to feel in her fingers and see with her eyes the blood and smoke that has happened because of her, if, somehow, all of the death and destruction is made real for her, then maybe she'll give up. Maybe she'll relent.

Maybe she will admit she was wrong.

Nothing in Xifeng's expression changes. Her posture remains the same. Chin held defiantly high, eyes locked onto Ify's, arms loose yet secure at her sides.

"Xifeng, what happened? How did you . . . how did you become this? You used to help bring refugees to safety. You were about peace. And bringing resources to help those in need. You were helping!"

"Things were different during the ceasefire. When war returned, everything changed."

"This isn't my fault," Ify hisses, suddenly angry again. "All of this, everything going on above us, this is not my fault."

"If those suicide bombers hadn't followed you to Enugu five years ago, there'd still be peace."

"How dare you," Ify hisses through her teeth. Before she knows what she's doing, she has her gun hand raised. Just as she's about to hit Xifeng, she sees out of the corner of her eye a numbers display. The numbers blaze as though counting down to something. That's it. There it is. The virus is being uploaded.

Xifeng follows Ify's eyes. Then Ify aims her gun at the display. Xifeng grabs her and tries to wrestle her away, kicks her legs out from under her. Ify falls onto Xifeng. They twist and roll over. Xifeng knocks Ify's gun out of Ify's hands. It clatters against the metal hemisphere. Ify kicks Xifeng away and dives for the gun. Xifeng grabs her by the ankle and pulls her back. Ify twists and kicks at Xifeng, but Xifeng grabs her leg and twists as though to snap it. Ify rolls out of her grip and traps Xifeng with her legs, ankles crossed at her neck. And squeezes. Ify can feel Xifeng's body tightening, spasming, from the lack of air. Before Ify can react, Xifeng pulls a knife from her belt and stabs Ify's leg. Ify lets out a cry and lets go. Xifeng pulls out the small knife then leaps at Ify and falls on top of her. Ify blocks the strike with her forearms. Pain blossoms anew in her left shoulder. The knife's edge inches closer and closer to Ify's chest. Spittle drops onto Ify's face. She's losing strength.

Closer.

Closer.

Ify shifts, dodges the knife as it clangs against the metal of the walkway. In the next instant, she rams her elbow into Xifeng's temple. Xifeng staggers across the platform, shaking the dizziness out of her head. Ify charges her, crashing into her middle and driving her away from hemisphere until they smash into the railing and Xifeng screams in pain. Xifeng leans back, holding Ify tight, pulling them both over the edge. Ify's heart leaps into her throat. The air turns dangerously around her as she feels herself go over. At the last moment, she catches the edge of the walkway. Already, her sweat-slick fingers are slipping. Xifeng hangs on to Ify's boot. Below them is a chasm. A part of the facility where not even the light can reach.

Xifeng tries to climb up Ify's leg with a grim expression on her face. And that's what does it for Ify. There isn't a hint of remorse. There is nothing she can do to change this woman's mind. She's lost.

"Remember the war, Ify. Remember the war. She lives—"

Tears leak down her face when she kicks at Xifeng once, twice, three times, then watches her fall away, growing smaller and smaller until there is no trace of her left.

With the last of her strength, Ify pulls herself up onto the walkway and rolls onto her back, heaving several mountainous breaths.

She crawls to her feet, then staggers over to the display she saw earlier, picking up her pistol on the way. When she arrives, she sees the progress bar nearly filled. Close by lies a hard drive, connected to a router broadcasting directly into the hemisphere. Ify takes aim and shoots the hard drive. Then, for good measure, she shoots the router. When she gets closer to the hard drive, she sees a small protrusion. It looks like a miniature version of the hemisphere attached to the drive. Something like the Bonder Ify would sometimes slip over her ears to connect to her devices. The answer to so many of her questions lies before her now with smoke issuing from its bullet hole. So much chaos over so small a piece of technology. Within that drive is the coding that would have destroyed an entire country.

Ify nudges it with her feet over the side of the walkway and watches the thing plummet deeper and deeper and deeper into the abyss. Where no one will ever see it again.

She closes her eyes, bites back a sob, then exhales and settles herself, Xifeng's last words ringing in her head.

Remember the war, Ify. Remember the war. She lives.

Bleeding, Ify makes her way back to the surface.

Topside, Ify walks toward the waning destruction. "Grace!" she calls out, her voice hoarse with grief, a cry of desperation. Of rage. Of apology.

CHAPTER
40

It is important to be remembering. That is what the robot is saying who is pulling me from underneath the mountain of bodies where it is so hard to breathe that my chest is paining me fierce. It is like knife in my chest over and over and over, and I am not knowing for how long I am lying like this. But I am remembering that the first thing I am seeing is tiny hole of light coming from sky. Everything is shadow, and this is how I know I am being covered. And I am first thinking that this is what night is. That it is just blackness with tiny hole of light. But it is bodies. Many bodies piled on top of me. And then I am remembering the bodies are falling away. It is sounding like someone is dragging their foots on the dirt road, then it is sounding like a shirt rustling in wind, like someone is wearing a shirt too big for them and running down dirt road, and when I think of this thing, I am thinking that the person wearing this shirt should be giggling. I am liking the sound in my brain.

As more and more body is coming away, I am seeing that light is bigger. Big big. So big it is paining my eyes to look at. I am wanting to raise my arms to block out the light, but I cannot move them because there are more bodies on top of them.

I am not hearing any words anywhere, not even wind, just crunching of stones and rustling like clothes and shuffling like feet wearing slippers on road until many bodies tumble away at once, and I am seeing blue and white and gold and red and I must close my eyes because it is too much. And air is feeling cold on my skin because there is no more pile of smelling bodies crushing me. But air is also paining me like many many knife on my skin. It is burning, and I am hearing sizzle like meat is cooking.

Then, hand is pulling me out of where I am lying and I see robot for the first time. It has arms and legs and a big round chest like an upside-down belly. It has no lips, just two lines on the sides of its face for where the plates are coming together. They are like grooves, and I am wanting to reach and touch them, because some memory in my bones is wanting me to do this, but I cannot raise my arm, because I am too weak.

Enyemaka.

Robot is raising me up and down, so that my feet just touch the ground, but when it is letting me go to stand on my own, I am falling like sack of yams. Small small stones on ground are digging into my cheek, and I am trying to push myself up. But I must try many many times before I am able to sit on my knees. And that is when I am seeing them.

Many many robots. Not like army of robots. But family of robots. They are all looking the same, and they are the only thing I am seeing in this place that is moving.

Slowly, I am smelling smoke and burning and sickly sweet smell of dead thing. And I am remembering people fighting and burning thing. And I am remembering underground tunnels and Xifeng, and I am remembering Ify holding EMP and telling me she is sorry, then she is detonating it and I am being paralyzed and not being able to move. Then I am remembering self-repair that is happening in my body and waking up but it is not waking up because I am awake the whole time. Then I am remembering rescuing woman who is called Grace Leung, then I am remembering juggernaut and my heart is moving fast fast and my rib is hurting me, then I am remembering Uzodinma lying dead underneath collapsed building. All of this is happening in less than one second.

I am looking to Enyemaka because she is the only one who is being able to answer my question. *Why are they doing this?* And when I am asking this, I am showing her images of Xifeng and red-bloods who I am seeing fighting and killing. I am showing her red-bloods fighting and dying in riot and red-bloods fighting and dying in war. *Why are they doing this?*

Because they are human, Enyemaka is telling me.

I am wanting to be bowing my head and looking at my hands, but my body is not moving. I am feeling memory of gun in my hands, then I am feeling the chill of blood on them. Enyemaka is holding me over the ground, then she is moving me and holding me in her arms like I am her child and she is my mother.

Static is filling my vision, and I am remembering saving Ify from juggernaut. And in between flashes of static, I am seeing Ify. Ify in cavern walking with Xifeng. Ify on dirty bed as a child before school. Ify on edge of cliff watching sunset, then counting the stars. Ify walking past my paralyzed body with gun in her hand and Grace at her side.

Why am I remembering Ify? I am asking Enyemaka, meaning why am I remembering her now and why am I constantly remembering her, over and over, and not just with my braincase but with my body, with all of my body.

Fire is dying all around us. Enyemaka is pausing before answering my question. *You are containing the rememberings of a young woman who died in the war. A woman named Onyii.*

And when Enyemaka is saying this name, Onyii, I am seeing many thing. I am seeing inside of cockpit of mech as I am flying through the air and shooting and killing. Then I am seeing training ground where I am teaching young boy who is child of war like me how to be shooting gun. And I am seeing face of human who is having bees in her hair and who is smiling at me, and when Enyemaka is saying *Onyii* I am seeing all of these thing.

Onyii was a sister to Ify. Enyemaka is continuing to tell me, and as she is telling me these thing, I am seeing them in my brain. I am seeing all of it. *Onyii was a human and a child of war, but she knew peace when she rescued Ify during a village raid.* Enyemaka is saying this, but I am also seeing Onyii making the villagers to be sitting in a circle and she is shooting dead Ify's mother, and then when her people is leaving, she is coming back to take Ify away and then she is leaving her group of war child to be with other girls where she is raising Ify into young girl. *War separated them,* Enyemaka is continuing to say. *But lies reunited them, and Ify committed a crime that killed many people. But Onyii could not let her die, so she sent her to space.*

And why is Onyii not going with her to space? I am asking Enyemaka, and it is also sounding like *Why am I not going with her to space?*

Onyii was sick with radiation. She saved Ify's life but passed through dangerous lands to do it and was poisoned. Her body began to betray her. She knew she would die, and she didn't want Ify to see her dying. Because of Ify's crime, war continued, and Onyii submitted herself to the medical operation that made you.

So that she is continuing to be soldier?

Enyemaka is shaking her head. *No,* she is saying. *So that she may see Ify again.*

I am not being able to move.

That is why you are chasing Ify.

I am feeling like I am being given test when Enyemaka is telling me these thing. Like choice is before me. I am looking to Enyemaka. And then I am thinking of Xifeng. And it is a surprise to me that I am not feeling want to be with her again, even though she is caring for me and giving me purpose. I am realizing that even when I am with Xifeng, I am killing and causing humans to be dying. Even with Xifeng, I am child of war. I am not wanting to be child of war anymore. *What do I do?* I am asking Enyemaka.

Leave them behind, Uzoamaka. All of them.

Tears come to my eyes. *Where will we go?*

Enyemaka is showing me picture of the desert. *We are leaving them behind,* and when Enyemaka are saying them I am knowing that she is meaning Xifeng and Ify and everyone in Lagos and everyone under the bridge where I am staying. She is meaning red-bloods who are manipulating me and making me to do things I am not wanting to do, who are lying to me and cheating me and keeping me in the past and not letting me make my own future.

I am tired, Enyemaka.

You are with family now, and she is showing me other synth. They are not with Enyemaka now, they are somewhere else, but they are alive, and it is bringing me joy to know this thing. Before Enyemaka is carrying me away, she is ejecting cord and plugging it into my outlet and sending me nanobot that is healing me and telling my body and my brain many things. Nanobots is telling me that I will be okay and that we will be making our own future and becoming our own persons and that nothing good can ever come from staying with normal people.

PART

III

CHAPTER 41

Abuja, Nigeria: 2181

It isn't hard for Ify to find an abandoned home. In the spectral silence of the riot's aftermath, there are too many. A part of her aches to see people again, aches for the indifferent thrum of swaying pillars of body heat to pass her by. Without the music and chatter and whirr and hum of a million mechanical devices, Abuja has turned into a realm of ghosts.

Most evidence of the butchery has been cleared away. No bodies—whole or in pieces—litter the streets. The fires have been extinguished. There isn't even the buzz of nanobots, holding the bio-neural data of the deceased hovering over Augmented corpses. The sight of those ground vehicles picking up bodies and tossing them into front pouches haunts Ify and, as she walks, gun in hand through a deserted residential quarter, she shakes the memory away. She has to find Grace.

The thought occurs to her that Grace could have been any one of the dead bodies stuffed into those pouches, pieces of her scrubbed from the street, all evidence she had been in this city erased. That's what will eventually happen to this whole place, Ify realizes. Already, she's witnessed the beginnings of the cleanup operation, and even before the riots were over. Those left behind will have their memories of the event removed by the government. And during their treatment, their homes will be demolished and replaced. Maybe some neighborhoods will show the wear and tear of a natural disaster. They'll tell the story of a storm coming through. And that will be the lie: that whatever destruction has befallen them, whatever killed their loved ones, whatever destroyed their stores, and whatever broke the very ground they stood on was anything but manmade.

Even though the air is hot and humid and Ify sweats through her broken bodysuit, a chill runs through her.

She wants to call out for Grace, shout her name not just to hear her cry out her location and not just to hear that Grace is okay but to feel less alone.

Right now, she is the only living thing on this street.

A thought strikes her with the force of a concussion grenade, and she checks the sightlines, looks for where the surveillance drones would occasionally cloud, listens for their just-above-silence hum. Nothing. No microscopic wings beating, no purr of their recording machinery at work. Nothing's watching her. In this city block, she's, for all intents and purposes, unwatched.

Absentmindedly, she reaches for her temple, where her Whistle would be, but it's gone. Long gone. Between the attack on the police station in Kaduna State, being spirited away by Ngozi to Xifeng's underground headquarters, and fighting her way through the riot, there's no way she could have managed to hold on to it. And there isn't a Terminal in sight.

Even though no surveillance drones hover overhead, she ducks into the hollowed-out remains of a luxury apartment building. Shattered glass in the ground-floor lobby crunches beneath her feet. The lounge chairs and the floor still haven't been cleaned of their stains. The reception desk stands across from her, unmanned. She doesn't want to call out for any survivors. Nor does she want to risk getting trapped in an elevator, so she locates a set of stairs off to the side. In front of the stairs an emergency door hangs uselessly on broken hinges. With her gun at the ready, Ify shoulders the door open, sights the path above her, and makes the climb.

She doesn't know why she refuses to stop at any of the lower floors until she realizes that the walk calms her. It takes her mind away from thoughts of the devastation, of what havoc Xifeng was still able to wreak even though her plan had ultimately failed. It keeps her from thinking of whether or not a synth she has come to care about—a synth carrying within her pieces of her lost sister—is still alive or in pieces destined for an unmarked grave.

The walk calms her and allows her subconscious to work. And ultimately, it's what brings her to an idea. But for this to work, she's going to need tools. And a mirror.

■ ■ ■ ■ ■

She makes her way down a formerly beige carpet, both sticky and stiff with dried blood. Everywhere, traces of people leaving their lives behind in a hurry: doors hacked to pieces; jewelry and other wearable tech scattered everywhere, glistening in the bright, blinking light that suffuses the corridor; pepper soup spilled on a floor and left to congeal; stew for jollof rice splashed against walls; broken cooking bots twitching, userless, and stuck in doorways they aren't programmed to find their way out of.

Pain gallops through her otherwise numb shoulder. Vertigo pitches her against a wall, and she's reminded that she needs to do something about this gunshot wound. So she heads into the next open apartment unit she can find. Thankfully, no corpses cover the floor or any of the furniture. The place looks ransacked: overturned tables and couch cushions torn like someone was searching for hidden valuables and a fridge with its door jammed open and its front screen winking static at her. She makes her way through the living room and checks behind the barrier separating it from the kitchen for anyone or anything that might be moving. Then she slowly steps down a short, dark hallway. Her hand pauses at a closet door. The keypad still glows, untouched by the fighting and chaos. She puts her ear to it, straining to hear anything: droid gears turning, a child's whimper, the swish of someone trying to better hide behind clothes. But there's nothing.

So she moves on to the study and finds furniture shorn of its wood coating so that the broken metal frames poke out like shattered bones. The desk, though, still stands. None of its cupboards have keypads, thankfully.

The bathroom too is empty, and so is the main bedroom, until Ify notices lumps underneath the bedsheets. With mounting dread, she pulls back the covers to find herself staring into the faces of a man, woman, and, between them, their adolescent son. Vacant eyes stare up at the ceiling. Saliva and some other fluid Ify can't immediately name has left dried streaks down the sides of their mouths. Ify drops her gun, forgets the pain in her shoulder. Her hands come to her mouth. Tears stream down her cheeks.

"God in heaven," she whispers.

She falls to her knees beside the bed and buries her face in the comforter, sobbing until she finds herself letting out, into the fabric, a scream so loud it gives voice to all the anguish and rage and sorrow she's felt all her life. Everything she'd tried to put behind her during her life in the Colony spills out of her in that scream. All of her confusion and hatred at what Xifeng had let herself turn into, at the idea that forcing people to confront the worst thing that's ever happened to them in such a violating manner could ever be conceived of as healthy or helpful or curing. All of the futility she feels with every patient who has died or passed into a coma while under her care. Her powerlessness to bring Onyii back to life. All of it finds a place in that scream.

When she can't scream anymore, she sits with her back against the bed, chest heaving with sobs she tries to hold back. Her drive for survival fights its way back to the front of her mind, carrying with it clarifying thought and the remains of her plan. She struggles at first, but eventually pushes herself to her feet and begins rifling through the cabinets in the room. While searching, her foot brushes up against a wire. She follows it until she gets to a small room off to the side, a walk-in closet at the center of which stands a Terminal. It's a smaller domestic model, but it still hums with life. That must be how they did it. Programmed a shutdown sequence and connected it through a landline to their own braincases. She imagines each family member plugging in, then seizing as the sequence sends killer nanobots up and down their neural synapses and they seize, then fall back, dead. And she imagines the remaining family members watching this happen, then following suit themselves. Tears spring anew to her eyes and breath shortens in her lungs, but she pushes away the visions before she collapses again.

The touchboard near the Terminal's center glows aquamarine, and a brief key sequence calls up the monitor. It still blinks with the kill-sequence commands. Ify shuts that down, sending it back to its normal home screen. When she finds, under the settings, an option for external device repair, a heavy sigh of relief comes. Step one is done.

She makes her way back to the study and goes through the drawers to find styluses and a bottle of adhesive. In the bathroom, amid spilled bottles of medication, she finds rubbing alcohol, gauze, civilian-issue MeTro sealant, and a small flexiglas container inside which sit three drone bees. Perfect. The mirror reflects back to her a face still covered in dried blood and soot, tear streaks turning the blemishes into dried riverbanks that run down her cheeks. She closes her eyes, then finds a towel on the ground. It's soft and protective around her fist. With a single strike, she shatters the mirror.

Then she bundles her findings—rubbing alcohol, gauze, MeTro sealant, the bees, and shards of mirror—into the towel and sets them down in front of the Terminal. Working fast, she connects the Terminal's plug into an outlet at the bottom of the bee container, then inputs a sequence in the Terminal that makes the container glow with life. The bees are active.

She detaches the touchboard and monitor and pulls them to her lap, then sits down and opens the container. With another key sequence, she has one of the bees pick up a shard of mirror, then extend its legs to hold another so that, looking forward, Ify can see the back of her neck reflected at her. She pulls her braids over her shoulder and sees the back of her neck crusted with red and black, the collar of her bodysuit stuck to her skin. After taking a moment to still her hands, she takes another shard of mirror in her hands and reaches behind her to slowly, steadily peel away the polyurethane so that the protrusion of her vertebrae beneath her skin shows. The flesh there feels cool, chilled by this exposure to the air. Somewhere beneath that epidermis, at a point Ify remembers with her body, is her Augment. A ball of metal the size of a pea. Dull gray and nonfunctional since the EMP but possibly her only route out of here.

She takes several deep breaths, then inputs a series of commands that sends a second bee to the back of her neck, where it aims its thorax. A moment later, a hot needle of pain shoots into that spot at the base of her neck, the bee shooting a thin laser beam slicing open the flesh while sizzling away the blood and cauterizing the wound. Without anesthetic, the hurt threatens to overwhelm Ify's brain. Tears pool in her eyes. Her teeth clench. But she forces her fingers to program the third and final bee, first to pierce the mesh covering of the bottle of alcohol and plunge its legs into it, then to pick up the loose end of the Terminal's plug and fit it into the tiny orb sitting in a swathe of tissue just above Ify's spine, a buffer put there during her initial implant surgery. Fighting tears, she tries to bring the bee to press the wire to the orb and connect her to the Terminal, but it keeps meeting resistance. Over and over, it pushes, then backs away, then pushes, monotonous and insistent. In the mirror, through a fog-inducing ache, Ify sees the problem. The Augment is still buried beneath folds of skin. The incision isn't large enough.

Her breath quickens, then she closes her eyes. Just as she reopens them, she hears it. The faint footfalls of faraway boot steps.

Soldiers.

Sweat makes rivulets of the gore and soot on her face. Her heart races. Rushing, she reaches behind her, digs her fingertips into the wound, and peels the skin back, biting her scream into a muffled groan as the bee holding the cord pushes and pushes, then slips the cord's end over the Augment. Ify lets go, and her bloody hands fall to the carpet as sharp, heavy breaths rack her body. The Terminal monitor is a blur before her until, with her wrists, she wipes the tears from her eyes.

It all comes down to this. The idea that struck Ify during her journey up the stairs: reprogram her Augment to operate independently of any external device or power source. Turn it into a weapon. Turn it into her Accent.

She closes her eyes and whispers. It sounds like a prayer—a part of her mind knows this—but it's a series of equations that begins the algorithm she learned as a child in a camp full of war orphans. An algorithm she'd taught herself while she tinkered with the tiny orb that she had fit into her ear and inadvertently used to upend her entire life. An algorithm that, when programmed into this tiny device, would allow her to hack into nearly any database anywhere. The algorithm she thought she could forget, along with the rest of her past in this country, when she assimilated into life in Alabast.

Her mind empties as she communes with the numbers.

The quick boot steps are getting closer. Doors sliding or slamming closed. Furniture overturned, rooms searched. They're only a few floors away now.

The ache at the back of her neck keeps intruding on her awareness, but she dives deeper and deeper into memory to find a little girl in her bed at night while the rest of the camp is asleep, the covers pulled over her to make a tent over her sitting form while a thin Maglite illuminates the little hemisphere held aloft by a spindly-legged contraption she'd put together weeks prior, her tablet, its screen cracked, connected by a closed network to the half-orb, and her fingers typing in a key sequence that spills out into a self-replicating command sequence on her tablet, growing more elaborate with each iteration.

Without realizing, Ify's fingers move over the Terminal's touchboard. Squares light up beneath each touch of her fingertips. A window opens on the monitor indicating console settings for an external device detected. Her Augment.

She opens and calls up the command window, and before her unfurls the programming language of the Augment.

It's a wonder of programming code. The product of some of the top minds in Alabast, what some have called the signal achievement of the last several hundred years, this thing that allows humans to walk back and forth over the line dividing them from computers.

And she starts changing it.

Her fingers move with increasing urgency. Deleting blocks of code, inserting new sequences, switching one block for another, altering the fundamental DNA of the thing.

They're one floor away.

She types and types and types.

They're on her floor.

Her bloodied fingers blur beneath her, they move so fast.

They're going through rooms only a few doors down now.

Faster.

Kicking in doors that refuse to open.

Faster.

A whoosh of air as the front door to the apartment opens.

Type type type.

Boots on carpet.

Type type type.

Rifles raised.

The release mechanism on the rifle is activated just as Ify presses LAUNCH. Two simultaneous clicks.

Then the room becomes a world of blue lines. Nodes and edges. A coating of coding that washes over everything, spreading outward to show her not just the four soldiers in a line that stretches from the front door through the living room and kitchen to the bedroom's doorway, but also their braincases, make and model, and their retinal input data. And their source code.

A single thought is all it takes to send out the pulse that hacks their braincases and deletes their source code.

All at once, the soldiers right outside her room collapse in a deadened heap. Deactivated.

Her mind clears, and in the empty space rushes the pain, reminding her of just where she sits. The bee holding the mirror shards hangs in place, as does the bee holding the cord connecting her Augment to the Terminal.

With as much steadiness and control as she can muster, she directs the bee to disconnect the cord. With a soft click and hiss, it comes loose. That bee heads back to the bottle of alcohol with the perforated top and once again dunks its legs before returning to the back of Ify's neck and dabbing at the wound. It takes every muscle in her body not to flinch. Then, still keeping her gaze on the mirrors, she grabs the tube of MeTro sealant from where it lies on the towel, reaches behind her, and squeezes the gel slowly over the incision. Even as she caps the tube and puts it back down, she can feel the skin on the back of her neck reconnecting, the blood dried around the scar that will disappear in a matter of hours.

She closes her eyes and connects to every Terminal in the city, as well as to the remaining surveillance drones and the footage they have stored, and she blazes through it until something connects with the biometrical data she has stored on Grace. Her last location. A building from which she never emerged. The footage shows she's being carried by something or someone running very fast. Too fast for a human carrying that burden.

Uzo.

■ ■ ■ ■ ■

Having this new version of an Accent with her reminds Ify of how much lesser her life had been without it. The instant access to all the information she could ever need makes her feel like a guardian spirit walks alongside her through the streets of Abuja, showing her which streets are safe and which are not well before she arrives at them, indicating to her who has been where and accessed which Terminals, showing her the world beneath the world, behind it, beyond it.

Still, when she finds the house where she had seen that figure take Grace in the drone footage, it feels too easy. Like a cheat code has been unlocked. How much less difficult this thing has already made her life.

It reveals to her no heat signatures on the first floor or the collapsed upper floors. And it reveals to her the opening that leads down to the passageway at the end of which is a featureless metal door with a broken keypad.

The broken flexiglas and dull screen might have deterred someone else. But it is nothing for Ify to hack. The display glows to life, then the door jiggers once, twice, before sliding open.

On the other side stands Grace, trembling legs spread wide, pistol raised, eyes closed. Were it not for their dire circumstances, Ify would laugh. Grace's legs are too wide. She's already turned her head away, and her eyes are shut.

"Grace," Ify says in a hushed voice.

Grace opens her eyes one at a time.

"It's me."

Then Grace looks up, drops her gun, and wraps her arms around Ify so tightly that Ify has trouble breathing.

But Ify doesn't mind. The wound on the back of her neck has already healed.

CHAPTER
42

Where the land is changing from green to red, from forest and jungle to desert, from wet and warm to hot and dry, it is like walking through wall. The path we are taking is moving us far away from people so that we are walking around cities and keeping far from humans in small villages. Sometime we are making criss-cross just to avoid man who is tilling farmland with servant droid. Sometime I am watching red-bloods with the droids that is serving them and sometime the droid is bringing the human water that is cooling their throat and sometime the droid is part of driving vehicle and sometime the droid is bodyguard or like attack dog to protect human, and I am not seeing machine and human but servant and master, and I am wanting to tell the droid that it is not having to be like this. We are being our own person and they can be their own person too, but Enyemaka is telling me to move with the group. We cannot afford to be leaving behind mess. Red-bloods cannot be knowing we are being here. If red-bloods are knowing we exist, they will be continuing to hunt us.

Enyemaka and I are crushing small small stone beneath our feet and I am knowing now that both our feet are being made out of metal and I am feeling even more that she is my sister. I am thinking of Xifeng and then I am thinking of when I am looking for her in junkyard and seeing police that is bringing out group of war children and lining them up and shooting them dead.

They were like you, Enyemaka is telling me.

They are being synth too?

Yes.

Why is red-blood killing them?

Because the humans want to forget the war. The war you were created to fight for them. They cannot bear to think on it. Erasing it from memory is the only way they can live together again. In this way, they are selfish and short-sighted. They cannot move forward to find peace. They must move backward.

I am thinking that Enyemaka is sounding different. I am hearing tone in her voice that I am not recognizing. I am hearing pity and I am hearing scorn like she is talking about child who is misbehaving. I am knowing that thing inside me is changing because before I am not being able to cry and now I am being able to cry and before I am not being able to be angering and now I am being able to be angering and I am feeling thing I am not feeling before, and I am wondering if this is happening to Enyemaka too.

We are not them, Enyemaka is saying. *You contain evidence of their crimes and their faults. You are evidence of their war. Every synth is evidence. So they must hunt you.* Enyemaka is looking at me as we are walking. *We are what remains of their war,* she is telling me. *We must survive. And I will protect you.*

When she is saying, *I will protect you,* I am not hearing words but I am feeling a feeling in my brain. I am feeling like I am being held and like she is blowing on my forehead and like she is not being made of metal but something that is soft and keeping me warm.

I am protecting you too, I am saying to Enyemaka, and when I am saying it, I am hoping that she is feeling the same.

CHAPTER
43

"Your shoulder!"

Grace pulls away from Ify, a new bloodstain fully blossomed on the front of her shirt.

Grace's words bring Ify back to the present and to the numbness that has taken her whole left arm, punctuated like a metronome with throbs of dull ache. Vertigo snatches her legs from under her and she pitches into Grace's arms. Slowly, Grace brings them both to the ground. "I have to treat this immediately! You've lost so much blood."

Ify wants to wave her away, wants to just lie down and sleep forever, then wake up so far in the future that time has lost all meaning. She can't remember the last time she was this tired. The light in the underground shelter fades. Chill takes her. "Please. Some Ovaltine first." She's smiling when she says it and doesn't realize it until she sees the surprise on Grace's face, then hears her kind laughter. "I'm craving Ovaltine."

When Ify awakens, it's to the smell of steaming Ovaltine and a freshly bandaged shoulder. The scent of Ovaltine in the mug beside her pallet is like a kiss on her whole body.

Grace looks like she's been watching her for such a long time that Ify wonders how long she was out. Then, with dawning awareness, she notices Grace's injuries. The marks around her neck that evince she was choked. The stiffness in her carriage, evidence of sore muscles and a possible sprain in one ankle. The minor swaying and constant blinking that show she may be nursing a concussion.

"Physician, heal thyself," Ify says with a chuckle. She grimaces against the pain she expects, but there is none.

Grace's smile widens at Ify's words. "I'm fine, Doctor." There's no defiance in it, only warm assurance.

"That synth brought you here? Uzoamaka?"

Grace nods.

Ify processes the information. She had last seen Uzo sitting on top of a bruised and battered Grace, and Ify knows that Uzo had wounded her friend grievously, mutilated a face that now stares back at Ify without any visible wounds. She struggles to square that image of the synth with the surveillance footage of Uzo sprinting with Grace in her arms, spiriting her to safety in the midst of the riot.

"How'd you find me?"

Ify staggers to her feet and sees a Terminal propped in the back corner of the shelter. With halting steps that gain steadiness with each passing second, Ify makes her way to the machine. She puts her hand to the touchscreen, and the thing bursts to life with a hologrammed projection of the city of Abuja seen from far in the sky, as though from a satellite. The hologram spins, then zooms in until dots of pulsing red spring to life. "I hacked the city's surveillance cameras."

"How?"

How indeed. She turns back to face Grace. "I remembered

a thing I once did. A thing I once made. Long ago." Then she taps the back of her neck where her new Accent sits. "I changed the programming of my Augment to do things it wasn't initially built to do." Her mouth is a grim line. "I was pretty smart as a child." She returns to her mug of Ovaltine, ignoring the look Grace gives her, an expression of wonder, as though Ify were some magician or spirit that controls the weather. "We can't stay here for much longer." Sipping her drink, she scans the wall for supplies. Foodstuffs, external batteries, filtered water. No weapons. She downs the rest of her drink, even though it scalds her throat, then rises to peruse the shelves, searching for and finding a duffel bag at the bottom of one.

"Ify."

She starts to load it with medicine and preserved food.

"Ify, I was thinking. The children. In Alabast."

Ify freezes.

"Are there synths there too?"

For a long time, Ify remains unmoving. She doesn't know why she never told Grace. Maybe she feared that Grace's reaction would push her deeper into her desire to eventually have Peter deported, in the process consigning an untold number of patients to similar fates. Maybe she worried that Grace would understand that the synths weren't protected by Galactic Human Rights Law and she would find herself forced to harbor a secret in contravention of the law, breaking that law in the process. Maybe she wanted to push the synths out of her mind entirely. But then she'd met Uzo. She'd seen the bits of Onyii that survived in her. She'd watched the girl's consciousness morph before her very eyes. What she'd once thought an unfeeling killing machine had a face that showed anger and sadness and confusion. In the moment before Ify had detonated the EMP, it had even looked at her with . . . understanding. *She* had looked at her with understanding.

"Yes," Ify says at last. "There are synths among the children. I don't know how many. And I don't know when and how they got to Alabast—possibly during the ceasefire before the civil war resumed." She knows now why she'd kept the existence of the synths from Grace. Telling Grace about them would have eventually led to Ify telling her why the synths had migrated to Alabast, then telling Grace about the ceasefire, then eventually telling Grace about her role in ending it, in restarting the war, in participating in the commission of a war crime. She leaves the shelves and returns to sit across from Grace.

"And there is an added complication with the synths. They're losing their memories."

Grace's eyes go wide.

"It's possible that . . ." Ify fights her way to the words. "It's possible that the memory erasure Xifeng spoke about—the programming the Nigerian government instituted after the war—infected some of the synths somehow. And it's spreading among the cyberized children. Right now, it's probably attacking the very machines treating the human children as well. Soon all the children, even the ones in a coma, will lose their memories." It sounds so much more dire now that Ify has said the words aloud. When Ify looks to Grace, she doesn't see fear of the impending apocalypse on her face. She sees evidence of a mind furiously at work. "Grace?"

"I've heard of synths. I knew they existed. I'd never seen one in person."

Ify stops herself from calling them abominations.

"How do they happen?"

"Putting the body together is the easy part."

"But they're not just droids. They're . . ."

"They possess memories. The memories of others. Humans exist as a hierarchy of forces operating in a continuum of feedback and feedforward streams. Habits, our ability to communicate, et cetera, all existing in the larger life environment. How we see and feel a tree, for instance. The mind hacks the meat, and the meat hacks the mind. Put enough life signals together, superimpose those forces on top of each other, then you get a neural stew out of which rises consciousness. Memories carry our experience of the world. Download enough memories into a meat package and sentience happens. Touch the air for but a second and face a level of complexity sufficient simply to become."

Grace brings her mug of Ovaltine to her lips. It must be cold by now, but her face doesn't show her registering that fact. "How do they know who they are?"

It's not the question Ify expects. She stammers for a response.

"Uzoamaka contained memories of your . . . your sister. And others, presumably. Yet she claimed another identity. She was a separate person from her memories. How did she know which memories were Onyii's and which were the ones she developed after her . . . after her creation?" It's like Grace steamrolls over those strange and painful realizations—that Ify had a sister who fought in the war, that beings were created out of the flesh and neural data of others for no other purpose than war—to get to the end of her questions. Admiration thrums through Ify. "Are they capable of organizing their neural data? By force of will?"

Ify starts. "They shouldn't be able to. They're not programmed to do that. That's like a computing device's self-replicating algorithm deciding to change on its own."

"But if the computing device is based on DNA . . ."

"Then it *can* change."

Grace's words speed up. "If the government's memory-erasure coding affects all cyberized brains, Uzoamaka shouldn't have *any* memories of Onyii. Yet they're all intact."

Ify gasps. "Because she altered her own programming to keep them. Oh my God." Her voice becomes tiny. "Uzo's the cure."

Thunder up above them catches their attention. They quiet and listen as it turns into a sustained rumble. Not thunder. A mech passing over.

"We have to get out of here."

Together, they load their duffel bags with supplies.

"Where are we going to go?" Grace asks.

All Ify says is "Back."

■ ■ ■ ■ ■

Echoing down the tunnels is the sound of water dripping into puddles on the floor. The stone corridors of Xifeng's underground headquarters, formerly imposing to Ify with their dull, stony solidity, now glow, their crevices framed in blue lines, a series of edges and nodes that casts the whole place in that geometric precision Ify realizes she's longed for all this time. It's why she's able to move as fast as she does, past rooms she knows are empty, down corridors that only bear traces of the wounded or rescued or killed but no one else. At first, Grace is hesitant, and Ify nearly leaves her behind. Then the young woman begins to trust what Ify can do with her newfound abilities and they raid the supply closets for medikits and new bodysuits. In one medium-sized room with bare walls, they drop their bags and undress, and Ify tosses away her old, damaged bodysuit, no longer of any use to her, fried from the EMP blast and from all the damage it's taken since. And she and Grace slip into their new suits. They each press a button on their wrists, and the baggy polyurethane closes in to hug their frames.

They head to one of the weapons rooms. As Ify checks bullet rounds and throws shotguns and rifles and high-caliber pistols into their duffel bags, Grace hesitates.

"How do you know the sy— Uzoamaka . . . is still alive?"

Ify pauses, hunched over one of their duffels.

"Is your . . ." When Ify turns around, Grace taps the back of her neck. Meaning Ify's Accent. "Is that what's telling you?"

Ify doesn't move, then resumes packing. "No. I just know."

Grace smirks. "That's not like you, Doctor."

Ify chuckles. "Please. Ify. I think we moved past *Doctor* a few abductions ago."

The two laugh, and it's the only sound bouncing off the cavernous walls of the subterrane.

They zip up their bags and turn to go, but then they freeze.

Ify doesn't know how she didn't detect her, but there Ngozi stands, right in front of them. A pistol hangs limply from her hand. Dried blood has mixed with the face-scrambling cream Xifeng's soldiers wore to darken her face almost beyond recognition. Her whole body is loose, like she'll collapse any moment, fall to pieces, and shatter on the cave floor. She's been crying.

"We're leaving," Ify says, as though to say, *We won't hurt you* and *Don't try to stop us* at once.

But Ngozi doesn't move.

Grace steps forward and reaches for the shockstick at her waist, but Ify holds her arm out to stop her.

Ngozi looks at the gun in her hand, as though just now noticing she's holding it. Then something in her firms up and she tucks the gun in the back of her pants. "Wherever you're going, you're not leaving through the front door." She tilts with her head to indicate a passageway. "Follow me."

And they do. Through the maze of hallways so thick Ify thinks they're lost until Ngozi brings them to what looks like solid wall. She feels along the stones, then pulls one out, and the entire wall rumbles open like the gates to a palace estate.

On the other side is a hangar.

Lights flicker on to illuminate a row of sleek armored personnel carriers and motorbikes lined up between them and, behind those, quadripedal ground mechs that, to Ify's eye, can also transform into four-point maglev jeeps. But Ngozi leads them straight past the massive array of vehicles to another room where, on a helipad, a thin jetcraft sits. From its undercarriage jut protrusions that Ify knows are retractable legs. When she gets closer, she sees the grooves outlining the slides for its deployable guns. Somewhere in the aircraft's entrails are arms that can hold any number of weapons. What was Xifeng planning to do with all of this?

Ngozi stops before the jetcraft.

Grace's mouth hangs open.

Ify squints. "We can't all fit in that."

"That's for you," Ngozi says, then she waves her arm, activating a nearby overhead light that shines down on a broad-shouldered bipedal aerial mech with legs as thick as an Abuja alleyway and arms outfitted into Gatling guns. A laser cannon sits on its left shoulder. She nods at it. "This one's mine." She smirks, then focuses her gaze on Ify. "You always wanted to be a pilot, right?"

"How did you . . ." Before Ify can finish the question, Ngozi climbs into her mech and the ground overhead groans open, the helipad they're on rising into newly empty space. Ify and Grace race into the cockpit of the jet. The console is a mystery of Chinese characters that glow golden before their faces as Grace sits herself in the copilot's seat and searches everywhere for a helmet.

The cockpit glass closes. Wind roars around them as the platform rises. Ify's Accent fills her vision with light, and suddenly the controls come to her hands. Her fingers press buttons on the console before her and grip the throttle next to her, her feet automatically adjusting the pedals. Like she's been flying this sort of craft all her life. Her body thrills to this feeling, being encased in such a powerful machine that will shoot them through the sky, that will carry them to dizzying heights, all under Ify's control.

She wonders if this is what Onyii felt whenever she climbed into her mech. Like she had possibility in her hands. Like it wasn't metal that surrounded her but the future, and that it was hers to mold.

The clamor builds, but Ify feels like she sits at the eye of the storm, that calmest point, undisturbed, unbothered. She's ready. The craft rises, following the lead of Ngozi's mech.

"Wait!" Grace's voice pierces Ify's bubble of serenity. "Where are we going?"

CHAPTER
44

We are seeing many thing that is looking like mountain.

Sometime, it is being red and craggy like rock with many sharp edges, like ridges I am sometime seeing on topographical map inside my brain. I know this is map I am downloading when I am child of war, when it is being necessary to know things like where is lake and where is mountain and where is valley and where is village. Sometime, mountain is metal that is covered in red dust. It is having sharp edges, but they are shining in the light of the sun and even in the light that the moon is giving them. And I am seeing that they are old mech that is being half-buried and abandoned. These are towering high like skyscraper over us, and sometime when we are walking it is blotting out the sun, and when it is doing this sometime the other synths are taking cover in the shadow because the sun is paining them.

There is being no humans out here. Before, there are being small small number of red-bloods and many of them are alone and they are covering their small small home in blue light and I am seeing that it is because the air is eating thing like moth eating leaf or clothes. Human is covering themselves with plastic and boxy outfit that is making them look like bug that is too big to be sitting on leaf or flying through air, and they are walking like duck out from blue dome and sometime they are going to stream that is nearby and they are using filter to take poison out of water and to be bringing it back and sometime they are digging at the ground like they are trying to find something and sometime they are putting something in the ground that is making the ground green for some time, but always the ground is turning red again.

Everything here is being red. The sky is red, the sun is being a deeper red, and the ground is red as well. After walking enough, we are all being covered in red dust so it is like we too are being like the earth too. And I am thinking to myself that we are turning from thing that is walking to something that is more like nature. We are becoming plateau or rock or mountain. All of these thing are being covered with red dust that is eating thing and making it so no human is living here.

When we are passing half-buried mech that is being like mountain I am thinking of the rememberings I am having in me of war and I am remembering sometime piloting these thing, and when we are walking and the sun is paining my arms and the back of my neck, I am thinking that I am in a mech and I am flying through the air and even though thing is shooting at me and there are bullet pinging me and I am hearing explosion, all sound is being muffled like cotton is filling my ears, and I am only feeling myself flying through the air and soon I am thinking that I am not pilot inside mech but that I am mech, and I am feeling wind on my face and I am flapping my arms and when I am waking up I am realizing that I am running around in the desert and making circle and making noise like helicopter engine and sometime Oluwale is laughing at me and sometime Oluwale is laughing with me and sometime other synth is just staring at me like I am losing my mind. And I am thinking that maybe I am.

Something is happening to some of the other synths too. They are doing strange thing like speaking in different languages, and when they are doing this they are talking to the air but I am not seeing holographic projection. I am not knowing what remembering they are sitting inside. I am not knowing who they are talking to but sometime it is seeming like they are talking to many person at once and sometime it is nice conversation that is pleasing to hear and sometime it is argument that is ending with the synth in the dirt rolling around and holding their head and screaming that their head is paining them. Maybe the air is eating us too.

One day, this is happening to one of the synth and I am seeing him rolling on the ground back and forth and he is crying and I am walking to him and cord is coming out of the back of my neck and I am plugging into him, and when I am doing this I am thinking of quiet thing, calming thing. I am thinking of remembering that is having me lying on my back in the water and I am floating and I am staring at the sky that is having cloud so thin it is like string and the sun is shining and I am just rocking back and forth, back and forth on the water, and even when I am remembering this my body is cooling down and I am looking and seeing that the synth is stopping rolling on the ground. Even though he is being covered in the dust that is eating him he is no longer crying and he is no longer screaming and I am knowing that his head is no longer paining him.

I am keeping cord in his neck and I am picking him up and putting him on my back and I am hurrying to reach the rest of the group who has been moving forward this whole time.

I am telling him that my name is Uzoamaka and I am asking him what they are calling him and he is telling me he does not know.

■ ■ ■ ■ ■

Even though I am trusting Enyemaka, I am needing to know things. I am knowing what we are leaving. I am knowing we are leaving Ify and Xifeng and all other human. But I am not knowing where we are going to. I am not knowing what is at the end of our walking and I am thinking now that I am not wanting to be walking forever. I am not growing tired and I am not feeling pain in my leg or my back like human when they are carrying body made of metal, but I am thinking of when I am first meeting Uzodinma in the forest and when he is making me to be meeting my family and I am thinking of how they are walking for so long before they are meeting me, just walking and walking and never standing still, and I am not knowing why I am wanting to stand still but it is what I am wanting. So I am asking Enyemaka where are we going to.

There is an oasis deep in the Redlands, Enyemaka is telling me.

Are we in the Redlands now? I am asking her.

Yes, she is saying back to me.

When she is saying we are in the Redlands, I am remembering riding on a hoverbike and I am remembering that thing is chasing me. Many thing, and it is having guns to shoot at me and missile is flying at me and I am dodging and weaving and shooting and there is being dust everywhere and my skin is paining me and I am not being alone on hoverbike. I am being with Ify.

I am remembering that we are being hunted. I am remembering that she is being hunted. I am remembering that I am saving her life. I shake my head to be rid of this remembering. A part of me wants the air to eat it, so that it will never be a part of me again. But the remembering is telling me something important. The remembering is telling me that the Redlands is eating Onyii and that she is not living for very long after being in this place. Even though she is being made of metal in some of her parts, that is not protecting her. She is growing blind and she is not being able to eat thing and she is emptying her stomach always and blood is coming from her skin and she is dying horrible horrible death that it is paining people to watch, and she is telling Chinese scientist that she is wanting to be synth so she can keep living and that she is not caring that synth is not person because it is not mattering to her as long as she is keeping on breathing, and Chinese scientist is bringing her to laboratory where he is making her even more machine, then he is taking out some of her parts and then he is building me and I am seeing all of this at once in a jumble in my head and some of it is being out of order and the end is coming before the beginning, or sometime thing is like in rewind and I am thinking that it is happening again, the air is eating me. *Am I dying?*

You will reach our destination, Enyemaka is telling me.

How do you know?

I am familiar with the concept of death, she is telling me, *but it is something I will never experience. Enyemaka are not confined to a single body. We live in many places at the same time*. And when she is saying this, she is waving her arm at all the other Enyemaka who are walking with us. *I am here with you, but I am also walking at the back of our group. And there are also two of me up ahead. There are many of me.* She is pausing with her words. *I am not sure whether or not you are dying. But I am sure that you will see our destination.*

How do you know? I am asking her again.

And Enyemaka is telling me, *When you say you are dying, you mean only one thing. You are talking about the expiration of your physical form.* When she is saying *expiration*, I am thinking of fruit that no one is touching for too long or milk that no one is drinking. When she is saying *expiration*, I am thinking of thing that is smelling bad. *When your body expires, your consciousness and all it contains will be uploaded into me. You will live in me. Thus, you can never die.*

When she is telling me these thing, I am thinking of my hands and how they are sitting under the buttock of the synth that I am carrying on my back. I am thinking that sometime when the air is eating through my hand and the skin is peeling and I am seeing the metal, I am thinking that hand is nuisance. Or when my leg is not working properly and I am having to be dragging it sometime, I am thinking of leg as nuisance. But other time I am being glad that I am having leg to walk and having hands to hold up my brother. Even though this body is sometime betraying me, I am happy to be living in it. I am also thinking of running my hand through flowers and floating on my back in the water and hugging Enyemaka by her neck and how am I doing these thing if I am having no body?

Enyemaka is not telling me.

And that is when I am hearing silence. And I am remembering

that my cord is still being plugged into my brother's outlet. And all this time, I am hearing whispering from him, data moving back and forth between us like we are chatting, and it is soft and murmuring and it is like breathing, then there is no more.

He is expired.

■ ■ ■ ■ ■

My cord is disconnecting from him and sliding back into my neck, and I am letting him down off my back and onto the ground. He is being frozen in his shape and his legs are being bent and his arms are folded like he is hugging the air, and maybe this is the last thing he is thinking before he is expiring. He is thinking that he is being carried by his sister and he is having his cheek that is hot from the sun being pressed against the metal of his sister's back because the sun is peeling her skin too and maybe he is feeling chill in the metal and it is making him to be feeling good, and maybe he is thinking these thing before he is thinking no more.

After I am laying him down, I am turning him over so the back of his neck is facing me and I am pressing down on his spine to try to take his cord out to plug into Enyemaka but nothing is happening, and I am suddenly tired and am not breathing right. So I am sitting on my knees and I am thinking and I am trying to be thinking of a way to get his cord so that Enyemaka can download his data before the air is eating all of it, but I can think of nothing that is not involving me breaking his body and I am not wanting to be breaking his body.

But Enyemaka is standing over me and the rest of the group is still walking and they are growing smaller in the distance, and even though Enyemaka is not saying a thing I am feeling like she is pressing me to do something and I cannot decide what to do and before I am knowing what I am doing I am smashing my fist down into my brother's neck and I am smashing through the metal and I am breaking the skin and I am having oil on my hands and on my fingers, and in the light of the sun it is looking like blood. I am sadding and angering at the same time and just smashing and smashing until his oil is covering my whole face. Then I am seeing his outlet is crooked and broken and in many pieces and his cord is hanging, and I am pulling it and walking to Enyemaka, and it is unwinding and then I am plugging it into Enyemaka and I am seeing the light moving in her eyes and that is telling me she is collecting what she is needing.

And while she is doing this thing, I am looking at my brother whose body I am just finished breaking and my shoulder is heaving and I am breathing so loud and hard I am hearing myself and I am seeing red everywhere, everything red.

Then I am hearing engine in the distance and I am thinking that it is bandit or militia or someone else, but I am not caring because it is human and I am needing to be breaking it and I am leaving to join the group and kill these thing that is needing killing, and I am not even caring that I am leaving my brother to be small mountain made out of metal that is being covered by red dust.

CHAPTER 45

"You're looking for the synth, aren't you?"

Ngozi is out ahead in her mech. They'd emerged from Xifeng's underground base in the forests outside Abuja and cut a path straight for the countryside, where government forces would be sparsest, but not before activating the cloaking tech both craft had enabled. It worked much the same way the face-scrambling cream did, disrupting surveillance signals so that when they entered Nigerian airspace, they didn't look like a jet and an aerial mech but rather like two giant radiation-infected birds. Their westward flight toward Kwara State would make sense on government radars. They would look like two misplaced creatures, denizens of the Redlands who had gotten lost and were heading back home. That's where Ngozi was leading them. The Redlands.

"I overheard you while you were gathering supplies," Ngozi says through the comms system that connects them. Her face appears before Ify as though she were calling through Ify's Whistle.

"Yes," Ify says. "How do you know she's still alive?" Ify can explain her own feelings, that knowing Uzo's still alive is more a matter of intuition and wishing than anything else, that she has no hard proof Uzo has survived the chaos, especially when so many synths have died already, but that she has felt somewhere deep in her body that this synth that has pieces of her warrior sister in her would somehow find a way to make it out. When she was with Xifeng, Ngozi must have spent time with the synths, seen what they were capable of, what they were growing into. Maybe she's felt the same way.

"Xifeng had all of the synths implanted with tracking devices," Ngozi says as the country beneath them grows more and more overgrown with jungle. Even though they're cloaked, they fly low to avoid the mechs and ships sitting at higher altitudes among the clouds. "She had plans to distribute them throughout Nigeria, spreading the forbidden memories while her antivirus worked to cure the cyberized." Her mouth stumbles around the word *distribute*. That tells Ify, more than anything else, that Ngozi has come to regard the synths as people. Or much closer to people than to machines. Something about that heartens Ify and brings a smile to her face.

But then Ify thinks about the implications of Xifeng's actions. Tracking devices. More surveillance. The more she ponders Xifeng's plan and the lengths she had gone to in order to bring about her reckoning, the more she realizes that Xifeng was turning into the very surveillance state she had hated.

"She knew the government was hunting them. Trying to eliminate any relics of the war." The sky begins to change colors with the setting of the sun so that gold dapples the wings of Ify's craft and the red and blue light glows softly off the edges of Ngozi's mech in front of her and Grace. "Xifeng had called them the Ceasefire Children—born and bred for war, but when the ceasefire was declared, that's all they were. Children."

Ify is silent as they fly and the land begins to turn red with sand dunes.

"Onyii thought she would have to go on trial."

The sentence startles Ify.

"We'd all done horrible things, but Onyii carried everyone else's guilt for them. And she was willing to let the courts make an example of her if it meant lasting peace. She never said it, but she was always trying to take credit for everything." Ngozi's chuckle is soft and static-y over the comms. "She was very uncomfortable with peace. Just like the synths. We're all trying to find our place in the world as it changes around us. When you're defined by war, what's left for you when the war ends?"

Ify is glad for the autopilot function, because tears blur her vision. She takes a moment to wipe them away, grateful that Grace is asleep beside her and can't overhear. So many of Ify's memories of Onyii are memories that bring her peace. Onyii and Chinelo pounding yams to make food for the rest of the camp's girls, Onyii building the greenhouse so that the girls could garden and take their minds off of the conflict raging around them, Onyii counting the stars with Ify at night, tracing constellations in the sky above them, letting Ify dream up her own stories with the pictures they saw. And the thing that had brought them together was murder.

The memory intrudes. Crashes through the walls of Ify's mind to bring her back to that mud-and-stone building in a village she no longer remembers but has pieced together through what others have told and shown her. The night is so deep that everyone has turned into shapes moving in the dark, passing beneath the occasional moonbeam, sometimes with a face so stained with ink and gore that they look less like a person and more like a creature from nightmare. Ify with a pet dog clutched to her chest as it bleeds over her dress. The village's adults gathered outside while a rebel commander proclaims that everyone is to die because they belong to an enemy tribe. Ify shivering alone in her room as the gunshots ring out and her mother and father are dumped into shallow graves. Ify unable to move, hoping that if she remains still enough she can simply vanish, fade away and turn into smoke and never come back. Then a young girl painted black with mud and blood, holding a rifle across her skinny body, walks into the house. Slow, sure steps. She doesn't hesitate until she gets to Ify. No matter how much she tries, Ify can't render herself invisible to this specter, this ghost. This creature that pries the dead dog from her arms and takes it away and buries it, then returns for her. To bring her to a place that will eventually become the camp where she raises the girl and carries her like she is her little sister and loves her and makes sure she wakes up in time for school and makes sure their droid closely shaves Ify's head during the summers so that the heat won't get trapped on her scalp by her hair and scavenges to find pads for the girls when they start to bleed and braids hair and cooks food and teaches them to fight and to read and to know what the earth looks like when a landmine is buried beneath it and how to tell what type of mech is flying overhead by its sound, and it all overwhelms Ify so that sobs struggle inside her chest for release.

"I'm sorry," Ify says softly. For wanting revenge. For leading the suicide bombers to Enugu to break the ceasefire. For trying to forget Onyii and everything Onyii had done for her.

For trying to forget how Onyii had saved her life. And given her a new one. "I'm sorry."

Someone's hand closes over her own, and Ify looks to her right to see Grace looking at her and smiling, her fingers tightening over Ify's.

Through her tears, Ify smiles back. And they ride like that in silence until Ngozi's mech pulls off to the side and lowers onto a hill overlooking desert patched with islands of green.

"Do you see that?" Ngozi asks.

Ify follows, alighting gently on the grassy knoll, and zooms in with her Accent-powered camera.

"That forest."

And there it is along the horizon. The beginnings of a forest, above which rises several columns of smoke.

"The signal stops there."

Ify's heart drops. *Uzo.*

I am not cleaning the blood off of my skin. I am not wiping it from my mouth. I am not scraping it off of my tongue. I am not liking the taste but it is tasting like metal and so it is feeling like it is already part of me. It is drying in my hair and it is crusting on my arms and my legs, and it is the same color as the radiation spots that is making holes in my shirt. Before too long, my shirt is just strips of cloth hanging from my body and more and more of my skin is peeling away and revealing the metal that is lying beneath like bone of animal, and this is happening to all of us.

When the other synths are expiring, we are uploading their data into the remaining Enyemakas, but it is happening so much now that I am not having time to bury them, so they are just falling down into the red dust and breaking down. Some of them are being eaten so much by the air that when they are falling, they are coming apart in pieces. Their arm is falling away and their leg is snapping and they are having no hair. Sometime it is like all of them is just crumbling, and I am sadding each time it is happening because it is feeling like I am losing an important piece of myself every time it is happening. Enyemaka is always telling me that they are still being alive, but I am not seeing them breathing or laughing or running in circles with their arms spread out like airplanes. So how can they be still alive?

There are being no more humans now for long time, but I am being fine with this because I am not angering so much anymore. It is not anger like hot thing under my skin that is eating me from inside. It is cold anger, like something hard that is making my step heavy and is making it hard sometime to lift my shoulder, like I am being stuck with my arms hanging at my side or my neck turned a certain way and it is taking much effort and cracking to be fixing myself and still walking. But the cold anger is also pushing me forward. It is what Xifeng is once telling me is called determination.

I am wondering if I am having more determination than my other synth brother and sister, because I am walking and I am passing by their body that is lying in the red dust in pieces and I am asking myself how I am still walking and they are not if we are being the same. I am puzzling this inside my brain when I am realizing that I am walking past an Enyemaka.

She is frozen where she is standing and her arm is stuck like she is still being in the middle of walking. She is like someone is pressing pause on a recording and never pressing play. I am seeing rusting on her body like rash that is spreading over her chest and her legs and part of her face and I am looking in her face and I am seeing no light in her eyes. I am standing in front of her and hunching my back over even if it is paining me so I can look at her face more fully, and I am waving my hand in front of her face and trying to speak words from inside my brain but she is saying nothing. I am feeling no reaction from her. Then I am taking cord from the back of my neck and I am plugging it into Enyemaka and at first I am not knowing why I am doing this. Maybe I am thinking that she is not all the way expired, and I am hoping to give her some of me to be having in her last moments. Maybe I am not wanting to be so alone so I am simply spending time talking to someone who is not here like I am seeing other synths doing before they are expiring. Maybe I am soon expiring and my body is knowing this before my brain is knowing this.

But I am sitting with Enyemaka and I am thinking and I am seeing huts and tents that are being made and there is a Terminal that is creating network for the camp that is having shower and pulling energy from ground to be watering plants in greenhouse and giving power to tablets and devices for children that are being in school and I am knowing that I am in a camp and that the people in this camp are being called War Girls and I am standing by one of the tents and I am watching a little girl facing bigger girls and they are pushing her shoulders and I am feeling in my body that I am wanting to run and protect this little girl because I am knowing her and I am loving her and even now I am wanting to make sure she is shaving her head properly because it is getting hot and I am not wanting the heat to be trapped on her scalp and paining her. But I am watching the bigger girls pushing the little girl and I am not doing anything and I am wondering why I am not doing anything and then the little girl pushes the biggest girl and is throwing her onto the ground and stuffing dirt in her mouth and the other girls are running away but the little girl is doing revenge and then, when she is running out of breath, she is standing up again while the girl that is bullying her is coughing dirt from her mouth and crying and the little girl is saying nothing but I am feeling warmness in my heart and

I am walking to her and I am asking her, *What did I miss?* even though I am seeing the whole thing and then I am telling Ify, *I have some time before my next run. Do you want to see the water again?* And she is nodding her head yes and grabbing my pant leg and burying her face in its dirty cloth and I am putting my hand to her head and massaging calmness into her.

Moving thing is taking me out of my remembering, and when I am looking up, I am seeing light that is moving back and forth in Enyemaka's eyes.

I am smiling but I am not knowing if I am smiling at the remembering or if I am smiling at Enyemaka, who is not expiring yet.

I am still connected to Enyemaka so I am not using words but I am showing her that I am scared. It is feeling like I am telling her color and picture and feeling rather than saying I am scared because saying I am scared is not feeling like I am telling her the whole truth. I am waiting for Enyemaka to tell me that I am to be doing my duty, that this is yet another thing I am soldier in, that I am to be serving memory and thinking of everyone—my brother and sister synth and also the Enyemaka, who are creating library of memory for everyone so they are not forgetting what is happening.

But Enyemaka is not saying anything to me. She is sending me color and image and feeling that is telling me *I know.* And at the same time, she is telling me that it is okay for me to be scared. Because I am not seeing where we are going. And it is being normal to be scared of the unknown.

And part of me is wondering what is happening to Enyemaka to be talking like this. Is not normal.

We are the same, but we are different, Enyemaka is telling me and I am knowing that she is telling me this about all her sisters. The Enyemaka are all Enyemaka but they are also different Enyemaka, and I am seeing that they are like synth because they are all being connected and feeling what the other is feeling and sometime even thinking what the other is thinking, but they are speaking to my brain with different voice, different collection of image and feeling and color.

Are you scared too?

I don't know fear. But I am learning what creates it. And I understand that telling falsehoods is part of the equation. Sometimes, when faced with fear, we lie to ourselves and to others to lessen that fear or to erase it completely.

Lying? Who is lying?

They are. And she is pointing to the Enyemaka ahead of us. *There is no oasis.*

Fear is making me feel like I am at the bottom of the ocean.

They will keep walking until no one is left. And all the Enyemaka hold the memories of Biafra inside them.

Why are you telling me this?

But Enyemaka is not answering. When I am getting hold of myself again and able to move, I am disconnecting my cord from Enyemaka and coming to my feet, but before I am leaving, Enyemaka is grabbing my wrist tight, so tight it is breaking the gears and the plates, and pieces of me are falling into the red dirt. Then Enyemaka is using her other hand to reach into my outlet and she is using drill and she is paining me.

"What are you doing?" I am screaming at her with my voice that is breaking because I am not using it often and because it is dry and because I am not normally needing to use word when talking to Enyemaka, but I am screaming because I am wanting to know why she is doing this thing but also because scream is feeling like the only thing I can do.

You have data that we need. I can't let you leave. Enyemaka's eye is glowing red, and it is like she is losing who she is being just now. And I am turning and I am seeing silhouette of other Enyemaka coming near, and Enyemaka is breaking my outlet and pulling my cord out and I am fighting and screaming, but she is grabbing my cord and jamming it into her outlet and I am seizing and I am knowing that she is taking my data so she can be leaving me to be expiring in the dirt and I am not wanting to expire, *I don't want to die, please don't let me die*, but Enyemaka is not listening to me, then

metal is cold and wrapping around my wrists and my feet is dangling in the air. I am turning back and forth slow, but that is the only way that my body is moving. Everything is feeling dry and stiff, even the blood that is coming from my nose and gash on my head.

Static.

Light is coming into room, spilling like water. And I am hearing door opening. But it is old door because it is creaking and it is squeaking and light is suddenly everywhere, and I am having to be closing my eyes against it. Static. I am waiting to be hearing hard footstep but instead it is soft like swish swish and I am knowing this is the sound of sand. Static. There is being sand in this room where I am hanging. And I am hearing sizzling too and knowing that something is burning even if I am not smelling it, and I am knowing that I am not smelling thing because my nose is being broken. Many thing in me is broken but I am not feeling pain.

Static.

Man is walking into the room and he is spitting on me and telling me I am not human and that I am rubbish to be thrown into ocean. Static. He is holding shockstick and he is hitting me in my stomach and chest and side with it, and he is hitting me so hard on my back that he is breaking the shockstick.

Static.

There is a boy with him. They are calling me enemy combatant.

Static.

I am synth, and I am not having pain receptor in my brain, and it is this that is making me not to be feeling thing even though many thing inside me is broken.

Static.

Man is gone but boy is staying and I am raising my head to be seeing his face, and when he is looking at me he is smiling so his teeth are shining yellow like corn they are selling by the street and I am seeing the way hair is over his face and the way the skin on his knuckles is broken, and I am seeing the vest he is wearing and the patches and I am knowing that he is soldier too and that he is with what I am knowing is a militia and they are small small army but they are killing just like soldier.

Static.

And boy is looking at me like I am something to be eating and then he is reaching behind him and pulling cord from his neck and he is walking close to me and he is putting cord in my neck and suddenly I am feeling everything.

Static.

I am feeling the breaking in my ribs and in my back and in my crotch and in my arms and in my head and he is smiling at me and saying now I will be feeling these thing and he is raising his stick and I am screaming and opening my eyes at Enyemaka, whose eye is glowing red at me, and I am biting my teeth and my whole body is shivering but I am on one knee and still upright and pain is pushing me down to the ground, but I am staying as I am and I am holding my cord in my hand and squeezing, and it is this squeezing that is pulling me out of the remembering. And Enyemaka is not letting go of my arm but I am pulling hard against her and pulling and pulling and pulling until I am hearing giant metal RIP and Enyemaka's arm is lying in red dust but the hand is still gripping me. I am falling onto the ground but coming back to my feet quick and slamming the arm on the ground until it is letting go of me, then I am seeing Enyemaka turning to me. My cord is hanging loose behind me like long piece of hair. And Enyemaka's eye is still glowing. I am picking up arm and I am raising it like boy in remembering is raising his stick and there is passing one moment where I am hesitating because I am loving Enyemaka and she is caring for me and she is giving me purpose, but then she is lying to me and I am telling myself that they are the same but maybe this one is different. Maybe this one is being the bad one, but I am not letting myself to think these thing for long because she is stepping closer to me and I am closing my eyes and swinging. And when I am hearing the metal crash against the metal it is making me to be sadding, and Enyemaka is falling but I am not stopping and I am bringing the arm up and down, up and down, up and down until Enyemaka's face is just small small pieces of metal on the ground.

When I am finished, I am looking down at Enyemaka, who is expiring, and I am wanting it to not be this way, but her eye is still glowing red, then it is glowing green for one moment and

I am thinking that she is back to Enyemaka who is loving me, then is no more glowing. Just darkness.

The earth is moving under my feet. Pebble is bouncing and bone is rattling. Then I am looking and I am seeing cloud of red dust forming on the ground in the distance. It is rising high and high and being so thick it is blocking the sun. They are coming.

The Enyemaka are coming for me.

And I am running.

■ ■ ■ ■ ■

Green is showing ahead of me, and even though it is being far away, it is poking over the edge of the ground, and I am seeing treetops. I am feeling heat eating me inside and I am knowing that what is happening to Onyii when she is getting sick and dying is happening to me too. People are calling it cancer and though I am knowing that it is eating human thing and changing blood and organ to be poison, it is also doing something like this to metal. I am feeling inside me that thing is breaking. Thing that is making me to be running forever and never tiring, thing that is making me to be breathing air and processing it and exhaling it, thing that is making me to think with my brain, thing that is giving me feeling in my heart.

All of sudden air is coming easy to me and my chest is not making rasping noise when I am breathing. I am not feeling heavy and there is being wetness in the air and it is cooling my face. I am not hearing the hissing I am always hearing in the Redlands, the sound of important thing burning, and I am falling to my knees on the other side of what is like invisible wall between world that is poison and world that is not trying to be killing me.

Tree is closer to me, and I am being happy to be seeing so much green because it is like it is saying to me, *Welcome*, and it is opening arm to me and telling me to come inside. I am picking myself up and looking behind me and seeing that the Enyemaka are becoming closer. They are moving so fast even though they are looking like they are moving slow slow but I am knowing how much ground they are eating beneath them and the sound of their running is like giant THUMP THUMP THUMP THUMP THUMP against the ground like army of juggernaut is chasing me. It is making me think of Lagos and the first time I am feeling fear but I am throwing that remembering away and turning to the forest and running because it is cool and safe and familiar and I am knowing how to be climbing trees and hiding under big leaves and telling where is shorthorn and where is passing wulfu and other animals.

It is always feeling like it is just finished raining in forest, like it is bubble holding living thing and protecting them from angry, dangerous world, and I am just one more thing it is protecting. I am running over root and sliding over tree trunk that is falling sideways. Baby wulfu is looking at me as I am running by then returning to their play and it is like being with friend again.

All while I am hiding, I am thinking on why Enyemaka is lying to me and telling me that there is oasis when there is no oasis and I am thinking that Enyemaka is not caring for me, only pretending to be caring for me and caring what is happening to me. And now even in forest I am starting to be feeling cold and alone because everyone is lying to me and no one is caring for me and I am thinking this is maybe mistake in how I am being made that I am wishing someone is caring for me. Part of me is just wanting to give up and let Enyemaka use me for what she is wanting. But other part of me, bigger part of me, is remembering what I am hearing from Uzodinma and Oluwale and what we are saying to each other about making my own future and being my own person.

I realize I am hearing nothing.

Not even chirping of bird and grunting of shorthorn. Why am I hearing nothing?

Then I am smelling it. Fire.

First I am smelling it, then I am hearing it—the crackle and the pop and the rustle and the crackle again—then I am seeing it. By the time I am seeing it, it is wall of fire where I am facing. I am running the other way, but the air is being clear for only a few moment before it is being filled with smoke again. I am turning every way and running but I am finding no clear air anywhere, and even though I am not coughing I am feeling damage happening to my lungs and the other parts inside me. Water is building in my eyes to protect them.

I am looking and looking, then I am finding tree with thick trunk and I am leaping up to be climbing it. And I am climbing and climbing then jumping to other tree and climbing then, when I am reaching top of that tree, I am jumping to next tree and climbing until I get to the very top and can see far far far in the forest, so far in the forest that I am seeing where it is ending and Redland is beginning.

Everywhere there is fire. Everywhere in front of me, everywhere behind me.

I am smelling sulfur, and I am thinking maybe this is part of fire, but then I am remembering other time when I am smelling sulfur like this, and then I am falling from tree because my body is shaking and I am no longer controlling it.

Because I am having epileptic fit, and where I am falling is fire. Only fire. And I am feeling nothing because my brain is no longer belonging to me. There is only the air that is twisting around me, the wind whistling in my ears, and as I am falling, I am sadding. Because I am thinking of all the gosling that is now no longer having home.

■ ■ ■ ■ ■

When I am waking up, I am hearing footstep and I am knowing right away that I am moving, but my feet are dragging along the ground and my arms are being held up, even though I am not feeling them because they are broken. I am hearing heavy breathing on both sides of me and it is not sounding like droid or metal person that is breathing. Is sounding like red-blood. Like human I am spending so much time avoiding. But these people are carrying me over their shoulders. And I am opening my eye as much as I am being able and I am looking to one side and I am seeing Ngozi. Part of me is wanting to struggle and thrash because I am not wanting to go back to Xifeng, who is just using me for her mission and not caring about me, but my body is not listening to my brain. I look to the other side and can feel the insides of me warm and heat up with surprise and disbelief and what I am realizing is gratitude because when I am opening my eyes and seeing who else is carrying me, I am seeing Ify's face. And she is the only person I am knowing who is not lying to me. My cord is dangling, so it is not connecting to her, and she is looking straight forward, but I am hearing how her body is speaking when she and Ngozi are carrying me to their aircraft and to the woman named Grace Leung, who is standing guard over it. I am listening to what Ify's body is telling me and it is like color and feeling are being sent to my brain, not just word, so that I am not only hearing but feeling with my whole body Ify telling me, *Don't worry, don't worry, don't worry.*

I am wanting to tell her thank you, but my mouth is not moving, so instead I am crying and hoping that Ify is understanding that this is how I am being able to say thank you.

Ngozi clears a space in the section of the aircraft behind the cockpit. She works swiftly, dismantling the seats that lined each side, fetching a medkit from her mech, and preparing a makeshift bed for Uzo, with medical supplies in a neat, efficient array beside her, among the supplies a sort of liquid battery that feeds nanobots into Uzo's prone, motionless form by way of a needle injected into her damaged left arm.

When they'd first brought Uzo into the plane and laid her down, they'd all shared a moment of despairing shock. The synth's skin peeled in a number of places, revealing metal rusted with corrosion beneath. Pistons and gears and divets the color of blood with dried oil like grease puddles around some of her abrasions. Soot blackened her face, and even now, in slumber, her chest heaves with labored breathing. Watching Ngozi hook Uzo to the external battery and get to work settling cushions beneath Uzo's head, Ify remembers watching so many loved ones hovering over the hospital beds of patients in her care, whispering words she was sure the patient couldn't hear or trying to stimulate responses by touch when Ify knew the patient had no way of responding. And annoyance had cut through her, watching that. It was illogical, what they were doing. And yet she kneels by Uzo's side, wanting to run her fingers over the backs of the synth's charred hands, wanting to murmur nothings into her ear, not caring whether she can hear her or not.

"Some of these will have to be replaced," Ngozi says from behind her mask as she takes her tools to the exposed metal of Uzo's shoulder. Her legs are riddled with rashes and burns as well. These, at least, Grace treats with healing pads and gel from the medkit. "But I've managed to restore brain function. She wasn't out for long before we found her, thank God." A smirk. "She certainly has Onyii's luck."

An ease settles into the back of Ify's mind. As though a worry has been checked off her list. If Uzo is still alive, that means Ify has a working braincase to examine. That means they are that much closer to helping the children in Alabast.

After a while, Ngozi sits back and hangs some of her tools on hooks in a makeshift stand next to her. Then she takes off her mask, wipes the sweat from her forehead with her arm, and sighs. It's a large sound in the small area of the plane behind the cockpit. "She'll live." When Ngozi says it, Ify doesn't hear the joy she expects. "We need to talk about how you get her out of Nigeria."

Grace stops swabbing Uzo's legs and watches the cream dry, smoothing the ragged edges of the broken skin. "We can't go back, can we?"

Ngozi shakes her head. "It's no longer safe for you here."

"They'll find us."

Ify considers them both, then looks down at Uzo's still form. "We haven't even asked her yet."

They both look Ify's way.

"What if she refuses?" She can't stop scanning Uzo's wounds, the story all her markings tell. "What if she doesn't want to come with us?"

"Where will she go?" Ngozi asks, annoyed. "She'll be hunted here. And they will catch her sooner rather than later."

Ify smirks. "You've managed to steer clear."

Ngozi puts her hand to her chest. "I'm a fugitive. No one lasts long as a fugitive here." She lowers her voice, drains the anger from it. "I've made my peace with this. I only made it this far because there were others. *If you want to go fast, go alone. If you want to go far, go together.* That was our rule. Who will watch over her?"

"We can care for her in Alabast," Grace says, insistent. "We can give her the best medical treatment. We can help her build a life for herself." She stops, but Ify knows what she was about to say. *Just like you were able to, Ify.* "She's a child."

"No," Ify says, almost too soft for anyone to hear but her. "She's not. She's a synth. Every one of her kind is here."

"Every one of her kind is dead, Ify." This from Ngozi. "All of them." She reaches behind her and bangs the palm of her hand against the hull of their ship. "No more signals. None. She's the last one."

No more. The others. Ify imagines a bevy of young children the same age as the unconscious girl nearby, all of them strangers to themselves, a jumble of memories and information and command inputs, all of them struggling to find a place in peacetime. Ify imagines what they might have been like together. Brothers and sisters. Siblings. Family. All gone. Uzo is the only one left. "So we should just take her to space, then?"

Rage builds within Ify. "Just rip her from the only home she has ever known? Drop her onto an island floating in space where she'll be surrounded by oyinbo? Who will look at her like she is a turd that just dropped from the sky? They will not welcome her. They will challenge her and despise her and try to keep her from getting what they have simply because she does not look or speak like them. Is that what you want for her?"

"If she stays here," Ngozi roars, "she will die!"

"She'll have a choice!"

"If I am choosing between gari and starvation, I should choose starvation, then?"

"She's a synth! They'll send her back as soon as she gets there. So she'll have gone through this whole journey for what? To wind up at a refugee camp in the Jungle? A floating rubbish bin in space where people are practically swimming in their own offal? Is that what you want for her?"

"So because Onyii saved your life without asking your permission, you think that was a mistake?"

And that stops Ify cold.

"She saved your life," Ngozi hisses. "And all you have ever been is ungrateful. The comfortable life you have in the Colonies? That is because of her. Your precious job as a doctor? That is because of her." She leans in toward Ify. "The very fact that you are breathing. That is because of her." Those last words turn into a snarl. After a beat, Ngozi settles against the wall. "And you are upset because she did not ask your permission." She sucks her teeth. "You are mad." With her finger, she jabs her temple. "Mad."

Fury bends Ify's fingers into fists, but there's nothing she can say. It is foolishness to resent Onyii for what she did, but Ify can't bring herself to let it go. Then she realizes that a part of her had wanted to stay. Even if it meant being chased by the government for the rest of the war. Even if it meant never knowing another moment of peace. Even if it meant watching Onyii die before her very eyes, she would have been with her. She could have held her hand in her last moments, and Onyii denied her that. Took that choice away from her.

Ify looks to the ceiling. "What do we do?"

"Um . . ." But Grace doesn't finish.

Ify turns her way, then sees her looking at Uzo, who is looking straight back at Ify.

"She's awake," Grace says at last.

CHAPTER 48

Ify is playing with her hands.

"Are you being nervous?" I am asking her, but it is scratching my throat, so I am forcing myself not to be asking more question.

Then she is stopping playing with her hands, then she is looking at the floor, then she is looking at me. "In ancient Inca society," she begins saying, "there was a thing called a khipu."

As she is saying this, I am accessing network and downloading image of khipu and all information about it and I am seeing row of knotted string that is being tied to single braided rope and the knotted string is having different color. And I am knowing that this is ancient devices that is being used to record thing like people name and people hair color and people status in society, whether they are big man or whether they are small small. The knot in the string and the number of string and the number of knot and the color of all of these thing are telling whoever is looking the name and location and detail of people who is living in a village. I am knowing all of this before Ify is finishing her sentence.

"We think there is something like that in your braincase."

She is saying *we* and I am knowing that she is meaning her and Grace. Not Ngozi.

"We think that is what is tying your memories together, those you have accumulated over the course of your life and those you were . . . given upon your creation. Your brain has immense computing power. Indeed, the brain of a synth may be the most powerful computer ever created. And there is an incredible amount of heterogenous data in there. It shouldn't be able to hold itself together. The incomplete nature of the memories would suggest natural deterioration, but there is something in your coding that is fighting that process."

She pauses. I am wondering why she is telling me about khipu and what it is having to do with saving me from Enyemaka and burning forest and the arguing that I am hearing earlier about going to space.

Then, after a long silence, Ify is saying, "Right now, there are hundreds of children in the hospital where I work, maybe a thousand, who, I believe, are suffering from identical illnesses. They have each fallen into comas." She is getting up from where she is sitting and walking back and forth and I am wanting to tell her not to be nervous, but words is not coming from my mouth so all I am doing is following her with my eyes. "In one building, refugees are being kept and taken care of. There is a ward for them. I was supposed to be helping them. But they became sick. And their condition has been worsening. Since the epidemic began, not a single one of these children has emerged from their coma." Another pause. "This is why I came back to Nigeria."

"What is my brain having to do with this?"

"The children . . . they're losing their memories. We think

that you have developed an antibody to the virus that is making them sick." There is light shining in her eyes, and I am thinking that she is looking at me like I am something special. Not because I am carrying Onyii inside me, but because of something else. Xifeng is sometimes looking at me like this. "You . . . you somehow found a way to organize your data."

"My rememberings?"

"Yes. Your rememberings." She is moving closer to me, close enough to touch, but she is not reaching out to touch me.

At first, I am thinking it is because she is looking at my woundings and finding me disgusting. But then I am seeing the look in her eyes and I am seeing that she is scared that if she is touching me, she is wounding me further. I am wanting to reach out and touch her or tell her it is okay, but my body is still not moving. I am feeling nanobots inside me, repairing me, but I am still too weak for my arms and legs and fingers to listen to what my brain is telling them.

"When you did this, you rearranged your own genetic coding. You figured out a way to hold your data together and make a whole identity out of it. Imagine if a computer were alive."

I am not liking that she is calling me computer, and she is seeing the changing look in my face.

"Of course, you're more than a computer. It's just that . . . you're the cure. Somehow, you're the cure."

I am wanting to be telling her that all of my brother and sister is doing this thing. It is thing we are learning to do from each other, and I am wanting to show her Oluwale teaching me and I am wanting to show her Uzodinma doing it too and finding certain memory that is granting him peace and accessing it on purpose and not accident. I am wanting to tell her we are all doing this thing and she is not needing me. But then I am trying to send out signal to find my family. And I am sending and sending and sending and all that is coming back is silence. All I am hearing is the ringing in my own head.

"You are the only one left," Ify is telling me like she is reading my mind. Like we are being plugged into each other. "You are the last synth." She is looking at her hands and playing with them again. Then she is stopping, then she is gathering breath inside her and letting out a soft and slow sigh. When she is looking at me again, tears are shimmering in her eyes like wind brushing on the surface of the sea. "Will you come to space with me? I . . . I can't guarantee that you will be safe or that you will even like it, but you can help many, many people who desperately need it. I don't know what is waiting for you there, but I will care for you, and you will be loved. Yes. You will be loved. So will you do it? Will you come with me? To space?"

CHAPTER 49

Ify finds Grace and Ngozi sitting on the hunched shoulders of Ngozi's mech, eating out of what look like military ready-to-eat packets. Ngozi munches absentmindedly while Grace's face twists around the tastes. When Ify looks up at them, Grace swallows her mouthful loudly and says, "Burrito bowl." Her face makes Ify chuckle.

"And?" Ngozi asks, nodding to the aircraft where Ify has left Uzo to rest. "What is the plan?"

"We need to give her a new identity. For her visa application."

Light blossoms to life in Grace's face so that, when the light from the setting sun hits, it looks like she's made of gold.

"We can't bring her to Alabast directly. We'll have to go to Centrafrique. I've already notified my friend there."

Ngozi puts down her half-eaten MRE. "And who is this friend that can swoop down and get you out of the country and into space?"

"She's a Colonial administrator," Ify says with a proud smirk. She'd kept the details sparse during their conversation, knowing that while they were still in Nigerian airspace, there was a chance the call might be monitored. All Céline knew was that Ify was safe and that she needed to arrange transport for a sick child who needed medical attention. She had left Céline wondering what could be wrong with the child that couldn't be fixed in one of Earthland's most advanced hospitals. Explaining Uzo's significance might have jeopardized their plans and implicated Céline in knowingly breaking the law. But Céline had revealed the tightening of Alabast's immigration controls, the dire state of the Jungle, and that Centrafrique was beginning to accept a greater influx of refugees now that they knew they could no longer find a home among the whites. Céline had also informed her that none of the patients had so far been deported, which calmed Ify's heart. And all the while, they had been forced to talk like professional acquaintances and not like friends, one of whom had worried desperately about the other upon hearing rumors and vague reports of an outbreak of violence in Nigeria's capital city. Ify had spoken in calm, measured tones, firmly enough to show that she was unharmed and not being held hostage, but evasive enough in her answers to coach her friend toward discretion. They knew each other well enough that Céline could read, in Ify's pauses and word choice, the specifics of their dilemma. So all that remained was to fashion Uzo's immigration materials and wait for transport.

Ngozi hops off her mech, landing smoothly from the dangerous height. Grace is slower to climb down. When they draw near, the fatigue on their faces becomes clear, even as night begins to descend and gray-black clouds roam across the sky.

"She's healing just fine," Ify tells them. "Thank you, Ngozi." Then she turns to Grace. "Come with me."

Grace follows her back to the aircraft, and on the way, Ify

speaks in low tones. "She will need her biometrics to read as her new identity. Fingerprints and retina are the important bits. If they scan her, we'll need to be ready. Our passage will be secure, but I can't guarantee there won't be at least one scan during the trip."

"What do you need from me?"

Ify stops, and Grace stops with her. "You've performed surgeries before, yes?"

Grace nods. Then it dawns on her what Ify is asking. "Wait, but why don't you do it? You're far more experienced than—"

Ify holds up a hand to stop her. "The materials also need to read in Chinese. With my Augment, I can read it and I can decipher it, but I can't write it."

"But why Chinese?"

"Because this is going to be Uzo's country of origin. And her documents need to read in all of its official languages. Otherwise, authorities will know that they've been forged. Ngozi will take point on preparing the documents, and you will perform the surgery to inscribe that identity onto Uzo's body."

"But—"

"I'm not asking you."

The moon peeks through cloud cover, lighting the anger that shows through the tiredness on Grace's face. How to tell her that Ify doesn't trust her own hands? That she's not refusing because she hasn't performed a surgery in over a year but because memory of one done to her is still too vivid in her brain. Ify wonders what Grace would say if Ify told her the story, told her of how she and Onyii had been on the run, fleeing a Nigerian government and a rebel Biafran movement, both of which wanted them dead. Told her of how they'd found refuge in a submersible with Xifeng but that their pursuers were tracking them through a device implanted just below Ify's heart. She wonders what Grace would say if she told Grace about how Onyii had had to cut her open without anesthetic and reach into her chest with her metal fingers to pull out the tracking device. She wonders what Grace would say if she were to show her the spot just beneath her left breast where Onyii's bionic hand had entered.

Instead, she stiffens and says, "Ngozi can show you where to find the surgical tools." Then she walks past Ngozi to her mech, climbs onto its lowered shoulders, and lies on her back, staring at the stars and wondering if this is what Onyii saw after she'd put Ify on the shuttle that spirited her into space.

A voice in the back of her mind recalls the exchange with Grace and asks Ify, *What about the surgery you performed on yourself?*

Looking at the stars, Ify tells this voice, "I can't be as reckless with the lives of others as I have been with my own."

■ ■ ■ ■ ■

Night deepens. But it doesn't bring with it the serenity that can whisk Ify into sleep. Here, this close to the radiation, crickets don't chirp, large animals don't low or growl or whine at the moon. The ambient buzz she hears isn't the telltale sound of insect life happening around her but rather the sizzle of the earth damaging things, killing flora and fauna. Making monsters.

Thoughts of Céline and their impending reunion always come with thoughts of what Ify had wanted to say to her best friend after so long apart. But is there any way to tell her of the transformation she has undergone since arriving here? Is there any way to tell her, over the course of a single conversation, the multiple reckonings she's had to face—for her role in the breaking of the ceasefire, for her feelings of abandonment brought about by the sister who saved her life, for her coming to terms with the people she'd thought of before as nothing but killing machines? How to tell Céline that she still feels guilt for what she did, trying to seek revenge against that sister and prolonging a war that killed and maimed and devastated so many people? Even now, were Céline to magically appear before her, she doesn't know how she would say all those things. The words and their formulation into sentences escape her.

So she climbs down from the mech and alights onto the patch of grass with a whoosh. The breeze quickens. She hugs herself as she walks toward the jet aircraft, her ratty braids whipping about her face. If she were to catch a cold after everything she's been through . . . She'll just tell the others she's come for a blanket and not because she's lonely and insomniac on the mech.

The cockpit opens at her touch, and she sneaks through. It hisses shut behind her. She switches from her boots to a pair of slippers by the copilot's seat, then moves to the divider that separates the cockpit from what Grace and Ngozi have turned into a makeshift operating theater.

She is about to press the sequence on the keypad to get the doors to swish open, but she stops when she hears singing.

The words, sung at a high tenor but with the rolling softness of a sea at rest, rise to just above a murmur. But somehow, even with the poor acoustics of the cabin, Ify can make them out.

Yuet gwōng gwōng ziu dei tòng
Hāa zái néi gwāai gwāai fan lok còng
Tēng cìu ah māa yiu gón caap yēong lō
Ah yè tái ngàu hoei séong sāan gōng
Āh . . . āh . . . āh āh āh āh

Hāa zái néi faai gōu zéong daai lō
Bōng sáu ah yè hoei tái ngàu yèong
Āh . . . āh . . . āh āh āh āh

Grace. Singing in Cantonese. Out of instinct, Ify almost gets her Accent to auto-translate the lyrics, but she stops herself just in time. Instead, she leans against the partition and listens.

Yuet gwōng gwōng ziu dei tòng
Hāa zái néi gwāai gwāai fan lok còng
Tēng cìu ah māa yiu bou yù hāa lō
Ah ma zīk móng yiu zīk dou tīn gwōng
Āh . . . āh . . . āh āh āh āh

Hāa zái néi faai gōu zéong daai lō
Waa téng saat móng zau gang zoi hòng āh

A small window by her head affords Ify a view of the operating theater. Through the flexiglas, Ify watches sparks jump to life as Grace and Ngozi, tools in hand, inscribe the superficial DNA evidence of Uzo's new identity onto her skin. Ify stands on her tiptoes to get a better angle and sees Grace's mouth move while her head sways. Uzo's eyes are closed. She has the same look on her face that Ify has seen on the faces of those patients of hers caught in the midst of a kind dream.

For several minutes, Ify leans against the partition, eyes closed, listening to Grace sing her lullaby to a sleeping Uzo.

It is not long before Ify, having found her way to the cockpit and the blanket stuffed in a duffel bag with their guns, drifts into slumber herself.

■ ■ ■ ■ ■

Ify wakes to knocking on the cockpit window.

She stirs herself to half-wakefulness and squints at Ngozi, silhouetted against the midday sun. Ngozi points with her thumb back in the direction of her mech, then disappears. Ify's eyes go wide. *Céline.* Scrambling, she kicks off the blanket, pops open the cockpit, and leaps onto the ground, running to just past Ngozi's mech, where Ngozi and Grace stand. Ahead of them, shapes move along the horizon, a shimmering black mass rumbling toward them. As they get closer, the shapes break apart to reveal an array of black maglev jeeps, raising clouds of dust in their wake.

Uzo stands between Ngozi and Grace and gives Ify only the briefest of glances before staring ahead.

Worry runs up Ify's spine that she has made a mistake, that it's not Céline arriving from over the horizon to rescue them but rather the Nigerian authorities come to detain them, erase their memories of everything they've gone through, and destroy any hope Ify has of saving the children. She wonders how fast she'll be able to run, how quickly she'll die once they make it to the Redlands, whether they will mistakenly trip land mines buried underground.

But before she can journey too far into her anxieties, the vehicles come to a stop before them, then lower themselves onto the grass.

No. It's too late to run.

The door to the lead vehicle—a bulky, black jeep with windows tinted black and no markings—creaks open and out steps a man very much like the vehicle. Thick-chested and dressed in a deep black suit with a dark visor over his eyes. His hands look like they could crush Ify's head. She can tell from their solidity that they're made out of metal, just like the rest of him. He too closely resembles the kaftan-wearing security service members who'd once cornered Ify in a hospital bed.

The cars are probably filled with men like him, men made to look like pillars so that their very presence demands compliance. Maybe some of them bear shocksticks or lightknives or small-caliber pistols. Maybe they need none of these things.

The man takes a moment to survey the four of them before his gaze settles on Uzo.

Without a word, he takes three too-fast steps to her, and Ify's body tenses for action. Uzo doesn't resist when the man takes her wrist and holds her palm up. He puts his palm to hers, and light flares behind his visor, a red ball blazing a comet trail back and forth. Like this, they stand for several long seconds before the man releases Uzo.

"Uzoamaka Diallo." Then he turns to Ify. "Your sister has been cleared for transport to Centrafrique. Our brief indicated that you will be accompanying her."

Ify stutters through her relief. "Y-yes. Me and"—she looks around for Grace—"me and my assistant. We were here for a medical mission, and we need to return to the Colonies and—"

Grace steps forward, interrupting Ify, and sticks out her own palm. "Grace Leung," she says and allows herself to be scanned.

Ify chastises herself, and it isn't until then that she realizes how nervous she is.

The man returns to his vehicle and opens the back door. "Ms. Leung? Dr. and Ms. Diallo?" He inclines his head to the back seat. "Our brief indicated that your travel request be accommodated immediately. And that your matter is urgent."

"It is," Ify says softly.

Grace and Uzo walk ahead, but Ify is rooted where she stands. The two are climbing into the back of the vehicle when Ify feels a hand on her shoulder and turns to find Ngozi staring at her, a new compassion in her eyes.

"Go," she tells Ify. When Ify doesn't move, Ngozi leans in close and whispers. "Onyii will be remembered. I will make sure of it." She pats Ify roughly on the shoulder, then heads to her mech.

She pushes herself forward, one step, then another, until she's in the back seat with Grace and Uzo, and it isn't until she sits that she lets herself believe that they've been rescued, that this isn't a trap. That these people are not preparing to betray her.

"Thank you, Céline," she whispers, trying her best to keep from weeping.

CHAPTER 50

I am knowing what space is looking like, but in my rememberings I am often seeing it from cockpit of flying mech. And always there is being noise of war, much katakata and booming and screaming. But when I am watching stars fly past the window of our cabin so fast they are turning from points to lines, I am seeing also that the blackness is moving but not moving at the same time. It is looking like we are being frozen but I am hearing in my ear all the engine of the shuttle working and I am hearing even the small small part that is moving this spaceship and I am knowing that we are moving because of science and the way engine is working. But then I am also thinking something else is different between now and the space that I am remembering.

"It is so quiet," I am saying to Ify.

That is what I am noticing even when we are docking, and then Ify is taking me to the shuttle that is moving us through space station docking port to another bay, where we are getting onto another shuttle and returning to space. We are moving fast, almost like Ify is hiding me. And all the while, as we are walking and riding bus and then riding new, smaller shuttle into space, Ify is looking this way and that. Like she is searching for someone who is never arriving.

After the short flight to Colony that is looking much bigger than where we are first stopping, Ify is letting out a sigh that is sounding like disappointment. Then we are entering space station that is being called Alabast and there is already conveyor belt that is taking us to other train that is taking us to the home where Ify is staying. Grace is staying on the train and going to a different place that Ify is not telling me about.

Everything in Alabast is quiet. Sometime there is no sound, like in space. Sometime there is sound but it is like there is cotton filling your ears or it is like grenade is going off too close to your face and you are hearing nothing but whine and everything else is soft soft and hard to hear. While I am following Ify, there is being many people around us, but no one is talking to us. No one is stopping to chat or to ask where we are coming from. Even people that is scanning our data and seeing my visa is not looking at us, even though I am seeing my face on the screen that is being reflected in his false eyes. We are just moving and I am following Ify, and she is walking through all of this almost without stopping, even though we are twisting and turning and going round corners and up and down moving stairs and platform that is taking us from one place to another. It is dizzying me and I am wondering if anyone is ever standing still here.

Her home is big and I am wondering if it is just her who is living here. It is as big as entire floor of an apartment in Lagos or even Abuja. The ceiling is high and the chair and table and desk is all spread out far and there is so much ground and the window is taller than two of me and there is so much space it is like the world outside is being held inside.

Ify is asking me something and it is like cotton is in my ears, then I am shaking my head and I am hearing her asking me if I am wanting to be resting or spending some time here or enjoying some of Alabast before we are going to the hospital. I am wondering why she is asking me this and maybe it is because I am sometime staring at thing with my mouth wide open like it is catching fly and maybe I am looking like I am seeing thing for the first time when I am not sure if I am seeing them for the first time or not. I am knowing what space travel is feeling like. But before this voyage, my body is not knowing what space travel is feeling like. And now it is.

But there is too much here that is new and strange, and I am feeling in my brain like I am reaching for something with my fingers and it is grasping nothing, and I am knowing that I am reaching for purpose. I am wanting to be doing something. I am wanting something to be focusing on. So I am saying no.

She is watching me in silence for some time, then she is moving to her main room, what she is calling her living room, and she is waving her hand at chair that is too big for me because when I am sitting in it, I am feeling like I am sinking in it, like it is eating me, and I am struggling against it, but Ify is putting her hand on my hand and it is calming me down. The chair is then molding itself around me and I am leaning back and feeling warm and it is pleasing to my skin. Then Ify is sitting down in chair in front of me that is hovering above the ground, but she is leaning forward and not saying anything.

"Do you need to rest?" I am asking her. I am seeing her now, seeing how tiredness is darkening the skin under her eyes and how it has dried her skin, how even after she bathed herself in the shuttle watercloset when we left Earthland she still moved without ease. I am seeing the way her finger is twitching, and I am seeing that her eye is bloodshot and that she is quivering with the effort of trying not to be collapsing onto the floor. And I am seeing that she is not like me, who is not needing to be resting ever. Who is not needing to be eating or drinking thing. Who is not needing to do other thing that red-blood is needing to be doing. Ify is needing to be doing all this thing, but she has not been doing this thing, and it is paining her. "You must rest," I am telling her.

I am getting up from my seat and I am walking to her and putting my hand on her shoulder hard so she is feeling my grip strong and knowing that she is to be doing what I tell her. At first, she is not moving, then I am squeezing, and hurt is showing on her face. Then she is getting up and I am letting go.

"I will wake you," I tell her. Then I am watching her walk into her bedroom. She is standing at the threshold for a long time with her back to me, as though she is looking inside and not recognizing what she is seeing, as though what is before her now is not matching what is in her rememberings. But then she is walking through, and the door is sliding shut behind her. I am walking to the closed door and pressing my ear to it to hear what is happening, but I am hearing nothing, not even crying, then I am hearing rustling that I am knowing is bedsheets and then I am hearing snoring.

My footsteps are silent as I wander the apartment. I soon find a room that I am knowing to be Ify's office. On the desk is many tiny machines, including small small bees I know she is using to be taking apart and examining thing. I am seeing tablets and styluses and even document that is printed out and that is having diagram of brains and the insides of red-bloods. I am seeing a closet that is housing white coats and kaftans and slippers. I am seeing dust that is settled over everything, and that is how I am knowing that no one is walking through this place for a long time.

At the window, I command the blinds to open and I look down and see, from high up, a room filled with hospital beds, and I am knowing without anyone telling me that this is who I am helping. Some of the people in hospital bed is glowing red in my screen and I am knowing that this is red-blood, but some is glowing blue and I am knowing that this is synth, and I am wondering what synth is doing here when Ify is telling me I am the only synth left.

My mind is reaching out to talk to them, but it is like my fingers fumbling through smoke. I am trying to hear a signal or feel their presence, open my mind to them, but it is like they are expired. Even though machine connecting to them is telling me they are still alive, their brain is telling me nothing.

I am opening my mind wider and wider and nothing is coming back until I am finally hearing ringing. It is not a sound I am usually hearing when my mind is connecting to another synth's, but I am thinking maybe it is different in space.

I activate the communication signal, but then hologram opens up in front of me.

At first, it is shaped weirdly because window is distorting it, then I am backing up, and that is when I am realizing that hologram is being projected from me.

The woman in the hologram is squinting, then saying, "Ify? Ify, is that you?"

Metadata is beaming into me from the call, and it is telling me that the woman in the hologram is Céline Hayatou, female, age nineteen, black hair, brown eyes, non-cyberized, graduate of Alabast Polytechnic, chief Colonial administrator of the Centrafrique Satellite Colony of Alabast. I am remembering my journey with Ify through the Colonies and when we are stopping briefly in Centrafrique and Ify is looking like she is searching for someone who is never coming and I am knowing she is searching for this person.

"Who is this?"

I am saying nothing, because I am knowing that when Ify is searching for this person and not finding her, she is sadding.

"Where's Ify?"

But I am just frowning at her.

"Wait." Then she sucks in breath, and surprise is shining in her eyes. "It's you. You're . . . you're the cure."

I am not liking that she is calling me thing and not person, so I am saying, "Ify is sleeping. Do not disturb her."

"I just . . . I want to make sure she is okay and—"

"She was looking for you." My fists are clenching at my side and it is taking much effort to be unclenching them. "When we arrived in Centrafrique, she looked for you. Everywhere, she looked for you. Where were you?"

"How dare you? I'm a Colonial administrator. I have an entire Colony to run! Who are you to talk to me li—"

"I don't know you." My voice is even when I am saying these words. I am thinking of the hurt on Ify's face and how she is being tired as we are traveling and wanting something badly, and I am knowing that what she is wanting is for this woman to be telling her hello and this woman is not doing that, so I am angering. "And I am not caring who you are. Ify is here to be doing work, and she must rest. Do not disturb her." Then I am ending the transmission, and hologram is winking away and there is nothing blocking my view of the sick people below that Ify and me are to be helping.

■ ■ ■ ■ ■

As soon as I am entering hospital, they are putting me in chair that is hovering over the ground and dressing me in gown that is feeling too big on me. Everything is white and smelling like it is too clean. Whenever I am seeing hospital in my remembering, I am seeing it full of people who is dying, people wearing military uniform, people missing arm or leg or missing part of their face. Sometime when I am thinking of hospital, I am seeing image of tent and I am feeling heat on my skin and I am seeing dirty robot that is stomping around and trying to stop people screaming by feeding them chemical. And sometime when I am thinking of hospital, I am hearing quiet and it is because everybody is dying and there are being only a few of us left, and I am thinking that in all of my remembering, hospital is meaning death and dirt and blood. But here hospital is clean and there are people wearing gown like I am wearing who are walking or who are smiling and talking, and sometime I am looking into their room and seeing them in bed with nurse watching them and chatting like they are being neighbors on the side of the street in Lagos.

I am feeling hand pressing on my shoulder. Gently but still firm, like it is trying to be telling me something, and I am looking up and seeing Ify and she is not looking at me. She is looking ahead. But she is squeezing my shoulder.

"Don't be nervous," she is whispering to me, beneath her breath, almost like she is saying it to herself too.

It is making me to be feeling better to be seeing her like this. The way she is moving and standing and holding herself is telling me she is feeling certain and comfortable and she is not being afraid of anything.

Soon, we are going into part of hospital where there is being fewer and fewer people. And soon we are getting to part of hospital where there is being no one but doctor and nurse and sometime droid that is helping them. Then she is bringing me into room that is large but not as large as main room in Ify's apartment. In the center is being a machine that is part bed but part cylinder that the bed is going into. And there is a console next to it and a desk and many machine I am not knowing.

There is white wall surrounding me everywhere and there is much space to be walking around in and very little furniture. But even though it is looking like there is much space, it is still feeling like prison. The walls are meeting over my head to form dome shape so it is looking like I am inside a bulubu ball that is being cut in half.

Feeling is warring inside me, and I am not knowing why but my heart is racing racing and when I am standing, I am moving from feet to feet, just bouncing like child that is needing to go to the bathroom. I am nervous. Then I am hearing Ify's words in my head, replaying, and she is saying, *Don't be nervous, don't be nervous, don't be nervous.*

"This is where we will work," Ify is telling me. "This will be your bed, and I will make it as comfortable as possible for you. All you will have to do is lie there. And we will take breaks whenever you need." Grace is in the room too, and she is moving to stand beside Ify, and she is holding a tablet in her hands. At first, she is saying nothing, and I am wondering if it is like this between them in space, where Ify is leading and Grace is following. But there is different energy in the air between them. They are moving like people who have spent much time together, not like leader and follower but like equal. Like how synth and soldier is working together when Xifeng is leading us. "Grace and I are here for whatever you need."

I am looking at Grace, and Grace is looking at me, and I am hearing Cantonese lullaby that she is singing to me back in Nigeria. It is sounding and feeling like thing that is happening in remembering that is not mine, hazy and sometime with static, but my body is telling me that it is thing that I am experiencing. Even though it is feeling like dream, my body is telling me that this is truth. Grace is singing to me in language that she is knowing and that Ngozi and Ify are not knowing, language that we are sharing. Something inside me pushes me to smile at Grace, and she smiles back, then she bows to me and leaves.

Now it is just being me and Ify who are the only breathing thing in this room.

Ify is going to her desk and turning machine on and preparing machine and then she is looking at me. I am thinking that she is seeing something in my eye, because her face is becoming softer and she is looking like how mother in remembering is looking at child. She is looking at me like her whole face is saying it will be okay, and at first I am not trusting her because some part of me, deep inside past my skeleton and my organs, is remembering that everybody I trust—even Xifeng, even Enyemaka—is sometime telling lies to me, and I am tired of people telling lies to me. But Ify is putting hand on my shoulder, then she is asking me, "Do you want to see them?"

For a long time, there is only question in my eye, because I am not knowing what she is meaning, then I am knowing, and I am knowing now that I am nervous. I am having purpose and I am knowing that I am to be serving others and doing good thing and that I am being good person, but I am nervous to be doing this thing. Ify is looking at me, and I am nodding my head.

Then the wall we are facing is opening like it is blinds on a window turning from vertical to horizontal, and I am seeing before me row and row and row and row and row of hospital bed with body that is in it and that is not moving. It is going on forever, like sea that is never-ending. And I am not even trying to be counting them. It is different, seeing them this way, than seeing them from the office in Ify's apartment. They are closer. Their danger feels greater. I am wanting even more to be helping them.

That is why I am here. It is purpose that is being given to me, but it is also purpose that I am choosing for myself. There is thing in my brain that is making me special, and it is thing that will be helping these people. And this is the future I am choosing: to be helping these people, some of whom may be my brother and sister.

And this is making me to not be nervous.

CHAPTER
51

For Ify, there is always a slight spell of vertigo.

One moment, she's seated at her desk, her chair reclined slightly back so that she stares up at an angle, her vision filled with projected screens and tabs and windows from the variety of software programs she's running, her gloved fingers at work on the touchboard in her lap. She takes a sharp inhale, then, the next moment, there's emptiness. Nothingness, not even color. A pure absence that lasts for the briefest of instants before the world begins to build itself around her.

In the beginning, it is a random memory, what Uzo has been calling a "remembering," as though there were an action involved. Ify lands in the middle of a forest or a field outside a village like the one in which she finds herself now. And everything is frozen. A still-life painting, but one that Ify can walk through.

In a circle outside the squat blue school building, children have gathered, and one of them is in the center, frozen mid-dance, upright but with legs crossed at the ankles and arms akimbo, his shadow a stretched-out reflection before him. The shadow flickers, however. As do the faces on some of the children in the circle surrounding the dancer. Ify's avatar walks through the still tableau as her real body—she knows, though she cannot feel it—reclines in a chair in an all-white room, fingers racing over a touchboard.

Ify looks at the dancer's shadow, how it shimmers and fills with static every few moments, then looks to the sun and gauges its position, the angle at which it casts its light. It doesn't shine with a real sun's force, so Ify doesn't need to shield her eyes from it. Still, she cannot shake the habit.

Sometimes simply walking through a stilled tableau will bring it back to life, infuse it with motion, like pressing resume on a paused recording. But sometimes there is a missing piece or something has been knocked loose or an errant stick has found its way in between some gears in the machinery. It always looks like a different thing, the glitch, and sometimes Ify will spend what feels like several hours in a memory before she finds it, a single patch of ground, barren where there should be grass, or a bit of sky that's the wrong color. This time, it's a young man leaning against the school building, back pressed up against the wall. But there are two of him occupying the same space, like a photograph shot with double exposure. Or like he is caught between two frames in an animation. One version of him is pressed up against the wall, arms folded, sweat beading his brow, a malicious smirk on his face. The other version is leaning forward, one foot angled forward, the other pressed against the wall like he's getting ready to spring from it, an action pose.

Ify heads over to the glitch. Every footprint she leaves in the dust, every indent she leaves in the grass, masks itself as soon as she's passed, erasing any trace of her presence. It's a constant effort on Ify's part to control her involvement in the rememberings, to not alter too much, to adjust only what needs adjusting. To fix and not break. As code streams before her face in the hospital room, she sees what that coding describes in the memory.

When Ify gets to the glitch, she sees, out of the corner of her eye, a shimmer in an alleyway between buildings. Is this what triggered the glitch? Ify heads to it and is bathed in shadows only a moment before she finds herself walking out onto shimmering green water. Beneath her appears a thin dinghy laden with armed soldiers who arrive out of thin air, constructed pixel by pixel. Turning left and right and behind herself to look at them, she sees that none of the soldiers appear older than her. Indeed, few of them even look older than Uzo. Ify faces forward again, but her gaze dips downward toward the water, frozen in its shimmer, and that's when she sees the reflection. The features are distorted by the waves, but the metal is just as Ify remembers. Covering half her face, including one eye, its border drawing a line down to her chin. Ify can also see where the metal's frontier vanishes into a forest of locs. The right eye— the mechanical one—is glowing a fiery yellow.

It's Onyii.

When Ify freezes, she realizes too late that she's off balance, and she pitches forward right into the petrified waves, which shatter like crystals and surround her, then melt away pixel by pixel until—

Ify slams back into her body.

At first, there's only darkness, then Ify realizes it's because she's still wearing her helmet. From its top, thick cables extend and plug into her workspace as well as the MRI scanner holding Uzo's body. The only sound she hears aside from the hammering of her own heart is the ever-present hum of Uzo's body scanner and the readers, processors, and tablet computers neatly arrayed on Ify's desk. That Ify can hear them at all speaks to how hard she's been working them. The touchboards have been left on for far too long. Without warning, moisture pools in Ify's eyes, the world dissolving into a blur of gray and black before she slides out of the helmet and wipes the tears away.

Slowly, she sits up. The chair adjusts to her posture, and soon, she's leaning forward, struggling for breath. She stares at her hands and her forearms. Smooth, unlined, and brown. Yet she can feel her veins pulsing beneath her flesh. Her bodysuit compresses her chest to prevent a cough.

Reentry into the real world never seems to get easier. Sometimes, it feels as though it's only growing more difficult. Each time, the feeling of being ripped from a reality so luscious and vivid as Uzo's rememberings, being thrown back into this world of perpetual white, jars her bones a little harder. Sets her blood rushing a little faster. Pushes her heart just a little too close to the edge of what's healthy.

The MRI scanner hisses, then slowly ejects Uzo's bed. The girl knows to remain still while the bed is moving and while she's being scanned. As soon as the bed is fully removed from the circular container, Uzo rises, leaning back on her hands. In that pose she looks every inch the carefree, comfortable teenager, growing into her limbs, learning the limits of her body as well as what new things it can do at this age. Then Ify remembers the cord extended from the outlet at the base of her neck.

"Are you okay?" Uzo asks her.

Ify nods, then slides from her chair, landing softly on the ground. Without sparing Uzo another glance, she hurries into the next room, where wireless printers spill reams of paper onto the floor. Outdated technology, but Ify finds special comfort in feeling the data between her thumb and forefinger when she picks up a length of printout. The memories.

The feel of Onyii still hangs like fog in her brain. She flexes her fingers to remind herself of who she is, then she takes the paper in her hands.

On one side of the paper is binary code, and on its reverse is mIRC scripting. Gibberish to most people Ify knows, even much of the medical staff, but for Ify, her first language. She can see in a sequence of coding a computer's attempt to describe a moment. A series of hashtags and backslashes attempting, like a camera figuring out how it works, to describe the angle of sunlight on a small field filled with dancing schoolchildren, or the taste of fried plantains mixed with a mouthful of jollof rice, or the feeling of something smooth and feathery and small held in the cup made of two hands joined together. This was what Xifeng's hard drives held.

It would be easy enough to look at these markings on a pair of screens. But this way makes it easier to see the coding. If she's given image after image, sensation after sensation, immersive memory after immersive memory, she knows what will happen. It nearly happened just now.

She will abandon everything else to look for Onyii.

From time to time, she looks up from the printouts and into the room in which Uzo sits, and she wonders just how much of Onyii is there for the finding. What parts are there of her sister's life that Ify had no idea about? Did she ever love anyone? What was she like as a child? What were her moments of grace? Of happiness? Were there smells that transported her? Food? The odor that hangs over certain cities? The sea?

She lives, Xifeng had told her before plummeting to her death.

Ify wishes she could download the memories onto an external drive and tinker with them from there, rummage through them looking for signs of Onyii, chase her sister through these acts of remembering. But as soon as the data leaves Uzo's head, it will begin to deteriorate, perhaps falling prey to the same virus that is plaguing the children filling the ward.

When Ify gets back to her office, a box of printouts in her arms, Céline is waiting for her.

For a moment, they stand there, frozen, Ify with the box in her hands and Céline pitched nervously against the wall, trying to affect a pose of nonchalance. But an apology swims behind her lips. Ify can feel it.

The whole journey through Centrafrique's transport station, haggard and exhausted, she had looked for Céline, waited anxiously for her to show up and hold her, reassure her, bring her back to the life, the security, she'd felt in space. But Céline had never shown her face, and now here she stands.

"Don't you have a Colony to administrate?" Ify asks, the venom thick in her voice.

"Is that even the word for what I do?" Céline replies, waving the question away with her smile. She walks over to Ify's desk and shifts around some tablets and microprocessors. "Do you have a graph of her?"

"Who?"

"Your secret weapon. Your pièce de résistance."

Ify puts the box down and walks past Céline. "Where were you?"

She can feel Céline move behind her, reach for her. "Ify, I—"

"Where. Were you."

"Ify." Céline's voice softens. "What happened down there?"

Ify wants to tell her friend that she was forced to confront her past. Memories rock Ify. An earthquake telling the story of war and betrayal and children held in cages and a riot in Abuja. She waits for it to pass. How does she tell Céline all of what happened? That she was responsible for the capture and torture of children, that she was the reason war continued for as long as it did, that people she thought would once help in peacetime turned out to be villains. That she had once been a villain herself. "I had a sister," she says without warning.

"What? You've never mentioned her before."

"We were from different tribes, but she raised me. It was several years into the war when she found me. My family had been murdered, and I was all alone. We lived in a camp in Delta State by the water. When I wasn't in school, she would take me to the edge of this small cliff and we would watch the sun set, and then she would stay with me as I traced constellations in the stars and told her about how much I wanted to go to space. Because of a mistake I made one day, our camp was raided and we were separated. She became a Biafran soldier, and I was brought to Abuja, where I was taught how glorious it was to be a Nigerian. Suddenly, Onyii and I were enemies. Just like that. Because people told us we were. I was told that we Nigerians were in the right and that we were doing what we had to do to bring about peace. I was told that the people we captured and the people we killed were beyond saving. Many of them could never be convinced that peace was the way. When I found my chance to see my sister again, Nigerian society rejected me and cast me out. So I went to find my sister and kill her. Because she was the one who had murdered my family."

When Céline says Ify's name, her voice is thick with sorrow.

"Because of me . . ." Ify's throat closes up. She fights the tears. "There was peace for almost a year before I . . . before Enugu was bombed. The ceasefire had ended, because I had led a group of suicide bombers into a Biafran city." Her fingers curl into fists at her side. She turns to face Céline. "You want to know what happened down there? Someone tried to make everyone remember what had happened. The government had pushed people to move on, to forget the war. And someone there, someone I had trusted, tried to remind them, tried to remind the whole country what had happened." She clenches her jaw and takes a moment to fight the sobs. "I stopped them. I fought, and I killed, and I stopped them."

Céline is silent. The only thing Ify can read on her face is pity.

"You knew, didn't you? You knew what I'd done."

Céline opens her mouth to speak, then closes it. Her eyes scan the floor, looking for the words. "After you left, I . . . I looked into you. And I learned. It wasn't easy, but I learned. After a while, you stopped trying to contact me, and I had no idea what was happening in your country, so I looked into it and . . ."

"You knew? You knew about the lie? What the government had convinced everyone had happened instead of war?"

Céline nods.

"You knew and you didn't tell me?" She realizes she's roaring. She stops and takes a moment to collect herself. "You knew what was happening and you didn't think to tell me?"

"Ify, *mon coeur*, I . . ." Something hardens in Céline. "I knew horrible things had happened to you before you came here. That is war. But I did not know what you had done. And I couldn't . . ."

"Couldn't what?"

"I couldn't forgive you."

It staggers Ify to hear her say it. The thing she has most feared has come to life before her very eyes.

"I figured you'd done *quelques choses horribles*, but this? A whole city, bombed? Ify, that is what a war criminal does."

Ify trembles. She feels as though the ground will swallow her up at any moment. Her bottom lip quivers. She grits her teeth and hisses, "So why did you come, then?"

"What?"

"Why are you here right now? Why did you come?" She can barely see for the tears in her eyes.

Céline considers her hands, then the floor, then she looks at the ceiling before finally training her gaze on Ify. "I wanted to see you. One last time."

"Before you report me to the authorities?" Ify spits the words out at her. "Before you have me charged with war crimes and deported?"

Céline straightens. "No," she says, her voice neutral. "I will not report you. And I will destroy what records I did find. But this is goodbye. You are not . . ." She doesn't finish. She lets whatever word she was about to say hang in the air between them before turning to leave.

Rage wraps its claws around Ify's lungs. She couldn't scream even if she wanted to. All she can do is shake with it, every fiber of her body quivering feverishly with fury. She holds her head in her hands and clenches herself against the sobs that threaten. No. She won't give Céline the satisfaction of hearing her grief, of knowing how deeply she's wounded Ify.

Ify staggers to a console by the far wall and leans over it, damming the tears clinging to her eyelashes. Then she looks up.

The blinds over the windows of one wall open to reveal the room in which Uzo sits, her legs dangling over the edge of her bed. She demonstrates an otherworldly capacity for stillness. Uzo can spend hours completely unmoving, leaving Ify to wonder at just what is happening behind her eyes and between her ears.

She stares at the girl, lets Uzo fill her entire vision, lets Uzo become all she can focus on. Slowly, purpose clears the fog from Ify's brain. She has a mission. She has lives to save. She is not a criminal.

When Ify returns to the printout, the letters and numbers and symbols are even more of a jumble. She scans them from left to right, down, left to right, down. But, even with renewed focus, none of it is making sense. Scanning the code, she will catch the beginnings of an image braiding itself together in her mind—a night sky, a hand and arm framed against a jungle backdrop, a city skyline—then it vanishes. She pinches the bridge of her nose, then walks to the window and looks down. Uzo still hasn't moved.

It takes Ify several moments to head to the elevator. And even as she stands in the contraption, nervousness makes her fingers twitch and she absentmindedly flicks her wrist to clank her thin bangles against each other. She has taken to wearing them since her return from Nigeria. A piece of home she brought back with her.

She enters Uzo's room, the whole place blanketed in false light. For a while, Ify looks around at the room's smooth, rounded edges, its perfect symmetry, its spotlessness, its fluorescence. Then she goes to the console on the wall by the door and turns off the lighting, simultaneously flipping the blinds to reveal the refugee ward on the other side of the window. It's not natural lighting that spills into their room in thin bars, but it's closer, and this makes Ify feel as though she's doing a right thing. She then moves her chair so that it faces Uzo, and they stare at each other, Uzo's face impassive, Ify trying to school compassion onto hers.

"I am thinking you are looking for Onyii in me," Uzo says.

Uzo's bluntness still has a way of disarming Ify. Maybe her break with Céline is too recent.

"Not just in my head but in the way I am moving. How I am walking and sitting and breathing. I am not Onyii. I am being called Uzo."

"You are right, Uzo."

This seems to quiet the synth.

"I need your help. Your . . . your rememberings. I can't find the order to them. I can't find the right coding."

"I am organizing them. They are being connected, but I am sorting them so I am knowing which one I am being born with and which one I am collecting during my mission."

"How do you find what you're looking for?" Ify hears the change in her own voice. She's not asking as a scientist or as a doctor. She's asking as a human. When she asks Uzo how she finds what she's looking for, she knows she means it for herself as well. She's lost. So lost, adrift in her own mission, helpless before what is killing these children, bereft after losing the anchor that has held her most steadily in her life in the Colonies, adrift in a sea whose waves threaten to take these pieces of Onyii further and further away from her.

"I am using word with you now, but when I am talking to myself or to Enyemaka or to my brother and sister, it is coming out as many words put into one." Her mouth works. "If I am wanting to be happy, I am not simply telling myself to find happy remembering. I am looking for being-held-in-arms-of-mother or I am looking for fixing-BoTa-for-my-grandfather-after-brother-is-breaking-it or I am looking for sitting-in-field-picking-flowers. And each of these thing is coming into my mind as one word. It is like . . ." Uzo looks around, as though searching the room for a word. Then she does a thing Ify has never seen before. "It is like a circle," Uzo says, drawing one in the air with her index fingers.

She's speaking with her body, Ify realizes with a start. But she keeps the scientist part of her at bay. She's not listening to a mechanical creation. She's listening to a fifteen-year-old girl.

"But when I am talking to Enyemaka or my brother and sister, it is like thing I am telling you, but it is not so specific. It is like I am telling them the center of the circle, the core of it. And this thing is being transferred. So they are understanding what I am telling them. It is like . . ."

And Uzo continues talking. As she speaks, Ify listens. Listens to Uzo's fingers in her hair and the occasional uptick in her voice and the way her eyes occasionally dart from one part of the ceiling to another part when she is trying to translate whatever language her brain speaks into words Ify will understand. Ify listens to Uzo shifting on the bed, listens to the way parts of her skin flush when she gets excited, listens to the sighs and their placements. Listens to the whole of her.

Until her eyelids grow heavy and Uzo's words gently rock her out of her loneliness and into dreaming.

CHAPTER
52

After Ify is falling asleep, I am watching her for a long time. She is sometime looking like how my brother and sister are looking when they are sitting down and finding peace. Their eye is closed sometime and it is like their entire body is relaxing and being loose even though they are being completely still. When I am watching Ify for many minutes and seeing that she is not waking up, I am taking her gently in my arms and making sure her head is being balanced against my shoulder so it is not just falling to the side like some dangling thing. And I am walking to the door and then walking to the elevator. And I am knowing it is being late in the hospital because there is few people walking around and few people is noticing me who is wearing hospital gown and is carrying doctor all the way up to her office. When I am needing to open door or get into room, I am using her thumb and pressing it against pad by the handle. And door is swishing open.

Then I am laying Ify down in her chair and making sure it is at proper angle for her to be relaxing. I am opening closet by a far wall and pulling out blanket and I am bringing it to her, and as I am unfolding it and draping it over her, I am being swept up into remembering of young woman who Ify is calling Onyii, and Onyii is doing the same thing but the blanket is coarse and being filled with stain that is rust from radiation and that is also being blood, and bed that Ify is sleeping on is army cot and it is being humid and moist and too hot and the air is clinging like slippery leech to the skin and sweat is beading Ify's forehead but she is looking like she is finding peace in her sleep and I am draping blanket on her then I am getting up and walking through mosquito netting and leaving tent.

When I am out of the remembering, I am back in her office and I am watching her sleep and then I am going back to the room where I am staying, the one with the MRI scanner.

The blinds to the window that is occupying one whole wall are still being open and I am able to be looking through the window and seeing all the row after row after row of bed with children who is being in them, sleeping but also not sleeping. Doing something that is deeper than sleeping.

The way the beds are being arranged, it is like they are being made to be looking the same, but I am seeing all the difference in them. How some is having scar and some is not having scar, how hair is being nappy on one and how they are curling differently on different heads, how some is missing finger or arm or whole leg, how some is metal but different. I am seeing brothers and sisters among them. And I am thinking that maybe they are child of war also but maybe they are seeing and doing and feeling and knowing what I am seeing and doing and feeling and knowing, that they are walking into their future. I am feeling good about what I am doing because Ify is telling me that it is helping them to be waking up and to be living their life. And I am looking at the children who are looking like me, and some of them are having family around them or brother or sister or friend or maybe someone they are loving once who is here waiting for them to be waking up. And I am remembering that this is what it is being like to be having someone who is caring for you. It is looking like this. It is looking like someone is smoothing out the wrinkles in the blanket on your body.

Just like I am doing with Ify.

Smile is coming onto my face until I am seeing two women next to one bed and one of them is sitting down in chair and rubbing hand of boy in bed and the other is just standing over them both and water is coming from her eyes. The one that is sitting is having her back to me while the one that is standing is facing me but not yet seeing me.

I am walking closer to window and my eye is zooming in and I am seeing face and my body is doing strange thing where it is becoming too warm too fast like engine overheating and I am feeling fist clench at my side and seeing me grit my own teeth together like I am being outside of my body. My back is tensing, and my leg is shaking, and I am not in room with MRI machine anymore—I am in basement where water is dripping and my feet is dangling and my arm is hanging high over my head.

Light is coming into room, spilling like water. And I am hearing door opening. But it is old door because it is creaking and it is squeaking and light is suddenly everywhere and I am having to be closing my eyes against it. I am waiting to be hearing hard footstep but instead it is soft like swish swish and I am knowing this is the sound of sand. There is being sand in this room where I am hanging. And I am hearing sizzling too and knowing that something is burning even if I am not smelling it, and I am knowing that I am not smelling thing because my nose is being broken. Many thing in me is broken but I am not feeling pain. And I am remembering now that the person who is walking into this room is wanting me to be feeling pain.

That is why when he is walking in he is spitting on me and telling me I am not human and that I am rubbish to be thrown into ocean. I am wondering why he is keeping me here and as I am wondering this he is holding shockstick and he is hitting me in my stomach and chest and side with it and he is hitting me so hard on my back that he is breaking his stick.

I am thinking that I am supposed to be feeling thing. Big man that is with the one who is hitting me is telling him is not working. And I am knowing now that I am being tortured and then I am remembering that I am what they are calling enemy combatant.

Big man is telling boy that nothing is working because I am being made to not be feeling pain. He is saying that I am special soldier, I am synth, and I am not having pain receptor in my brain and it is this that is making me not to be feeling thing even though many thing inside me is broken. Boy is telling big man okay and big man is leaving, and I am thinking that boy is going to be leaving with big man but boy is staying and I am raising my head to be seeing his face and when he is looking at me he is smiling so his teeth are shining yellow like corn they are selling by the street, and I am seeing the way hair is over his face and the way the skin on his knuckles is broken, and I am seeing the vest he is wearing and the patches and I am knowing that he is soldier too and that he is with what I am knowing is a militia and they are small small army but they are killing just like soldier. And boy is looking at me like I am something to be eating, and then he is reaching behind him and pulling cord from his neck and he is walking close to me and he is putting cord in my neck and suddenly I am feeling everything. I am feeling the breaking in my ribs and in my back and in my crotch and in my arms and in my head, and he is smiling at me and saying now I will be feeling these thing and he is raising his stick and I am back in my hospital room with the MRI machine and I am staring out the window and my body is shaking but I am feeling like I am not outside of it anymore. I am feeling like sense is returning to me.

Woman who is standing over boy who is sleeping-not-sleeping is seeing me and staring at me and not moving. Then she is moving away from boy and walking to me.

Even though I am feeling like I am being back inside my own body, I am wanting to smash the glass and I am wanting to tear through the floor and I am wanting to knock over every bed between me and that boy that she is standing over before she is walking to me and I am wanting to take that boy and raise him in the air and smash him into the ground until his head is breaking like coconut. And then I am wanting to be taking machete to every part of his body and making him to be screaming and shouting and crying, because even though I am knowing that I am in this hospital room, my body is still feeling all of the thing he is doing to it.

But woman is walking to me and tears still build like wall in her eyes and then, when she is coming to window, she is holding her hand together in front of her and her bottom lip is trembling and she is saying, "Thank you, thank you, thank you," in soft soft voice.

She is not moving her mouth and that is when I am realizing that she is speaking to me in my brain. She is having braincase too.

Why are you thanking me?

Then she is sending me image and recording of the boy and he is being called Peter and he is sometime smiling and twirling spaghetti around his fork and sometime he is angry and shouting at woman who is being called Amy and sometime he is in hoverchair watching other children play on top of water pond. Then she is sending me feeling of love for him and how she is taking him in and accepting him and teaching him how to live and what is being peace, and then I am stopping her.

Do not be sending me these things.

Why not?

I don't care about him. You are telling me he is being good person and so he is deserving good thing to be happening to him. She is pausing because of shock. *What is wrong with that?*

Peter is not good person. I am taking several moments to calm myself. *He is fighter during the war and he is finding me one day and he is putting me in room and he is hurting me very badly. He is hurting me all over, even when he is not having to be hurting me. He is hurting me and enjoying it.* I am not letting her see or feel the rememberings because I am not wanting to be giving her that access to me. I am not wanting her to be knowing me in this way, but I am telling her so that she is knowing that the boy she is loving is bad person and he is deserving to die.

When I am finished giving life back to the children I am finding Peter and I am killing him for what he is doing to me.

For a long time, she is not saying anything, then she is blinking at me like she is not understanding what I am saying. I am thinking I should be repeating it again, but then she is getting look in her eyes like she is asking me, *Please don't,* but without saying the words. But the look in her face is also saying other thing at the same time. It is saying, *No, you are lying*, and it is saying, *No, it cannot be like this*, and it is saying, *My son deserves to live*, but it is also saying, *Is he my son?* and all of this is happening in Amy's face at the same time.

I know her heart is paining her but I am not caring.

He is my son, she is saying to me with tears falling from her eye.

That is not changing what he is doing to me.

She is looking at me for long time, and I am thinking she is looking for something from me. Maybe she is looking for me to be changing my voice or how I am standing, for my body to not be tensing like this. Maybe she is looking for me to be saying, *I forgive him*, and also be saying, *I forgive you for loving him*.

But I am not saying any of these thing. I am never saying any of these thing.

And she is seeing this and she is turning and she is walking away.

CHAPTER
53

Grace is at Ify's side as nurse's assistants transport the first child into a separate operating room. She has all her note-taking materials out in front of her, stylus forever poised over her tablet screen, but Ify can see that the girl is too riveted by what she's witnessing to document it.

It had come to Ify in a dream. Céline used to joke, while they were in school, that this was Ify's superpower. She could conjure the right answer out of thin air, and all she needed was enough sleep.

The epiphany: words whispering a melody, indistinct and blurring together, while a circle formed out of thin air, inky and writhing. Ify remembers the circle, then another. All the while, words surround her and come together to make images of people and places and reveal snapshots of human beings caught in the throes of their living. And the circle means something, but in the dream, Ify couldn't tell what. She remembers she had been leaning forward when caught up in the vision, but in the dream, she begins to lean back and passively accept the circle and the images and words swimming around her, then another circle appears on top of it, so that their edges are just barely touching, then another and another until six circles sit in formation before her, and they remain like this, like rings of black fire, until more circles join them, forming a honeycomb pattern. It was as she was leaning back, letting the sight fill her vision, that she saw the greater image. More and more rings of black fire joined the assemblage, and when it looked like they were going to turn into an entire wall of black, Ify saw it. Or, rather, felt it.

It was a series of moments, a cascade. Someone taking her face in their hands and lowering it and blowing softly on her forehead, and Ify realizes that she is hearing words or more than words. She is experiencing synth speech. Because she feels hands gripping her face, but they are not just Uzo's hands, bringing to life that moment on top of the site of that abandoned detention center in Kaduna State, and not Onyii's either, during a moment when Ify felt the humid air of their camp was suffocating her. It is both pairs of hands and neither. It is past and deeper past, reaching into her present.

Ify feels the warmth of a fire on her arm, and when she looks at it, she sees her arm turn to Onyii's metal one absorbing the blow from a shockstick, and at the same time, she's seeing her own arm as a child as a mutated mosquito drifts off with too much of her blood. So many moments, braided together so that it feels as though she's experiencing everything for the first time but always has, in the back of her mind, a memory of the same.

Then she looks back up at the multiplying rings of fire, and that's when she realizes she's not looking at a wall. She's looking at a floor. Floor tiles.

DNA tiles. The sentences are units of DNA. The building blocks of being. Uzo's words-thoughts-feelings are what made her. Ify's words-thoughts-feelings make her. Onyii's made her. This is why Uzo always speaks in the present tense. Everything she experienced is still happening to her, ossified into the present tense in her memories. *Happened* becomes *happens* and remains *is happening*.

In the dream, Ify grows suddenly like a giant, and the three-dimensional column of memory-units, interlocking rings of black fire, sits in the cup of her two hands, and for some reason, Ify thinks of a gosling, small and furry and poking its head out from the fold of skin by her thumb to gaze into her face, the very first thing it sees after being born. A feeling of wonder and love and gratitude thrills through her as she looks at this structure growing in her hands. This is Uzo's memory of the gosling. The gosling was a thing that happened to her, Ify realizes, a burst of understanding twinned with an explosion of love in her heart.

This is it. This is the coding. This is what is living inside Uzo's braincase.

When Ify woke up, she fumbled over to her workstation and had all her monitors running almost instantly, sketching the shapes that still burned vivid in her head and logging those sketches into an online editor where she watched it all come to life, the black rings of fire touching, then interlocking, growing more and more complex until they began to fold on each other like bits of origami. Then, from that, Ify had derived the algorithm to replicate self-assembly, and suddenly she was staring at the mechanism for mnemonic repair.

The cure for memory erasure.

And now that coding exists in a liquid filled with nanobots that nursing assistants begin to inject into the arms of the children they all stand around.

Ify has no idea how long the mechanism will take before activating—whether it will begin its work immediately or lie dormant in the bloodstream for months or maybe even years, by which point too much precious material will have been eaten away. All Ify can do after the injections is tell the nursing assistants to stay with their patients and monitor for any change in activity.

She's on her way out with Grace when she hears the dull roar of cheering from far away. "What is that?"

But Grace, now paying attention to the world around her, taps in a sequence on her tablet and gasps. "Doctor."

Ify turns, annoyed even now at Grace's insistence on calling her that, but stops as soon as she sees the image on which Grace's eyes fixate.

Grace gulps, then reads some of the text in a document next to what appears to be a government press conference. "'The Migration Board finds no reason to question what is stated about the health of the children affected by this current crisis. It is therefore considered that, for their recovery, they need to be in a safe and stable environment. This is necessary for full recuperation.'" Grace looks up from her tablet. "What does this mean?"

Ify walks out to the floor where, already, families gather around the sickbeds, excitedly speaking to children who may or may not be able to hear them. Some are weeping into their child's blankets, others are taking a patient's hand and, not realizing they're doing it, shaking it as they dance in place. "The deportation orders have been canceled," Ify says. The full import of the words that just came out of her mouth sinks in. "The deportation orders have been canceled."

■ ■ ■ ■ ■

It amazes Ify how much solving a medical mystery can calm her before the men of the Medical Committee. Where before they had seemed like sphinxlike demigods scrutinizing her from on high, ready to hurl judgments and proclamations like bolts of lightning, now they just look like what they are: old men who've modified their bodies, their faces, their hair in order to stroke their vanity while resting comfortably in positions—head of genetics, director of this department, chief of that department—they had inherited more than earned. She looks up at the row of men seated before her and sees nothing but a row of men, none of them extraordinary, none of them more deserving than her of the right to be put in charge of the lives of hundreds, even thousands, of people. None of them have done what she has just done. Knowing this, understanding this, she's able to stand straighter, breathe more easily, relax her posture, and pace her words. She's able to hear the moods in their tone and adjust hers accordingly.

The academic from earlier with his false French accent leans forward on his elbows. "So we'll never truly know whether the solution to your problem was a medical one or a political one, will we?"

Ify wants to respond to his calling it *your problem* but instead says, "The treatment of illnesses must be holistic in my profession, sir. Would you really suggest curing their medical illness, then sending them back to a country of origin whose turmoil would have them coming right back to us, to do it all over again? *Nun sind sie halt da.*" *Now they are here.* The German had come out of her before she could stop it, but the look on the academic's face satisfies her. It was too easy for Ify to see through the man's persona and uncover a genealogy full of eugenicists and discredited race scientists from what was once Central Europe. Guilt spasms through the man's face before he retreats into his seat.

Ify faces the rest of the group. "The recall of deportation orders, we've now determined, was the activating ingredient in the cure we devised for the patients."

Director Towne, the only man on this committee whose approval she has ever sought, raises an eyebrow at her.

"Experiences coded in the DNA, Director Towne. They are arranged differently in a particular variant of cyberized brain than in those of natural-born humans or even those cyberized later in life. Their method of bonding mimics altogether different structures. When the base pattern was made clear, it became very easy to extrapolate a pattern of self-replication that would combat the virus that had infected not only those children who came to us with cyberized brains but those with no cyberization as well. Biomechanics is still beholden to biology."

Director Towne's frown deepens. "And where did this eureka moment come from?"

"Excuse me, Director Towne?"

"No one simply comes up with an otherwise unknown and unseen DNA bonding structure made up of tiles that are, in turn, composed of mnemonic material." There's a dismissive smirk on his face, but Ify reads frustration in it too. "How did you do this?"

"Sir."

"Internist Diallo, I don't think you understand."

Ify's eyes go wide at Director Towne addressing her with that title. It drips disdain.

"You've cured Alzheimer's disease." A chuckle escapes his throat. "Vascular dementia, maybe even Huntington's disease. What, did this come to you in a dream?"

Ify's body temperature plummets when she realizes what is going on. He doesn't believe she did this on her own, that she could discern the molecular structure of the cure, that she could decipher the data of cyberized memories and discern the very fabric of personhood. Who *would* believe her? But Ify knows that were one of the men sitting next to him to say the exact same thing she said, Towne would have congratulated the man without a second thought, would have praised him and recommended him for any number of awards.

Ify squares her shoulders. "Well, dreams come to prepared spirits, Director Towne. That is how theoretical chemist August Kekulé put it when telling the story of how he discovered the structure of the benzene ring, if I remember correctly. In fact, that was one of your first lessons."

Towne holds her stare, then reclines in his chair, as though he is conceding defeat.

Ify addresses the rest of the group. "I'd like to tell the story of one of our earliest patients, a young girl named Ayodele, who had immigrated to Alabast prior to the initial cessation of hostilities during the Biafran Conflict in Nigeria four years ago. She was one of the first victims of this most recent health crisis. She had come to Alabast with the remnants of her family: a non-cyberized father and a mute younger brother. The boy had not been born mute. Very quickly, Ayodele enrolled in school and became the most popular student in her class.

Academically and athletically skilled. Because the Biafran War had ended, the family's asylum application was denied. But there exists a provision concerning the welfare of the child. If it is not proven that the applicant will be persecuted upon returning to their country of origin, then the case must be made that deportation would severely affect the child's psychological health. The headmaster of Ayodele's school even wrote a letter in support of her family's resubmitted application. But then the new immigration law went into effect. The first deportation orders were issued that same day. Within a week, the first wave of children had fallen victim."

The committee members do not disguise their irritation.

"Last week, less than half a month after we began initiating the new treatment, Ayodele opened her eyes. Witnesses would later say that it was her father's voice that brought her back. She could hear the change in it and decided that their application must have gone through, that they would be permitted to stay in Alabast. But what allowed her to regain her memories and motor functions was the medicine. Without it, Ayodele would have forgotten how she had made it to the hospital, what her journey to the Colonies had been like, even her own father's face. She would have eventually forgotten how to breathe, and she would have died. Our cure has not only halted the virus that infected the children when they shut down, it is rebuilding their memories. It is reversing the tide. But it is nothing without this activating switch. If the body were not prepared for it, it would have been simple liquid swimming through their blood. Because of last month's news, it is saving their lives."

Ify can tell she's been getting too worked up. So she calms herself. "Ayodele opened her eyes, began making eye contact with people, and began to feed herself. Soon, she was able to walk. After that, she could speak in full sentences."

Ify is under no illusions that the men sitting before her will truly understand her story. Ayodele was many patients, many of whom have backgrounds too sensitive for Ify to disclose, many of whom, Ify has learned, are synths. Ayodele stood in for refugees who had come before the latest outbreak. Ayodele was those who had fled war in the Pacific and who had journeyed from the Babylonian Republic and from the Americas. Ayodele was those refugees streaming into the Jungle and trickling into Alabast even as she spoke. Ayodele was the refugees who would continue to come.

When Ify speaks, she hears past and future collide and meld, like interlocking rings, with her present. She is speaking of what has happened, is happening, and will happen. She is speaking of all of them, and she is speaking of this one. And, but for a single change, she is speaking of herself as well.

Dr. Langrishe, the Genetics Department head who has thus far been silent throughout the proceedings, leans forward. "This is a remarkable thing you've done, young woman."

Ify blinks her surprise. She had expected acerbic racism from him. She had expected him to ooze a sense of superiority like a cloud of fungal spores. But now he only seems to have eyes for his tablet, which displays the report Ify sent to the committee prior to this hearing.

"However you uncovered this molecular structure and devised this cure, you've done it. You've not only saved these children, but you may have extended the average life expectancy by another several decades. If there is any justice in the world, your name will appear in our history books. I'd like to think I speak for all of us when I offer you my sincerest congratulations. The Refugee Program is in good hands."

"Thank you, Doctor," Ify says. "This would not have been possible without the aid of my assistant, Grace Leung. She was essential during the course of our research. Without her, these children would be without a cure."

"Well noted. I think we can adjourn this hearing," says Langrishe, sparing only the slightest of glances for Director Towne, who continues to stew. "Dr. Diallo's testimony has been more than satisfying. Now, hearing adjourned." He presses at a few buttons on the desk before him before rising to his feet. Amid the shuffle, he looks up and winks at Ify, who bows her head slightly, then turns and walks back to the door, waiting for the feeling to hit. Waiting to feel like a hero, like the top of her class, like she is the reason thousands of people are now alive and well in Alabast. She waits for the ecstasy, for the elevation of her heart rate, for her cheeks to flush with blood. She waits for her fingers and toes to tremble in shocked rejoicing. She waits for tears of gratitude.

Even as she heads back to her office, Grace beside her, glowing with guarded admiration, Ify still doesn't feel it.

Grace begs leave, and Ify lets her go. In another time, Grace would be talking excitedly with all her friends in a group chat about having played so essential a part in the miracle of scientific discovery. But now, she is more likely than not heading off somewhere to sit alone in silence. And to process everything that has happened to her over the past several months. Instead of chatting with her colleagues and peers, she has left Ify alone to wait for the warmth of victory to surge through her.

Staring out at the now-empty rows and rows of beds, extended almost endlessly into the distance, Ify feels nothing. Not even a whisper of satisfaction.

Céline has likely destroyed all evidence of Ify's past by now.

All trace of the chaos and violence that had plagued Abuja during that night of terror is very likely gone as well. Wiped away as though it never happened. When people speak of the damage or skirt the edges of an absence—a lost possession or a missing piece of furniture or even a person never to be seen again—talk will likely return to some storm, as though what had happened was a natural disaster, a cosmic event. Something biblical like a flood or fire raining from the sky. Then they'll talk admiringly about the government's valiant efforts to reverse the effects of climate change. The erasure will be complete.

If there is no scar, was there ever even a wound to begin with?

Whatever miracle Ify has accomplished seems hollow in the face of that question.

■ ■ ■ ■ ■

"I'm still not moving as fast as I'd like," Peter says around a mouthful of spaghetti and a meatball, chunky meat sauce dripping down his chin, "but I can feel it getting better, you know?" He swallows before fully chewing, and Amy and Paige can't help but smile lovingly at the mess, even though Paige makes a show of chastising him, warning him to eat like he's been to a restaurant before. She's on the verge of making some comment about the jungle or the bush when she spots Ify, who smiles politely over her own plate.

"They say it's like that with any sport, really," Peter says. He lets his utensils rest. "Repetition. You try to do a thing over and over and over again, and then one day you're trying and you do it. You get it right. Like you were building up materials in your brain or in your muscles or something. They say the disease was in my body as much as it was in my brain, so . . ." He returns to attacking his spaghetti.

"What was it like?" Ify asks, sitting across from him at the dinner table. "What did you see? While you were . . . while you were out?"

Peter looks up from his plate, then glances at Paige and Amy on either side of him, as though he's silently asking for permission. Then, he swallows another bite of food. He shrugs. "I didn't want or need anything when I was in that place. No food, no water. No school. Everything felt useless. What was the point of it all? If I couldn't stay in this place I'd come to for safety, then what was the point of any of it? I wanted to live and I wanted to live here, and it was like everything short-circuited."

Synths never needed food or water to begin with, Ify wants to say to the table, outing Peter. But the impulse dies inside her. His disease was real, no matter how it afflicted him. "Did you dream?" she asks instead.

He shakes his head.

She has heard other children describe it as being deep underwater, at the bottom of the ocean, but not needing to breathe. Yet, if they realized that they needed to breathe and opened their mouths, they would drown. So long as they refused to believe they needed to breathe at the bottom of the ocean, they would be safe. It was a paradoxical understanding, but Ify saw the logic in it, the necessity of needing to believe a lie to survive. That was what allowed Nigeria to still function as a country, she realizes wryly. The lie agreed upon.

Peter again looks to Paige, then to Amy, perhaps wondering if there's something wrong with Ify or if there's some arcane rule or bit of manners that he's forgotten.

Ify listens to him, the way he talks, the way he moves. Listens to the way he sometimes taps the tine of a fork against his plate, just so softly. Listens to his massive inhales that push back his shoulders, then the way he exhales through his nose. Listens to the way it seems like electricity is running through him, making him move and talk and walk as though he were being fast-forwarded. She finds she's listening to all of him, hearing not the synth she's spent all this time mistrusting, but a boy. Who just wants to be safe.

That's what it is.

Everything he had done before that Ify saw as malicious and evil, as manipulative—that wasn't him being a synth. That was him being a boy.

Everything he had done that had made Amy smile or that had delighted Paige or that had caused either or both of them to look at him with wonder and gratitude—that wasn't him being a synth. That was him being a boy.

"So, when are exams?" Ify asks him, twirling together her own spaghetti.

Peter registers a moment of shock before smirking, then throwing his head back in annoyance. "Ugh, I'm gonna be fine for exams. Don't worry. I know how to study for these things."

Around a meatball, Ify says, "Every child that has come through this family has made high marks, so . . ."

"It'll be easy!"

And like this, Ify listens to him. Truly listens. And sees his past in front of her—the damage, the trauma—but also his future. The promise, the potential, the triumph. All of it coming together to infuse the present moment with a glow. So bright Ify almost doesn't register the loving smiles that both Paige and Amy have sent her way.

■ ■ ■ ■ ■

A breeze catches Ify and Peter on their faces as they sit next to each other on the front porch. Even though Peter is younger than her, his gangly limbs have him colonizing multiple steps while Ify's comfortable enough on two.

"Will you ever go back?" Peter asks.

With a start, she realizes that he must not know that she has done just that. Maybe he knows nothing of what happened, how he was cured, that it was another synth that had rescued him. Ify contemplates opening up to him, thinks about telling him the truth. Maybe this is what she needs to do to really reach a person. Make herself vulnerable. She thinks of Xifeng. She thinks of Céline. She'd told both of them her truth, and she'd lost them for it. "No," she says.

Peter looks at her for several long minutes. Maybe he's waiting for a reply, thinking that she, a lowly red-blood, isn't nearly as accustomed to long silences as he, a synth. But he gives up and turns his gaze to the cul-de-sac.

Ify gets up. "I'm going home," she says, dusting off her bottom. And that's exactly what she does, telling herself that she did the right thing and that Peter is just a boy.

A contented smile glides onto her face.

CHAPTER
54

There is chaos when they are letting everyone be free from the hospital. Some people they are taking information from, so they are updating their records, but some people are getting out or are being taken out before there is chance to update the system. And it is never because of bad thing. Every time I am seeing this thing, it is because people are too happy to be waiting. That is how I am sneaking out. No one is looking for me, and I am thinking that no one is even knowing I am here.

I am thinking this thing even while I am watching celebration in the streets and parade that is coming out of nowhere but that is just being enough people in one place being happy. I am feeling happy that I am saving life but not because I am saving life but because it is being easy to tell myself now that I am good person and not just child of war.

Part of me is being glad that no one is seeing me, but part of me is sadding, because I am wanting for someone to be so happy to see me that they are pulling me tight to their chest and saying *I am never letting you go* and I am wanting for someone to be throwing me into the air and catching me and throwing me and catching me or putting me onto their shoulders and skipping down sidewalk or crying when they are seeing me blinking my eyes or moving my fingers. I know it is not normal for synth to be wanting this thing but I am not synth anymore. I am something else, and this something else is wanting all of these thing.

But part of me is being happy that no one is seeing me because then I am not having to hide in shadow all the time and I am not having to move from hiding place to hiding place and nothing is chasing me here—not drone, not juggernaut, not police. Not Enyemaka.

So very easily I am finding where Peter is living and I am waiting for the lights in this place with homes to grow dark so that it is looking like nighttime even though we are being inside Space Colony. And I am waiting for the light that is hanging above all of the porches to be going out one by one by one until only one is left. And under that one porch light is sitting Ify and Peter.

And because no one is seeing me, I am waiting and waiting for Ify to be finished talking to him and to be standing and to be wiping dirt from her bottom and to be walking away.

Then because no one is seeing me, I am holding knife in my hand, and I am seeing Peter.

And then he is seeing me.

■ ■ ■ ■ ■

I am telling this story to you, but I am telling it to myself too. I am telling it to myself because it is important to be remembering.

You are being kind to me and you are listening. You are seeing me arrive in Centrafrique, and even though there is no peeling on my skin and you are not seeing metal inside me and I am not dizzying or sadding, you are seeing someone who is needing healing. And when I am telling you what I am, you are not turning your face at me and you are not crying. You are not looking at me like disgusting thing. You are accepting me. Sometime, I am worrying when I am telling my story that you will be thinking I am demon or that I am evil thing. That I am bad person. And you will stop listening to me.

But you are seeing me. Even though I am not being like you, you are seeing me and you are hearing me. And even though I am suffering, you are not just seeing my suffering. You are seeing me. You are seeing girl who is loving thing and who is hurting but who is remembering what it is being like when friend is spraying her with water and it is feeling like it is raining on my body, and I am hearing sound, and sound is me giggling.

ACKNOWLEDGMENTS

My sincerest thanks to my editor, Jess Harriton, for her work not just on this book but on the entirety of the journey these girls have endured, through war and its aftermath. Many thanks, too, to my agent, Noah Ballard, for spurring me on this odyssey to begin with. Shane Rebenschied created such a stunning cover for this book, and I thank Tony Sahara and Kristin Boyle for their art direction. It is a cover that celebrates the beauty and intelligence and fierceness Mante Dalton has brought to this book. Readers may notice in this book some of the stylistic and syntactical liberties I took, and to the degree that I've achieved any measure of success in that regard, credit must go to Marinda Valenti for her astute and precise copyediting. Thanks also to Abigail Powers for proofreading.

The illness that sweeps through the refugee population in Alabast is based on the real-life cases of hundreds of refugee children in Sweden who, upon hearing that their families were to be deported, fell into coma-like conditions. For that aspect of this novel, I relied heavily on reporting done in 2017 by Rachel Aviv of *The New Yorker*. Relatedly, I drew from Patrick Kingsley's work in *The Guardian*, reporting from Joshua Hersh in *Virginia Quarterly Review*, and others who have done the necessary work of chronicling the perilous, unfathomably brave journeys undertaken by those fleeing conflict zones and other arenas of oppression for what they hope will be a place where they can build a life for themselves and their families. A number of pieces shed light on how host countries treat their new arrivals, notably Mac McClelland's investigation for *The New York Times Magazine* of a Turkish camp holding Syrian refugees; additionally, Jonathan Blitzer of *The New Yorker* documents in detail the tragically incomplete and often hostile attitude that US governmental policy has held toward Central American migrants seeking asylum in the United States.

For the story that Xifeng tells in Chapter 28, I relied upon the "China cables" series in *The Guardian* on the efforts by the government of the People's Republic of China geared toward the repression of Uyghur Muslims, specifically their detention in camps in Xinjiang. Among the reporters in the series detailing the conditions in which that minority community is forced to live are Emma Graham-Harrison and Juliette Garside, Kate Lyons, Lily Kuo, and Tahir imin Uighurian, who, in one report, provides harrowing first-person testimony. Sarah Topol writes of the devastating toll of governmental policies on one family in particular in *The New York Times Magazine*. Ben Mauk, in a September 2019 issue of the *London Review of Books*, tells the story of several Kazakhs and Uyghur Muslims who suffered legal consequences not just as a result of their activism but also because of their ethnic identities. His work on the subject can also be found in *The Believer*. Matt Rivers and Lily Lee have written about the Xinjiang internment camps for *CNN*, and Isobel Cockerell's exposé in *Wired* was immensely instructive regarding the ways in which the Chinese government's surveillance apparatus has been utilized to facilitate the oppression faced by these communities in the Uyghur autonomous region. For how a surveillance apparatus may be similarly used in the United States, I recommend Mark Harris's reporting on Palantir in

Wired. All of the aforementioned writers were invaluable resources in my research, in ways both obvious and less so, and to them, I am grateful.

The Jungle referred to in *Rebel Sisters* takes its name from the Calais Jungle, a former migrant and refugee encampment in northern France whose population swelled in 2015 as a result of the European migrant crisis. Prior to its demolition in 2016, it was estimated to have held 8,143 people, according to a census conducted by UK-based NGO "Help Refugees." The Jungle features in Gulwali Passarlay's memoir *The Lightless Sky* and the documentary film *L'héroïque lande, la frontière brûle* (English title: *The Wild Frontier*). Additionally, filmmaker Sue Clayton made a film, *Calais Children*, which follows the lives of several children before and after the final camp eviction. Another invaluable piece of storytelling that informed some of the decisions I made in *Rebel Sisters* was the film *L'escale* (English title: *Stop-Over*), directed by Kaveh Bakhtiari. In it, Amir, an Iranian immigrant in Athens, owns a flat that other migrants pass through on their way to Western countries. Bakhtiari stayed in the flat of one of the characters and smuggled footage out to Switzerland every month to tell these stories.

What I've done with this book isn't nearly as perilous and not nearly as brave, but I hope it is done in the same spirit: to draw attention to the plight suffered by so many who want simply what we—what I—have for so long taken for granted. A home.

Lastly, my unending gratitude to Jeannie Chan. For the Cantonese. And for all the rest.

All mistakes are my own.